VARIETY

and

MYSTERY

Variety and Mystery

This is a work of fiction. Names, characters, businesses, places, events and incidents are either the products of the author's imagination or used in a fictitious manner. Any resemblance to actual persons, living or dead, or actual events is purely coincidental.

For permissions or correspondence contact the author, at:
gardinercdorsette@gmail.com
F I R S T   E D I T I O N
Published in 2024

Paperback ISBN: 979-8-9899100-3-8

Library of Congress in Publication Data

Name: Gardiner Dorsette
Title: Variety and Mystery
Case Number: 1-13486822021 | February 2024

Category: Fiction, Folklore, Short Stories

Written by: D. Gardiner

Designed & Formatted by: Eli Blyden | www.EliTheBookGuy.com

Printed in the United States of America.

To the great grandchildren

Contents

Star Paragraph List

Pages

p. 51

p. 68

p. 94

p. 96

p. 114

p. 203

p. 263

p. 357

p. 379

p. 388

p. 455

p. 478

p. 552

p. 557

p. 558

p. 563

VARIETY

and

MYSTERY

Author and Writer Doctor Thinker

D. GARDINER

Introduction

Anything written by someone can be a history, a mystery, or a mere talk. If you have undeniable evidence in what you see and read, and that evidence provides vital proof, it is surely a history and you can keep it as such. If you are unable to discern what you read and understand it properly, that experience, in accordance with your knowledge, can help you understand that it is a mystery. If that naturally appears to be some common words, in accordance with your knowledge, then surely you are dealing with a mere talk. Whether what you read offers you little or great, it is not bitter. The wise ask to find even a few ways to visualize a benefit, which will undoubtedly touch the heart and help you find the maximum of every existing wonderful thing that a reader can enjoy.

People can reveal anything about others, but for their own affairs, only if someone knew what the matter was, they may express just what they eventually knew because pleasures and interests to the future do not reside in the account of wrong or bad actions. That is why woe to anyone who dares say what a person is not supposed to say. Such an analogy might be used in my case and in any others because humans want to live happily, regardless of their wrong past. Therefore, whatever the reason for what is said or written, it can be a history, mystery, or mere talk.

A boy was about three to four years old. One evening, his mother gave him a plate of food. Someone else, a member of the family who had developed some serious bad ways, was near the boy. He drew a piece of meat from the boy's plate, and the boy tried to grab that meat back from him. Unfortunately, he put a hot, soft boiling pepper on the boy's plate. Mistakenly, the boy thought that was the meat, and before the predator could take it back, the innocent boy ate it. Immediately, his jaw, ears, chest, heart, eyes, nose, and head were trapped under fire. His mother, who was trying to help him, did not know what was happening to her boy. She had no clue of what was happening to him. Anything she put in his mouth turned out to be a fire, tasting as hot fire and cramps his chest. The mother, a wonderful and beautiful responsible mother, had no chance to know what had happened to her son at that moment. The boy was afraid to tell his mother what was happening to him, and she died before the boy could tell her what happened to him that night and who had caused her to spend the entire night trying to console her baby boy.

If that person has to tell or write anything about this story, no one can be sure if he can gather enough strength to say what he eventually did to that boy. Because he himself wants to feel good and happy, it clearly shows and proves that things people write can always be true history, mystery, or mere talk. Good ways are to protect the children, even sometimes with your own child. Teach them not to fear telling you what others do to them that is bad. In some parts of the world, people compare small children with little dogs just for loyalty. No one can be sure if that is the best way to say it. They may say it to prove how nice children are; a little dog respects his owner, protects him, never leaves him in bad times, and remains his loyal friend even if they become poor forever. But a child can do much more than a little dog.

Blind Beggar and the Little Boy

This is the story of a little boy with a blind beggar man. The little boy did not have a parent to take care of him, and the blind beggar man was homeless. In that case, both were homeless and in need. The little boy needed a parent, and the beggar man needed a guide. They became good friends because the boy needed a parent, and the blind beggar man needed a guide. They often begged at the public marketplace. One day, they had a chance to listen to the news on an open radio in a business. It should have been wonderful news for both of them, but no one expected such an event to occur. The news mentioned that the king of the nation was at the beach with his family and had lost a ring, a ring that was very important to the king's family. The news further stated that any man who finds the ring will have the opportunity to marry the king's first daughter. They both heard this news.

When leaving the marketplace where they were begging, they went walking by the shores to the place where they usually sleep at nighttime. This time they walked closer to the sea on the sandy beach. The boy sees a shining light in the slow waves of the sea. As he approaches, he can clearly see that it is a ring. Then he remembered the news they had heard at the marketplace. The little boy says to the blind man, "I found the ring!" He said this because a reward had been offered by the king to any man in the nation who can find the ring and bring it back. The reward was to marry the king's first daughter if the ring truly belonged to the king, and if it was the one he had lost at the seashores while on a recent visit to the beach with his family.

The news stated, "This is the word of the king to the nation: I am the king of the nation who has lost a ring that carries my own name. I lost it while I was at the beach with my family for a visit. If any man finds it and brings it to me, I will marry you to one of my daughters, and you will become the second person in my palace as the vice king."

When the boy tells the blind man that he had found the ring, the blind man asks him to let him feel the ring. The boy gives the ring to the blind beggar man, and the blind man puts it into his pocket. He then said to the boy, "Let's go to the palace of the king." The boy guides him, and they go to the palace of the king.

At the entrance of the palace, the security guards, thinking they were there just to beg, tried to stop them from entering the gate. The blind man opened his mouth and exclaimed to the security guards, "You're trying to stop me!" And he interrogated, "Don't you know that a reward was offered by the king for any man who finds his lost ring at the seashores?" Upon hearing this, the security guards opened the gate for him to enter. As you can see, at that moment, the blind man doesn't say "us" but actually says "me." The security guards take him inside, while the boy had to go back to the street to continue begging. They carried the blind beggar to the king with the king's ring in his pocket. Thus, he became the biggest winner of all time. However, he forgets to ask himself how the boy is doing and how he feels about the situation.

So, it is not sweet for the boy that the blind man forgets about him, even though the boy saw the ring, found it, and grabbed it with his hand. Now, the blind man is qualified to marry the first daughter of the king and become the second person in the palace as the vice king, all while disregarding the little boy's trust and innocence. Despite their poverty, the boy had trusted the blind man as a parent without any regret.

Before his parents died, the boy overheard them talking about an important plant that has the power to cure certain diseases immediately. He listened attentively and remembered both the plant and the diseases it can cure. Unbeknownst to the boy during the preparations for the blind man's marriage to the king's first daughter, the king himself was struck by a serious disease. As a result, the wedding date was postponed until the king's health improved, as there was no known cure for his ailment. The king then issued a different bid, offering his second daughter's hand in marriage to any man who can cure him.

Seven days after the boy guided the blind man by the king's gate, he heard a different news about the king's illness. The news reported that the king has a disease that doctors were unable to cure. At this point the king put out a bid similar to the first one, stating that any man who can cure his disease and prove it will be married to his second daughter.

The boy knows how to cure the king, so this time he went to the palace alone without the blind man for him to guide. Upon arrival, the guards took him inside the palace, granting him the opportunity to see the blind man, who was now the second person in the king's palace as the vice king and the future husband of the first daughter. The boy was received by many high-ranking individuals in the king's palace, who gave him a seat among them. They begin to ask him questions to ensure that he is indeed capable of curing the king. The boy confidently answers yes and states that he can cure the king, but only if they can provide him with what he needs to perform the cure immediately, as time was of the essence. The boy informs them that the only potential challenge they might face would be obtaining what he requires for the cure, which can complicate the situation for the king.

In response, they said to the boy, "A king's life is in danger. What shall we not do to save our king?" The boy then opened his mouth and stated that he immediately needed the head of a blind man to cure the king. Upon hearing this, the blind man himself speaks up and says, "He said the head of a blind man, but he did not specify my head." At that moment, everyone turns and looks at the blind man. By uttering those words, the blind man revealed that he was the one they were seeking to carry out the task.

The blind man was then beheaded with a mighty sword, and his head was handed to the little boy. However, the boy did not actually use the head of the blind man for the cure. Instead, he employed a plant that he had known about from his parents before they passed away. He successfully performed the cure using his secret knowledge. The boy's ordeal of misery came to an end, and he became a joyful boy who married the king's daughter and occupied the seat of the vice king as the second person in the king's palace.

Everyone can draw their own judgment from this story and find a valuable lesson for themselves.

Sometimes the people you trust are not the ones who truly have your best interests at heart. In a town, there lived a brilliant young man with his mother and sister. They loved their neighbors and lived peacefully. However, one jealous neighbor came over and concealed himself behind a wall. He called out to the young man, claiming to be his god and instructing him on what he must do to avoid being killed. The young man was warned not to disclose this to anyone. He was given three choices to stay alive: kill his mother, kill his sister, or start drinking alcohol. Despite his intelligence, the humble young man falls into the trap set by his devilish neighbor.

The young man contemplated the options in his mind. Killing his mother was detestable to him, and he couldn't bear to harm his beloved sister either. So, he made the decision to drink alcohol in order to preserve his own life. He continued to drink, and one fateful day, he became drunk. In his intoxicated state, he ended up killing his sister. When his mother tries to intervene and help, he tragically takes her life as well. He carries out the terrible acts that the jealous neighbor had wanted him to commit, destroying his family.

Sometimes, nearly everyone may seem good on the surface, but it is important to exercise your own judgment based on what you learn, observe, and hear. These experiences provide valuable lessons to reflect upon. Ultimately, many events occur without a good reason or no reason at all. It is through discernment that one can navigate such circumstances.

King and His Vice King

A king and his best friend, who also served as his vice king, went fishing together. This was the first time the king had gone fishing, so the vice king had to show him what to do. This is not a problem because they are longtime friends and rule a nation together. The king had chosen him as his vice king when he became king of the nation and had been ruling for a good period of time, so there was no problem. But, there was no guarantee that accidents would not happen. When they started fishing, the vice king showed the king how to cast the line so he could catch some fish. On their first attempt, both of them doing it together, they get a big fish, but unfortunately, the king lost one of his fingers in the process. The incident saddened them, and they did not return with the same joy they had set out with. The king blames his vice king, and things turn bitter. The king then makes the decision and sends his longtime friend to prison.

While the vice king was in prison, another nation waged a big war against their nation, conquering every part of it and taking everything with them, including the king and all capable men. After the war was over, the conquerors left the nation and did not take any prisoners, which allowed the vice king to stay in his nation but remain in prison. As for the king, the conquerors took him as their spoil. However, at the border, they had to ensure that they were not carrying anything impure or sick.

When they checked the king, they found out that he was missing a finger. They made sure he did not enter their nation and instead sent him over to the border. A law prohibited them from touching anyone who had lost a body part, so when they discovered the king's missing finger, they loaded him and dumped him over the border. The king walked for days and nights until he finally reached the capital of his nation and was restored as king. Now, the king sent someone to liberate his best friend, the vice king, from prison and asked him to forgive him for sending him to prison. The king now understood that the accident had saved his life from the enemies. The vice king also thanked the king and said that if he had not been sent to prison, he who had all his fingers, by now, could have been killed in the enemy's prison. Now they continue to rule.

Some years later, the king becomes more powerful than any other king who had ever existed before him. He actually wants to be sure that he can keep the power, so he does whatever he can to maintain it. When he becomes old, he wonders who will replace him. He calls some wise counselors to meet with him and seeks their advice on who will be the next king for the nation. Unfortunately, all of them have the same idea: there was a man who did not exist in the nation. After meeting with them separately, he realized that they all had the same idea, which scared him. He said to them, "If you are sure we don't have that person in the nation, he must exist somewhere else. Find out if he may exist in other parts of the world."

After a few days, they put on a list more than four nations where they had heard of at least one important person who was similar to the one they were thinking of. At this point, the king asked them, "Can someone else from a different nation replace me as king for this nation?" One advisor replied, "That must not happen. We must do something to stop that from happening before it's too late."

As a result, they prepare for war and engage themselves in a battle with one nation after the other just to find and eliminate the person they think might become the next king of their nation.

Years go by, and not much progress has been made. For that reason, it is not a purpose of expectations to win any war, but rather to stop that person from taking over as king of the nation. Even though no mathematics in the world has control over the loss a war can cause, everyone knows that it is something very complicated and one wouldn't want to be in the middle of it. So, evidence of progress is not there, but the goal of the king is not progress. Ultimately, he doesn't want any enemy to succeed him as king of the nation. If that happens, they know what it can cost the nation. Therefore, he wants to make it clear that it must not happen. Perhaps he remembers that he was out before, so he doesn't want that to happen anymore.

Well, as time goes by, one day his half-brother succeeds him as the king of the nation. This is the person they had envisioned replacing him as king. So, what made them think a half-brother could never be a king of the nation to replace his half-brother?

Eventually, his half-brother succeeded him as the king of the nation, the very person they had identified as his replacement. Why did they think that a half-brother could never replace the king?

Well, the half-brother was not honored among them, as a half brother who was not honored, even his friend did not expect him to become a king. When he was young, he was considered rejected by his father. He was a subject of hatred or a curse among them. However, when his father died, he was the only son who was there to bury his father in a graveyard. He was not honored in the family, but he was honored in his neighborhood. His rejection within his family did not diminish his wisdom or his dreams for the future. It did not create any obstacle against his visions.

One of the reasons why it is not right for someone's thoughts and beliefs to prevail over what a child cannot be is that no one is conceived during a bitter time, but conceived in the womb of their mother in the joyful moment as it should be. Not only for the child you love, but for all children.

Father Requested Counselor for His Sons

A good father had seven children, four of whom were girls with no problems at all, but the three sons caused plenty of problems. The father was very concerned about his sons, and upon analyzing their cases, he had in mind that two of them were heartbreaking and the other one was not too bad. So concerned about his sons, the father requested to see some wise counselors regarding his sons. When he met the counselors, he explained to them what was happening with his sons. The father said to the counselors, "I have three sons. Two of them have some disastrous problems, but the other one has a problem that is not too serious as the other two." The counselors asked him what the problems were, and he explained to them. The first one lies too much, the second one hates other people, including his own neighbors, and the third one is a fool, which is not too bad.

The counselors answered the father and said: "If the first son likes to lie, you can only send him to law school. When he becomes a lawyer, he can lie without any problem for you. Rather than paying for his lies, they will pay him for his lies. For the second son, if he hates people and doesn't love others, have him study the Bible. When he gains that knowledge, he will love everyone, including his neighbors. Unfortunately, for the third son who is a fool, we don't know any solution. There is no cure or treatment for fools on Earth."

When the father heard the results for the first two sons, he was greatly happy. But when he heard about the third son, whom he thought was not bad, he wondered greatly. He sends them to school, but his wonder does not diminish for his sons. After some years, two of them are doing well except for the fool. Most of the things that you might visualize as small are not actually the way you were seeing them. Reality is finding the way to administer them, either way, you are viewing things that will not eventually change the reality of the matters just for yourself.

The first son, who becomes a lawyer, practices law for some years, but eventually decides to quit. He revealed that his father had put him in law school because he used to lie a lot, and he thought the knowledge of the law would help him to stop lying. However, his profession as a lawyer only drags him deeper into the lie, which he becomes detested with. He believed that people should have the right to represent themselves in court, and it was not right to force someone to hire a lawyer if they did not feel the need for one. In some cases, judgments are made by lawyers and judges before listening to both parties, which is not right. Also, when someone is asked to change their mind by pleading guilty for a shortcut, it's not right. Whenever you plead guilty, someone else is considered right and wins. If you're sure you're not wrong, why plead guilty? Someone else is taking over your right.

The lawyer has turned himself into a garden man now and is eager to learn about all sorts of plants. He is not taking long to learn because he wants to control his garden. He starts building some sheds for his plants and tools, and he plants all kinds of vegetables and beautiful flowers in his garden. In this garden, he raises a beautiful family with peace, respect, and dignity. There are no questions about his past lies when he was young or his past lies as a lawyer. Now, he is dealing with a beautiful family living in a beautiful garden with all sorts of beautiful things that you can see with your own eyes.

After many years, a tornado forced them to evacuate their home. They were afraid and wanted to leave everything behind, so they decided to cross a river on foot to reach a different city. However, when they arrived at the river, it was like waves of the sea. They cannot allow themselves to cross that river; eventually, the only chance they have is to endure the destructive tornado. After three days, things started to improve, and they decided to visit the city they had been prevented from reaching by the river. However, they learned that the same tornado had destroyed that city. It was now nothing but ruins. This experience reinforced their decision to abandon lies and live a life of honesty, as it was the only way to ensure their safety and protection from any future disasters.

The family returned to their city and continued to cultivate their beautiful garden. One day, a visitor from a different nation visited the garden and invited them to a festival celebrating the colors of each nation. As for their nation, they had no idea they were chosen. When they arrived at the festival, the first thing they did was look around to see if there was anyone of the same color as them. When they couldn't find anyone, they resigned and left. After some days, they received a letter saying that the festival had been canceled because they were the only ones missing with that color. However, the festival was now rescheduled for a later time for them to attend. By then, they understand the reason why they were the only ones with that color, and they feel more confident and open for the next time they will attend. This time, they enjoyed it to the fullest.

When the family returns home, they receive a visit from a brother who used to hate his neighbors. He arrives with his family, including two small children. While they are talking, the children are playing in the garden. One of the children gets stuck between two trees and cries for help. No one was paying close attention to his crying for help; however, a neighbor hears and comes by and takes him out. His father thanks the neighbor and says he sees now the good reason why his parents wanted him to love everyone else, including his neighbors.

The brother had been trying to become an engineer, but was not doing well in school, having failed his tests six times. He becomes discouraged about that dream and decides not to return to school. But while he was deep in thought, he happens to look upon a smooth wall where he sees a spider attempting to climb up. Every time the spider tries, it falls back down. Sometimes it almost makes it to the top, but falls back down to the floor again. This went on approximately six times until finally, on the seventh attempt, the spider successfully reached the top. Upon seeing this, he said to himself, "If that spider could have enough patience to climb the wall seven times and eventually succeed, then he can go back to school and pursue his dream of becoming an engineer." And he returned to school, eventually passing his exams, and becoming an engineer.

Beautiful Daughter of the Family

A beautiful daughter was born into a family, unfortunately her parents died while she was still an adolescent. She had to stay with her big brother who took great care of her. Years later, she married a man, and because of her knowledge as a good nurse, she became a super and excellent mother to her children. So far, they were doing very well, taking care of their children with the knowledge they had. She had a good sister and three good brothers, two good uncles, and a good aunt. She gave birth to nine children of her own. After the birth of the last one, she suddenly becomes unhealthy, while some of her kids were still very young babies. After more than a year of illness, she died, leaving her children behind - children whom she loved more than herself, and who loved her more than anything in the world. You may know that there are not enough words in the world to fully express the depth of this love. But for good kids, good fathers, and good mothers, it is more fulfilling when you can see and embrace them. During that period of sickness, while she suffered and endured before passing away, her brothers, uncles, and aunt were always there for her; especially her aunt, who was there with her all the time.

When you lose a battle, it is time for the wrong friends to say goodbye. But it is more important than ever for the good ones to support the kids, especially the very young ones. She made a request before passing away, which was an honor. Sometimes things start well but do not finish well. Some of the kids cope with a very harsh life but, like a mother hen who eventually dies and leaves behind her chicks, some die and some survive. While many hopes can perish, whoever does not die continues to live and exist. Whatever events may happen or have happened to anyone in life, if for any reason you disagree, you do not have to agree, especially if you can prove you are not inheriting your ancestors' beliefs.

Lift your eyes to the sky and look at the birds and gaze upon the lilies of the field. Ask yourself where their mothers and fathers are, and if that is the case for you, be the same. We can never forget while we are living, so be good, strong, and take courage. Most of us know that any good family can be displaced for one reason or another. While the children are growing up, each one of them forsakes their own way to cope with life. One of them makes a lot of friends and becomes a part of several good groups of people and tries to forget the past events that were bitter for the heart. Less than a year after the death of his mother, one of his big sisters suddenly dies. Certain problems never end, but no one can be familiar with every problem. Whether you have faced a severe problem or not, life is still there to pursue as a goal. That is the only hope to make it out. As time goes by, most of us want to learn something to make life look better.

The person who has several friends to keep him strong, had one friend who became a registered nurse and was continuing her studies to become a medical doctor. One day, she did not feel well and eventually went to see a doctor who conducted some medical tests to determine what was wrong. The following week, when she returned to the doctor, she learned that she has a heart disease and needed immediate surgery to prevent her from dying too soon. However, there was no doctor available in the country where she was living to perform the operation. Her doctor provided a letter for her to obtain a visa from the counselor to travel to another country for the surgery, but her request was denied more than three times in a two-month period.

Despite the financial resources available to her parents, she still passed away in less than three months. This can make anyone fear for the nation, but for her parents and her good friend, it is a serious loss that could have been prevented if those responsible had taken the loss of other people to heart.

The friend who lost his mother and sister begins thinking about what could cause an ambassador to refuse a visa to a person in danger during an emergency. He believed it was a flaw in his own country and that there was not enough awareness about the potential for similar tragedies to occur again. He decided to leave his country for another, where he remained for an extended period of time. Whether or not he did the right thing by executing his idea, no one can say, but as for the heartbreaking experiences that people face, they have no limits, whether from one person to another or from one nation to the next. When the young man arrives in the country he had chosen to go to, he has to face a different language, try to find new friends in a different neighborhood with a different culture, and find different ways to deal with life. The enthusiasm and opportunities he had as a child remained with him throughout these events. Good or bad lives cannot be blamed on anyone. Ideas, thoughts, and thinking are blind to the future. If only, who writes in our time, can write a book that everyone can read before their birth and see how their life will be, then they can choose whether or not to be born. Believe it, many people would choose not to be born if that were possible. However, we know that such a miracle is not yet possible.

When someone is a candidate for an important position in a nation, if they only talk to the middle class and millionaires, the conversation will make a chain between middle class and millionaires. Then, even if they are a billionaire, when they talk with those who are financially and materially poor, they may say they are poor so that everyone can believe they will help them. When they talk to untouchable millionaires, they may try to prove that they too were born into wealth. This shows that whenever someone says they are poor, they may not actually be poor, but rather they want to be paid by the poor for their words and their time spent talking with them.

Whoever has a chance to say that they have been somewhere is certainly no longer on the road. But if you are still on the road, you do not count because no one can see you. After five years, the young man returned to his native country where he was welcomed. However, after only half a year, he goes back to the foreign country, and then three years later he moves to a different nation. Someone can fight for his life or to change his life, but that doesn't mean an eternal life, and sometimes you may encounter more problems. No one can win anything by shifting from country to country. Almost everyone who does that can prove a good reason for it, but doing such a thing can become a way for them to avoid what we should call misguided, misled, and betraying themselves. No matter how it happens, it can be called an event of life over which nobody gains control. From far away, your love for your loved ones may fade where there are no flowers or blossoms, but just a positive thought for your dear loved ones.

Days and years go by fast, and the kids are no longer called kids. Now it's time for them to close their eyes and minds to the past and see things positively. Good luck to anyone who makes their way clear, but those with bad luck may see their luck travel behind them. One thing for sure is that if someone becomes a blind person, that person will worry a lot about their blindness. That is normal because when you were born, you did see everything with your good eyes.

Supposedly, at the time of your birth, you did not see anything and everyone else was born in the same way. Actually, nobody talked about being blind or seeing; would you even know that you were supposed to see anything or worry about your blindness? Surely, the answer is no. Whether the situation you are living in is characterized by fear, poverty, or not being good at all, if it is true, you cannot make any changes at all. You must live your life as you were born to live that way.

Caterpillar Guest of the Ants

One day, a person was observing a caterpillar that had fallen from a tree leaf in a garden full of vegetation. Some ants were supervising the caterpillar and asked for his visa or permit to visit their homeland on the ground. The caterpillar had always seen the ants working on the ground while he was in the shadow of the trees, so he refused to talk to them and immediately turned his back to try and get back on his tree. The ants tell the caterpillar that they appreciated that he is going back to his tree because that is the best way for them to receive a guest like him.

The caterpillar thought everything was over, as someone always said, "The important one doesn't walk fast." On his way back to the tree, the caterpillar walked very slowly and began to climb his tree. However, while his last part was still on the ground, the ants addressed him and said, "You were our good guest, and you deserve something good from us. But for now, we don't have anything good enough to give you. We can only give some kisses." The caterpillar looks at them and asks, "On my back? That's okay. You are so kind." Meanwhile, the ants said, "Oh yes, you are already ahead. You don't have to turn back just for our kisses." The ants go ahead and start kissing the caterpillar on his back. Those kisses were the last ones the caterpillar received in his life.

The ants put the caterpillar under arrest and took him to their queen for judgment and discernment about whether or not he had the right to turn his back on them and be in a place where he was not supposed to be. Now the caterpillar is in prison and unable to talk to the ants. While his case is under investigation, the ants are looking for better ways to view the future. While the caterpillar is in prison, he starts complaining about ventilation and says that he can't breathe. The ant guards suggest taking him to a doctor to determine the cause of his breathing problem, so they take him to the doctor ant's office. The doctor asks the caterpillar how he is feeling and he replies that he can't breathe. The doctor says that he will find out what the problem is and after some tests. The doctor finds out that the caterpillar has too much liquid in his body. The only solution was to draw out some of the excess liquid, and the caterpillar agreed.

The ants begin by drawing all of the caterpillar's juices. The only thing you can see is the ant's festival, not even a little ruin of the skin is left behind. In less than half an hour, there was nothing visible to identify the caterpillar. A poor caterpillar living by eating only vegetation, how can he believe the ants should have mercy in his regard? That is a mistake which cost him his life. The caterpillar is not the only one because humans also make similar mistakes. The caterpillar's wife and children are looking for him. A fire ant informs them that he saw the caterpillar in the ant prison, but the ants are looking for the caterpillar's family to release him to them. The caterpillar's wife leaves the children at home and goes to the ant's territory and meets with the ant agents about the case. They tell her that her husband will see the judge the next day, and if she spends the night there, they can leave together quickly. She agrees to stay, but she experiences breathing problems overnight while she is with the queen. The queen calls Doctor Ants Scheme, who arrives quickly and suggests an operation. All the ants gather together to perform the operation, but after half an hour, Mrs. Caterpillar is nowhere to be found.

Now, only the children are left behind. Their father left without notice, and their mother has disappeared too. They don't have any parents, but they still try to crawl on the trees. One day, a bird comes and talks to them, and they become friends. They are happy but remember their parents telling them not to let the birds see where they are living. However, now that they have no parents, they accept the bird as their friend. The baby caterpillars become good friends with the bird, who promises to teach them how to fly so that the ants cannot harm them anymore. They all agree, and while they are learning, a neighbor caterpillar catches some birds eating her babies' caterpillars. Now, they understand why their parents told them not to be friends with the birds and not to let them know where they are living.

Birds always come to them early in the morning. Now whenever the baby caterpillars see birds, they hide underneath the tree leaves so that the birds cannot find them anymore. You can benefit from a wrong friend, but you will lose more than what you are benefiting from. Most of the time, what you're going to lose is your own life. Therefore, it is not a good chance to take. The baby caterpillars have already learned from the birds how to fly, but only a little bit. That little bit is not enough to turn them into big birds like the bird had told them they would become, but it's just enough to make them fly. They are too weak to be called birds. Actually, they are called butterflies. The main point is that, as a benefit, they are no longer caterpillars who cannot walk fast or fly, and the ants cannot catch them anymore. But they are beautiful creatures that you don't need to be afraid of or worry about eating your garden plants. Everyone wants to see their beauty all the time.

Caterpillars that become butterflies are very intelligent, just like people who can learn from negative experiences. Caterpillars learned a good thing from birds. Three weeks later, a family invited the birds of the sky to a show in a garden, where the most beautiful bird will receive a prize for its beauty. Butterflies hear about this and are the first guests to show up at the beautiful garden. Meanwhile, all the big birds are coming over. When the contest begins, the butterflies hide themselves under the tables. They are greatly confident they will be able to win, and when it is time to give away the prize, the butterflies come out and start flying all over the place. Even the birds who thought they were more than heaven and more beautiful than the rainbow are forced to change their minds. The owner of the garden show is a little bit scared because all of the big and rich birds are sitting there. It was embarrassing for him to honor the little butterflies over the big birds. Then, the big birds actually understand the owner's embarrassment and become quite ashamed. Because of this, the big birds dash out one after the other. It is a good time for the butterflies. But that isn't the end of all. After the dance, the drums are heavy. The butterflies enjoy their gifts for their beauty. But are butterflies really considered among those real birds?

While going out, all the big birds hid themselves by the very front door. Only they know what they plan to do. Now the owner of the garden said to the butterflies, "Unfortunately, I made a mistake by not inviting you. But as you can see, you are most welcome to the show and, fortunately, you are the winners. As for your gifts, I know butterflies always travel with antennae, so I will give each of you two brand new pairs of antennae." The butterflies were very happy and thanked the owner of the garden before finally saying goodbye.

Now the butterflies have extra antennae and can go anywhere they want with no problem. But there was a different problem at the back of the very front door. Nearby, the big birds block the way out by flying one behind the other and say, "Congratulations, birds. Oh, you deserve honors for your beauty, butterflies." The butterflies hear these words and relax. The big birds then say to the butterflies, "Let's leave together. Whether we come from the same festival or not, nobody loses anything whether they win or not." The butterflies agree to travel together with the big birds.

On the way to their homes, the birds asked the butterflies, "To what family of birds do you belong?" The big birds said, "We've never seen that kind of beauty before." The butterflies replied, "We just look like our parents, who were beautiful." When they approached where the butterflies used to live as caterpillars, the big birds said, "Let's rest here a little bit on those trees. Maybe we might find something to eat." While resting on the tree, all the big birds started laughing and saying, "If only we could find some caterpillars." One of the birds asked the butterflies, "Do you eat caterpillars?" One of the butterflies answered and said to him, "Our family and we only eat where we live. Other than that, we never let anyone else know what we eat." The birds said to them, "We are friends not only from today but from a very long time." One of the birds said, "Do you remember when your parents disappeared at the ant's prison?"

By means of that question, butterflies understood where they were, but it was too late to turn back. Unfortunately, the big birds catch the butterflies and cut off their antennas and wings. They then eat each antenna and wing of every butterfly, and drop their bodies on the ground for the ants. Now, remember who the butterflies are and where they were. Why did they lose their intelligence? Maybe because they wanted others to call them birds and forgot about their own safety, becoming too charming with their untouchable beauty. More importantly, if you are not invited, don't go anywhere.

Butterflies did not receive an invitation but they still go to the show and win gifts, which also wakes up jealousy among the birds. Content yourselves and with what you have. Butterflies were once caterpillars who knew nothing about beauty or flying, so what more could they possibly need? Some people are never content with their position in life, which can turn a smart person into a fool who ignores wisdom.

When butterflies reach the ground, they are no longer able to walk or fly away. Ants come across them and ask, "Are you some mystery or gift that has come from the sky for us? How come you are here and unable to walk, climb a tree, or fly away?" Caterpillars have now transformed into neither butterflies nor small birds. They have lost the capacity to even be caterpillars. The ants take them to the queen for examination to determine their identity. After the examination, the queen declares that they are a gift that has come from the sky for the protection of the trees.

When butterflies were with their parents, brothers, and sisters, they were caterpillars. During that time, ants were ground workers who spent nights and days making trees grow. However, the caterpillars themselves would stay on the top of the trees to destroy the leaves. Now history is clear- they can run but cannot hide themselves. The time has come for them to come down and feed the roots of the trees.

So, what happens to the rest of the brothers and sisters of the butterflies? Well, they travel from north to south and never stay in one place for a year. They are nomads, thanks to their perfect antennae. Even their babies left behind are able to find their way and locate their parents. Meanwhile, the older brothers and sisters are thought to be keeping the beauty of some flower gardens.

Whenever someone travels from place to place, they may not necessarily acquire material riches, but they can enrich their lives through new experiences. The first butterflies did not necessarily have to go anywhere, and there was nothing inherently wrong with staying where they are. However, their downfall comes from betraying their own safety and risking their lives just to win some antennae at a festival they were not invited to.

The rest of the butterflies remember they were caterpillars. They still travel for their own safety and for the beauty of everywhere they can be, as some beautiful guests, regardless of no payments or gifts. Sometimes, you may never hope for anything back for what you actually do, and you are continuing to do it without any regret.

Parents and Children

In some parts of the world, parents let their children know that if they deliver them to the world, there is no way to repay that. That can be true, but the reality is that we can find a little difference between delivering and giving life. Anybody can deliver or make a delivery and turn themselves back away without care. So, in order to merit anything as an honor, you do need to take good care as you can.

As for the parents who have in their mind that their children are there to be the non-paid slaves to them, in those places, children work hard enough before they can form their own family, without any pay, and they are doing that without any regret at all, because they did not hope for anything as pay from their parents, according to what their parents told them. But parents who take good care of their children are the only ones to say they are giving life to their children. As for those who do not care, they are only delivering children to the world. If that is all you can do, you might be considered as one who does their best, but you must educate them so that they can understand that you have some limits as a parent, because some days they themselves might have to be parents.

A father who had seven children with his wife died suddenly one day while some of them were still kids. He was a farmer cultivating his farm outside the city. Now, he is no longer present, and the wife has to take care of the kids. With the help of the older ones, she is able to raise all of them. She lives a long life until they themselves take care of her as their own mother. That was all she had under her possession and what she could do for them at that time. They never had a chance to pursue higher education, but they understood the limitations their mother faced in providing more. Parents who are not rich often have a clear understanding of what they want to do for their children, but they are often limited in their ability to accomplish their aspirations for their child. Regardless of age, all children must learn how to respect their parents and love them with a good heart.

If you were raised in a country that you consider good, you may not fully understand the circumstances faced by others. However, if you have the opportunity to travel to different places, you might have a different idea. Most of the time, people have children, but it may not be exactly what they desire. Children come into their lives, and they embrace their role as parents. There are countries in the world where many people struggle to provide for their children, but they lack the means to control the number of children they have. For some, they may not even have one child, while others have multiple children without the opportunity to adequately care for them. No one knows what they will eat for the day, and some may go without any food at all.

A young man was with his mother at a supermarket when they approached a crowd of people outside. They were following a man who had been arrested by the police because he cut off his five-year-old son's ear. Why did he commit such a horrible act? The father explained himself and said, "The little boy was going to play with some other children at a neighbor's house, and as children often do, they started complaining about each other. The neighbor children accused that boy of eating their food." Upon hearing those words, the father becomes so enraged that he actually cuts off one of the boy's ears. It is truly heartbreaking.

They ask him where he has put the ear so they can reattach it, but he claims to have forgotten where he had dropped it. However, it was later found in his pocket. As you can see, when a parent is unable to take care of their own children and lacks any assistance, it becomes a serious matter that affects their lives and even their souls. Now, The father of the boy deserves to be in prison. Everyone can see and acknowledge that. What will become of the boy while his father is in prison? Not many people can answer that question. However, despite the problems with the neighbors and whether they accept him or not, the boy might always turn to them rather than suffer from hunger on the streets. These kinds of problems cannot change the love and care that parents have for their children, nor can they change the love that children have for their parents. It is just heartbreaking.

To prevent most of the problems, your bravery should be manifested through enduring situations. Other than that, you might need to be slow to anger, because no one deserves reproach for pity.

When something wrong happens, people will not consider your anger or the time you were mad, but they will only consider the result of your anger and what you eventually do. If you have a certain situation, that situation belongs to you and your family, and if they are facing a situation, it is also your situation. Therefore, it is always regrettable to witness such miserable problems as the one mentioned.

A good woman lost her husband suddenly to death, leaving her as the only one to care for five children in a house close to the main street of the town. How can she raise her five children without a father? Every day, she sets up a table at the front porch of the house where she sells a small amount of merchandise to those who want it. This is how she raises her children, acting as a superwoman and a respectable parent. She never gets angry with her children or anyone else. She manages to send all the children to school with her own courage, and they continue to live peacefully. Eventually, all the children get married and form their own families, and she has a long life filled with joy, seeing her great-grandchildren growing up.

One of her daughters passed away after getting married, but she had a son before her death, whom the grandmother also raised among her children. Patience and hope can take you to places you never thought possible in life. Maybe she never has a chance to buy something of the best quality for herself, but she always buys something good for her children. Her strength and splendor lie in her hope for the future. After raising all her children, she finds great joy in her heart and laughter on her face. Her honor and glory reside in providing her children with a good education, not in things she could never afford. She avoids the wrong friends and seeks what is good for her children, proving that she was always there for them. This makes her a brave person who deserves the respect of all.

Respect and dignity do not reside in anger or madness, but in self-control, patience, and blinding yourself from unnecessary things while hoping for the future not only for yourselves, but for those who will be part of the future. History or mystery, take a good point for yourself, and follow a good path of life.

Both ways, children can benefit from parents, and parents can also benefit from children. In order for a parent to benefit from a child, that parent needs to prepare their children in a good manner. That way, your children benefit from you. On the other hand, those children shall never wait until you get old to help you. But if there is a need, your children will help you with great happiness.

There was a woman whose husband died without notice, leaving her with plenty of children. She took good care of all of them. The interesting point is that she lived for more than one hundred years. Supposedly, if she did not take care of her children, there is no way someone who did not take care of their children could live that long under the care of the children. Maybe they might have wanted to do even better, but they may not have had enough possibilities to do so. As for that woman, all her children have taken care of her with their own resources until they take her to her grave, her final resting place. But they are proving themselves as good children with great courage to contribute to their dear mother who was always there for them.

A man who was apparently a good man had three children: one son and his twin sisters. For some reason, he didn't think he did enough to help them. Whenever he talked, he would always say that when he gets old, he knows they will reproach him when they have to help him. But before they can reproach him, he will hang himself on a tree with his own pocket bandana.

As his children grow up, the father becomes sick and continues to suffer for a long time. Eventually, he sees his life as contemptible, betrays himself, and hangs himself on a tree. When you are not able to talk, people don't know what is in your mind. But for that man, what he actually does is his own plan that he has always talked about.

The main point is, if he had taken care of his children as he was supposed to, that plan would never have entered his heart to affect him. The important thing is that his children love him very much and make great efforts to have him buried like everyone else. It was his own plan to accomplish, and no one knew how to stop him from carrying out his own plan.

His big brother was a popular man who was respected by everyone as a good person who did good for anyone in need, regardless of where they came from. He was the first one to pass away peacefully in his own home. By the way, no one has control over how anybody can die or whether they should die. Everyone carries their own yoke, and many conversations are for good moments. Often, no one knows when someone has lost control of themselves.

Human Power Limit

The power of humans is limited to good times only. Your good time is when you are able to do anything you actually want to do without interruption. Whenever you are the one who must perform acts of obedience, you become less powerful. A man who spends a lot of time in the middle of a mountain contemplates many things. He has the chance to see powerful people become weak and weak children become very powerful.

In the midst of the mountain, he sees a big, mighty tree with branches floating out to the ceiling of the heavens, while small trees have nothing to compare to. After some time, all the branches of that big tree appear to be dry, as if waiting for a few winds to destroy them, while the very small trees become majestic trees. He also sees people who own beautiful homes and others who live under trees. Then, a great flood arrives and covers three-quarters of the area. People who were sleeping under the trees scramble upward to higher ground for their own protection. Meanwhile, those who own pretty homes seek shelter inside. In the end, the homeless have their lives as gain, and the owners of the beautiful homes perish in the flood.

Look at all kinds of beautiful trees in a splendid garden with beautiful flowers and fragrant blooms, beautiful birds of all kinds and colors, and various fruits for human consumption and for the birds. Every day, the birds come to admire the beautiful flowers, but then they leave. What makes the birds know when to admire something beautiful and when to leave? If people had left when the flood was happening, they would never have died at the wrong time, and they would have had a chance to reoccupy their homes.

While walking in the midst of the mountain, he sees a big fire burning all over the place and around him, but he is not worried. At that point, a violent wind and rain came over. He stays under a big tree and doesn't even get wet. In this way, he thinks that nobody can survive if they are not on the top of the mountain. When the low ground starts rising up to the sky, he waits to see how he is actually going to be raised up. However, this operation was stopped by him and he raises his eyes to the heavens, seeing nothing more than a beautiful place to sit.

You can always see a beautiful place from your journey, but you might never arrive without encountering some unexpected situations.

Pool Coin Millionaire

Two young men were following a ravine when, at a certain point, they came across a pool of water. However, it was a very dirty and murky pool. Both of them decided to dive in and submerge themselves under the water. When they resurfaced, one of them has a flat object resembling a coin, but this coin has a value of several million dollars. The other man opened his mouth and said, "One million dollars is too much for only one person to live with." The man who found the coin heard what he said and decided to give it to him. The man who received the coin was very happy to take it from the one who found it.

Later, after becoming rich, he says that the man who had given him the coin was a fool. Almost everyone would agree and call him dumb or a fool. However, it is supposed that he never wanted to become rich. What is bothering him? Some months passed after this event, and they never remained friends because a fool cannot be a friend to a millionaire. But whether he is a fool or not, wise people say that the one who never asks a question is the true fool.

The millionaire was so delighted to mock a fool that he didn't have a chance to ask him how he was going to live himself, as for him, a million dollars was too much for one person to live with. When he gives the coin to him, it is no longer too much but too small for him. After another year, the laws in the nation change, and it is announced that the coin belongs to the government and had disappeared during a time of war. Now, the millionaire is under arrest and must explain himself clearly to prove his innocence. To do so, he needs to present concrete witnesses. This is the perfect opportunity for the millionaire to seek out the fool and have him testify in court as his former friend. When the day arrives, the millionaire's family takes the fool with them to the court.

At the courthouse, many jurors were present, awaiting the proceedings. When questioned, the wealthy millionaire explains the circumstances of finding the coin and presents the fool as the individual who discovered it and gave it to him. The judge directs his inquiries towards the fool, asking about the coin. The fool confirms that he found the coin underwater and gave it to the millionaire. The judge, skeptical, shakes his head and calls upon the jurors to deliberate. One juror raises a hand and expresses familiarity with the witness, stating that he has known him as a poor man for a long time. They question how the witness can suddenly be the one who finds the valuable coin and gives it away. Other jurors join in, asserting that even if the witness was unaware of the coin's value, the millionaire should not have left him in misery. They label the millionaire's claims as a significant lie and predict that his plan will not succeed. Consequently, the judge reaches a verdict: the millionaire will not be set free and will be taken, along with his family, to serve a lifetime in prison as mandated by the nation's laws. The millionaire and his family now face captivity, while the poor man, in his poverty, remains a free man. This outcome serves as a reminder that when one believes that others possess too much, it often reflects an underlying desire to possess those things oneself. However, perceiving things in this manner will lead to a life where most of the days do not truly belong to oneself.

They said, "That is a big lie you are trying to make. Then you will not accomplish anything." Now the judge has concluded. The millionaire will not be set free and may not be allowed to return to the courtroom. In accordance with the nation's law, they are taking him and his family to work in prison forevermore. The millionaire, along with his family, faces captivity, while the poor man, as he is, remains free. Now, whenever someone believes that others have too much, that is not a good sign. It is likely because you feel that you should be the one to possess that thing. But if that is the way you see it, most of your days will not truly be yours.

That man's words put himself in prison. Remember, he was the one who said that even a million dollars is too much for one person to live with. That was not true in his heart. If it were true, why did he keep the coin only for himself when the guy gives it to him? So, that doesn't prove he had the right knowledge, but rather that he was envious of that money, displaying wicked covetousness. As you know, if you try to hold onto too much power, the power itself will capture you. When they took the millionaire to prison, the poor guy was there in court with him. Before they locked him up, he signs a deal for the poor man to oversee his wealth until he can get out. But he will never get out. Eventually, the poor man might become a millionaire over time. Not just a millionaire, but also wise rather than a fool. Remember, respect and dignity do not reside in anger or madness, but in self-control, patience, blind yourself to the things of others, and hoping for the future. The winds are not for your ears, the rain is not for your head, the fire is not for your body, and the rising waters cannot flood you out.

Scam Man

A man lived in a city. Compared to most people in that city, he was considered rich. He owned three large houses and had a significant amount of wealth. However, he was not very intelligent. One day, he met a scam man who claimed to know how to make people rich in less than a day.

Intrigued, the man asked the scam man to explain the magic behind it.

The scam man suggested they meet at the man's house to demonstrate how it could be done. Both of them agreed, and the man and his wife met with the scam man. The scam man proceeded to show them his method for making money. He explained that in order to become rich, a person had to give him a certain amount of money as an investment. The more money they gave, the more they would receive in return. The scam man promised returns ranging from tens of thousands to hundreds of millions.

The couple realized they didn't have the amount of money they wanted to pay the scam man to put them among the richest billionaires in the world. Then, they decided to meet a businessman and make a contract with him. They handed over three property certificates, one for each of their houses, as collateral to borrow the money. The certificates served as a guarantee that they would repay the borrowed money. Then the couple decided to get hundreds of thousands of dollars on each house with a contract for only a one month period of time. If they do not return that money after one month, those three homes will belong to the businessman. Now the contracts are done, the couple actually got the money they wanted to get the deal done.

With the contracts in place, the couple received the money they desired, and they are happy with that. Now is the time to get back to the scam man. That is what they do: they go ahead and find the scam man and have him come over to their house just to make enough money for them, so they can become the richest people in the world. Of course, the scam man is more than happy to come over to their house, but only during the night because they don't want anybody else to know how they are getting rich so quickly.

The scam man himself has many reasons he doesn't want to show up during the daylight.

Good deal for both parties: a time money plus a time fool equals a couple without knowledge and poor overnight. After the scam man gets the money, he disappears from their sight. Now, the money maker cannot be found. The couple's distress remains hidden until a cursed child reveals their plight to a friend. The only truth is that after one month, the couple becomes homeless. If they sleep in a house, they must ensure it belongs to a compassionate person willing to help them with their problems.

Remember, if you do not die, you still exist, and if you are actually breathing, you are still alive. They are dashed out with no words and make their ways far out. They don't even have a word to describe their own miseries until people who knew them before, like their children and friends, are able to help them fly to a neighboring country. If only they were content with what they had, they would never meet such misery on their path. But envy cannot give any other fruits than engraved situations. Eventually, their minds were blinded by the wrong kind of ambition that cost them to annihilate their own wealth, wishing not only their children to get a good lesson from that but everyone who knows these situations exist.

They were living in a large city, which was a chance for them to know about scams and wicked people, but their envy to become the richest people in the world guided them as a strong power that turned the false into a truth and later struck them like a strong wind. What should make a sensible person think that, a person who knows how to fabricate his own money without any trouble is going to lose his time to come to your own home overnight just to make that big money for you and collect a very small amount he already has from you to get that done. If good sense is supposed to be used, they should ask him to make that big money and collect the small amount he wants from that big money himself, and you can get the rest of that money. They allowed him to get their money because they themselves have a strong belief in the magic of that scam man.

They had in their mind magic anyway that could help them. But that kind of thinking makes nothing more than sustenance a fool's thought. Such a deal erases the time spent at school when you were very young and also erases your continuing progress to learn more for the future. The real truth is that the couple thought they were the only people who had not yet found a good magic man, but now luckily they finally found what they need, which is a good magic man. Now they are going to be the richest people in the world. By means of that, they are diving themselves to the bottom of the ocean without a judgment of themselves as they are supposed to be smart people. Now they have a feeling of winning while having lost.

One day, a young man went to a business where he encountered a businessman who was talking to him about a business he wanted to invite him to enter. The businessman explained to him how that business functioned, then he waited and listened carefully to him.

After he finished listening to what the businessman had to say to him, he tells the businessman that if he entered that kind of business, it meant he would tell his parents, who used to put him through school, that they were fools and he was the only one who had sense. He actually said that after the businessman told him that some billionaires wanted to help others get rich, but they are doing that by collecting a small amount of money from them.

You can start with two thousand dollars, and if you want, you can start with a million dollars. You can make more money by giving them one thousand dollars and after one week, they will give you a check for one hundred thousand dollars. If you give them one hundred thousand dollars, they will give you a million dollars.

The businessman said to him that everything was going well for many people he knew. That was true; some checks have been given to the first people who entered the snare, but that person was only wanting to make sure that he can catch as many people as he can at a time. He actually wants so many people to get involved in that business.

So many people who did not understand if that was a snare are going out to anywhere they can borrow money, either from the bank or from friends, and they borrow as much money as they can find, and give it away to that person so they can get rich faster. But after the big money enters, people continue to give away and stand by, waiting for their millions to come out. So, a big thing is happening, but not a big amount of money. It is a big headache for everyone who was waiting to get rich fast. A double headache for the one who borrowed so much money with the hope that they were going to get rich.

Now, the money they borrowed to contribute to their fast wealth is no longer considered big money but rather too much money. They are no longer able to afford that kind of money. The phone number for that person no longer works because these funds are sufficient. None of them are able to contact that person anymore. Furthermore, people who used to own houses are no longer homeowners. Likewise, those who used to own businesses are no longer business owners. All the beautiful vehicles have become relics of the past, and even people are not easily seen anymore.

More than a month since the businessman invited the young man to enter the business, the young man, who had no knowledge of what had happened, encounters the businessman and asks him, "How is the business going now?" The businessman responds with a vague question, asking the young man what kind of business he is talking about. From that moment, the young man starts to suspect that something might be wrong. By acting in such a manner, he instills a feeling that something significant has occurred.

Another person approaches someone who doesn't even know him and tells him that he has won a lottery ticket, but he needs to pay some money before he can receive his winnings from the lottery manager. He then asks the stranger to help him pay that money, promising to double his money once he receives the millions. The man asks him how much money he needs, and the person replies that he wants thirty-five thousand dollars. The man advises him, saying it's quite easy. He suggests going to the people where he used to play the lottery ticket and winning, and asking them to collect the thirty-five thousand dollars from his substantial winnings and give him the rest. That way, he wouldn't have to borrow any more money, and he wouldn't have to share his money with people he doesn't even know for no good reason. The man doesn't show anger towards him because he gave him sound advice, and he believed that the man would heed his words and credit his lie. Whether they believe it or not, someone else falls into the trap. Almost everybody who falls into the snare of the scam are individuals who already know what is going on but believe they may be the lucky ones to cross the most dangerous bridge without paying a high price. There is no way out without sacrifices. Just stay clear of scam snares.

Wrong thinking, wrong reflection, and wrong beliefs lead to misleading and betrayal. In a nation under the blue sky, there lived a good businessman who believed in himself as a good person. He never worried about thieves, gangs, or wicked criminals and robberies. He went about his business without any concern for the possibility of wicked actions. No one believed that such things could happen to him. However, one can only rely on good times, as the bad times often lurk behind. Other people started doing the same type of business as him. They put eyes on his business, but he didn't pay much attention to them. It was an error not to safeguard himself against them, as these individuals had their sights set on him. His downfall could make a significant difference to their own business. They have him in their heart as a bad person for them, and one day a scam artist comes to them and tells them that the good businessman is paying money to have them killed. The scammer says that if they give him that money he will give it back to the businessman, nothing will happen to them. They actually believe this wicked person and think that ensuring their safety is better than facing death. They fail to understand that the scammer is just trying to make money off of them. They have become so blinded by their hatred for the businessman that they can't see the truth.

Now they go ahead to form a plan for themselves to determine what would be best for them. They approach other wicked individuals and pay a smaller amount of money to have the long-time reputable businessman killed. The news spreads quickly, and they are satisfied with their destructive act against the businessman, thinking it will bring them good times.

Contemptuous covetousness, subdued by a loathing man, destroys an honest individual. Sometimes wickedness does not stand for long, as those who engage in it eventually come to realize the consequences. Both the one who paid to kill the businessman and the one who received the money understand the gravity of their actions. They all know the inevitability of the grave. Those who are left behind can learn a valuable lesson from this experience.

If only a deceased person could find a chance to come back and start a new life, even a fool could become the wisest person on Earth. Concerns about sustenance may be the greatest worry, but there is nothing wrong with having or not having wealthy material possessions. However, when it comes to a person's life, it is untouchable. Just as you love and cherish your own life, others also love and value their own lives in the same way. Every person on earth possesses only one life, and for this very important reason, everyone cherishes and love's his own life, and honors and respects the lives of others. One day, a man stood by the side of a road under construction. He noticed a very long chain that had been there for a very long period of time. Upon closer inspection, he observed that some parts of the chain were on the ground, while other parts were under the ground. Some parts were hidden in the shadows of a shelter. As he continued to observe, he noticed that when the construction workers used a machine to pull the chain out, he had a second chance to see every section of the chain. He looked and saw that the section that had been under the shelter was new, the section on the ground was almost new, and the section that had been buried under the ground had rusted.

Actually, when they pulled the entire chain out, it was no longer divided into multiple sections. It was seen that there was only one chain being used. Whatever way you can see it, believe it; the way humans perceive it is that a single chain can have different parts—some in the shadows, some in the sunlight, and others far away. But if an event is about to occur that affects the earth, it will concern every human being. Every single human existing will be affected.

Two little boys were trying to hunt birds when one of them injured a bird in the midst of a flock. When one bird got hurt and couldn't fly, that bird started crying and every other bird flew back to see if they could help him fly, but could not. Unfortunately, the other birds were unable to fly with the injured one, but they helped it find refuge under a large rock where the boys couldn't find it anymore. The bird cried out for help, and the others made great efforts to try and help him. Most of the time, humans die without help because no one hears their voice. Sometimes it's because others are unwilling to offer help due to their own personal reasons. One thing that can be certain is that no matter how much money someone may pay at the hospital when they get sick it cannot be denied that doctors, nurses, and their assistants are helping them. Even if someone believes they don't need help from others, suddenly finding themselves on the ground and unable to move, someone comes along and takes them to the hospital. Isn't that enough to call for help? That for sure, no one can refuse the help of others, and no one can live without the help of others.

During a tornado, six children playing in a shack behind their parents' homes became trapped when the tornado struck the shack. Five of them were able to flee, one child couldn't make it as he was blocked by some debris. Their parents were not present at the time, but the remaining children started yelling for help. Neighbors rushed over, and one of them successfully freed the trapped child. At that moment, neither the child nor their parents could deny the need for their neighbor's help. They couldn't possibly repay the neighbor enough for their assistance. All they could say was, "Thank you" for saving the life of their child. Even though the boy had serious injuries, being alive and receiving treatment is always better than death. One can never imagine how happy those children felt when they realized their good hopes in their neighbors. A great thanks goes out to the neighbors for saving the boy's life.

Both scenarios demonstrate the importance of considering our neighbors. Even though you may not feel the need to engage in a relationship with someone you don't know or if you're not a friendly person, the truth is, as long as you don't hate or harm anybody, you haven't done anything wrong. Some people don't have faith in their neighbors, but when they face problems, their neighbors often come over to help if they can see the issue. There was a rich man who had a house near a sea canal and kept his boat there. One morning, he slipped from the top of his boat and fell into the deep water. Crying for help, nobody in his house can hear him, but two construction workers on the other side of the canal see him and swim over to assist him.

The man had been looking at his beautiful boat. As he started getting old and there was some water coming onto the boat, he slips and finds himself in the water. There's no shame in crying for help, so he makes an effort to grab the boat. He was happy to see other people coming to help him. All he could say was, "Thank you very much," even though he might have to see his doctor later to make sure there were no complications from falling into the water. It's hard to imagine, but such situations can happen where someone may die close to their home without anyone inside having a chance to witness the problem and offer assistance. By then, it may be too late to do anything.

Head Without Body and The Cow Man

A farmer and his family were doing very good on their farm. They had all kinds of fruit trees, vegetables, and animals, most of which were good to eat. The farmer had a wife and a daughter, and they lived in a big house built by a local builder.

They had everything they needed to live with their family. However, the farmer had one issue—a problem with sharing meat. Whenever he wanted to eat an animal, he wanted to eat it all by himself. Whenever there was meat, his wife and daughter were not there. One day, he wanted to eat a large cow, but he felt embarrassed to eat such a big cow alone. So, he went somewhere nearby and called out his own name, and his wife answered. He asked her, "Where is your husband?" and she replied, "My husband is not here right now." He then told his wife, "I am his God, and I have a very important message for him. When he returns home, tell him to go far into the farm, build a shack house for himself, take a big cow with him, and eat that cow alone. Don't let anyone else touch the cow. Once he has finished eating the entire cow, he can come back home. Please make sure you tell him because if he doesn't do it, he will die with his family." After leaving the message, he returned home without even waiting for his wife to inform him of the news. He was the first to know if anyone had left a message for him. Then his wife told him everything that the voice had said. After listening, he started crying and told his wife and children that they had all worked hard together, so how could he do such a thing just because God commanded him to eat the entire cow alone? He would rather die than to do such a thing. He just wanted to hear what his wife had to say so he could go ahead and eat the cow. His wife replied, saying it would be better for him to eat the cow alone than for their entire family to die together. So, go ahead and do what God asked you to do. When you are done eating the cow, you'll come back to us. Then he is very happy with what his wife said, whether he is playing or not, he is happy to eat the cow by himself.

Now he goes far away into the farm and builds his shack house. While he builds the shack house, his family still helps him because they believe it was God who told him to do so, and they want to follow what God's told him to do. After the farmer finishes building his shack house, even though his family helped him, they cannot be there when he's going to eat the cow. Good chance and courage, on the first day, he makes sure he has enough food and water so he won't have to leave his meat until he's finished eating it all. And that's exactly what he does. He goes to the farm, gathers whatever kind of food he wants, and puts it inside the shack house. As for water, he does the same, making many trips to a water source to collect enough water. He decided early not to move until he had eaten all the meat.

Making his last trip to the water source, he notices a crab freshly walking on the sand. Although he believes he has enough meat for now, curiosity gets the better of him, and he sets out to find that crab. He follows the crab's design in the sand until he finally reaches a point where the crab is under a rock. However, when he lifted the rock, it was more than the original crab, it was a head without a body! He sees it is not a crab and he drops it to the ground and turns away. The head speaks to him, saying he cannot leave it behind because he was looking for it under the rock, and he must take it home. The man realizes it's just a head and assumes it can't harm him, so he grabs his water and tries to go home, leaving the head behind. But the head insists that he must take it home or face eternal death. Ignoring the warning, the man refuses to listen and the head commands him to fall dead. He collapses, appearing lifeless for a moment, then the head commands him to come back to life, and he revives.

Now the head demands that he take it home with him, or he will be dead forever. The farmer, being a lover of meat, not only listens to the head but obeys it as well. He actually takes the head with him to his shack house, where he plans to eat the big cow all by himself. Upon reaching his shack house, he believes that he owns the shack house and the meat because a head without a body cannot eat anything.

Now the head and the farmer are in the shack house. The farmer tries to put the head outside, but the head says, "No, no! Put me inside on a seat." By the way, the man only has one seat in the shack house, and now that seat no longer belongs to him. The man doesn't want to die anymore because he has a big cow to eat. He reluctantly places the head on the seat and begins cooking his first meal. He prepares a generous amount of meat and prepares good food.

When the food is ready, the man tries to taste it, but the head says, "Don't taste my food. I am the only one who gets to taste it." The man opens his mouth and says to the head, "I own this food. What are you talking about? Why can't I taste it?" The head insists on its demand. When the man tries to taste the food, the head commands him to fall dead, and the man actually falls dead. After a minute, the head commands the man to come back to life, and the man awakens.

Now the head instructs the man to place all the food within the reach of his mouth. After the man arranges the food within the head's reach, the head orders the man to fall dead. Once again, the man falls dead. After consuming all the food, the head commands the man to wake up and return to life. The farmer wakes up, and the head instructs the man to make more food right away. But each time the man prepares the food, he doesn't even have a chance to taste it. This continues, and the man actually starts getting smaller because he is not allowed to eat and is forced to cook food for the head every hour without being able to taste or eat it. Anytime the food is ready, the head says fall dead and just after the man is done, has to put the food where his mouth can reach. Now, the man is not only thinking about how he cannot eat his meat he loves so much, but he starts thinking about a good reason for him to share the meat with his family, so they can eat and he, himself can eat too.

After one week, the head had consumed the cow and all the other food the man had in the shack, then they dashed out to find the man's family. However, the head begins to watch him closely as he tries to leave. The head asks him, "Where are you going?" Now the man answers, explaining that he has a family—his wife and children—and he hasn't seen them for one week, so it's time for him to see them. The head says that the man must take it home as well. Now, the man starts crying because he is already too small from not being allowed to eat, and now he has to take the head with him. For the farmer, that will be the end for him and his family. As he is thinking about this, he remembers when he lied, saying that if he didn't eat the cow by himself, they would all die. While he continues to cry, the head asks, "Will you take me home or not?" The man says no, and the head commands him to fall dead. The man falls dead. After a minute, the head commands him to wake up, and the man comes back to life. Now, the head insists that the man takes it home, and the man has no other choice but to take the head to his house.

The farmer carries the head on his shoulder as they make their way home. The head has been eating a lot of meat and has become plenty heavy for the man to carry, while the man himself has not eaten anything at all. To carry a heavy head like that is a punishment for the man, but he must carry the head or die. After a very long day, despite his misery, he finally reaches home. However, when the man's family sees him, rather than being happy, they have a double surprise. The man has become nothing but bones and skin, and he now has a double head.

Now the man's wife and daughter must help him in putting the head down from his shoulder. As he tries to explain what has happened to him, the head interrupts, and insists that there is no time for talking right now, only to make some food for it to eat. The head says that they must prepare a cow the same as the one it ate at the shack house, or a bigger cow for him to eat. Wherever they go, they must carry the head with them. If they don't comply, the head will make them dead, and when he re-awakens them, they must do what he wanted them to do because they don't want to die for real.

They bring the head along with them to the farm, and the head chooses the cow it wants to eat first at their home. Afterward, they return home to prepare the cow. After they are done with the preparation, they have to take the head back to the farm so it can choose the type of food it wants them to bring home to eat with the cow. The head chooses everything he can see, such as plantains, bananas, name root, potatoes, and taro. They make many trips, each time carrying the head with them because he doesn't want them to leave him out. The head ensures everything is ready, and then he says it is time for food.

So, this becomes the third surprise for the man's family, as they still do not know what has happened to him with the head. The man knows that he will not be eating anything, but his wife and daughter thought they were going to eat a meal. They didn't know because the head wouldn't let the man tell them anything. The wife tries to taste the food because she sees how her husband has gotten very thin. She says maybe he is probably thinking too much about having to eat the whole cow without his family, who had stayed at home. However, the real truth is a step closer, waiting to be revealed and shared with them. As the wife tries to taste the food, the head says that no one except itself is allowed to taste the food. Now, the man's family begins to wonder greatly. The head tastes the food and declares it to be good. Finally, the meal is ready, and the head tells them to bring the food where its mouth can reach. Hearing that, the man's family eventually understood what was happening, they started crying. The head tells them there is nothing to cry about and to place the food within his reach. The family refused to do that and the head commanded all of them to fall dead. In an instant, he ordered them to come back to life. This time, the head's commands are fast because it sees that its food is ready, and it wants to eat. As they come back to life, the head tells them to place the food by its mouth. Eventually, they position the food where the head's mouth can reach, and immediately after, the head commands them to fall dead once again. They comply, and they are once again lifeless. After the head finishes eating its meal, it instructs them to come back to life, and they revive. This pattern continues daily until the entire family is reduced to skin and bones.

One day, the man's wife had a chance to talk to a neighbor who was concerned about how the farmer's family looked. She actually tells the neighbor and he reveals that he knows the head well and can help them deal with the situation and overthrow its power. Now, she is very happy, but she wondered how this opportunity would become possible. The neighbor told the man's wife that she shall, every morning, when the head always wants you to take it to the shower. The head enjoyed the water, having lived in it before becoming attached to the family. After the head finished showering, it desired to have its hair brushed well and be placed under the sun for a short while before being taken back inside. The neighbor advised the man's wife to tie the head's hair up high, straight toward the sky, and position it on a tall chair outside the house to bask in the morning sun. After all, don't stay anywhere close to it. Put it there alone because there are eagles that are always looking for food during that time of the morning. If the eagles spotted the head without anyone around, they would fly down lower and grab up the head and take it as food to eat. Happy, the wife returned to the house in peace.

The next morning, early in the morning, they took the head to the shower, as it preferred bathing at that time. After the shower, they brushed its hair up and tied it straight up toward the sky, placing the head on a tall chair as its final resting spot without a body. They prepared the head the same way as the neighbor instructed. The head was happy because it could see everywhere from its seat. But, when it heard the eagles squawking, screeching, and crying from above, the head started calling for the man to come and take it inside. The head didn't want the man to know its fear of the eagles. The family pretended as though they didn't know that the head and the eagles were not friends. With each cry from the eagles, the head called out to the man more desperately. However, this time, they kept telling the head to wait a moment, making the head seriously mad. It didn't want to have them to fall dead because it didn't want the eagles to attack while they were lifeless. As the eagles flew lower in the sky, the head began crying out for the people to come and bring it inside the house. During their refusal to bring the head inside the house, one eagle plunged down and grabbed it by the hair, getting its claws around the knot tied to the head's hair. The eagle soared into the sky, far above a rocky mountain, pursued by plenty of other eagles. When they reach the highest part of the mountain, the knot tie loosens, and the head falls onto the rocks below. At that moment, the head shattered and sprayed like water across the mountain, where the eagles, along with other animals, participated in a feast. It was a moment of peace for the farmer's family, and they expressed great thanks to their helpful neighbor.

Never forget that your problems will catch up with you in a way that will not make you happy. But, in the end, someone might agree that they benefited from the problem. Let's imagine a man who has a wife and only one daughter. They are a family and possess many animals that are good to eat. But whenever the man wants to eat one animal, he plans only for himself, leaving his wife and daughter with nothing to eat. So, who can he blame other than himself? His family has no reason to blame him, as he is already blamed by the head without a body.

Right now, the man is finally completing his education from the Head-Out-Body University. Through this experience, he learns the importance of sharing with his family. He now understands that his wife is the one who finds ways to free them from their problem. He also understands that his neighbor deserves respect for the ingenious way he liberated them from the head without the body, and loves him with all his heart.

Now, when the time comes to eat the big cow, the entire family will have a chance to laugh and enjoy themselves. They have been working hard both at home and on the farm, especially in taking care of the animals. The lessons learned from the Head-Out-Body University have taught the man not to abuse his family.

The head can only think and take action because it has no heart. When a person thinks about something, their brain can send and receive signals from their heart to assess whether it is something they should do or not. However, it is something totally different in the case of the head without the body. The head can only think and act immediately. Whatever the level of your knowledge, the things you ignore are greater than you because they are not ignoring you or your actions.

The farmer had his head, but he did not have a good brain, which led him to betray himself and believe he misled his family. That is why he gained valuable knowledge at the Head-Out-Body University. As for his professor, the head, he did not have a heart but only a head. Eagles possess both a head and a heart, making them highly intelligent. No other bird can surpass them. They can see better than any other creature on Earth, and they are more wise and capable. No other birds can beat them.

Eagles fly higher than most other birds that have ever existed, and their vision allows them to observe everything on Earth from a great distance. This makes them crucial contributors to the liberation of the meat-loving man and his family. Regardless of the situation you find yourself in or the circumstances you observe, it may seem that there is no solution to it. However, that is not the case. The solution is simply unknown to you, but it is undoubtedly close by. You just don't know how to grab it.*

When your eyes eventually grow too dark to perceive the light, A light is shining somewhere, especially for you. When you cannot see the green color, some green trees are planted somewhere, especially for you, bearing your name. When you are alone, many others are honoring your name, especially you. When you isolate yourselves, someone very special is still looking out, especially for you. When you think you are done And over, many still consider you the most special one. You are what they live for. Many eyes witness a bird struck by a predator, but that bird, in its time, dies in its secure spot.

Builders of a Big Tower

* A big nation in the world decided to build the greatest tower that has ever existed. To ensure that the tower is constructed according to their vision, they carefully selected the most skilled builders whom they believed were capable of building this dream without any difficulty. They were confident that these chosen builders would not make any errors at all. During the construction phase, everyone was happy to see some good construction.

However, not long after reaching the midway point, frustrations began to arise among the selected individuals. These frustrations quickly spread and affected everyone involved, both on the field and in the offices. In the midst of the construction and amidst the confusion, everyone wanted to be the one to provide the best solution for achieving the greatest result.

Many other contractors continue coming, saying that they are best suited to make good repairs to the foundation and get the construction back on track the way it is supposed to be. With so many bids to choose from, they chose those they deemed most qualified. When the repair jobs started, everyone was filled with optimism. Unfortunately, just before completing the first quarter of the project, the tower deteriorated, becoming worse than ever before.

Now, they decided to try another approach by bringing in some different contractors to take charge. They placed these new contractors ahead of the previous builders. Despite making multiple selections through various bids, these particular contractors confidently stated that there was no doubt their work would be perfect. However, as soon as they began, they proved to be unfit for the task, unable to set the tower on the right path.

These dreams turned into hopeless aspirations. For over a century, the project continued in the same manner, without a trace of success. But, time and money ask for no pity at all.

After trying so many different contractors for the tower and never being able to find the right one to complete the project, they became exhausted. Despite their fatigue, they were determined to see the tower built and couldn't retreat until they witnessed a great accomplishment in the work they had already started. Actually, they decided to take more bids, even from those who had never been considered before, and as a result, all contractors began to come forward, including those who had previously missed their chances. They didn't want anyone else to outshine them.

After carefully reviewing numerous details, they discerned that they needed to give a chance to someone who had never been given an opportunity before. The initial builders and contractors acknowledged their past mistakes but emphasized that they should be the ones to repair the tower due to the valuable lessons they had learned from their errors. They believed that they had acquired enough knowledge by now to successfully accomplish the construction of a good tower.

After conducting multiple revisions and interviews, they finally chose a new contractor whom many of them thought might be qualified for the job. Now, the main concern for the former builders and contractors was whether, if this new contractor succeeded, they would lose future opportunities to secure other jobs. They worried that when the next tower needed to be built, it would be the new contractor who would be chosen. They wondered how much setback they would have to endure before reclaiming their positions. Despite the potential compromises, they agreed that they should do whatever it took to regain the job. Now more than ever was the time to showcase their abilities, capacities, and dedication.

Everyone needs to learn from their past and become better for the future. This was important because repeating the same mistakes could undermine their progress and hopes for achieving anything positive. Time was passing fast, and minds could change, along with unforeseen events that were not on the shortlist. Only those who were alive could make plans, but if they were not executed, the plans would be deceased or carried out by someone else.

During the time the new contractor was on the job, many words would be spoken, but who could accurately predict what would happen? Someone might try, but even the most ordinary things could sometimes betray the future. One thing was certain, though: it was not yet time to find fault with the new contractor's work. Of course, a construction area might always have some dust that could be complained about, but if you were involved in the project, you wouldn't worry about the dust. It would only be a problem for visitors and those living near the project site, who would be unhappy because of the dust.

While waiting to see whether the tower would turn out to be a successful project, the former builders and contractors, including some recent candidates who had attempted to secure the job, were preparing themselves to become more desirable candidates for future opportunities. However, they held the belief that if the current contractor performed well, they would continue to choose contractors of the same kind. They were now facing another period of waiting, hoping to witness a setback that would enable them to achieve their objectives.

It is very difficult to witness a job that many people from the past were not capable of accomplishing being realized by an unexpected person. While in games, many people prefer to see their own choices, the reality remains stable for almost everything you want to do if you are the one doing it without interruption. The main point cannot be changed without a valid reason. At the end, everyone might agree on only one point, even when some ideas may be different. After experiencing denials, everyone can come together to see how a better avenue can be established to satisfy their plans, which they don't want to give up.

There is a time to hope, a time to gain, and another time to give up, accept, or agree to what should not be done on your behalf. But the more occupied you are, the more important your time becomes, not only for yourself but also for others. Life can hold great significance for those at the tower, those attempting to build the tower, and those who believe a tower can protect them and their loved ones. They appreciate the times that prove all the efforts made before have not brought them closer to a positive realization and may never yield any rewards at all. After hundreds of years, no one has found a positive way to complete the tower, which proves that all efforts have been in vain. Anyone who wants to attempt the same will encounter the same outcome.

There is only one person who can be defeated, and that can be a heavy burden. But when many people experience defeat, everyone can draw strength from it. While building a big tower may never reach the standards of a nation, let alone the world, the focus should be on creating something acceptable and forgetting about being better, because "better" is the enemy of what is good. If you have something good and you strive to make it better, there's a possibility that you'll end up destroying what you've worked hard for.

Three Young Professionals Compete
for a Pretty Girl

Years later, in the present day, three professionals were living in a town. All three of them were young men. One was a laboratory doctor, another was a general inspector, and the third was a scientific man. When they all wanted to get married, they found themselves competing for the same young girl. But now, each of them needed to understand that he was not the only one trying to marry the young girl. Likewise, the three young men were not the only ones who wanted to marry her. But, because they are for the most good professionals the competition is primarily between the three of them. This complicated matters for the young girl as she had to choose between three professionals.

Individually, each one of them needed to make their own effort to be the right one to choose. Now, each man has made up his own mind. The science doctor stated that he will pay close attention to every creature in his line of work to determine exactly which one he should imitate, believing that this will lead him to victory over the other two men. After close observation, he decided to imitate the honeybee.

The inspector man said that he would inspect every other professional's creature, believing that this would help him identify the perfect creature to imitate and become the winner. He proceeded to conduct thorough inspections of every living creature he encountered, hoping to find his inspiration. After his last inspection, he decided to imitate the spider.

The laboratory doctor said, as a doctor, he will focus on finding a creature that matches his own profession, believing that it will be the ideal one for him to imitate. As he said, he goes out and looks.

After he does his search, he selects the mosquito as the creature that best represents his profession.

While the scientific honeybee, the inspector spider, and the laboratory doctor mosquito start making their trips to the girl's house, her parents, who owned the house, would often see them but dismiss them as mere insects of different kinds just passing by. Initially, the homeowners think these were passing insects, but as they continue to see them so many times, they begin to suspect that these are different insects each time. The wife continued to see the insects and got very scared because this is the first period they continually notice these insects there. They might call pest control to investigate to see if some insects have taken place somehow at the house. If this turns out to be true and they call pest control, all three professionals will be destroyed.

The science man, determined to imitate the honeybee, believed it to be the most intelligent and skilled professional. He hopes that by imitating the honeybee, he can develop greater abilities and surpass his competitors. On the other hand, the general inspector, during his inspections, discovered the spider is a very marvelous creature who can work very fast, build protective structures, and find food for itself. As such a hard worker, the spider is a worthy creature to imitate

Meanwhile, the laboratory doctor has a specific criterion for his choice. He sought a creature that can perform tasks similar to his own profession, leading him to select the mosquito. Despite its small size, the mosquito possessed all the necessary tools and instruments required to carry out its work as a laboratory doctor. The mosquito preferred not to carry heavy bags, but it had everything it needed to practice its profession effectively.

After all, the three men were confident in themselves. Individually, each one believed he was the most qualified to marry the girl. In order for one of them to win her over, they all decided to meet together before the girl. They decided to put on a joint show, allowing them to discuss among themselves which one will capture the girl's attention the most. When they arrived at the girl's house for the show, the homeowners, a man and a woman, were not present. This was the first show witnessed by the girl, and the men had plenty to say amongst themselves. After the men left, a neighbor who had observed them approached and informed the homeowners about the presence of insects in their house. The homeowners expressed gratitude to the neighbor for bringing this to their attention. They discuss the situation among themselves and make the final decision to call a pest control company.

The pest control company, known as "The Last Shows and Competitions of Insects," agreed to inspect and treat the house. An appointment is set up, and the job is done at once. The process will take about a week before the covers can be removed. While the house was being treated, the company placed an advertisement that read: "Fest to all insects." During this time, the science doctor honeybee, general inspector spider, and laboratory doctor mosquito will pay their visits.

This time, the three men will not arrive at the same hour but separately. The general inspector spider makes the first trip and upon reaching the house, he notices the invitation. He goes in and occupies a corner close to the ceiling. The science doctor honeybee arrives at the next hour and also sees the invitation. He claims a spot underneath the roof soffit for himself. Finally, the laboratory doctor mosquito makes his appearance. As a doctor who always carries his instruments, he doesn't want to stay in one place. He flies from corner to corner, exploring different areas in search of potential clients to draw something.

While flying inside, Doctor Mosquito approached the corner where General Inspector Spider was stationed. The mosquito rested on the wall, and at that moment, General Inspector Spider was on duty. He approached Doctor Mosquito and said, "I must inspect you, Doctor Laboratory, before you leave." Doctor Mosquito responded to the inspector, "You cannot even fly. How can you inspect a doctor who can fly?" Mosquito tried to fly and escape, but it was already too late. Mosquito's wings are ensnared. After the inspection was conducted, the inspector discovered that Doctor Mosquito was not a licensed doctor. Mosquito had been traveling from one hospital to another, drawing blood without a permit. Now, Doctor Mosquito has to stay in prison until he can see a judge. After the judges decided, Doctor Lab had to remain imprisoned for a certain amount of time.

Scientific Honeybee wanted to visit a beautiful garden in the field and tried to find a free way to enter and exit. In doing so, Honeybee discovered the corner where General Inspector Spider's office was located. Honeybee rested there for a little while, and General Inspector Spider approached, standing a far distance away from Scientific Honeybee. Inspector Spider identified himself as the General Inspector Spider. Honeybee detected Spider's mouth moving and tried to leave because Honeybee can't see anyone and can't hear anything. However, as he is trying to leave, he understands everything.

When Scientific Honeybee can't move due to the snare set by Inspector Spider, Honeybee asks the inspector what is going wrong. The Inspector Spider, a little scared of Scientific Honeybee, said, "As you know, the government puts laws in place and continues to reinforce them every year. I don't want you to misunderstand the new laws, which is why I want to briefly inspect you, but you are not under arrest." Now, Inspector Spider sees his chance to be the better creature imprisoning the other two competitors. As he sees it, there are no mistakes. He is the only one who can benefit that pretty girl. As for Doctor Laboratory Mosquito, he can't stay in prison for too long. He always needs some ventilation to help him breathe, which he doesn't have at that moment. He just died at that moment. As for Doctor Scientific Honeybee, he becomes upset in prison because it was his first time being arrested and imprisoned. He continues to hurt himself on the prison walls until he also dies. Inspector Spider wakes up and walks very slowly, conducting inspections to ensure that both Doctor Laboratory Mosquito and Doctor Scientific Honeybee are dead. After completing the inspections, he confirmed that both are dead. They are no more. Now, only General Inspector Spider remains. He'll see if he can claim the girl as his prize.

Doctor General Inspector Spider continues his work while the pest control company controls the insects in the house. They control Doctor General Inspector Spider before he marries his dream girl, the most beautiful girl in the eyes of so many, especially these three untouchable professionals. None of those three men obtain a chance to even see when a different mouth is eating the fruit they work so hard to acquire, until a road leads to their downfall. In conclusion, the wise shall not compete because competition never truly wins. If you apparently win through excessive power, when it's time to rest, you might not enjoy your trophy.

All three professionals are destroyed due to the condition of competition. Early in the morning, they come to clean up the house while a beautiful dove arrives. That dove has the unexpected chance to win all the cases without a single competitor. The dove is now getting married and forming a very smart family living in a mountain close to a valley plain where people cultivate a lot of rice. The dove's family became the most famous family ever to live in that area. Every morning, the dove family takes a shower and goes to the top of the mountain to sing a song for the glory of a beautiful day. The dove family always sings their beautiful song for the glory of those who cultivate the rice around that valley, making them the most fortunate doves in the area. They no longer have to worry about eating any more bees, spiders, and mosquitoes.

Garden Talks to Owner

A man with his family lived near a valley where the dove family also lived. He has many lands and cultivates a lot of rice. While cultivating the rice, the man was also planting a little vegetable garden, mostly beans. Being busy with his rice field, he didn't have enough time to take care of the small farm. One day, he finally decided to visit the neglected garden that he had planted months ago. At the time he's coming he looks and sees that little garden looks good, but he thought that little garden did not produce because he did not take care of that little garden. As he got closer, he exclaimed, "My garden is looking good!" Surprisingly, the little garden answered him, saying, "The way I was there, did I have an owner too?" When the man hears the garden talk, he is shocked and runs off with non-stop speed. While still running very fast, he sees another man carrying a bundle of wood, he hurries up so he can reach that man.

The wood man, noticing his fast pace, waits for him. When the garden man catches up, the wood man asks why he was running so fast. The garden man explained that he had a little garden but hadn't had enough time to take care of it. Now that he had a little time, he went to take a look. To his surprise, the garden looked good, and he exclaimed, "My garden looks good!" In response, the little garden answered by saying, "The way I was here, did I have an owner too?" This question left the garden owner astounded.

The wood carrier then questioned whether that was a good enough reason to run so fast. The bundle of wood that the wood carrier carried replied, asking if the wood man wouldn't run in the same situation. Hearing the talking wood, the wood man didn't have time to contemplate what he had just said. He only had time to drop the wood and run away. Actually, rather than one man running, two men are running with two different but similar pieces of news. When you're not the one singing, all songs are easy for you. When you're not the one dancing, all dances are easy for you. However, when your time is near, you're never adequately prepared to dance or sing better. While the wood carrier accompanied the garden owner, many others passing by listened to their news. Just imagine, if only one person carries the news, not many people will be interested in hearing it. But because there are two of them, everyone took their words to heart. Among people who did not hear the news, some of them continue to make similar mistakes.

Two Brothers Become Kings

Two brothers were outside their parents' homes when the older brother saw a beast. Upon closer inspection, he realized it was a serpent, although not a large one. He grabbed a rod and attempted to kill it, but the serpent opened its mouth wide, revealing its forked tongue. Fearing for his life, the older brother ran away from the serpent. The younger brother, however, said they couldn't run from such a small serpent, but that he would kill it. So, he got the rod and approached the serpent, but as he got closer, the serpent did the same as it did to the big brother; opened its mouth wide and put out its forked tongue. Now, the younger brother himself had to run away, leaving the serpent alive. Sometimes, a small mistake is not something we ponder, but it can prevent a bigger mistake.

As the two brothers grew up, the older one became the king of their nation, and the younger one served as the vice king. A problem arose between their nation and another nation. The president decided to resolve the issue by sending a special envoy to the other nation, and the other nation did the same. They should have imagined resolving the problem in a few days, but with good common sense, they could understand if they were making any progress or not. As time went by, they declared that progress was being made, and the situation was becoming calm between the two nations. They had no reason to worsen things further, as everyone agreed that good dialogue was the solution.

If anyone sees a beast and turns away from it, it is normal. But when you try to kill that beast, it fights back for its own life until you retreat and run away, leaving it with its life. You must understand that in that moment, you are the one who is defeated. When the older brother saw the serpent, he initially tried to kill it but then changed his mind and left without running away. However, when his brother attempted to kill the serpent, they both ended up running away as the defeated ones.

The arguments between the two ruling nations can be compared and may be similar in the same manner. If only the two brothers had remembered or learned a lesson from what happened to them, it would demonstrate the importance of paying attention to whatever is on your path as a human. The two brothers continue to rule the nation, and everyone in the nation agrees that they are doing a good job. There is nothing to worry about in the nation. The problem with the other nation seems to have a good result, and both parties continue to do their work efficiently.

According to the agreement between the two brothers, the time has come for the power to shift from the older brother to the younger brother. The older brother will now become the vice king, while the younger one, who was the vice king, will rise up and become the king of his nation. They have executed the promise between them, and whenever a change is made in power, the new leaders will also make changes to the laws of the nation. A problem that was on its way to resolution will now become a focal point for that nation and the other nation, to determine whether the present situation will cooperate with the previous agreement that was progressing well. However, the younger brother has decided to make some changes. As you know, to make changes, you must also consider demolishing what you already have in place. The new king is actually going back to the basics of the situation to determine what he wants to keep or reject. At the same time, the rulers of the other nation have realized that they themselves need to be prepared to make whatever changes are good and necessary for themselves.

Actually, the two brothers do not remember their little history with the serpent. When the younger brother comes into power, he decides to escalate the situation with the other nation because, in his view, they cannot reach a better agreement to prevent such a catastrophic moment. The new king makes the decision to engage his nation in war with the other country, despite the different ideas of his own brother, the vice king, the former king, and other high-ranking members of the kingdom. After more than a year of misguided efforts from both countries, war seems to be the only option in their eyes.

So, a big war starts between the two nations, lasting for more than a year and resulting in significant loss of life and wealth for both sides. Eventually, the other nation gains control over the limited territory of the two brothers' nation and finally enters the capital. At this point, the two brothers have no choice but to accept defeat, not only for themselves but for the entire nation they had ruled for many years.

Two possibilities emerge: either the pursuit of perfection is the enemy of achieving something good, or there is a failure to pay attention to a reality that can affect more than just one person or one nation. When the two brothers were fleeing from the serpent, they were running from their garden to the house where they lived. Now, they are fleeing from their positions of power, seeking refuge and hiding. If one can analyze the situation thoroughly, it might lead to a reexamination of the initial agreement they had with the other nation.

Now, there is no longer a question of any agreement between the two nations, but only a question of what kind of favors that nation may obtain from its enemy. Whether they should consider it as hostility or anticipate what may happen, all depends on how they manage the overthrow of the two brothers from power. When the two brothers used to run from the serpent in the garden to their homes, they never blamed each other because nobody missed anything. But now, that may not be the same because there are too many questions about to arise, not only concerning the two brothers but the entire nation. The two brothers were running from their positions of power, but when they were running from the serpent, the serpent did not pursue them. The serpent only wanted to protect its own life, just as they wanted to protect their lives. This time, the other nation decided not to pursue the two brothers, but a serpent doesn't miss anything just to make someone run away for their life. So, if you are running from war, you might have to pay somehow, which means experiencing double loss. The other nation seizes enough wealth from the two brothers' nation to cover their expenses for the war that the younger brother had caused between the two nations. When the brothers learn that the enemies are leaving the country, they hurry to return to their positions as king and vice king before someone else takes over.

They were not thinking about additional situations, but while entering the capital of the nation, they were captured by only three soldiers of the other nation who were left behind because they were still in the field when the other soldiers left. They had no other chance but to find their way back home, and now they were thought to be the ones to carry the two big spoils: the king and vice king. Meanwhile, the two brothers and former rulers were under arrest by the three soldiers. The five individuals had to cross the valley where many intelligent doves resided. The two brothers used to hide near the valley, and when they ate rice, they always shared some with the doves. As a result, the doves didn't have to fly far to find their food, and they were very happy to have the men as neighbors. When the doves saw the men under arrest, they flew onto a tree and began singing a beautiful song. In that song, they expressed gratitude by saying thanks to the glory of a beautiful nation where strangers couldn't understand their language, "Ooh king and vice king". You did not grant anyone a license to hunt any doves in that valley. There where you are for your own glories, please, playing like you were both dead.

The two brothers heard and understood what the doves were saying because it was the same language spoken in their country. Both men pretended to be dead, playing along with the doves' the two brothers were dead. Since the soldiers had no means of transportation and no one else was present when they arrested the brothers, they freed themselves from the burden and decided to make their way home without the king and vice king as their spoils. As for the doves, they remained perched on the tree, observing the scene. They sang a different song this time, they say, happy are those who keep friends with the doves of the valley, as they would never be carried off as spoils by enemies to another country. When the enemies are listening to the news, they should wonder a great wonder. Please wake up and go ahead and eventually restore yourselves in power.

The two brothers woke up and made their way back home. In order to reach the capital of the nation it would take two days' time. This time, they made it overnight. Before resuming their jobs as king and vice king, they focused on loving the beasts rather than killing them. Anybody can learn from the beast, just as the doves in the valley teach even the kings to love and respect their neighbors. We should never engage in a moment that undermines our neighbors' lives, but instead embrace different ideas.

When the two brothers returned to their positions as king and vice king, they became the best rulers the world had ever seen. They brought peace not only to the human population but also to the animals. The nation had good leaders to guide them, and If they hadn't overlooked their initial lesson, no problems would exist. This is a great thanks to the lessons learned from the birds of the sky who were plentiful in wisdom.

As the two brothers grew old, the nation pondered over who would rule next, as they did not want to repeat the grave errors. They understood that wisdom should be the main focus, as the lives of everyone were in jeopardy when wise leaders didn't rule. If you are certain you are a bird and you don't have wings, don't try to fly. By doing such a thing, you are inviting defeat upon yourself. Just stay on the ground until your wings can finally reach you, and then everyone will recognize you as a bird. *

> **When a bird is out of his wings, he is the first guest of the dust, and the insects like ants and mosquitoes. When that bird is able to fly away, there is no regret in his heart at all. When your eyes are too red to see the roses, when your heart is too small to carry the moon, when your mind cannot brave the freezing ocean, when your memory cannot touch the atmosphere, when your desires cannot travel among the stars, when your senses cannot feel the sun, lay down wherever you are and make a beautiful dream which is important to you and for the world.**

Young Man on the Roof

* A young man was always wanting to work on the roof of a building, but his legs are too short to cross the soffit and reach the roof. One day, with the help of some friends, he finally manages to reach the top. However, he is disappointed to find that there is nothing for him to do there. He stands and watches others working instead. Being a boy, he finds ways to pass the time and not feel bored. He gathers some friends and starts playing dominos.

As the game progresses, the boy realizes that he has more dominos in his hand than the other boys. Now, he doesn't want them to win the game. He blocks the game, hoping to win by counting the points. However, after blocking the dominos game, all he sees in his hands are big pieces like doubles and larger ones. This means he can't win anything. Determined to win the game instantly changed to a card game. They play two rounds, but no one has won yet.

Because that boy wants to win, he doesn't want to lose even though he hasn't won anything in the first two games. For that reason, the games are played so the last winner wins everything. Now the boy is confident that no one else but himself can win the last game. And by winning the last game, he will be the only winner of all the games.

As everyone is playing to win, it's difficult to determine who will win the game. However, good sense can be put to the test. The chances of winning are better for someone who hasn't won a single game yet. With patience, one can see the ant's womb. With faith and patience, the boy continues playing his game, hoping to be the last winner who takes everything.

While playing, the boy looks around and does not see his big brother, who was with him earlier. Concerned, the boy gets up and starts searching for his big brother. He searches everywhere until he spots his brother standing somewhere, unable to walk because someone seriously injured his right shoulder. Frustrated, the boy expresses his anger, stating that if the person responsible for injuring his brother is aware of his existence, he should either die himself or take revenge for hurting his sibling.

While the boy walks past his brother's house, it appears that someone had placed a sharp tool as a snare where he had to walk. The tool cut the boy's right foot near his ankle joint. When the boy looks and realizes that his foot cannot be replaced, he feels a deep pain in his soul. He accepts that this is how he will be for the rest of his life, walking with this disability. He believes that he will never be of any good to himself again. However, both his life and his big brother's life are on bitter tracks, and they now need to find the strength to prove to themselves that they are not defeated. They were born as men from a brave mother, and they should continue to be brave. If it should become worse, they must reinforce their power and strength.

Unfortunately, the brothers may never be together or fulfill their old dreams, their existence will cease only when they return to the dust. Everything will sleep as it did before they were born. As for the games, they are not over yet. The boy is still waiting for his last game to be the winner. He is determined not to give up, despite the bitter moments or the challenges of life. He will carry on with the game until the end, even if he has to fight for his big brother or risk becoming a victim himself. Embarrassing moments are like the sun, providing nourishment for the skin that needs it. Defeat serves as a refreshing water, and a strong wind is for the weak legs.

While the boy is still growing up, he is more than happy to befriend another boy who lives nearby his house. One day, they went to a river together. When they reached the water, that friend hurt him badly in the head and then ran away, leaving the boy behind. The boy helped himself out of the water and sat on a stone until he felt well enough to make his way back home. When he felt good enough, he returned home and never asked his friend about why he did such a thing. When his friend didn't hear him say anything, he came over and apologized, saying he didn't mean to do it. The boy only responded with a yes, but he never tried to keep a friendship with that kind of boy again. Sometimes, a simple action can tell many things. Maybe that boy is not the one who can be a real friend. The boy already knows that, but he didn't realize it until he saw his friend's actions. He chose to keep himself away from the bad boy.

Some years later, the bad boy's true identity showed the person he truly was, not a good person. Suppose the boy had forced himself to stay friends with him? That would never be a good friendship. Most of the time, it's not easy to listen or learn from what you see or suspect, but it's always better to run when you see a rope rather than be killed by a venomous serpent. The boy is still focused on winning in the games, not losing, even though he may not have gotten any spoils yet. Just like when a bird gets caught in a snare and manages to fly away, the bird catcher doesn't win anything. If the boy has enough knowledge to keep himself away by understanding his friend's actions, it shows how much he values his cause to win without regret. Whether young or old, a person can always learn from others, just as they can learn from someone else's mistakes. That's why sensible people can learn from anything, including trees and animals.

Goat Steeler is Back to Prison

Two men have been sentenced to prison, one of them for his non-stop stealing of the farmers' goats. Actually, he has one year to spend in prison before they can let him out. The second man has one year and one day to spend in prison before they can set him free. These two men went to the tribunal, and the judge told them about the time they would spend in prison. However, they themselves didn't even know how many days make up a month. When their sentences were pronounced by the judge, they thought it was a short period of time. Every single day, these two men believe they will be released from prison on that day. But as weeks go by and they are not being released, they start getting upset and very impatient. They are nowhere close to seeing the end of their prison term.

After a week in prison, whenever the prison guards come by, the two prisoners want to know if they will be set free that day. Every time they ask the guards when they will be set free, the guards try to explain to them, but without a good result. It's because these two men don't know how many days in a week, let alone anything about months and years.

When a month is over, the two men are still in prison. Now they are saying that it is worse than death, complaining at every little chance they can find. But the reality is that they were never told two words: the word "long" and the word "punishment." They never understood that they were there to receive a long punishment. They didn't even know if they were there to be punished, and they have no concept of weeks, months, or years, but they can understand the concept of a long time. Now, after two months, the men are discouraged, saying they will never be released from prison. They believe that nothing is possible for them anymore except to stay in prison forever. But even as they say they are resigning themselves to staying in prison forever, every single day they think is the day they might get out of prison. The only thing they have a chance to hear the guards say is they can get out of the prison. For them, it's something they think could happen at any minute because they are not able to understand anything at all.

After six months, their families visit them, and now they are sure about their freedom. But when it comes to counting the time, every day is the day they have in their minds for their release from prison. Now, after about nine months, too many hopes without results, the two thieves are impatient. However, they have a good chance because there are two of them, not just one. The amount of time they have left to spend in prison is all they can think about and complain about. But they have forgotten the reason why they are in prison. It may be a good chance now that they have only a quarter of their time left behind them.

Time refuses to go fast when you are waiting in line and goes slower when you are under the yoke. These men have more than a million dreams at a time. Twelve months are near the corner for the man who was sentenced to one year in prison. The order was given to the prison guards to bring him to the tribunal, and at that time, the judge set him free. Now he is happy to go back to his house after spending a full year behind bars. The judge at the tribunal explained to him that he only spent one year in prison because it was his first offense as a thief. However, if he steals again, his sentence will be three years in prison. But the man doesn't know the reality of what three years in prison entails.

So, what he was waiting for was the time to be liberated, and now that time has come. It's time to leave the prison and say goodbye to the prison guards. The man is free, and his freedom takes him away from the prison's watchful eyes. Nobody knows how long it will take for him to return to prison, if he ever returns at all. He was in prison far away from his home, but now everyone can see that it's better for him to be released from prison. He finds the road to his house and continues on his way. As he nears home, he passes by a goat farm across the road. While he is passing by, a goat with an allergy to thieves' sneezes. The man becomes furious, saying that he spent all that time in prison because of goats, and now, just after being released, he hasn't even reached home yet and the goat sneezes on him.

Then he tells the goat that if it does that one more time, he will remove that allergy from its nose. While he is still talking, the goat sneezes again, more than three times. The man becomes even more bitter and runs over to the farm. He takes hold of the goat by its neck and strangles it to death.

While that man was killing the goat, the owner of the farm approached. The owner of the farm called for help, and they tied up the thief and took him back to the prison he had just been released from. Now he's in big trouble. He is upset because he believed he had a valid reason and thought the judge would let him go after hearing him out. He was sure he had a reason. The thief arrived back at the prison on the same day he had been released.

When approaching the prison, the prison guards asked him what happened to him so early. He answered the guards and said that even if it were them who had spent all this time in prison for goats and were just released, if a goat were to open its nose and sneeze on them before they even reached home, they would take that sneeze away from its nose so that it would never do it again.

The owner of the goat doesn't know all these details. All he knows is that he caught a thief who was trying to steal his goat, as thieves always do when stealing the goats of farmers. Many questions arise about this thief. After spending one year in prison and being released, he hasn't even returned to where he was living and has already stolen another goat. This proves how much of a nuisance he is to the farmers. His time is going to be longer than he expected.

The farmer goes back to his house and is very happy that he caught one of the thieves who had been stealing his goats for a long time. Now there's no way for him to steal any more goats for a long time because he won't be getting an early release. The farmer and his family rejoice because they have been working harder and harder every day while the thief continued to steal their goats. Now the thief is in prison, and he thought he would win the case where a goat was at fault for sneezing on him after he had spent so much time in prison for goats. In his opinion, the goat should have had pity on him, and the goats should have hidden themselves when they saw him.

If the thief were to win that case, only the judge would know. But the thief himself believes he can get away with it this time. After a few days, they take the thief to court. The first thing the judge asks him is his name. The thief identifies himself as the person who was recently released from prison. The judge then asks him why he has returned, as he has already served his one-year sentence.

The thief explains to the judge that this is a different case that happened to him on his way home after being released from prison. He tells the judge that he knows what it's like to spend a lot of time in prison for goats and then be set free. He almost reached his house when a goat standing on its owner's land sneezed on him. The thief tells the judge that even if he were the judge, he should have taken that sneeze away from the goat's nose so that it would never do it again to anyone who had spent time in prison for goats.

The judge asks the thief where the goat is now. The thief answers and says that the goat was given to the prison guards, who returned it to its owner. The judge says he must see the goat. The guards informed the judge that the goat was killed and couldn't be kept for long, so they made a reasonable decision and allowed the owner to take it with him. The judge asks the thief how the goat ended up being killed.

The thief responds to the judge, stating that when the goat sneezed on him, he grabbed its neck and strangled it to death. The judge tells the thief that he previously claimed the goat had sneezed directly on him. The judge points out that the thief shouldn't have been so close to the goat in the first place and that it is not permissible to enter someone else's property to harm their animals. The judge reminds the thief that for a first-time offense of stealing a goat, the sentence is one year, but if he returns for another theft, the punishment will be three times greater. The judge also notes that the thief has now become a criminal by entering someone else's property and committing such a crime.

The judge concludes by stating that the thief will need to return to the courtroom to face charges for his theft. Moreover, the thief's actions of entering the property and killing the goat result in additional charges carrying a life sentence.

When two individuals go to a courtroom for a judge to decide who is right or wrong, both believe they are in the right. However, it is an unfortunate surprise for the one who firmly believed they would win the case, only to hear that they will spend the rest of their life in prison. The thief man is now going to prison without a chance to voice his complaints because he knows he will never be released again, and he cannot impose his own laws on his neighbors' goats. All his hopes now rest on a miracle that may eventually allow him to escape, but miracles are neither easy nor often.

The thief 's family is heartbroken to learn that he was so nearby but never reached home. Now, all his great hopes have vanished. He only thinks about meeting his friend who was in prison at the same time as him, even though his friend has only one day left before being released, while he himself was already released. Therefore, he lacks the ability to comprehend the significance of a single day at this point.

As for the man who was supposed to be liberated after one year and one day in prison, when the prison guards went to release the goat stealer whose one year was over, they told him he would be released in one more day After the guards left, the man stayed by himself and saw his friend being released from prison. Now he was the only one left, trying to count his time. He thought about one year and one more day, finding three words on his fingers for one more day and only two words for one year. He believed that three was greater than two and that one more day in prison was much longer than one year. He decided to end his life, but as he attempted to do so, a prison guard visited him to give him his final word about his release. The guard had no knowledge of the prisoner's intention, and the prisoner's plan failed at that moment.

The guard spoke to him extensively about his release the next day, but the prisoner couldn't understand the expression "less than one day" the guard used to describe the remaining time. It was his only significant problem. Early in the morning, when the prisoner was on his process to end his life, the prison guards came to release him. Unable to breathe, they thought he was simply sick and took him to a hospital. After a few days, he was sent back home instead of to prison. Now he understood the meaning of "one more day" and "less than one day," but he still didn't comprehend larger units of time like months and years.

After his release, he had the opportunity to learn about the story of his prison friend who had been released before him but unfortunately returned to prison. He himself became a part of that story, for his lack of knowledge. However, he was back home, and this time it wasn't easy to go back to prison. The man decided to let everyone know that he was not the same person and would never return to prison. He explained the misery he experienced for something that held little importance. From that point on, if anyone had to go to prison, it wouldn't be him; it would be someone else. He was determined to say no more to prison, forever and ever.

Everyone could rejoice knowing that he would never go to prison. However, it was heartbreaking for someone to go to prison, not even reaching their home and returning to prison once again.

Man Learns from Vegetables

A man never had a chance to observe the reign of vegetation for a day. While he was in an airplane, he looked at the earth and saw how organized and beautiful it was. This led him to decide to visit a forest with the intention of abandoning his community and living there. What were his main motivations? His main motivations were the unity he perceived in the vegetation, which he doesn't have among the people in his community. He often sees problems arising between people and believed that the community of plants was better than that of humans. He decided to take his family and join the plants.

By the time he plays closer attention, he eventually observes that plants sometimes crowd together, causing damage to one another. Big trees stop the growth of smaller trees, and branches would crush each other. After all, they were united to form a marvelous beauty and provide shade for the protection of one another, more than just for humans and animals. What a valuable lesson! The man said to himself that he had finally learned how to minimize his problems with others and live together with unity and peace, for the benefit of themselves and their children. May the world become wise by learning from what it hears and what it sees. Human problems do not often stem from nature or wild beasts but from other humans. Sometimes, humans can be worse than a tree stopping a small tree from growing.

Wild beasts do the same thing to other small beasts. Physically, humans may not crush your head, but they can crush your business, which represents your efforts to survive, through their actions and words. They refuse, rebuke, minimize, lie, scam, and more. Just like when you have two plants of the same category in the same soil, one grows and bears fruits while the other doesn't grow enough to produce fruits, something is wrong. The same applies to humans. If two people engage in the same kind of business in the same town, and one is successful while the other is not, something is absolutely going wrong. A body, and with some bodies, are putting you down.

One day, a bad neighbor takes his good neighbor's dog and dumps it in a forest. The dog travels from farm to farm with no way to go. The dog learns how to live life in that kind of way until it is adopted by a farmer. If you must live your life like everybody else, then live as if you were born to live that way. The measure of life is not dependent on what you are or own. Peace of mind is what wise people cultivate all the time.

If you can tell where to hide when a tsunami arises from the sea and joins together with a deluge from the sky, wisdom is yours. Then you are wise, and you can be the last one to see that, but knowledge of that can be hidden behind your understanding. Many centuries ago, there was a village on earth where they chose an elder person to rule that village and every other nearby village. They ordered a handyman capable of being with him and watching over him at all times. Do you want to know why? They wanted to make sure that if he missed his steps and fell down at any time, they should make a written note about where he fell down, the time of the fall, the date, month, and year. More importantly, they noted how many times he fell. This was because at that time, when someone important fell down, they had to do the math. Sometimes, if he had to spend seven years in power and he fell down six times, that meant he would not be in power for the other six years. He would only have one year to complete his time. After that period, he would no longer be able to rule. Six other villages would step ahead of his village, and his village would be seven rows behind. One word can be put into more than a million sentences. A clever or intelligent mathematician can tell the world and the universe.

Imagine sitting on the side of a long road where many people are walking, some fast and some very slow. At a certain time, some who were very fast become slow, and others who were very slow become the fastest. The volume of speed cannot determine how fast you can win; the number of times you may stop can reduce your chances. Running without control diminishes the energy you need for a last-minute push. Stand and look at the one who others see as the powerful person who can rule the world. In just twelve inches, which is one foot in measure, that person can fall down to the ground more than two times. Supposedly, if there were a law to punish a foot that betrays its owner and lets them fall, believe that most of the big rulers should have both of their feet in prison while the rest of their body rules their nation.

Not only a foot often betrays its owner, but in reality, no one, whatsoever, is betrayed by an enemy. That always happens by a friend, a member of your family, or a person you trust and have confidence in. One beautiful young girl lives with her first and only lover and becomes the mother of many children. The man becomes a polygamist. Eventually, that mother has to work hard each time to make money, but the man always takes the money and spends it on the other women. She works on the farm to earn her money, but the money is never there for her children. The man gives it away to the other women. Her brothers help her and give her some animals, but they all go to the other women. Believe that a woman who abuses those kinds of ways may not live for long. Yet she is dead. After her death, that man even sells the lands she inherited from her parents to build houses for the next woman. And he puts the children she had with him into serious misery and poverty. Instead of helping, he diminishes and reduces them. He is not only betraying his first beautiful love but also the kids. Wishes are not awesome but horrible things. She loves him so much she acts as if she were blind, deaf, and dumb. When other people eat the food you work hard for, they also hate you. They want to see you die so that they can establish themselves on everything you possess.

Sadly, that history can be compared to a mother chicken who freshly hatched her eggs and has her beautiful chicks, and suddenly a predator arrives. By trying to protect her chicks, she loses her own life and eventually leaves the chicks behind without any protection. With the first training they received from their dear mother as a trophy for them, it all depends on how that lesson is not neglected among them in order to survive or not become the next meal for those predators. As humans, the same people you help every day are the same ones who eat your bread every day. They are also the ones who want to harm you. If you have never been a victim or if you are a victim, you can continue to help, but never put in your mind anything wrong that could shrink you from doing good for anyone who truly needs it. Just be wise. You are the one who must protect yourself. Please yourself to do so and live in peace, being a happy person at all times. Stand, look, and see. A rich person takes his boat and goes fishing, while a poor person takes his fishing line and goes to the shores. In the end, look and see. Both come back with some fish they needed. The wise conclusion is that two people went fishing and caught fish.

When you are far away from certain things, you don't even believe they can truly exist as a reality until someone you trust can convince you. It is true that in some parts of the world, from the time a child starts standing up and walking, that child starts working as an adult, day and night, for their parents without pay. They often don't eat anything, not because they are so poor, but because that is how their own parents treat them. Some of them have different mothers, and their fathers make them slaves to work for the other women they have. They don't buy any clothes for them or send them to school. If the children become weak and sick, they are not taken to any hospital, they must die at home. If they are beaten three times a day, it is a festival for those women who do not own the child, and it is considered fine by anyone else because they believe they are doing nothing bad or wrong at all. Some children live in such a state for more than thirty years. Whatever the children own, their fathers take it and give it to their women. They say that children never have anything, and whatever children have belongs to their women. Often, they claim to possess animals for sale and consumption, but as for the children, the children must work for them because they cannot eat them. In regions like this, only twenty-five percent of the population believes in education. Some others do not send their children to school at all, and some say that sending children to school brings misery to the nation, so sometimes the government must force them to send their child to school. Those who are afraid of the government, their children might have a chance to learn how to read and write. Children can and should help their parents, but for those who are aware of this kind of abuse, it is, of course, too bad to appreciate.

In places like that, if you are a girl, you are assigned to go wherever the water source is and bring home water as much as they use per day. If you are a boy, you must go to the farm as much as they want in a day. There is nothing wrong with living according to where you live or stay, but a lack of knowledge could cause you to abuse your own children. This is a view not only for rural areas in developing countries. The absence of knowledge is the source of every kind of poverty and misery. When it's not someone else's fault to destroy an individual or a group of people for whatever reason they choose to do that. Be wise and see all things green for the future.

There was a father who was not good enough but had plenty of children. Some of them were old enough to get married, but that father didn't want to spend his money to get them married. He encouraged them by saying that it would never be too late to get married and if they were not married at an early age, they would not miss anything. Many of his best friends wanted their sons to marry his daughters, but he just didn't want to spend his money to marry them, so he refused them. Spending money for his children was not like drinking water. As time went by, all his friends started distancing themselves from him. And all his older sons started doing what was good for themselves and got married. When the father saw that all his older sons had left him, he started complaining to the younger ones who were still with him and said to them, "In a while, I will not see you anymore because I'm not lucky with any sons at all. You guys are going to do the same as your big brothers." Not long after, his daughters also decided to give him some troubles. They started getting pregnant, and suddenly he became a grandfather of so many kids. Some daughters not only gave him one kid but more than one. Now, when that father wants to complain, he says he doesn't have luck with his daughters. Then his young sons make jokes and say, "You only don't have luck with your sons because they are not giving you any babies for you to take care of, but you have plenty of luck with your daughters who are giving you a lot of babies to take care of." The father didn't want to spend his money to get them married, and now he must take care of them with their babies as his gifts, which makes him more fortunate in the region.

Imagine that the father didn't want to spend his money to get his child married. Now he has to spend every day feeding the kids, buying clothes, paying for hospitals, and paying for school. Not only for one kid, but for multiple kids. And he still must spend for their mothers. Many other people may prefer to get them married to someone who loves them so that they can have their own family and take care of their own family.

Mistakes you already made cannot be avoided, that's why they're called mistakes. If you go somewhere to hide from it, that means you're punishing yourself. If you take your time to repair it, that means you're paying for it. If you are trying to live with it, that means you are enduring it. You cannot go underneath it; it has to be your burden no matter how much it might weigh. Don't underestimate what one error can cost you, many years from the time you commit that error. In the case of that father, one thing was good: he always endured his mistakes and did not try to do the same thing with the other children.

The grandfather has lived for more than eighty years with more than hundreds of kids, grandkids, and great-grandkids. He repaired himself enough for his kids, his neighbors, and friends to call him their counselor and seek help from him. If you run away from your burden, you will never be honored by anyone by any means until the end. But if you endure your burden to the best of your ability, it will make you look like a crown of beauty over the head of a mighty king. A very good king who cultivated enough knowledge to rule a world full of wonderful people. A king where his people don't have to dream about miserable events or any blackmail to end their beautiful dreams and their sense of comfort and confidence in him.

You don't want to be like a father who has a five-year-old son saying he lost confidence in his father because when he saw somebody do something wrong to his big sister and she was crying, he was crying too. Then he thought his dad was going to ask them what happened, but instead his father just beat both of them for crying. That father did not act as a good father at all, nor a good judge for his children. Actions like these encourage any malicious person to do something definitely wrong to your children. When they lose your support and confidence, the children feel nothing more than trash, good for nothing. They are afraid of their parents and afraid of their parents' workers. Morally, they are like burying a life in a deep pit.

They are living a bitter life in a pit every second of their life instead of the happiness they were hoping for from their own parents. Now, it's time to think twice for miracles as they grow. Raise your eyes and look at the sky, look at the heavens. When the clouds approach, there will be no more sun. But the sun still is at the same spot. Whenever the clouds go away, the sun will shine again. When it's raining, you can't do everything you want to do, but rain never lasts long enough. When night falls, you can't see without a light, but all of these won't last for life. Everything will fade away and clear your path for a better life.

If you go to a park where you can contemplate everything you see, maybe you can draw a good lesson even from animals. But when you are going somewhere and you know where you are going, don't even take a second to look at a dog that's heeling or a bird that's singing in the garden. That can be a reason for your loss in the second. You are on the road precisely for the place where you have your destination to reach.

Sometimes your own friend can tell you to stop going to school or stop studying something, and they can even tell you that you don't have to learn a trade or a profession. They want you to just go out and fest! Will you agree with your friend? In our days, almost everybody in the world wears clothes, but each one of them wears clothes that fit them. Does your friend fit you like a piece of clothing you are wearing? If not, make your way to the light because friends are not always there for each other's misery. Don't allow yourselves to be dragged down, as time may be too short to repair anything.

Deceptions can be everywhere, especially when people have to face others. Naturally, you can be more resilient when you are professionals or when you believe in your trade. You can push back intimidations to the place where they belong, the way they come from. If you enter a salon that doesn't suit you, don't be surprised if you feel out of place and have to forge your own path.

A family went to a furniture center to see some furniture they admired so much. They thought if they couldn't get that furniture right away, someone else might get it before them. They made offers to put that furniture on hold or layaway for them. Unfortunately, they later found out that they couldn't possess that furniture because the agreement didn't match both ways. Some months later, the family decided to visit that furniture center again and to their surprise, the same exact furniture was still in the same spot, unsold. Now they have a good idea about why all stores have so much variety—it's because everyone has different tastes. Nothing is lost, even if something is left.

Is there any closure on your way? Anything blocking your path? Use your good sense and be wise for yourselves. Make a detour where something better lies ahead for you. That arrives sometime, you'll be more motivated, very fine, and more prepared for any future to come. If the past remains in your mind often, it's because you're not content with your present moment or time when things are ready, better or good. All the guessing will be over and won't be remembered forever.

A river cannot flow without a connection to a source of water and can never join the ocean without a canal. Similarly, a person's joy cannot happen without some connection to others. In the same way, you can also find those who can cause the worst problems for others. It's up to you to follow the good way for your own protection.

A tree's first protection can be its shadows, but it can also provide various benefits. Some trees produce blossoming flowers, while others produce different kinds of fruits that benefit humans and animals. If this doesn't work in certain regions on earth, there are causes or reasons that exist.

Insects like bees have the ability to produce honey, but humans can do much more than that for the benefit of others and for a long time. When a person dies, that is the only time you stop benefiting from others because you also return to dust at that moment. They can no longer receive anything from you anymore.

Crazy Woman in the Park

Once, a person was visiting a place like a park where many people were passing by. Some were just trying to relax because they were tired, others were stressed out, and some were simply visiting out of curiosity.

While everyone was paying attention, a donkey was honking. In response, a bird sang from a tree, and then a woman, known as a crazy woman, spoke up and said, "The donkey said he would bite, and the bird says your mouth is long." Although they thought she was crazy, she made a joke that made everyone laugh.

When animals talk, not many people can discern what they are saying. Therefore, among the people who were there, nobody knew whether to believe that woman or not. The only thing everyone could be sure of was that the woman had the opportunity to relieve some stress in the minds of certain individuals nearby. If you are someone who knows how much stress is released when someone laughs, then you already understand the impact she had on each person there. Stress flew away for free, and a lot of good can be done with zero cost to you as compensation.

Imagine going to a movie theater where you have to pay money, but this woman doesn't even receive a thank you for what she ultimately accomplishes — releasing them from the stress that occupied their minds and replacing it with a story for them to tell later, all because of a "crazy" woman. It's important to see and understand that people can learn from any creature under different circumstances.

You may fight multiple times to satisfy the person who does good for you, but most of the time, you will never be able to do that. On the other hand, never expect anything as good from the people you help. By chance, it may happen, so don't place any expectations or hopes on that. Instead, continue doing what is good for those in need.

A young man was visiting a farm while a farmer was about to feed his cows. He paid close attention to what the farmer was doing as he took a big loaf of hay to a separate cow that was by itself. When the man tried to share the loaf by breaking it into small pieces, the cow got mad and pushed the farmer away from its food by placing its forehead on him. The man thought the cow had turned into a bad cow for the first time, but before that, she was a good cow. Do you think the cow is a bad cow or not? The cow is actually a good cow. Believe that if she were a bad cow, she would have harmed the farmer by using her horns to push him or doing something worse. So, what is the matter supposed to be? Believe that she is just telling him that she is no longer a baby and to stop treating her food as if she were a baby. Just give her the food and let her eat it the way she wants. She doesn't want to harm him for real. Sometimes, animals do that to their own offspring as a form of discipline. Some animals require a lot of respect, whether they are small or big, as they can seriously harm people, as you know.

There was a boy who saw a small lizard catching a black spider, despite his mother always telling him not to touch animals. He put his finger between their mouths and got bitten by the spider. He thought he had been bitten by the lizard until his father revealed to him that it was actually the spider that had bitten him. The lizard had actually grabbed the spider from behind to prevent any retaliation. But the poor boy, lacking sense, didn't back away from that bad punishment and instead stuck his finger in the mouth of the captive spider. At least from that time, he learned from his own experience to listen to his mother, who tells him not to touch such creatures. Now, he will surely have to tell his friends so they don't make the same mistake. Now the boy understands the meaning of "eyes see, hands not touch." Instead of blaming only the spider, the boy now respects both spiders and lizards. He initially thought it was the lizard's fault, but now he has learned to respect the lizard as well. Of course, the lizard was the chief in that situation. He had never touched them before, but the boy often got stung by wasps and bees.

As for the spider, it just tasted more bitter. The boy didn't have any sense at that time, but now he is accumulating knowledge day by day and learning from his mistakes, growing wiser until he can avoid small bad events.

A girl went to a garden park with her mother. When she saw a beautiful rose, she tried to grab it but her finger got pricked by thorns, and she started crying. Her mother consoled her and told her that there are no roses without thorns. Before you can possess a rose, you need to learn how to pick it up without touching the thorns.

As an adult, do you already know how to pick up a rose without touching its thorns? Don't make any mistakes; proceed on your path with caution and consider your relationships with others, as well as with yourself. Has someone dear to you ever unintentionally hurt you? Have you ever unintentionally hurt your loved ones and felt regret? The reality is that you won't be able to avoid every little difficulty in life. Some of them are part of the human condition that everyone has to deal with, live with, and accept just the way it is, like daylight and dark night. If you prefer to see it as darkness during daylight, then you must simply wait for the nighttime.

These conditions are hours to come, and your patience must obey. It's almost similar to eating and drinking water. No matter how much you've eaten and drunk at present, it won't change anything. If it's supposed to be four hours until your body needs food and water again, after four hours you will feel hungry and thirsty. If for any reason you don't respond to that need in time, your body will charge you a late fee, resulting in gastric issues, weakness, poor vision, and much more. If you want to deal with the situation, there will be no negotiations; you must adhere to the routine or pay the penalty. Your requirement is to take the original road to resolve the situation. The only exceptions are eating and drinking. If you don't eat and drink, doctors and pharmacies will collect the late fees that your body system charges to your account. Suppose you are not satisfied with going through them in reality? Everyone's advice may prefer resolving the problem and preventing future issues. The first step is to eat and drink on time, avoiding late fees, penalties, weakness, poor vision, and maintaining overall good health for that case. Then create a different and brighter future.

Friend Abandons Friend

Two friends were not able to find food for themselves, so they decided to make a trip to the suburb area to meet a farmer and ask to work for him in exchange for some food to survive. As they approached the gate, the owner saw them and asked them, "Who are you? Are you hiding here just to steal from my farm?" They answered and explained that they had come from far away and were only seeking work to survive. One of them claimed to be skilled in weeding grass, planting corn, and eliminating pests like rats, mice, and snakes, while the other one said he is only a watchman.

The farmer took the one who knew how to plant corn, weed grass, and kill beasts to assess what needed to be done, while the watchman stayed at the gate waiting for his friend. After going through the tasks, the skilled worker was hired and given a place to stay at the farm and completely forgot about his friend waiting at the gate. After waiting for too long, the watchman eventually decided to resign and continue his journey alone, with nothing concrete to strengthen his mind about what had happened to his friend. He cannot make it inside, for say he might find a little information about his friend. He hoped his friend would come out and explain the situation, but he couldn't find any trace of him.

After walking a few miles, a shop owner who had passed him on the road twice finally stopped and asked where he was going. The watchman explained his need for work to survive, and the shop owner offered him a job as a watchman for his shop. The watchman gladly accepted, as that was his expertise. They realized they needed each other, and an agreement was quickly reached. The watchman was hired by the shop owner and found a place to stay.

He excelled at his job and gained the appreciation of the people he interacted with. After two years, the shop owner acknowledged his dedication and offered him a two-week vacation to visit his hometown and friends. The watchman was grateful for the generous gift and happily prepared for his trip, knowing that he would be paid during his vacation. It was the first time he considered himself on vacation.

To his surprise, he encountered his forgetful friend, who had been hired by the farmer and was now in trouble due to the farmer's passing and a conflict that arose among the heirs. They decided to kick him out to avoid complications. Despite the friend's disregard, the watchman sympathized and accepted his fate without any notice. He left the place with only the clothes on his back, heading towards the gate. Just before he reached the gate, with a group of people behind him ready to close it, he saw and remembered the little bench where he and his friend had once sat before the farmer hired him. His friend was now forever resting on that bench. For the second time, the watchman sat on the same bench, this time alone, with no friend to talk to and no hope of ever seeing his friend again.

While he placed his bag between his feet, at that crucial moment, the guard opened the gate and threw his friend outside. He was so stressed and had no idea that the watchman had been sitting there for two years, waiting for him. The rat killer quickly stepped out, breathing heavily, and asked the watchman how he was doing. The watchman replied, "I'm still here, watching and waiting." Now he opened his eyes and saw that his friend had been waiting for him for two years, just as he had thought. Sometimes deceptions can be complicated, but now they both had a story to share with each other, a chance to rescue and reconcile.

In the end, history had taught them a valuable lesson: if the farmer were to return for the watchman, they could both leave the farm behind, empty and without any doubts. They would be expelled from the farm gate, left with only the clothes on their backs. How can someone always blame their friend for their mistakes? Are you strong enough to let the future speak for both of you? Or do you always let your quick anger guide your actions and take control of you?

Imagine that, at this very moment, it is the man who was abandoned behind the gate who opens his bags and shares some good clothes with his friend who had abandoned him. He left a man who understood his situation and could have joined forces with him. Despite everything, the watchman didn't complain. Later, he gained a deeper understanding of the situation and had no regrets at all. Nobody wants to prepare themselves to be abandoned by a friend or rebuked by someone else. In this case, there is no room for regrets because if both men had stayed at the farm, they would have been cast out without mercy or hope, with a dark path ahead on their journey back home to where they are from.*

> ***An excellent friend is one with mutual understanding, one who can counsel and comfort when others need it the most. Errors and mistakes of all kinds belong to imperfect humans. If you are a perfect person, it's easy for you to know. If your teeth never bite your tongue and you never hurt your toes while walking, then believe that you are perfect and you are also declaring to be the first perfect human on earth. If you don't, and you find no one else, be adhered to convert every wrong way to a transit of good heart and contemplate the whole world with a bright eye.***

*As the men return to their hometown, they remain good friends, but the watchman becomes the only hope for the farmer. The watchman is there for his two-week vacation, and when it is over, he must go back to his job. The farmer has no other choice but to leave with the watchman so that the watchman can make a request on his behalf before his boss, something he had forgotten to do for him at the farm. Upon arriving, he makes the request for his friend, but it is not accepted. However, the watchman is granted the privilege to keep his friend with him. Instead of being a farm worker, his friend might become a household helper, with no trust issues between them. They had waited behind the gate for a long time, but now they find enough food, drink, and a good place to sleep thanks to their good friendship.

However, life is not just about taking care of a friend. Sometimes, a friend may not want another friend to take care of them. When that happens, it is a mistake made by someone, either by them or by others. If so, make a good dream and turn it into a reality that you can enjoy, and others can appreciate, admire, and honor. Do not neglect any good responsibility within your capacity. Time goes by quickly when you are in control, but it goes very slowly when someone else is in control. When others pay attention to you, your time goes by quickly, while their time seems to go slowly. On the other hand, when you pay attention to them, their time goes by quickly, and your time feels like an eternity. People often underestimate this reality.

Sometimes, as we turn and leave behind our childhood, we feel strong, especially noble, and very powerful. We may even forget that all powers, in general, are only temporary and limited. We close our eyes for a moment, and when we open them, we see our children, who were once small, now big and strong enough to hold our hands and lead us where we may not want to go. Beware not to make too many mistakes. If you sow the wrong seed while the land is open and clear for your path, that bad seed will grow and block your way, causing your legs to weaken and your feet to stumble.

Luck is like a bird that builds its nest during good times, so it doesn't have to rush during bad times. Although good runners do not often win, accidents are not often severe.

Stand eventually to the courtyard of a mighty residence when suddenly eyes witness a world tsunami. One part approaches from the northeast, while another part joins from the south, forming a great circle over the entire world. No habitat, plant, tree, human, or animal stands a chance to prevent or survive its destructive path. The circle continues to rapidly expand, eventually forming a narrow tunnel that connects the earth to the heavens.

Within that tunnel, formed by water and wind, there is only one person and a tree. In less than a second before the tunnel closes, that person jumps under the tree for protection and a chance to survive because that was his last choice as a defense to survive. If the tree is also engulfed by the tsunami, there would be no way to survive under the troubled waters. Breathing becomes impossible, and you may become one of the deceased. Jumping under the tree itself is not a guarantee of safety, but every living creature fights for their precious life, even in situations where victory seems impossible.*

Uncomfortable situations are not welcome but always arrive without notice. Supposedly, one day, suddenly, all sectors are forced to live in the same way. You can imagine a name for the addition of all, grabbing you by a finger and traveling with you as if dragging on a single cable in the sky. It's a truly rapid trip, for instance, a trillion miles per hour, and you complain about it trailing you too fast. You look behind and see much fire where you just about left, now you become admirable in your effort to stay alive. Your appreciation is abundant with no reserve for the personality. When you speak, you are listened to, and when you speak with, where you stand, you join. When you walk away, you are walking with thought becoming yours, knowledge turning yours, and the dream is yours. When your eyes close, you are closing your eyes. Beside a king, you are a crown of beauty. Among the most beautiful, you are the rose. By looking at your eyes, you consume enough light to cross the darkness under the very deep ocean, swimming together with the mighty marine animals without any wonder to harm, traveling among the stars with no fear of asteroids. Where we are is where we belong, and who you are is what you are.

*Nobody can naturally walk without two feet if they were born with them. Suppose you were not born with any feet at all and had never seen anyone else born with feet. In that case, you would never think about missing any body parts, and you would continue to live without regret for any part you don't have. So, if your nose doesn't allow you to enjoy the scent of blossoming flowers, simply admire them as your own unique benefits. If your own eyes prevent you from contemplating the beauty of the moon, let your mind enjoy what you cannot see and touch. If your skin feels against your flesh, let your senses triumph over it, as if you were born to live that way. When the sun refuses to touch your skin and the trees don't cast any shadows on your path, embrace yourself for who you are, as you have never needed them to live. Though you will survive without them.

I know of a medicinal plant that can be found almost everywhere in the world. If you pick a leaf from it and divide it into as many pieces as you want, then drop them anywhere on the ground, each single piece will grow into a separate plant. Many people living on Earth have been divided into pieces by others, resembling the spreading of this plant. However, wise individuals transform their pieces into lessons, acquiring enough knowledge to help themselves and those in need. They assist others in navigating the many challenges they encounter in life.

The low degree of what you don't know is greater than anything you already know. No matter how much time you spend at school and whatever you learn, there are places where people never go to school. Unfortunately, if you have to live among them, you will discover that they know many things you don't know yourself. You might think you know better than them. Yes, there are some differences. You have a greater capacity to explain things and put them in order. They don't know how to put anything in order, and that is one of the biggest advantages you find from the time spent at school.

Imagine two neighbors, each with a newborn baby. As the babies grow up, one mother teaches her child how to dress and undress, while the other mother says, "I'm here for my child, and when he gets big, he'll know everything he wants to know." One day, both mothers go out, and the two kids play together outside. While playing by a pool of water, they become wet and cold. They want to change their clothes as the temperature drops to a very low degree. One child goes inside and changes his clothes, but the other child enters his home and doesn't know how to remove his clothes or put on different ones because his parents never taught him. The boy sits in a corner, waiting for his mother to come back home and change his clothes for him. You can imagine how much that boy suffers just because of the lack of early training he did not receive from his parents.

A person observed some mother chickens with their chicks. A mother would have her chicks for about two days, and when they reached two days old, the mother would clap her wings as a signal of emergency. Each chick would immediately hide itself and wait for a different signal from their mother to come back out. When they finally received the peaceful signal, they would come back out without any fear. The chicks cannot neglect the importance of this early training, as it provides great protection against predators throughout their lives. Wise people try to avoid anything that might bother them on their path.

On a road there was a man riding a horse at a fast pace. Despite this, he would raise his hand to greet pedestrians. Why would a man on a horse, going so fast, need to say hello to people on the ground? When he approached a bad spot, his horse jumped with him causing his hat to fall off. A pedestrian picks up his hat and hands it to him, and he thanks the pedestrian. Immediately after, a different man, riding on a different horse, this time that guy going straight on his horse and said nothing to anyone. When his horse jumped, his hat fell to the ground, but no one picked it up for him. All pedestrians moved to the other side of the road. Now, everyone understood why the first man had greeted every pedestrian. They watched as he got off his horse to pick up his hat, even though many people had passed him. The first man didn't have to get off his horse because he had greeted them earlier, so when his hat fell, they picked it up for him. So, when you are in a position of authority, pay attention to those beneath you and don't burden them excessively, like someone who puts their knees on someone's neck until they expire. A simple gesture of kindness can open an iron gate, but a disrespectful attitude can cause long-term, uncontrollable disaster.

Long time ago, people took a long time to learn many things, just like they do now. However, there are some differences today because you need to learn how to stand when you meet another person and whether to shake hands or not. This practice is quickly becoming history in our time. Teachers will ask their students questions about specific years, measurements in feet, and how greetings were done.

Dog Fights His Owner for Wearing a Mask

A good dog was about to fight with his owner. Does anybody know why that happened? The dog owner says his dog is a good dog, but when he walks with that dog, he always puts a muzzle on the dog's mouth so that other people might not be afraid of him biting them. So, now they require the dog owner, along with everybody else, to wear a mask at all times. When the dog looks at his owner's face, he sees the mask that looks just like his muzzle. He thought his owner stole his muzzle, and as a result, the dog starts a fight with his owner to get his muzzle back.

The other people who noticed the fight called animal control to put that dog under control. When they arrive, they don't expect the dog to talk, but they ask the dog, "What happened to you, dog?" The dog answers and says to them that his owner always puts a muzzle on him because the dog sometimes bites people. However, people never bite dogs or others like them, so people shouldn't have to be punished by wearing a muzzle. That's why he tried to remove his muzzle from his owner's mouth. The dog agrees that dogs sometimes bite people, and he must accept his punishment for what dogs always do. But as for his owner, his owner actually did nothing to deserve a punishment like wearing a mask all the time. After witnessing this every day, eventually, the dog accepts and understands that both he and his owner have lives, and what happens to him can also happen to both of them.

Long ago, people said there is no difference between people and animals when they are dead. But in many cases, there is no difference from life to life, whether beast or human. Reasonably, people are guided by principles, but training some animals can be extremely helpful to human lives. Animals always prefer their owners, no matter how they are treated. A man steals a family horse and keeps the horse for years, but that horse has his owner's loyalty imprinted somewhere between his waist that the thief cannot see. After about three years have passed since he stole the horse, he believes that everything is going smoothly for him. On a beautiful day, he decides to take the horse for a ride. Good for the owner and his horse, but unfortunately for the thief, while on that horse, it runs on a non-stop trip until it reaches the house of its original owner, with the thief still sitting on its back, then he stops.

The owner was congratulating that man by faking and said to him, "You are a wonderful rider, and you have a beautiful horse too." He answers and says, "Ooh yeah." Meanwhile, the horse, who sees his true owner, is yelling and neighing non-stop. The owner looks and sees his name at the same spot. By the means of knowledge, the horse belongs to him. He kicks off the stealer and takes his horse.

After one hour later, the stealer is no longer a horse rider. Rather than being a horse rider, he becomes a prisoner associated with many other prisoners. This time, he is imprisoned for stealing a family horse and keeping it for years. After all, the owner adds a different name to his horse, which says, "You steal me, I arrest you." Now, the horse stealer is in prison. After serving his time, he is finally released and supposed to be a free man. He is making his way heading to his town where he used to live.

By unfortunate chance, before he gets home, he crosses through a land by a park where they keep some horses. While passing by, a horse says, "Hee! Hee!" About three times, he turns back and grabs some stones, starting to throw them at the horses. The owner sees him and asks him why he is doing such a horrible thing, beating his horses. He answers and says to the horse's owner, "A horse is laughing at him because he went to prison for a horse." He said the horse saw him and laughed, "Hee! Hee!" Then, the horse's owner calls a police officer, and the police arrest him.

This time, a man who used to like horses enough to steal one has now become a threat from a different angle for the horses, trying to kill them. When they took him to court, he said that a horse, while he was on his way home from prison for stealing a horse, mocked him by laughing, "Hee! Hee!" Then, he tried to take revenge on that horse who disrespected him. The judge said to him, "You have the right to pass by." Then, the horse in the park had a chance to neigh or laugh. The judge said to him, "Now, for the second time, again, you are wrong and guilty. You must go back to prison." The horse beater says if he has to go to prison, they should put that horse in prison too because that horse mocked him first before he took revenge.

The judge says, "Not only for you because you are wrong more than once, that horse is already in prison when you hurt him. He is in a park, not on the street. Right now, you both are in prison. You should be satisfied enough, and remember a horse did not steal you, but you are the one who did steal a horse. Plus, adding to that, you are stoning a different horse. Then, you deserve your time in prison." Great thanks to a judge, a good judge. Horses and the horse's stealer are all under protection. Whether in prison or in a park, when both of them have a chance to be free, they will also live peacefully forever.

Time spent in prison is greater than the time he should have worked to purchase a horse. Wise people are patient and work hard to purchase what they truly need. If you actually want something, work hard and buy it. Don't steal it. So, you don't have to sleep in prison for anything if you don't steal it.

All Children Thieves, the Family is Cursed

To the extent that your unrighteousness takes you, your chance of becoming a curse is greater. Then, from there, your weeping is hiding not far away, waiting for you, and gnashing of teeth will be yours plentifully.

A young boy was visiting a different city than his own. He arrived as a stranger and talked to other boys, one of whom was a very bad boy capable of actions that even a big thief might be afraid to be involved in. While talking with him, the stranger boy tried to discourage him from all those bad things he had heard about him. He told him the history of a righteous person and the one who practices bad actions, like breaking into neighbors' homes and stealing what they have inside.

The bad boy replied to him, saying that he is a tourist because he is visiting the city, and he is not allowed to do anything. If he does anything wrong, they will make him leave. But as for him, that boy doesn't have to worry because whatever he does, he'll stay there because he belongs there. By answering like that, he proves himself to be a real fool without any cure. Rather than listening and turning to the better way, which could be a wonderful way for him, he is unwilling to understand. Belonging here can be a curse here, weeping here, and dying here.

The bad boy continues his bad ways as he grows older. He becomes a great thief and the greatest curse for his parents. Despite his young age, the boy thought that every day would be the same. He granted himself the liberty to steal without wonder or fear, turning himself into the most plundering individual. He was expelled from school for stealing too much. Each time somebody caught him stealing from their homes, he received a serious beating. He repaid the boy who tried to help him by stealing his bicycle and replacing its parts with those from a different bicycle he had stolen elsewhere.

Years went by, and they started putting that young thief in prison. When he was released one day, he would go right back to prison the next day. Each time they caught him, he received a beating. One day, everything might give him notice of his health. After a serious beating in a house he had broken into, the boy became sick in prison. When he was released, he had grown too big for his clothes. The boy could no longer walk properly with his big, low belly. All he could do was wait for his last day to come as fast as he had not expected.

Yet he belongs here, doing whatever pleases him here, weeping here, gnashing his teeth here, and drinking his curse here, a reproach for his parents. But they finally said goodbye to a miserable life and tribulation. Rather than being lost to the graveyard, he wronged others and found rest in peace forever and ever.

A great family becomes a curse for the community where they live when all their children choose the wrong paths for themselves instead of good ones. The father tries to maintain his reputation by distancing himself and leaving them with the mother only, but that only makes things worse everywhere. It is not the right solution. Their mother has to face the trouble each time the police come and take them away, and she becomes stressed out. As some are released from prison, others enter. Only one declares himself a good person, and all the neighbors agree and tell the police that he is good. They don't have to apprehend him when they come for the others. So, he is not a suspect in anything. He relatively triumphs as the only "good" one and can go wherever he wants without interruptions by the police.

Some of their cousins turn out to be the same, bringing no relief for the police. It becomes a grand problem for the community and a source of trouble for their mothers, as the police do not give up on them. The more the residents complain, the tougher the police become on the thieves. There are plenty of arrests and punishments, and finally, prison. They are released one time, only to return the next day or the following week, but never longer than a month outside of prison.

One day, a chief asks one of them about his brother who said he is not a thief. He answers and says, "Chief, if you see a dry leaf, you don't shake it. You will not know if there is any wasp nest. But when you shake it, you will know if there is any wasp nest."

Truly, one night, a thief enters a place and a woman who was there tries to face him with a weapon. Unfortunately, he seriously wounded that woman badly before he was forced to run away when the woman hit one of his eyes out. He quietly had to flee with one eye. The only son who never steals is he. Now with one eye, the police are looking for a person with a fresh eye wound from a weapon.

The police gather all the reports from that woman, who is in a hospital with some serious wounds from when the thief tried to kill her. The woman is taken to the hospital, and the thief and criminal travel to a different city. There, he stops at a police station to report four men who attempted to assassinate him, then he escapes from them with his life. He makes his case that four young men attacked him, and he had a chance to run, but one of the four already wounded him with a weapon. They ask him for a description, and he describes the four young men. However, he says he knows one of them and gives the name of the one he knows to the police, along with the address where he lives. He is the son of a family that everyone in the community knows.

When the police arrive at the house of that young man, his family tells the police that their son did not go out overnight. But the police put him under arrest and took him to the police station for further interrogation. The police continue to question him about the other three men who were with him when they attempted to assassinate a man on the road. While they continue questioning him, some police from another city arrive and talk to the other police about what they hear. Finally, they say they are coming over to have some inspection done on that man. After their inspection is complete, they declare that he is the right criminal they are looking for. Then, they must take him back to where he came from for theft and the crimes he actually commits and runs away. The police take that man back to the city where he was stealing and committing crimes against that woman.

Such a joy for parents and the young man who is falsely accused by a thief and criminal! A young man who spent his night sleeping in his bedroom, then arrested at sunrise for attempting to assassinate someone overnight and being handcuffed by the police for what he cannot explain. He is accused by the thief who is actually trying to defend himself and continues to make other people believe he is a good person who never steals, unlike his brothers. He pretends to be a good man and continues to steal and lie to everyone, presenting himself as the only son of his parents who never steals.

This time, a good and fresh breeze is floating and touches the ears of the innocent man and his parents. The great stealer is exposed publicly, rather than turning himself into a mighty and honorable righteous man while plundering others. His wrongdoing at the women's business renders him naked in the eyes of everyone as a great thief and criminal who attempted to commit murder on a woman at her own business. The brave woman fought back and wounded the thief, who is now exposed for all to see him as the thief he is, instead of an innocent accuser weeping and gnashing his teeth for what he doesn't know. Now it is time for the stealer to pay the price. The police tie him up so well that it's no wonder if he is weeping. It's time for him to taste what he did to others, his multiple wrongdoings against them.

Everyone is happy to see the fortunate young man who was falsely accused by the thief released to his parents and enjoying life with the family who regains their peace. Meanwhile, the criminal continues to answer the police interrogatives while they help him with his applications for his new hotel and receive mistreatments as a welcome to his brothers' and cousins' territory. Many people did not expect him to be visited at any time soon. As his brother said previously, "If you don't shake the banana dry leaf, you will never know if there are any wasp nests." That woman shook the leaf and found out that there were so many wasp nests. Some flew away to a different city and bit innocent people. Thanks to the police and the wound he received, they were able to track him and bring him back to where he made his first sting.

As for that stealer, he is a lucky one because at that time, a first-time criminal does not spend much time in prison if he doesn't kill someone or rape a child. The son who never steals goes to prison for much longer than his brothers ever did. But after spending all of his time in prison, he becomes a free man. In his case, it looks like the chiefs did a very good job because that stealer gets out of prison not only as a freeman but also free from a mindset to commit another crime or harm anybody or property whatsoever. Among those thieves, he is the only one who lives long because he quit his wrong ways. Instead of being the only son who is not a thief, he becomes the only son who lives long.

Now, no one should make a mistake by saying he is the only son who lives long among his brothers. When released, he returns to his parents' house and later builds his own house. No one ever suspects him of being a thief anymore. Maybe he is the only brother who can remember what he was facing during the period of time when his wrongdoings to others were bitter to his taste. It was a moment where it only depended on the chiefs of the police to decide whether they should let him live or not. From that time, maybe he made a covenant with his mind. If he didn't die on that road, eventually, when he gets released, he would take a different path, which he is trying for real.

More than that, he witnesses all of his brothers dying under his eyes for the reason of stealing and, off and on, going to prison. Not to forget his cousins. Each time they catch them before taking them to prison, they always get beaten more than once. In prison, if they want them to work, even if they are sick, they have to obey and do the work because they are stealers and can easily fake being sick. No one cares for you if you don't care for yourselves. When released, try not to come back for the same kind of actions. Quit stealing and own yourselves. That man draws a good lesson for himself for his own benefit that grants him a chance to see when his parents are buried in the graveyard. He wins the greatest gift, not to enter the pit before his parents lay down and die. Instead of his brothers who were entering the pits one after the other before even having a chance to bury the parents, the parents must bury them. As cursed, they are swept away in an uproar, weeping, and gnashing of teeth, and also reproach for unrighteousness and cursing the family's peace of mind and a strong hold is not their harvest. Sympathy for the wrongdoer, defrauded, that is their cultivation as seeds sown. Those seeds cannot change to joyful happiness and honor. Their children are subject to inherit a bad name.

Because most people understand the meaning of a name, every bad son of that family bears their mother's name and keeps their father's name for the good times. Each time the police apprehend one of them, he gives his mother's last name. If he goes to another place, then he gives them his father's last name. Therefore, the cousins who do not steal abandon the name that their bad cousins bear and shift to their other parents' name. That way, they don't have to carry the same name as the thieves.

It is not sweet at all when someone is trying to do what is good and right for themself, and someone who shares the same name chooses the wrong path and puts a red tag on that name. They change their last name and distance themselves from those bad ones. They turn into a bright light, continuing to travel a path through darkness, like a person with a cancer disease ready to sacrifice any part of their body to prevent the cancer from killing them. Good people can do whatever is good and possible to avoid any relationship with anyone who carries a bad name or is a wrongdoer, and anyone who sympathizes with unrighteousness.

Even if a good judge may show a preference for someone who steals a piece of bread rather than dies, they will not openly state it because it is still better to work for that piece of bread rather than steal it. Of course, you will be punished. If someone steals a plate of food and eats it right away, a judge may not give them the same sentence as a big criminal, but if you steal a plate of food when they are looking for a cattle thief, they will find your name in that same book. Everyone will call you a thief, just like they call the one who steals a big fortune. That was not yours; you should work for what you need, with no pity or mercy, regardless of your bad situation. The laws are there waiting for transgressors, and no one should be exempt.

If you choose a wrong path for yourselves, the only place that cares about your tribulations is the pit. When you reach your pit, there is no more reproach, gnashing of teeth, or weeping, except for you and those in the pit. If you leave behind anyone who was dear to you, that wound will stay fresh each time they must deal with anything related to your former path.

Somewhere on this planet, if a great-grandparent was committing a crime or stealing something, a son from that family can never try to have a girl to be his wife from the other family who already knows about that history. Neither are their sons allowed to get a girl from that wrong family to marry with. Those thieves can only go some way far to find somebody who was in the same bad ways as them, among those who carry the same reputation as them. Events do happen and time can change but good people keep their integrity and worthiness. A good lesson anyone can draw from that is whoever is from a good family and marries a thief among the bad things, your children will be the ones to inherit bad ways and may come to repeat the similar wrongs as the past was done by a parent. It is never too late to beware when you are not yet counted among the bad oranges who are rejected and towed far away forever. A million good actions will never restore and upgrade a bad name in this category, but a single bad action is enough to destroy more than a million good actions built through many years with a lot of strength and knowledge. Be wise and drink honey only from the real bees, then your taste will never be bitter for the rest of your life.

A young man grows up in a family where he was involved with something bad. Afterward, his parents decided to have him leave that community to somewhere else. Time goes by, he comes back as a rich person who has plenty of money and wants his parents to find him a young girl among those he appreciated for him to marry. But when his parents go ahead and talk to the parents of that girl, they tell him, "Your money cannot bury or cover your reputation and cannot purchase our daughter." What darkness! It is good to prevent because the cure is not sweet as the honeybees. The past of that young man forced him to turn away from that young girl. Someone else maybe, where they didn't know him before. His money cannot restore him to a good person among his neighbors. He has been rejected. He thought that at this time, because of his money, he can become the first stone to build the house of that young girl, and so that is not the case for him. They don't want to buy him as a limestone to build anything.

Poor Man Attempts Suicide

A poor man was living in a city where everybody was rich, compared to himself, because he had to work for his food every single day, if actually he doesn't work for a day he will not be able to eat anything also for that day. Eventually, he becomes so weak, not too many people want to give him any work. No one cares about his situations, and he doesn't want to steal anything despite his bitter period of life. He is carrying one name which is poor rather than carrying both the name poor and steal. Routinely he always makes some efforts to gain his food. At a certain point in time, he becomes so low morally, mentally, and physically, he loses his strength now he is dwelling in the shadows of the darkness where a miserable life becomes a burdensome for him to carry. The only way he can help himself according to his mind is to put an end to his miserable poor life. Imagine yourself to see a weak old person come to you and ask for work? In your mind you may ask yourself what can he do? Suppose he dies at your work, what can you do? Yet, because so many questions are set at the table, nobody wants to answer. They just don't let that man work for them.

So, nobody cares about giving him work anymore. No one says how he's going to eat and live. He keeps his integrity and worthiness. He preserves his name and never steals anything. This time, he becomes so discouraged that he finds a rope to hang himself on a tree somewhere. But he has only one sweet potato left for the rest of his life. Then he decides to eat that sweet potato as his last meal. He takes his time while moving very slowly because he doesn't have any more strength. He gathers some drywood, makes a fire, and puts his sweet potato on it. He keeps turning it over until it's ready to eat. Afterward, he puts it in some water to remove the burning skins. When everything gets soft, he removes his sweet potato from the water and takes it with the rope he has to hang himself for his last moment, as he has in his mind.

He climbs over a wall and gets onto a tree after settling himself on the tree. He actually puts a knot in his rope and puts it on his neck, then he sits on the tree just to finish eating his meal before he can kill himself. While he removes the burning skins of his sweet potato and drops them to the ground, he actually finishes eating his meal and reconsiders his action. He then takes a look at the ground and eventually sees another man sitting down and eating the burning skins of the sweet potato. The man on the tree pays close attention to the one on the ground and gains courage and strengthens himself. After the man who ate the potato skins walks away, the man on the tree gets off the tree and follows the other man. When he finally reaches him, he salutes him, and they begin a conversation. The man on the ground explains how far he has come from and asks if he can help him find some water. Then the man on the tree takes him to where he got his water to soften his potato. That man actually drinks some water, and the man on the tree also drinks some water on his extended time. Now the man on the ground tells him about his activities. He says that he is a person who used to work and just had enough to survive on a daily basis. Now that he's getting too old, people don't give him any more work to live or survive his life. He mentions that he has a friend in that city who is a farmer not far from where they are. He's trying to go to him so that life can be better for him. However, his problem on the road is that he is very hungry. He says that by chance or grace, he found some potato skins and has just eaten them. Now he is drinking water. He thanks him for the water and says that he's good to go to his destination.

The man on the tree said to the man on the ground, "If your friend is a farmer, maybe he can help me too because I also need some help to survive." Now both men are agreeing to travel together to the farmer. When they finally arrive, that is where a paradise was waiting for them. The farmer is getting old also and possesses many places at the farm where they can live because his children already got married and moved to different places. They have things like fruits and food of all kinds, and they can eat whatever they want. Work becomes exercise for them. They do work at the farm to put things in order for themselves. At that present moment, no more envy or thoughts to put an end to a self-life just because they cannot have food to eat and places to live.

Now, between the two men, who is helping the other? If the ground man did not show up, the man on the tree would have hanged himself. More questions arise. If the man on the tree did not drop his potato skins on the ground for the ground man to eat, would he not die hungry before he reaches his friend, the farmer? Which one benefits the most from the other?

Everyone knows for sure if the ground man did not eat the sweet potato skins, the man on the tree would have killed himself. Are you able to discern who benefits the most here where each life was in jeopardy? You might find that equal. *

> *What are your problems today, or how is your life? Are you happy, or are your problems continuing to multiply? It is for sure the man on the tree did not hang himself anymore after seeing that he is not the worst one facing the bad moment in life. After all, he has a last meal like his mind was pretending that, but the man on the ground has nothing at all despite that he did not envy to kill himself. Instead, he strengthens himself to make a trip to someone who knows him before to find the help he needs. The man on the tree gets his lesson, and he changes his mind. Both men comfort each other and make a way where a better life is waiting for them. Whenever darkness happens in your way, a very bright light is waiting somewhere, especially for you. If you are sick and no one takes care of you, some very special doctors are waiting for you somewhere. If you are actually eating in a trash can, at the same time, a beautiful table is set on your name. You are just encouraged to take one more step and be there by yourself.*

*As for these men, regardless of the harsh periods in their lives, they know that in life they have no reason to regret. They are still alive. They never had a stronghold, and they were not looking for wealth. So, the most important thing is what it costs to stay alive. After all, now they both live in a formidable stronghold, thanks to a happy friend.

Three Men Travel Through the Wilderness

Three men were living in a town who eventually faced a serious famine. At a certain time, they had nothing left to survive, so they decided to cross a wilderness to reach a different town where they could buy some food. It was far away, and the scorching heat of the sun beat down on them, draining their strength. Nevertheless, they continued with hope, aiming for a safe trip to that town. They had no food or water at all.

When they reached a serious point where they had lost all hope of reaching the town before dying of hunger, one of them reached into his pants pockets and found three small pieces of peanuts, estimated to be one and a half peanut seeds. They could each have a half seed of peanut. Upon offering, one of them said that a half seed cannot help him, so he didn't have to eat it. The other two men shared the half seed that he refused, which gave them each a quarter more. Now, the two men had three quarters of a seed each.

They continued their pursuit very slowly until night. Overnight, they found some relief as the heat of the sun diminished. Early in the morning, they approached the lane of the town with great hope that if they could reach it, they would no longer die of hunger and thirst. They managed to reach the city, and once there, two of them ate the food and drank the water they found. However, the third man could no longer eat as it was too late for him. He died right beside the food and water because he could no longer swallow anything at all.

Do you know that if he had eaten the half seed of peanut, he wouldn't have died? If he had eaten that half seed, he would have been able to make it just like the other two men. How many lessers cannot make it big? How many big ones who cannot share to lessers? At least take the time to go back hungry, but if you don't eat anything, you will die regardless of what you ate in the past. The other two men lost a friend, but they were grateful to have preserved their own lives.

Instead of eating a half seed of peanut, he preferred or chose to die. Believe that he never gained enough knowledge to understand how much food a life needs to sustain itself and for how long. In that case, if you put yourself to the test, you will realize the difference between eating a very small amount of food when someone else refuses to eat. If two normal persons eat at the same time, one consuming plenty of food while the other eats only a small amount, both of them will become hungry at the same time.

There is no obligation for anyone to do what others do, but sometimes it can be a matter of life or death. If that man were rich enough not to eat a half seed of peanut, why did he cross the wilderness in search of food? The two other men were more than happy to eat a meal consisting of three-quarters of a peanut seed each.

The two men survived the trip despite facing numerous harsh situations. If you know where you are going, hunger, the heat of the sun, thorns, and thistles are not enough to cause you to not make your way to your destination. If you do not make your destination, it may be a mistake by yourself or someone else that prevents you from getting there.

Wealthy Man Names Son Not Easy

There was a wealthy man living in a large city, and he had many kids with his wife. When their first son was born, they gave him the name Not Easy. As the wealthy family's first son, Not Easy began to grow, and at about age seventeen years old, his father, the wealthy man, suddenly passed away. Now, Not Easy, the son of a formerly wealthy man, had to live with his mother without his father. Not Easy possessed a lot of friends of all kinds to help him destroy the wealth he had inherited from his father before he had acquired enough knowledge to handle it responsibly. The son no longer had any respect for his mother as he did before, especially when his father was alive.

A short period of time after his father's death, his mother also passed away. Chaos after chaos, the son's name is Not Easy; he has lost his mother and father. Now, it is not easy for Not Easy. Not Easy, amidst so many friends but with zero understanding of real life, played all kinds of games for money. It didn't take long to see Not Easy building a small house in a different land for himself to live since his parents' homes were all gone. Lands have been sold off acre by acre. He could not keep up with his small house. He moved to his aunt's house, knowing that the money is over. There were no more houses or lands to sell, or any more money to spend with his friends. Every single friend disappeared, leaving Not Easy behind on his own.

Thanks to his mother's sister, Not Easy found a place to sleep and food to eat, but there was no guarantee of daily meals. Sometimes his aunt would be away or wouldn't cook any food, and Not Easy couldn't say he was hungry. He couldn't break any laws to satisfy his own stomach by saying he might not be hungry. Whether or not Not Easy found food, he would still be hungry later.

Imagine a person who is used to eating anytime he wants, but right now, he can't even count how many times he goes without a meal. Sometimes, a little taste of alcohol is enough for other people to overpower him and make him work for them. Not Easy has a difficult life. It's not easy for him to give up on life, and it's not easy for him to steal anything that belongs to others. He makes himself the hardest worker ever to exist, but unfortunately, alcohol always wins over Not Easy. Now, Not Easy eats only when he reaches his red line to pass away due to hunger.

He works from dark morning until dark evening, cutting wood and rocks to make limestone for people to use in building their houses. He works only by himself, until he can accumulate a pile of limestone, which takes him weeks, sometimes even months during the rainy seasons. When he doesn't go to the people, they come to him and give him a small amount of money as they place their limestone orders. By the time he has some limestone ready, whoever gets here first are the winners. He never has anything left to sell and make money from. The money he has already received for their orders has already been spent on playing games.

He keeps the word he has always said: he'll be rich. Rather than understanding when riches elude him and he becomes poor, wealth never lets him catch up anymore, sometimes forever and ever. Not Easy always tries to win; that's how he sets his mind, and he always looks like a happy man fighting with a good spirit.

One day, a person stands at a window where they can see Not Easy in his aunt's kitchen. They see Not Easy boiling water and adding vegetable leaves and salt for his meal. The person walks away slowly, hoping that Not Easy may never know they witnessed his actions. This person walks away with emotions after glimpsing into Not Easy's actions. As he has never touched anything that doesn't belong to him, which makes him qualified to keep his name, Not Easy, clean and not easy to steal. He refuses to give up his reputation and strives to maintain the honor of his family name.

Time is passing quickly after plenty of hard work, thanks to his good health. Not Easy has finally built a house for himself to live in on a land he inherited from his parents. He has only one neighbor.

So, life is not easy for the son of the wealthy man. Riches have been swept away, and poverty and a hard life continue with hope to get back on his feet and rectify past errors.

Not Easy is actually making some progress with his limestones, which people buy quickly from him. Unfortunately, one night a group of thieves comes to his neighbor's home to assassinate him. Not Easy, who hears his neighbor calling for help, rushes over trying to help his neighbor with no success. Not Easy has to flee for his own life. Not Easy approaches and sees the thieves. They also see him and say something to intimidate him, so that he won't report them to the police. But Not Easy is the only neighbor he has, so he reports the thieves to the police. And finally, he becomes too afraid to continue living in his house, as the police tell him it is no longer a safe place for him to live anymore. Not Easy quietly leaves his home and disappears, with no one seeing him anymore.

Some people said Not Easy lives in a different town, while others said Not Easy is dead. Who knows, he may have already been killed by the assassins. That is not easy for anyone to know and tell, but one thing is certain: no one has seen him anymore. Not Easy, the son of the wealthy man, is not easy to see anymore. But for sure, as part of his responsibility, he disappears with his family name and the name they gave him. Not Easy cleanses himself from theft, crimes, and other scamming activity.

Not Easy was young and foolish; he did not have enough knowledge to be wise as a man who can resist his bad friends and control his developing bad ways that led him to his downfall. Knowing what a bad friend can cost you is not easy, and gaining that knowledge can be very expensive. While you don't know when an event like an accident can sweep you away, never assume that your children are too young for you to explain to them how life can be and what lies hidden behind friends and their entertainments.

No matter how many fruits a tree can produce each season, when it dies, there will be no more humans, no more four-legged animals, nor flying birds standing by to say, "Let's take the same road." They will not take any chances with you anymore because you are over. Therefore, give your friends only what you want them to have from you, but don't let them have control over you and your inherited wealth. That way, they can never drain out the wealth you must live on, and you won't find yourself draining away and being swept to the ocean by a simple sinkhole.

If a name can sometimes have a serious meaning and have something to do with the life of the person who bears it, it is important for you and everyone else to know the meaning of the name chosen for a baby. Most people on Earth choose a name that matches a parent's name. Others pick a name that reflects a difficult situation they are facing, which might not be good for everyone, as later in life, whoever carries that name might face a worse situation. Be wise when naming your baby. If you name your baby "dog," don't be surprised if they behave and act like a dog. You cannot blame anyone else but yourselves because you are the ones who named your baby "dog."

One day, while speaking to another person, someone asked him what the meaning of his name was. He replied that he didn't know, and the person told him to find out the meaning of his name because each name has a meaning. That might be something he never searched for or wanted to know, or he might already know it. If you are familiar with mangoes, when someone says "mango," you know what it is. Similarly, if you are familiar with aloe, when they say "aloe," you know exactly what they're saying. Do not choose between reward or mercy when the salvation is yours to grant.

A person was young when his father killed his mother. Later in life, when he had a son, he gave him a name that means "this is the murderer." This son is the grandson of the criminal who killed his grandmother. When the grandson himself got married to a woman who became his wife, they had five kids, and she became pregnant. Then, the man killed his pregnant wife along with their five other kids. What can you say about his name? His name means "this is the murderer." The first crime committed by his grandfather was not enough. This man committed murder, and that's what his name means. Did anyone expect that to happen from him? Everyone can say no. So, what you don't know will never be mere just because you don't know it. You can only ignore it as a bird snare with no exit to skip out. That man enters prison and does not expect any future release with life. This is a murder erases his family, including himself, forever. Many people in the world have names that mean "hard life," and some of them change their names for some reason. If you are witnessing a hard life, you can soon see a different way in life.

Wishing for a miracle where everyone can see how their life is going to be before their birthday. This way, they would have the choice to be born or not on Earth. If you agree with life, from beginning to end, you agree to be born on Earth. But if you do not agree with that life, you can refuse to be born on Earth without any prejudice. So, if we could make this happen, imagine how many people would agree to be born and how many would deny life on Earth. The person who reveals this would become immortal.

Woodpecker, Spider, and Snake

Whatever your intellect may be, sometimes it needs to be guided by true wisdom other than that which can trap your own selves. This did not happen to the birds who were the first to use the internet and create websites long before humans. One bird is the woodpecker. While people use their fingers or thumbs to operate computers, woodpeckers were doing it long before humans. Woodpeckers would travel from tree to tree and build their own websites. They would create small holes as their websites, and when they were away, other small creatures would enter these holes and stay there, becoming the woodpecker's email messages within the cell of the tree trunk.

When the woodpecker returned to its computer, it would just enter its password, which was created for it by the inspector spider. After the spider had placed the password for the woodpecker, they became two partners who never met. When the woodpecker returned, it would remove the password, which was a part of the spider's webs, and consume the other small creatures that had served as its messages within the wood trees. What do spiders get paid for its job of placing the password in the woodpecker's computer? Spider and woodpecker were partners, but not to meet together. After the spider had completed its jobs, it would stand not too far away. Every time a message came, the spider inspected that message. Whoever entered into the cell, stayed until the woodpecker removed the password for him to get them. However, anyone trapped outside would be consumed by the spider before the woodpecker arrived. After the spider finished eating, it would move further away and hide, avoiding a potentially unhappy encounter with its partner, the woodpecker, who may not be pleased to see him as a partner on the web, not to meet.

Spiders were not only specialized in placing passwords, but they also built satellites as shelters to protect themselves from predators who want to eat them and provide living spaces. These shelters also served as traps to catch food for the spiders and also their strongholds. As for the woodpecker, he said his plumage doesn't like water or wind and he builds his stronghold on the trunks of majestic trees where predators like snakes could not climb by. They carefully selected a formidable and wonderful tree to build their stronghold, where they laid eggs, hatched chicks, and expanded their family. The woodpecker family grew into a large bird family on that majestic tree.

But, some snakes in the area were not pleased with the constant noises coming from the community. The snakes are slithering around to identify the noises and find they are coming from birds singing and chicks crying. Snakes had a strong appetite for birds. Each night, a snake would attempt to climb the majestic tree to reach the woodpecker family's stronghold. But every attempt proved in vain; they couldn't make it up the tree. Night after night they did not make it. Finally, they tried a different way, climbing smaller trees whose branches were resting on the majestic tree and then finding their way to the larger tree.

One night, the woodpecker family's stronghold turned into a festival of the great restaurant for the snakes who moved from cave to cave, eating the woodpeckers and their chicks. The snakes decided to stay and made the stronghold their home, leaving the woodpeckers who were not victims to fly away and attempt to return. However, the snakes refused to leave, recognizing the favorable conditions for catching birds on the tree. Even rats, trying to escape the water during the rainy season, found themselves on the snakes' menu. Time passed quickly, and the snakes were getting bigger, while the woodpeckers resigned themselves, quitting their former stronghold.

No more woodpeckers for those snakes to eat anymore. Now it is not easy for them to find food in the same place. Snakes search for food every night, often falling to the ground and quickly fleeing to other locations. However, everything is not quiet between the snakes and woodpeckers because woodpeckers have made a case and filed complaints against snakes for their losses. All the incidents have been reported to the C.I.D. and F.B.I. Also, the woodpeckers' partner spiders actively keep a watchful eye on the snakes.

When the snakes leave the tree, spiders inspect everything and place passwords on any open spaces, in case a snake returns so that it can be reported to the C.I.D. mongoose and the F.B.I. honey badger. Over time, spiders travel to the lower ground and construct satellites to block every path of the C.I.D. mongooses and F.B.I. honey badgers, leaving only the entrances that lead directly to the snakes' stronghold. It's an excellent revenge for the spiders and their partners, the woodpeckers.

A day later, with the C.I.D. mongooses on the right and the F.B.I. honey badgers on the left, the entire territory is thoroughly searched. The snakes are arrested and held accountable for their actions of plundering the lives of the woodpecker's family. Mongooses and honey badgers assure the woodpeckers that their family shall never be afraid because of snakes anymore, at least until more eggs hatch again in that area. Some snake eggs are still underground, yet to be discovered until they hatch and grow in the forest.

Now, woodpecker no longer consider building any stronghold among the snakes. They have been counseled to build on high pine trees and coconut trees that don't have enough branches for snakes to climb and cause them trouble and pain. After visiting some cells on banana trees, where his partner spiders have placed passwords for him, woodpecker looks at a banana tree and thinks it would be a suitable place to build a museum for his mother when she dies However, he decides to wait until his mother eventually passes away before building it, keeping his plans to himself.

When woodpecker's mother finally passes away, he flies directly to the chosen banana trunk tree to build the museum for her. However, he soon realizes that it's not as easy as he had previous thought. He faces a serious challenge for the first time in his tree management skills as a master carpenter. Every time he tries to drill the banana trunk with his beak, he encounters some webs that get in the way, preventing him from building the museum. It's the end of a dream, and the woodpecker must think twice.

Imagine if the woodpecker had shared his plan with others, stating that he would put his mother's remains in a museum cave inside a banana tree trunk. How embarrassing that would have been for him. Fortunately, thanks to the woodpecker's personality, he is the only one who knows the obstacles he is facing at this point. His defeat only makes him stronger, and there is no need for him to feel ashamed. Woodpecker flies back to his territory and constructs a beautiful cave as a museum for his mother to rest in peace forever. This time, he keeps his mother close to himself, and his partner spider builds an artistic and majestic satellite in front of the cave, with plenty of webs and passwords to prevent bugs like flies, ants, or others from getting inside the cave where his mother's remains are placed.

Woodpecker did not reveal his heart, and doesn't have to be ashamed. That is a good lesson for people to use as a defense against critics who aim to bring about defeat, humiliation, and deception. Most people believe in confiding in others, but where you don't need any counsel or help it is your choice whether to disclose or keep things to yourself. Remember, the first laugh will never come from the enemy, but from your friend. After all, people who don't know you are not worried about whether you are ahead or behind. Your friend you are on the road with is the one who wants you to walk behind them. If they wish to run, let them run and go so they don't have to see when you are walking slow or too slow.

In some countries around the world, woodpecker and his partner spider install their websites everywhere, even in people's houses. Early in the morning, woodpecker arrives and checks his email on the house's windows, roof, decorations, and anywhere else. They are always happy when Styrofoam work is done on your homes, as they will establish a good office department there for their family to spend some time, especially when they are escaping from the snakes in the woods and can take a break from their original homes in the forest. Snakes often rent homes from woodpeckers but never pay the rent, until mongooses and honey badgers intervene to enforce the laws. The mongoose and honey badger laws dictate that all snakes, without exception, should stay in a designated area so that when the mongooses and honey badgers arrive, they can easily find them. If they are not found easily, they will search for them wherever they may be hiding and eat them as meals. This is the law of honey badgers and mongooses when it comes to snakes. If snakes act unjustly towards birds, what can be said for lizards and frogs?

Sometimes people are aware of someone else who is suffering the most, but they choose not to mention them because they are not considering them for some reason. For instance, rats are highly sought after by snakes, but birds can receive some protection against the snakes because not many people are fond of rats due to their annoying nature. They have no mercy for rats.

A young boy liked to hurt animals. His parents told him not to beat the animals, but he did not listen to them. His father tried to discourage him by saying, "Son, if other people see you beating animals, they may think you eat the same food as the animals and that is the reason you try to beat them." The boy did not listen. His father tried a different approach and said, "If anybody sees a dog running away when they see you, everyone will say you are a bad person because dogs only run away when they see bad people, not good ones." The boy always believed that if he didn't hurt animals first, they would bite him. He continued hurting animals even when he was twenty years old because he hadn't fully quit.

One day, he saw some cats and picked up a stone. He hurt one of the cats, and it stayed on the ground as he approached it. The cat looked him in the eyes, unsure if he was the one who hurt him or someone who came to help. The young man stood there, looking at the cat until it walked away. At that moment, the young man felt deep shame within himself, and he vowed to never hurt animals again. He realized that he should have listened to his parents. Now, he listened to the eyes of a cat, bowing his head down in remorse for his wrongdoing.

Among the things parents say, some of them are very special. You cannot live without them in this world. If you miss them from your parents, you can find them in a good friend. If you don't have them from your friends, you can find them in the people in your environment. If you still refuse all those possibilities, the authorities will intervene and force you to have them. If you are foolish enough to resist and not learn those principles, the authorities will keep you confined somewhere for the rest of your life. This is because you cannot live outside without those principles.

A young boy, who sees his parents have plenty of money, believes that he doesn't have to attend school because he will inherit money. But what can you do with money in the world if you don't have enough sense? The boy doesn't want to learn; every day they take him to school, but he never studies his lessons or does his homework. In the entire world, if you possess money without sense, you are just possessing a pit. Your wrong friends will kill you and spend your money only in wrong ways. You should never expect them to do anything differently if you lack sense. Even if you don't have money, sometimes you can live better than those who have plenty of money for themselves. It is always best to have both sense and money. So, it is hard to say, but if you don't have sense, you don't own anything at all.

Some good sense can make everything much better, just like how some salt can make food taste better. A single pearl, when ready, looks truly wonderful and beautiful. Likewise, many different colors together can create excellence in beauty. This proves the importance of the varieties of everything in nature. At certain times, you can be able to understand something you never expected to understand. For example, a boy might be born with a problem or develop a problem in his system. When he eats, it seems like he is not breathing from his nose, so he has to breathe through his mouth while eating. This causes a lot of pressure and some annoying noises for those who are listening.

Some of his cousins thought he was just eating too fast. They tried to help him, but as he grew older, he never quit that habit. They believed he just didn't want to quit those bad ways because a doctor had never said that the boy couldn't breathe through his nose. Unfortunately, one day another cousin mistakenly used a medication and ended up with the same condition as his cousin. He was always blamed for the way he ate. Now he himself is unable to breathe through his nose, and he has to eat very fast to have a chance to breathe through his mouth. He must eat very fast and swallow his food rapidly to avoid suffocating and experiencing high air pressure in his throat, nose, and mouth. Now he has the chance to visualize the conditions of his cousin and realize that blaming him for his eating habits was unjust.

Rather than blame someone for things you do not know and understand, as your apology may not be enough, it is better not to add any bad comment at all. Now, if his cousin learns this lesson, every time he encounters someone with a similar situation, it will come to his mind and help him understand how people can be imperfect. Sickness, birth differences, or any other cause can be involved in such situations. If everyone were born that way, you would never know if it is a problem. So, enjoy the good life you have, whether perfect or not.

Two Cousins on a Trip

Sometimes, what a person can understand and see, others may not. Two cousins were on a trip on a ship when one of them saw the other dive under the ocean and never come back. You could never imagine how he felt seeing his cousin disappear under the ocean. Weeping, he sat down and continued to think about his cousin being lost during that trip. After about three days, as the ship was about to dock, he looked up and eventually saw his cousin came back. With joy in his heart, they were reunited, but he was still scared and wondered with great curiosity. He was afraid to approach his cousin. What had happened to his cousin under the water at the ocean? He couldn't explain anything more than what he had witnessed because he hadn't seen his cousin again until they approached the port of the land. He hadn't seen him die. His cousin had disappeared in the ocean and come back in time. What you see with your own eyes is what you can believe for sure. Sometimes, what people tell you can remain a mystery and won't be erased from your mind. That cousin can only remain a mystery because no one was at the ocean to witness exactly where he was at that point in time during the trip on the ship. The cousins didn't set foot on land together, and they never talked about that event. It was considered as if it had never happened during the trip. The cousin didn't have to report the loss of the other cousin anymore; he was happy enough to say they had a good trip and arrived on time.

A man stood in the courtyard of a monument and raised his eyes to the sky. He saw a stronghold city with awesome houses with wonderful beauty and excellence. While he continued to look at the buildings, he approached a person standing at the entrance. He thought that these magnificent homes might exist on the ground and reflect into the sky. He said to the man at the entrance, "Look at some kinds of houses in the sky." The man replied that he couldn't see them. The man persisted, and the other person denied their existence, saying, "Not everything your eyes can see, other people's eyes can see as well." The things were visible to his eyes, but not to the other person's eyes. Some of the things your eyes can see, others may not see. The man at the entrance walked away, while the man who saw that city in the sky continued to look at the heavens.

At this time, he recalls a previous experience when he was here before, at a time when a person was standing somewhere and placed their right foot in the front yard. That image was so big he couldn't see any further than his knee. The foot was entirely made of gold and shone with enough light to turn your own eyes into a source of light. He looked at it for about two to fifteen seconds and closed his eyes. When he opened his eyes again, they had turned into a source of light wherever he turned his face, and all he could see was bright light. This was because that foot was turning his eyes toward the light. Whenever he looked at a wall, it would shine as if a big light were turned on over it. Eventually, he had to keep his eyes closed until they could return to normal, like they were before.

When a river diverts as a landslide over a mountain, then he was walking below that mountain. Each time he approaches that river, the river would shift to a different place, and the former places would dry up. Many materials were lost due to this terrible event, which was as a landslide. The river diverted over the mountain, causing damage to vehicles, homes, and endangering the lives of people and other animals who encountered it.

When he was attacked by a monster beef cow with long horns that was trying to kill him, instead of staying to die, he ran from the beast, which followed him wherever he went, from street to street and home to home. Finally, he put an object on his forehead, and the monster beef cow started fighting with that small object, believing it could remove it. This allowed the man to peacefully make his way out without any interruptions from the wild monster beast.

Your eyes can be a light for you to see what other people shall not see and contemplate. They also grant you the privilege to identify right and wrong. Your knowledge can be the only wealth for you to possess during your entire life, but it can protect you and save you, helping you identify all kinds of snares that are against yourself. Nothing in your life can guarantee you more than good knowledge without deception. Many people think that when you go to school and learn how to read and write, you actually have knowledge. That is not all. The truth is, you are on the road to true knowledge, which you need to survive. Certain situations start from what you can hear even before you were born as a baby. Anything is true if you know how to manage it, and that can be some help for you at a time in life.

Two Boys Walk in the Forest

Two boys liked to walk in the forest not far from their parents' house. One of them was listening when his father told them what to do to survive if attacked by a wild pig in the forest. Eventually, while walking in the forest, a wild pig came forward and attacked them. At that exact moment, the boy's memory recalled what he had heard from his father. What did his father tell them? His father told them that each time they walk in the forest, they must make sure to have a long rod in their hand. If a wild pig attacks them, they should immediately use that rod to scratch its belly, and the pig will immediately lay down.

Thanks to their parents' advice, both boys had a rod in hand. They started scratching under the wild pig's belly, and the pig immediately lay down. The boys quickly ran away from the wild animal. If you only went to a great school or university, you would learn a lot but not enough at all. Because you never learned how to survive a wild pig attack.

If you have a big or small animal like a dog or cat in your house, even if you know you have a good animal, that animal can surprise you with its actions. At this point, you might think that the animal is at fault, but when you know the reality, it can be a different surprise for you.

Any animal, whether big or small, like a dog or cat, can kill a newborn baby. A dog can not only kill a newborn baby but also harm anybody, especially if it is an animal that doesn't want to see strangers. Among the people who are in great danger are newborns who have just arrived in the house. If you don't immediately make sure your cats and dogs see you with that baby, they can wake up overnight and kill your baby, believing they are killing an enemy like a rat or any other unwanted creature in the house.

It is seriously true and important to know and understand that if you are a lover of big animals and pets, whatever is in the animal's mind is to protect you. That's why, if you change your clothes and don't communicate with that animal, it can attack you when you come back to the house. If you haven't informed them and you become pregnant, that can be very serious. Make sure your animals see that you are pregnant, especially when you change your clothes. Let that animal see that it is you. After you give birth to the baby, make sure your animals see you and your baby so that nobody needs to worry about any problems related to your animals.

A pregnant woman grows bigger every day, and each time you change your clothes, you need to make sure the dog sees that it is you by speaking directly to the dog, especially when you are ready to go out. Make sure the dog sees you changing your clothes. That is the way you can protect yourself from harm by your own pets. When you bring your newborn baby home, do not allow any animals to approach the baby until you are sure those animals know they have a new baby to protect. Don't let your dog and cat mistake your baby for a rat or any other creature that has entered the house. Do what you need to do to make the dog and cat familiarize themselves with your baby before you can trust them with your baby. If you don't, they can wake up overnight when your baby is crying and believe they are dealing with an enemy, doing something unexpected to your baby.

As for wild animals, any wild animal that eats what comes into someone's mouth may no longer see that person as a real threat and may not even run away upon seeing that person. If a wild animal is living nearby, it may never want to attack you, but never assume that you can get too close to a wild beast. Beasts sometimes eat wherever they can find food. You never know when a beast might eat something that has come from a human's mouth. If that happens, the beast will not attack that person again, unless by mistake. After all, if you do not own animals, stay away from wild beasts. Prevention is better than trying to cure.

Old Man Tied a Man

A young man was bitten by a dog and had to go to the hospital. On his way back home, he met an old man. Both of them walked slowly—one due to their age and the other due to a real event. In reality, they were two people walking slowly without any specific details.

When the young man reaches a little further, he hears someone say, "Hahaha!! Old man tied him, he cannot go anywhere." The young man immediately thought that the person was addressing different people who had been tied up by the old man he met on the road. He said to himself, "How come people let that slow old man tie them up?" He continues on his way home. When he's about to enter his house gate, he hears his old father calling his younger son to give him a hand and help him get up from his seat. His father says, "Old man tied me out." The young man says, "Oh! That old person I met on the road tied somebody else, and he also tied my father."

The young man decides that he wants to know why the old man tied his father. He enters the house and actually doesn't see a rope.

He asks his father, "Why did that old person tie you up? And where is the rope?" His father tells him, "My son, today you are only twenty-five years old. In another fifty-five years, you will know why the old man tied me up, and you may not see the rope, but you will feel the rope." Hearing this, the young man is a little confused, but he explains to his father that he heard someone say that while walking on the road and thought it was the action of the old man he met before. According to what he says, his father explains to him what the expression "old people tied" stands for. Old people tied somebody means that the actual person is getting old, and because of their age, they can no longer do the same things as when they were young. Now his son fully understands what it means when old people tie somebody and prepares himself for his own time to be tied by old people.

While every young person knows that old age will eventually catch up with them, no one is truly ready to get old. Both men and women try their best to maintain a youthful appearance. They remove gray hairs, apply dark colors, and even undergo surgery to appear younger. However, energy drinks and organic food cannot reverse the passage of time or magically restore youth. People may compliment you by saying you look young, but they never say you are young or younger. Aging is something people fear because it brings them closer to their end. The spot no one wants to be in, especially one who doesn't feel ready to turn back to a non-existing state.

People without wealth are particularly afraid of dying because they worry about the financial burden it may place on someone else to bury them. This fear adds to their concerns during their remaining time on Earth.

In a variety of pearls that form a necklace, each individual pearl holds equal importance and value for the proprietor. A young man was growing up in a city where he was known by every inhabitant as the righteous man of the area. He never had any children. When age started to affect him, he became as blind, but not completely. He has a donkey and a cane stick to navigate where he wants to go. Holding the rope of his donkey, he would walk behind it, having the donkey to lead him wherever he needed to go and back home.

One day he had to remove his shoes because he had to cross a river. After he finished removing his shoes, he held his donkey rope and went on his way. When he finished crossing the river, as he always did, he put his shoes back on. He thought his donkey would be waiting for him, but instead, another man approached. The donkey moved further away, and the other man bent down and was replacing his shoes.

The donkey man was here first, he had finished first and put his hand on the man's back and said, "Let's go," just as he would say to his donkey. However, the man had not finished replacing his shoes and was not moving yet. In confusion, the donkey owner raised his stick and struck the man about three times, repeating, "Let's go! Let's go! Let's go!"

Now, that man, who believed he was probably being arrested by an authority figure, opened his mouth and asked why he was being arrested and immediately beaten. With a heavy heart, the humble blind man kneeled on the ground, begging the man for forgiveness. He explained that he thought the man was his donkey, who he believed was waiting for him on the side of the road.

Truly, many people passing by knew the blind man well and understood that he did not have any ill intentions. They intervened to help the beaten man understand the mistake. A good man, who never raised his hand over anybody, today, because he became blind, raised his baton and beat a man rather than his own donkey.

Imagine a righteous man who had never raised his hand against anyone, would, in his old age and blindness, be compelled to raise his baton and beat somebody just for bowing down to put on his shoes in front of him. Age has come over and tied him up, making him beat the man. Old man tied him up and had him do what he didn't want to do.

News spread across the nation about an old man who would tie people up where they couldn't do anything for themselves. There was also an old man who would arrest and beat people. Upon hearing this, parents started teaching their children how to respect any old man they see. If they need help, help them without complaint and do whatever they could to assist them, while never engaging in any wrongdoing towards the old people. This is why everyone, especially the younger generation, made sure to show respect to all old men and sometimes even honored them to the best of their ability.

Another incident occurred involving the blind man. He attempted to carry some items he needed on the back of his donkey, placing them in the pockets set on the donkey's back. However, when the donkey had to cross a high step at the gatehouse, the pockets slid off the donkey, causing all the items to go flying. The blind man had no idea how he would retrieve his belongings, and he exclaimed, "Ha! That old man tied me for sure." He returned to the road where someone helped him find his scattered belongings and placed them back on his donkey. Afterward, the old man continued his way, walking behind his donkey towards their destination.

Later in life, his wife became sick and eventually passed away before him. Since they did not have any children, representatives from the community gathered with others to discuss what exactly to do for him so he could have a better life. However, there were already two ladies who came every day to take care of the old man.

He never had a chance to see them physically because he is blind, but he always listens to their voices. The representatives decided to sell his large house since he no longer had a wife and purchased a smaller house where he could live by himself. The two ladies would continue to provide care for him at his new residence. While this decision was made for him, what about his own desires?

When the representatives believed they had accomplished what they wanted for him, the old man surprised them with his request. He told them that since he no longer had a wife, he couldn't bear to be without one. Among the two ladies who cared for him, he asked them to choose one for him to marry, so he could have a wife once again. His statement surprised them because they viewed him as someone on the path to the grave, but he had different plans. He acknowledged that his wife had passed away, but life continued for him. He didn't concern himself with when his life would come to an end; instead, he wanted to enjoy each day he was granted before his time was up.

Time went by, and his house was sold to another person since he had no children. The new owner noticed a dove's nest in a low tree at the back of the yard. Every season, the dove would return, lay eggs, and raise her chicks. However, during other seasons when the dove was away, a musician bird that never built its own nest rented the dove's nest to raise its own chicks. By the time the dove returned, the musician bird's chicks had already flown away.

One good day, the new owner decided to clean his yard without paying attention to or caring about the dove's nest. He removed the nest, which contained two baby doves. A friend passing by saw this and questioned the owner about why he had disturbed the nest with the baby birds. The friend tried to hang the nest back in its place but failed because the branch had already been cut down. The friend jokingly warned the owner that just as he had removed the birds from their nest and put them on the ground, someone could come and remove him from his house on his bed. The owner needed to be cautious.

A few days later, bad friends of his wife came over to his house, then they were sleeping on his bed while he slept on the floor himself, the same way as the birds. Eventually, he decided to dispose of his bed, taking it to a dump. The similarity between him and the birds was that he had lost everything: his family, especially his wife, and later, his house. It had nothing to do with what he had done to the birds, but because his friend had mentioned it, he couldn't help but feel some concern about his own situation.

As for the musician bird who always uses that nest, she flies over and over, looking at the baby doves on the ground. This problem concerns not only the doves but also the musician bird, who always has her babies in that nest. After the cleaning has been done, there is a big beetle grub, such as those who live inside the rotting wood, who are walking on the ground. The musician bird looks at the ground and sees the beetle grub walking, slowly ramping on the ground. The bird flies down to the ground to turn that beetle grub into a meal for her to eat. She starts by using her beak and beating the beetle grub on his back. Then the beetle grub turns himself upside down and lies down on his side instead of his belly. While the bird is pecking him out, he grabs her beak and locks the bird's beak between his teeth and his multiple feet under his belly and plots himself as if he is dead. He forms himself into a ring while he locks the bird's beak inside the loop very tight. Now the game has changed to a different phase. The beetle grub is continuing to play like he's dead; he no longer gives the resemblance of a beetle grub, anymore. He only looks like a ring. The bird is too weak to fly away with the beetle grub, who is much heavier than the bird. The musician bird, who always sings day and night when it's not raining, quietly forgets her role as a fantastic and wonderful musician. Now she turns into a great fighter to survive. She flaps her wings for like five minutes, then she becomes too tired. Then she resigns and lies on the ground. Now both of them play dead to survive from the game.

After another five minutes without any movements, the beetle grub thought the bird had died. He releases her beak, and she's the first to fly away and rest on a cable to the sky where a beetle grub cannot come to rest. The bird stays on the cable, thinking about his situation. Meanwhile, the beetle grub peacefully makes his way to his destination. The musician bird, who always uses the dove nest, notices the dove apparently on the way to losing her baby chicks. The musician bird thinks she is going to enjoy a big beetle grub as her meal. So, both birds are getting sad at the same time, although it may not be for the same reason. But all of their emotions stem from one source, which was the owner cleaning his backyard. Imagine if the musician bird had eaten that beetle grub without any problem, and a sad dove lay in the area where the musician bird was going to play his instruments incessantly. That should never be a joke for the dove.

Time is coming for those partners and neighbors to split up. The beetle grub, as for him, for sure, he cannot walk far, but it is not easy to know where he is located. The dove is probably in the neighborhood, and the musician bird can still be around, playing his instruments day and night. What about the owner of the house? The owner of the house has his candle continue to burn the same. He was a good man who suddenly got separated from his wife and married, unfortunately, a bad woman. He had two kids and later discovered that the woman withdrew all of his money from the bank and sent them to men she found on dating sites. Everything he had as money was swept away by that bad woman. However, she left him with his two children to start over in life. This time, the dove had two chicks on the ground, and the man himself had two kids with him too. So, life continues.

Science does exist. At one time, people believed the Earth was flat. Approaching a different period of time, they realized that the Earth is not flat. Even in our time, many things remain beyond the reach of our eyes to see.

Life is short, and people who desire justice must be cautious about how they wield power, whether it is over humans or other living creatures. If the man raises his kids like he is supposed to, perhaps he will have a chance to rebuild his life and skip the darkness caused by that bad woman.

Humans are prone to all kinds of errors, especially when they lack knowledge. People don't attend school solely to learn how to navigate every situation in life. Sometimes, you simply don't have to worry, as most problems are created by humans for humans. If you know where you are going, you don't have to stop and ask for directions because by that time, you have already reached your destination.

Family Sells Home and Own Clock Box

A family has a beautiful home where they live. However, at a certain point in time, the family finds themselves without anything and without any work to make money for their survival. Day after day, they become increasingly poor and have nothing at all to support themselves. Now, they are considering selling the house. They love their home so much, not only because of their emotional attachment to it, but also because everyone, whether rich or poor, needs a place to live.

Finally, when they can no longer afford to buy food for the family's survival, they make their decision to sell the house. Before selling it, they take a malicious decision. They decide to buy a solar system clock with a high-volume alarm. This alarm is set to open itself every night from nine o'clock p.m. until nine o'clock a.m. in the morning. They place the alarm inside a box and lock the box in the ceiling of the house, where it remains hidden from view. Only if someone were to go up into the ceiling, would they see the box, but not the clock itself.

When someone comes to buy the house from the family, they are informed that there is a small box in the ceiling that belongs to them and cannot be removed at the moment. They propose including this condition in the contract, so they can retrieve the box when the time is right. The buyers agree, and a contract is signed stating that they are purchasing the house, but the box remains the property of the original family and is not for sale. With the contract signed and the money received, the buyers express their gratitude and love for the home. The deal is done, and the new buyers prepare themselves and move in over the weekend.

Initially, everything is pretty much quiet until nine o'clock in the evening when a persistent alarm starts ringing, continuing for twelve hours until nine o'clock in the morning. This is far from pleasant and not a good start for the new owners. However, they believe it is just a temporary inconvenience. The following day, the same alarm pattern repeats, from nine o'clock in the evening to nine o'clock in the morning. Now, they make efforts to contact the seller, the previous owner. Eventually, they manage to reach him and express their concerns. In response, he asserts, "You are the owner of the house, I'm the owner of the box. You have nothing to say about my box."

The buyers find themselves unable to sleep through the night due to the incessant noise. Frustrated, they decide to take the matter to court, seeking resolution with the seller. In the final judgment, the judge declares, "You own the house, he owns the box. The contract states that. We cannot intervene in this matter; it is up to both of you to resolve it." This is the final judgment they receive.

When they hear this, they decide to abandon the house because they cannot live in such a situation. However, the former owner, who had been closely watching them, returns to the house on the same day the buyer makes his final trip out. The crooked family, feeling defeated, returns to the house. Now the malicious owner has the money to take care of his family and still has the house for them to live in. What a lesson for the family who did not fully secure the house they purchased!

Doing business with someone you don't know doesn't make you a real partner because you can never see what's in that person's mind. Honesty is not the fruit of wrongdoers. If you have a deal with someone, distance yourself from that person as soon as possible to protect yourself and whatever you think they might use against you. Don't allow yourself to be an easy catch for malicious individuals.

Even someone you know can change over time due to matters of the heart. People's hearts can change every second and make progress towards what they have in their mind, especially when they don't want to control their bad ways. These rule over them, kidnapping their mind and controlling their mind and thoughts. These inclinations govern their thoughts and actions. The only way to potentially catch them is through their actions. However, once their actions are completed, it's already too late for you to protect yourself against them.

A young man was caught stealing and later escaped from the police. His parents, who live on the island, have a friend who also knows the thief. After stealing and fleeing from the police, the young man makes his way to his parents' friend's house. When he arrives, he tells them that he was working with a bad person and accidentally broke an expensive saw while working with it. He cannot afford to replace the tool, so he decides to flee from his employer to protect himself from the pressure.

Arriving at the house with only shorts on, as he had crossed the sea by swimming, his defense doesn't seem very convincing. However, since they know his parents, they offer him a place to sleep until they can get the real story. They give him a section of a guest house, which has three parts to live in, like a triplex. The thief lives like a prince, enjoying free meals, drinks, and sleeping free instead of being in prison where he is supposed to be. It's a stroke of luck for him that the telephone doesn't work well on the island where he comes from, making him believe that the police won't find out about his location anytime soon.

Despite the fact that he should be in prison for breaking into people's houses and stealing from them, they provide him with new clothes to wear. He knows what he did and pays attention to every piece of news. A thief who should be in prison is granted the privilege of going to the beach among good people, making him feel like a hero. It's a little too late, but news about him is on its way. When he suspects that one of his cousins is coming from the island he fled, he realizes that the true light will soon shine upon him. Now, he focuses on fleeing to another place, but with a repetition of his previous actions. How will he make it this time? He does exactly what he is as a thief—grabs every pillowcase he can find, enters the other two guest units, and steals whatever he can carry with him. That night, he flees without anyone noticing.

Early in the morning, a neighbor calls and says they found a briefcase by their gatehouse on the roadside. When they investigate, they discover that the briefcase belongs to them. The thief, while fixing the things he stole on the side of the road, may not have had enough light and simply left the briefcase by the neighbor's gate.

When they checked the place where the thief had been, they were surprised to see that he went to every section, stealing everything he could carry, like clothes, shoes, and money. He was the wrong guest who should not have been there. As for those who suffered losses, they were there at the wrong time. The thief didn't want to get arrested when the news arrived about what he had done on the island he came from, but he made sure he repeated the same bad actions. Unable to go back to the island, he made his way to an unknown place for others not to find out.

It was too late when they found out that he was a thief. They should have never accepted him at all. The only advantage they had was that the thief couldn't carry more things than a thief normally can, and he didn't have access to the main house where the family lived. His limitations gave them a chance they would never regret. The owner of the house had a good friend on the island, but not a good friend's son who was a thief and a liar. That thief said he crossed the sea by swimming to arrive at the mainland. Many people say if you are a friend to someone, you are also a friend to their dog, but not always, because some people are allergic to dogs, especially the thieves' dogs. You'll never know when you can be the one to be their victim.

Pastor Father Devil

You can only know people's minds if you are those two boys who always try to scare their father when he's coming home from work every night. Each night, when they know their father is getting closer to the entrance gate, both of them grab flowers from a tree and shake them to frighten their father, as if a devil were attacking him. But the father always says to them, "I'm not afraid of you, devil. I rebuke you." However, there is a man in the neighborhood who calls himself a pastor. Every weekend, he takes his accordion and goes to a village with some other people, and they start a service from six o'clock p.m. to nine o'clock p.m. All they do is dance and sing, "We're not afraid of you, devil. Death to the devil. Crush the devil's head and rebuke you, devil." The pastor keeps everything he says in his mind.

One day, that pastor has an appointment with the boys' father at his home around the same time he usually arrives. The two boys are unaware of the appointment, so as they always do, they go to the gate to try to frighten their father. But this time, it's going to be a good different joke for them. When they hear someone approaching, they think it's their father. Instead of their father, it's the pastor. When the boys start shaking the flower trees, the pastor gets down on both knees and says, "Oho! Father devil, I always say that, but you see my heart, Father devil! Father devil, you see my heart! You see my heart, Father devil!" Now, without excessive force, the pastor is telling the boys that whenever he goes to that place, playing his accordion with those people and singing, he rebukes the devil, crushes its head, and steps on it, declaring death to the devil. He has never been serious. He is the one who is most afraid of the devil and even calls it father, claiming that the devil can see and know what's in his heart. Imagine how bitter that man, who calls himself a pastor, must feel when he realizes that he is telling the boys what is in his mind about the devil, whom he always curses.

Those boys have a special talent for coaxing people to reveal what they are hiding in their hearts and minds, particularly if those individuals consider themselves pastors or believe they are pastors.

Pastor Father devil, you see my heart picks up his instrument every weekend and goes to an empty house in a village. He starts playing his accordion from six o'clock p.m. to nine o'clock p.m. However, the empty house is also used by other people in the village for their own entertainment on weekends. They prefer to start at eight o'clock p.m., but the pastor's group refuses to leave until nine o'clock p.m. There is always a conflict between the two groups because sometimes the pastor wants to stay until ten p.m., and he often manages to start before the other group since he begins at six o'clock p.m. Each time the entertainment group wants to use the place and the pastor is still there, some of them hide and throw stones on the tin roof of the house to scare and drive them away. That's how they manage to claim the place for their own entertainment.

When that happens, the pastor always says to them, "If you don't want me to do what I've done to my lord, my lord will be talking to you." Then they reply by saying, "Your father devil sees your heart. You are not serious. Nothing will happen to us." Finally, since the village people had been using that place for a long time before Pastor Father devil, he decides to play his accordion outside, while the others entertain inside. The pastor is somewhat relieved to be outside too, as he is a little afraid that his father devil might come inside and catch him by surprise. The others often say to him, "Beat the dog and wait for his owner," which is why the pastor becomes so afraid. He knows that he has been afraid of his father devil when he and his people keep saying things like "dead to him," "rebuke him," and "stepping over his head."

When the pastor eventually meets with his people, they ask him a question, saying, "How many devils exist?" He answers them sadly, "Only one devil." They respond, "Okay, but how many father devils exist?" He tells them that there is only one father devil. They argue that there can be more sons than fathers, but they cannot understand why there are more fathers than sons. If there is only one devil, two father devils cannot exist. There cannot be more fathers than sons. Then the pastor says to them, "There is only one, no different from that." The people tell the pastor that they feel confused. The pastor asks them why, and they explain that there were two father devils on the trees, perhaps the pastor didn't have time to look up at the flower trees. There were two boys representing father devil when he put his knees to the ground and said to them, "Father devil, you see my heart." Surely, there were two of them. But we are seriously confused because you are telling us not to follow the devil, yet the only one we should follow is your father. But when you met the boys, you called them father devil. That means devil is your father, and you are following him.

By saying all these things to the pastor, discussions turn into disputes, and eventually, a separation occurs between the pastor and his people. He tells them that he only made a mistake by calling devil his father, but the people tell him that whatever comes from his mouth is in his heart and mind. They urge him to be with his father devil, as they are no longer children of his devil father. The boys who are not real devils carry the name of father devil just for acting, as a devil who may never exist in that way. However, the malicious heart of the pastor father devil is revealed through their acting as something they are not.

Now the pastor has nobody to make money from. He grabs his accordion and goes to a different city, this time not calling himself a pastor but a blind person. Every day, he goes to a street corner and plays his accordion, pretending to be a blind person in need of help to survive. Those who take the time to listen to his accordion playing give him money, believing that he is genuinely blind. They place the money in his pocket, and if any change falls, he quickly grabs it and adds it to his pocket. This way, he manages to make enough money to buy a house for his family, as almost everyone has to work every day to survive if they are not rich. He is not rich and makes sure he uses his fake blindness to make money every day, that is his work for him and his family to survive. He no longer needs a specific place to go or other people to sing while he plays his accordion. He no longer has to compete with those who want a place to entertain in a vacant home every weekend. The former pastor is now making more money, easy money, as a fake blind man. He saves enough money for anything he wants for his family.

One day, two thieves suddenly surprise him at night when they enter his home to steal what they want. Two things happen to them. Firstly, as you know, he has a scar from a father devil who attacked him. Secondly, he is caught off guard while sleeping. Due to these circumstances, he is unable to do anything but shake. When his wife sees that her husband is unable to help protect their home and belongings, she says, "Okay, my husband, that's what I always like about you. Whenever you start shaking, that's how I know you're ready to kill all those thieves." Hearing this, the thieves look at the man shaking like a leaf in the wind and become fearful for their lives. They quickly run away, leaving behind everything they were trying to steal.

As for the pastor, he is a deceptive man who always deceives others. Therefore, he never has peace of mind and is never strong enough to defend himself. Anyone who catches him by surprise, he immediately thinks it must be his father devil. In any case, thanks to his wonderful wife, the thieves do not win. They run away with their lives as spoils, but they have no way to steal anything. From the first part, the pastor lost his city where he used to live with his people because he was afraid of the devil, whom he calls father devil. For this reason, they lost confidence in him, seeing him as a deceptive man who betrayed them for a devil he calls his father. His fear cost him his city and his people.

However, the second time his fear saved him from losing everything in his house, where he and his family live. Perhaps his wife didn't want to criticize him for his weakness, so she found a good way to turn that weakness into something good. It's better for every woman to pay attention wherever possible, not to criticize her husband's bad ways, but to find a way to turn those bad ways into acceptable ones, if you can. Don't let what you can do die because of what you cannot do. The fake blind man has no regrets for having a wife who is intelligent enough to guarantee the security of the family the way she can. Anyway, sometimes you need a strong part to make a weak one work or a weak one to make a strong one work. So, life continues.

As for the thieves, they never come back here anymore because they don't want to get killed. They only want to steal things they can enjoy without having to work hard for them. But what a good person works hard for over many years, the thieves can grab all of it and finish it in less than a day.

The fake blind man continues to play his accordion and earn money. No one can say he is doing anything wrong because he is playing his own instrument. People like how he plays and listen to his music, and they give him some money. That's how everybody sees it.

One day, two beggar men arrive in the area where he plays his accordion and challenge him to be their partners. They assume he is blind, but in reality, he is not truly blind nor a real beggar like them.

The two beggars, one completely blind and the other guiding him, go from street to street and sometimes through the marketplace. One morning, while they are on their way to the marketplace, someone encounters them and greets them, saying, "Have a good morning." The sighted man replies, "Thank you." After the person leaves, the blind man says to his partner, "I heard him tell you to have a good money. It seems like he let you take that money from among the plenty in his bag." His partner responds, "No, he didn't give us any money. He just wished us a good morning." The blind man insists, "No! I heard him tell you to have good money. So, keep yours and give my portion to me."

Despite the efforts of the sighted man to convince the blind man that they did not receive any money, the blind man refuses to believe him. The blind man assumes his partner received the money and kept it for himself. This leads to a dispute over money that doesn't actually exist. Eventually, the two partners engage in a fight, and during the fight, the sighted man keeps the rod that he guides the blind man with, leaving the blind man on his own.

As a blind person cannot walk independently, the blind man tries to find something to grab onto so he can stand straight. Unfortunately, what he grabs is the tail of a donkey standing by the side of the road with its owner. Instead of standing straight, the blind man falls, and to his misfortune, the donkey raises its hoof and hits him on the forehead. Unable to see, the blind man thinks his partner hit him and cries out, "We had a discussion, but that shouldn't have been involved! Why did you hit me so hard?" Fortunately, his partner and other people come to his aid, helping him stand back up and informing him that he was not hurt by his partner but by the donkey whose tail he grabbed, which then kicked him with his hoof.

Another person standing by the street opens his mouth and says, "This is a good kick for the blind man." Once again, the blind man's ears fail to catch the word "kick" properly, and all he can hear is, "This is a good cake for the blind man." Cake as a cake made in a bakery. He believes they are giving his partner a good cake on his behalf. They had been fighting by a donkey that didn't want people to fight, and the donkey had separated them. However, the problem is not entirely resolved because the donkey forgot to kick the dust out of the blind man's ears, which is blocking his hearing completely. Since the blind man did not receive proper treatment from the donkey, it will surely create more problems for him as a blind beggar. Now, he has a hump on his forehead as well.

Both men are tired and looking for a place to rest. After ending their fight, they come across a small marketplace where people are preparing food for passersby. There is also a bakery and other stores. They find a spot in the shade to rest. Throughout this period, the blind man keeps the phrase "This is a good cake for the blind man" in his mind. He realizes it's a good opportunity to remind his partner about the cake, so he reminds him. However, his partner denies ever receiving a cake for the blind man. This makes the blind man very uncomfortable, and he quickly forgets what happened before. As he has done in the past, he engages in a serious discussion with his partner, which immediately turns into a dispute over a cake that doesn't exist. The blind man never had a cake for sure, but he refuses to accept it. After a lot of arguing, he still refuses to believe that he didn't have a cake. Finally, a fight breaks out between them, near the store where people are cooking food.

This time, there is no donkey involved. However, being blind, the man unknowingly approaches a fire where people are preparing food to sell. He feels the heat on his forehead, the same spot where the donkey kicked him, causing him intense pain. He starts yelling at his partner, saying, "You ate my cake, and now you're heating my kick!" This time, when he says "cake," everybody understands because they are selling cakes. But when he says "kick," they mistake it for the same word, "cake." They think he is asking if they heated his cake, and they reply, saying he didn't pay for a cake order. He can now hear that word very well and then says, "Someone gave my partner the cake meant for me." They tell him that no one gave his guide a cake on his behalf. It seems a similar confusion is resolving another confusion. He agrees that there was no cake for him, that is for sure. But now, the pain from the kick is intensifying rapidly, like a burning sensation. He experiences a lot of pain and complains.

At this point, there are no more discussions or disputes. Nothing remains except to take him to the hospital, where maybe they can offer him some relief and help with his pain. The blind man never knows if his problems are the creators of other problems and troubles.

Now, the blind man tells his partner that he cannot see and is mistaken in fighting for something he cannot see. Furthermore, he is partially deaf and unable to fully hear what other people say to them. He expresses that these troubles have created a barrier against their well-being and asks his partner to leave him at the hospital and go so that his partner can have a better life. He feels and understands that he has caused his partner so many problems and pain, and his apology can never be enough to heal the wrongs he has done. He simply wants one last favor from his partner, out of his partner's own willingness.

The guide listens to the blind man's request and takes him to the hospital to see what can be done to help alleviate his unnecessary pain. Upon arriving at the hospital, they head to the emergency department, burdened by their lack of insurance. They endure a long wait before they can receive assistance, despite it being named a general hospital. When the blind man is questioned about himself, he mentions that the only person who helps him is the one who directs him when he needs to go out. However, he caused that person too many troubles, and he no longer wants to go with him. The doctor asks what he plans to do if he no longer wants to go with his guide. The blind man responds to the doctor, expressing his desire to stay at the hospital. The doctor laughs at him and informs him that no one can stay at the hospital unless they are seriously ill. Once the patient starts feeling better, they must leave to make room for other patients. The doctors then turn to his partner and remark that the blind man is a source of misery for him, causing trouble all the time. The partner wishes to be free from that misery.

The doctors then address the partner, asking who he is. He replies, stating that he is a poor man. He explains that it is too much for him to be poor and also burdened with the blind man's misery. The doctors respond, saying they understand his perspective, but they also make an important observation: "Do you know that all miseries belong to the poor?" They emphasize that the partner's first name is "poor" and his last name is "misery." The partner looks at the doctors in the eyes, and they inform him that he is a poor, miserable man. Upon hearing this, both the poor man and the blind man leave the hospital and continue their lives outside. The key word is simple: miseries are associated with poverty. If you are poor, all miseries become yours. The poor man leads the blind man, and thanks to the doctors who clean his ears, he now has a good chance of hearing anything others say and avoiding fights with his partner and guide due to his lack of hearing.

More than that, in accordance with their situations, they sometimes belong together because they are both beggars and poor individuals who must deal with misery. It's never too late to quit some bad ways and bad attitudes. Then, the blind man quits his bad attitude and sticks with his friend and partner for a better way to live with peace, exempt from unnecessary trouble. They remember the fake blind man who avoided them when they challenged him to be their partner. There are so many stars in the sky, but they are not necessarily forced to be as one grape in a bunch. You can do whatever you can to upgrade yourselves for your own safety and protection against a bad life. Make sure you have the ability to identify yourselves naturally. If you are a category of a dog, don't put yourselves in the ranks of eagles. If you do so and cannot fly away, they might put you in a cage. Then, your liberty will be lost, and your possibility to run will be swept away like a stream over shores. Your beautiful dreams will sleep under the power of your enemies.

Don't forget that sickness and old age are your worst enemies in life. It doesn't matter how you see someone or how you look at them; that person may be the most reserved and private personality you could never expect them to be. Never accept a plate of food from a friend just to please them. If you have a need for that food, take it and do whatever you currently want to do with it. But if you only take it just to please your friend, before you finish eating, your friend will come over to you and say, "You took his food from him and ate it while he himself was dying of hunger." Your feelings will be as indignant as a poor dog in the wilderness because you did not do anything in your favor but to please a friend. If you want to please a friend, you're the one to give to them. Do not receive anything by believing you're pleasing anyone. You should only receive when you feel a need for what you receive.

A man always agrees with his wife on everything. During a period of time, he has to do some cement work on a house wall. While he is doing the work, his wife comes over and helps him. He is very happy to see his wife helping, even with the cement work. He gets excited and tells all his friends what a good wife he has, saying that she even helps him with the cement work at the house. Okay, every man should say that. Well, she is the wife, and nothing negative should be put into that.

Pay attention, some years later they go through a divorce. One of the reasons she grabs as a motive and her solid reason is that he made her work hard at the cement job, lifting buckets and blocks, which she was not supposed to do. That man did not have enough knowledge to understand when something is not right. He was to the point of being deceived and betrayed by his wife, and he never realized anything until she decided to definitively separate from him. She ensnared him when he believed everything was fine for him, accepting everything to please a wife who had a very bad heart for him.

The Lawyer Becomes Homeless

Since you can never read people's hearts, whoever you have to deal with, it is important for you to leave a little space for yourself to breathe because people's hearts can change every second, not just one person's heart, but everybody's on Earth. A person who is a lawyer has been betrayed by some jealous and selfish friends, resulting in him facing the authority of the nation where he's living. The matters take a long time to clarify, and he must spend a lot of money. He is also not allowed to practice his profession anymore, as his license has been canceled. By the time he is done with the court and all the actions against him, he no longer has any desire for a good life. He ends up living under a bridge where many other homeless people live.

Imagine yourself as a person who was a lawyer, now losing everything and unable to easily start something to survive. When that lawyer arrives under the bridge for the first time, it is the rainy season. He looks up at the bridge and notices a little spot that might be a better place for him to put his piece of cardboard so he can lie down. As he starts to put that cardboard down, another man asks him how long he has been here. He answers and says that it is his first day here. Then the other man says to him, "I've been here for twenty years. Look where I lay myself. You get here for the first time and you're looking for a better place to lay. If there is any better place, do you think it can be yours? Are you someone better than us who lays down on the ground?" While he continues to talk, and the former lawyer listens, the rain intensifies, and mud mixes with the water dropping down from a hole, directly onto the spot the former lawyer chose to rest himself on his first day. It seems like the first man already knew what would happen and avoided that section. In this case, it seems like the one who is talking to him is actually helping him avoid getting buried in mud on his first day in his new habitat.

So, after all, the lawyer is in his new habitat, among new friends, with new neighbors. All he needs now are new experiences to live and deal with, which his new friends are trying to teach him. They explain to him that as a lawyer, he needs to know some laws and live by them. Under that bridge, it's very important for him to know certain things because he is going to share that spot with a lot more neighbors, including the most respectful neighbors: centipedes, spiders, and snakes. With many others as well, it's up to him to quickly learn how to manage himself to avoid any trouble with one of these neighbors, which can be fatal for him.

Now the lawyer understands that he didn't learn everything he needed to live in this world. First, he made a mistake with his human friends who were always at his law office, which cost him his profession as a lawyer. Now he must learn a different law, which is how to respect certain animals' spots, so the animals may not attack him. He now understands that humans also need to respect other humans' spots. They did not respect his office, which was a spot for himself, so they disrespected him and disqualified him as a lawyer.

You know that when you are at a low place and you fall to the ground, you have less chance of a serious injury. But when you are at a high spot and you fall to the ground, you have a greater chance of a major injury. That happened to the former lawyer. If he had a low skill level, he could easily go to other places and work as a laborer to make a living. But it's not going to be easy for someone who has just been removed from the office as a lawyer to lower himself to that degree. You may think twice before you see that happen, for sure.

You don't have to be an expert or specialist to know that most of the people you see under the bridges or in any other homeless situations are not always individuals with low education or without a profession. They come from all levels of education. They end up there as a result of various reasons. Some of them make serious mistakes, some have mental disorders, and some are there because someone is jealous of their progress in life and uses their power of influence to manipulate friends in positions of authority. They abuse the system to downgrade these individuals, and eventually, they find themselves where their enemies are pleased to see them lying down.

Sometimes you encounter people who may appear good-looking but approach others asking for food. These individuals may not be seeking work, that's true. However, sometimes their physical appearance gives no insight into who they are internally. It can be no better than catching a bird, removing its feathers, and releasing it into the wild where it cannot fly anymore. By doing such a thing, you actually do more harm than just killing the bird. Although in some cases, certain birds can miraculously survive in the wild until they are able to regrow their feathers and fly again.

When someone makes a mistake that costs them a lot because they know they were the ones who made the mistake, it is easier for them to gather the strength to get back on their feet. However, when someone didn't make any mistake and it was someone else who caused them to be on the ground, that person is more likely to be discouraged for a very long time. People affected by mental disorders can also regain their footing if that disorder is over for some reason.

Only a fool has no cure. If someone is criticized because they are a fool, they will continue on the same path and get worse every time. There is no cure for a fool. While normal people move forward, foolish people continue to follow a circular path, leading nowhere.

A young man was hired to perform a certain type of work for a small amount of money, but he also received free lodging and food as part of the deal. Although the money wasn't much, if he were to have a job that paid a larger amount, he would have to use that money to cover rent and food expenses, which would likely be the same or even less. When his friends mentioned that they were working for higher wages, the man decided to quit his job because he felt he was earning too little.

Another friend advised him to ensure that he found a better job before quitting, as it's not wise to leave a job without having a guaranteed better opportunity in place, especially one that could cover his expenses for rent and food. However, his friend's words didn't enter his ears as he had hoped. The man moved to his cousin's house, believing what his cousin had told him: that he would find a better job at the same place where his cousin had been working.

Certainly, he was hired at that job, but how long would he stay? Soon after being hired, he rented his own house. However, a few months later, he lost his job and had to continue paying for his rent with the little money he had saved from his previous low-paying job. With little hope of finding a new job soon enough to support himself, he had ample time to reflect on the first job he had quit prematurely— a job where he didn't have to worry about rent and food.

The great lesson for him was that you don't discard your old clothes until you have purchased new ones for yourself. All the time he spent without working to earn money for his kids to go to school and to take care of his family, as he had done before and was supposed to do, cost him great family troubles. His wife eventually left him, and he had to move from place to place without finding stability. Until his children grew up, he was never able to support his children adequately as a good father. Most of his time was spent far away from them, and he couldn't send anything on time for their schooling or for them to do other things they wanted to do.

Sometimes life travels very fast. If you make a single mistake, life has already passed you by, leaving you trailing behind in a circle that leads to nowhere. Naturally, some people cannot succeed in life without someone else guiding them. If, for some wrong reason, they refuse to listen or adhere to another person, their life will immediately take a reverse course, and it will never be easy to get back on track.

The Thief Family

Most of the time, the life of a person dedicated to helping others resembles a foolish life. When you are someone who wants to help, you often don't take the time to identify fake people who try to take advantage of you and even attempt to destroy your life. There was a person living in a city where not many people had time to see other people's problems because of their own problems to resolve. A young man, who always wanted to help others, has a house. When he decided to move to a different city, he made arrangements with a friend to rent out his house.

During that period, a family of five individuals arrived and presented themselves as individuals hit by a serious event, requesting a favor from the man to rent the house to them. The man called the house owner and explained the situation. The owner, being a person who wanted to help, said, "Go ahead, don't let them suffer, rent the house to them." Later on, it was discovered that this family of five, consisting of a gang father, a gang mother, and one boy and two girls, had the worst reputation in that large city.

That family occupied the house for about seven years without paying a penny. The owner, who didn't owe any money on the house, became tired of paying taxes every year and not receiving any payment for his property. After that seven years, he decided to stop paying taxes. When the owner visited the house, he found it empty with doors wide open and no locks. Upon looking inside, he realized that those thieves didn't even leave the tiles that were on the floor. They took everything with them or sold it, including refrigerators, air compressors, heaters, and doors. The only things they left behind were the roof and the walls, but not without damages.

The owner made it outside very fast before he could remember how that house looked before

those people entered here. Buying a place and living here for less than a year and actually losing it by trying to help some thieves who presented themselves as good people. This is truly discouraging. Before allowing those thieves to enter the house, one of his cousins had warned him that he looked like a person caught in the snare of fake people. As you know, when someone dedicates themselves to help, they are often seen as a fool who cannot be helped because fools have no cure. If you are crazy, you can be cured, but if someone is a fool, only his pit can save him.

As deceptive people continue to deceive as many others as they can, a day of reckoning awaits them when they will be lying down in sheer pain, haunted by memories of their wrongdoing. Their memories alone will ignite a fire that will not stop until they are struck down. May the wicked perish. As for those who do what is right, they will never allow themselves to be discouraged by the actions of wrongdoers like those wicked people. Reproaches are reserved for those who plunder others, but honor and a strong moral foundation belong to those who are righteous. If you do not inherit something and have not worked for it, you must respect what does not belong to you.

You might want to be like a frog, or you might never like frogs, but frogs don't want any woman to put them out when they switch inside the house. You may want to know why. Well, there was a place where many frogs were living. Over time, people started building houses all over that place. As people removed the bushes, which served as the frogs' habitat, some frogs perished, but most of them hid under anything they could find to survive.

During the construction, the frogs continued to pay close attention and never suspected a woman who came to work. When the first house was completed, the frogs paid attention and noticed many women entering that house. Then, overnight, many frogs positioned themselves by the doors, windows, pool, and everywhere. When a woman opened a door, frogs jumped inside the house like rain. The woman grabbed a broom and repeatedly tried to put the frogs outside. Despite her efforts, the frogs returned and continued jumping from corner to corner, refusing to leave. This cycle repeated until she became too tired and left the frogs alone inside the home. Later, when a man came home, he easily put the frogs outside.

Why don't frogs want women to put them out of the house? Frogs say that if a woman puts them outside the house, it means they are not alive. As long as they are alive, women will never put them outside a house because women do not build houses. Men are the ones who build houses, and frogs will only obey a man when it comes to being put outside, as long as the frog is still alive. If a woman pushes them from one corner, the frog will not go outside but will jump to another corner. Perhaps frogs don't become friends with women for some other reason too, but something must be put forward as an excuse, just like when people don't like others, something is always presented to justify the reason for that.

Maybe women were stealing the frog's hips and buttocks to make themselves more beautiful than the frogs. This could be why frogs are never happy with women. Cucumbers never stop fighting with eggplants because of a similar situation. Wasps eat plenty of honeybees because honeybees can make honey, which wasps cannot do in comparison. So, jealousy will never end. A schoolteacher insults kids because they are wearing better clothes and shoes than he does. As a teacher, he is supposed to help them and teach them what they don't know, but his jealousy for what they possess, which he himself lacks, leads him to insult a kid and tell him that he doesn't know the name of the shoes he wears.

One day, the teacher asks a kid, "What is the name of that thing you are wearing on your feet?" The kid answers and says, "The thing I wear on my feet is called a hat." All the other kids start laughing, except for that kid and the teacher. They remain silent. It seems like his parents have already told him how to answer the teacher because the teacher always asks him the same question. At that point, the other kids don't have enough sense to understand what is funny, but the kid who answered and said his shoes are called "hat" knows what happened, and the teacher knows it too. He has a good feeling about it because the opposite of shoes can be a "hat". This is a great muzzle to stop a bad dog from biting the kids. From now on, there will be no more bullying or insults from the teacher to the kids. Kids come to learn, and the teacher comes to teach. It creates a tender atmosphere for everyone, with calm spirits and peace of mind.

A teacher can use the money he earns to buy what he needs the most, and parents can buy what they want for their kids to make them happy. What they have should not be a reason for a teacher to annoy them. Somewhere in the world, no one has the right to bully or insult another person, especially if you are in a position to help others. Interestingly, some parents are so intelligent that they don't waste their time complaining, and that's also good for the guilty ones who don't have to lose anything like their jobs. Instead, they bully the kids by saying something unpleasant to upset them. However, sometimes the kids behave wisely and reply with unexpected words in return.

So, if you don't want to hear that one more time, you must stop, relax, and do not bully them anymore. When your wrongs have been brought to light, you yourself are in the darkness.

Triple Friend Enemies; One is Not Innocent. Goat, Cat, and Dog

There was a dog who was a good friend with a goat at the goat's neighborhood. There was a butcher shop. One day, the dog decided to go to that butcher shop without any money to buy but with the intention to steal some meat. However, the only road for the dog to reach the butcher shop was the same one that crossed through the goat's backyard.

As the dog approached the goat's backyard, he walked with his back very low so that the goat couldn't see if it was the same dog who was his friend. Luckily for the dog, the goat pretended not to see the dog trying to deceive him and acted as if he had never seen the dog. When the dog reached the butcher shop, he didn't even ask for the price; he simply grabbed a big piece of meat and tried to turn his back away, believing that there were so many people present that he wouldn't be noticed among them since he was lower than everybody else.

When they told the dog that he wasn't paying, the dog had no time to talk, only time to run away. The butcher grabbed a cutlass and struck the dog. The dog thought that if he dropped the meat, it would give him a better chance to run away peacefully because he didn't want his friend, the goat, to hear his voice. Unfortunately for the dog, the man continued hitting him on his back with the cutlass until the dog forgot about his friend, the goat, and cried out, "No! No! No!"

After the dog finished crying, he became exhausted from trying to run before he got struck again. Now, the dog remembered his friend who was not far away. Very quickly, he tucked his tail behind his legs and tried to run fast enough so the goat wouldn't see him crossing the backyard. This time, the goat said, "My friend has a problem, I need to help him out." By the time the goat reached the backyard, the dog came face to face with him. The goat asked the dog, "What happened to you, my friend?"

The dog answered and said, "Oho! Haw! Haw! If someone really wants to give you a job, they must let you know in advance so that you can prepare yourself to do the work. They didn't tell me if they wanted me to work for them. I just reached the butcher shop, and they chose me to be in charge there. My friend, I said, 'No! No! Not now! Not now!' Oh, my friend, I have my owner's gate to watch twenty-four seven. How can people believe I'm the one responsible for a butcher shop? I will never do that, as you know. People like my owner sometimes can chain you up, put you in a cage for a very long time, like a criminal."

The goat acknowledged that it was true, and it's exactly what they were doing to him by putting him in their yard, restricting him from going wherever he wants. But when he gets out, he eats a lot of different grass before they put him back inside the fence. The dog is no longer worried about the conversation, as it can cause a lot of pain on his back. Moreover, the dog doesn't want his owner to know if he was out of the yard, where he is supposed to be all the time.

While the dog is running so fast, he meets a cat and gets very afraid. The cat jumps on a tree close to the doghouse. The dog, who has a lot of pain on his back, starts yelling as soon as he enters his owner's gate. When his owner comes out, the dog says, "Hooo! Hooo! Hooo!" The dog said he laid down here and a cat jumped on his back, scratched his back, and ran away. The cat runs away, but the dog doesn't want to leave the gate without his owner's permission, so he lets the cat go. However, the cat is now on a tree nearby.

When the owner of the dog looks and sees the cat on the tree, he runs to grab a rod from his backyard. The cat seizes the opportunity and jumps down, running away. When the man returns, the cat has already gone, so the dog cannot stay in one place. The dog keeps moving from one spot to another.

Hmm, hmm. When the owner takes a closer look at the dog's back, it's not so simple. A cat did all that to a dog while he was lying down. This is a bad cat. The man has to take care of his dog, which he is doing. A few days later, he goes to the butcher shop where he sees a picture of his dog on the wall with a message saying, "If you are the owner of that dog, you are allowed to meet with the butcher shop manager."

When the man enters the butcher shop manager's office to meet him, the manager shows the owner a picture of the dog holding a big piece of meat in his mouth. Now, the owner claims that the dog belongs to him, and he is the one who has to pay for the meat. The man agrees and pays for the meat. When he gets home, he pays closer attention to the wound on his dog and better understands what his dog tried to do to the cat. Now, he puts a chain on the dog's neck and takes him inside a cage because he didn't stay in his owner's yard all the time as he was supposed to. Instead, he traveled to the butcher shop to steal meat.

While the dog is imprisoned by his owner for making him pay money for the meat he stole from the butcher shop, his friend, the goat, never sees him anymore or hears anything about him. At one point, the owner of the goat decides to put the goat in a different section where the grass is growing much higher, and there are plenty of mice living under the grass. As the goat eats the grass, the mice become uncomfortable and start looking for somewhere else to live.

By that time, there is a great festival for the cat who waits by the fence each time a mouse gets out. The cat grabs one as his taxes he claims to be paying to him. When the goat is full and stops moving, everything becomes calm, and no more mice are seen for the day. The goat lies down, and the cat also lies down by the fence before going home.

During this moment, the goat has a chance to talk to the cat about a friend he had who he never saw again. He tells the cat that the friend was offered a job at the butcher shop. The goat asks the cat if he has ever encountered a dog like that. The cat replies, "Meow, I saw him a long time ago for the first time when he tried to mess with me. I had his owner put him in a cage so he doesn't mess with me anymore. Every night, when I pass by, the dog yells 'hoop hoop.' I make sure to keep my tail high on my back so that if the dog gets out, I can climb up a tree before he can grab me by my tail."

The cat tells the goat that if he doesn't know how to climb a tree, the dog can eat him whenever he gets hungry. The goat responds with a dismissive "Nen! Nen! Nen!" and insists that the dog is his friend. The cat warns the goat once again, saying that the dog will eat him soon if he doesn't find easy prey. The goat tells the cat that he doesn't think the dog eats meat because he was offered a job at the butcher shop and refused it. The cat questions the goat, asking why the dog would go to the butcher shop if he really doesn't eat meat? The goat answers, saying that the cat might be right, but he needs to see the dog in action to believe it.

The cat concludes by telling the goat that he will never have a chance to see the dog in action and believe it anymore. The day the goat sees it happen; it will be too late for him.

Dog will eat you anyway if you don't know how to climb a tree," the cat says. "The only thing I can do for your protection is to teach you how to climb trees and go to the top when dogs attack you." The goat agrees to learn how to climb a tree and becomes partners and friends with the cat.

While the goat eats grass, the cat catches the mice that come from the grassland. Once they are both full, the cat starts teaching the goat how to climb the trees. There is good progress from the very first week. The goat learns to put one foot on the tree while keeping the other three feet on the ground. By the second week, the cat had already taught the goat how to put two feet on the tree. It is a promising development in the goat's behavior.

However, suddenly, the dog escapes from his owner's cage and runs straight through his friend goat's backyard, passing by the butcher shop without stopping. The dog remembers what happened to him at the butcher shop and runs back to his friend goat.

The friends are happy to see each other. The goat mentions seeing someone who looked like the dog passing by, but he thought it was someone else. The dog confirms that it was indeed him but explains that he has friends at the butcher shop who wanted him to work for them. However, he didn't want to work for them. He only came to say hello.

The goat expresses concern, as he hadn't seen the dog for so long and thought something might have happened to him. The dog responds, saying that humans sometimes let dogs out, and other times they lock them in for a long time. But this time, they won't be locking him up anymore.

The goat tells the dog that he has also been put in a different section because there were too many mice in his previous area. He explains that the mice were constantly trying to enter the house, so they moved him to this section to eat the grass and drive the mice away. The goat mentions making a new friend named Cat, who enjoys catching mice while the goat eats grass.

The dog is surprised and asks, "Hoop" if Cat is a good friend to the goat. The goat confirms yes. The dog realizes that Cat must know where he was, including being locked up in the cage and everything related to his situation. He wondered if Cat was aware of his meat-stealing activities and where he was kept in the cage. He asked the goat if the cat was a good friend to him? Goat answers yes to the dog, and he confirms that Cat is indeed teaching him how to climb trees. The dog said are you serious? To which the goat says yes, he is serious. The dog contemplates the situation and realizes that if Cat shows the goat how to climb trees, it could be the end for Cat. The dog believes that if his friend, the goat, can learn, then he can learn as well. The dog decides that he doesn't want to be put in the cage anymore and changes his routine. He eats the food left on the porch, drinks water, and finds another place to sleep where he won't be easily caught. This gives the dog more opportunities to meet up with his friend, the goat.

Currently, the goat only knows how to place his two front feet on the tree. It took him about a week to achieve that, and within two weeks, he managed to place both front feet on the tree. The remaining two feet will take a maximum of two weeks to master climbing trees. Can the goat make it? Only time will tell. The goat is so focused on his friend he didn't see for a long time, the dog, and teaching him how to climb trees, that he completely forgets about his appointment with Cat for the exercise involving his third foot. How much do goats know about teaching a friend? So far, he only knows how to put two feet on the tree.

When Cat, who didn't forget the appointment, arrives close to the goat's yard and observes from a distance the goat who is trying to teach the dog how to climb trees. Cat watches as the goat continues to place his two front feet on the tree while the dog mimics his actions. Cat realizes that the time is right to see what they are doing, but from now on, Cat decides to rely solely on what he already knows. Likewise, his friend, the dog, will be the same. Cat acknowledges that both the goat and the dog will forever be limited to knowing how to climb with their front feet for the protection of cat's life, "Meow".

Cat makes his way back to where he lives, and the next day, he visits the goat's yard. The goat is happy to see Cat and believes that with his help, he will complete his training to become competent enough to teach the dog how to climb trees. It becomes a shared goal that both the goat and the dog eagerly thirst for. Cat tells the goat that this time he will stand on a high rock and jump onto the tree, and then the goat should do the same. By doing so, the goat will be fully capable of going anywhere he wants on the trees. The goat is filled with joy upon hearing this plan and trusts that Cat will fulfill his promise, as Cat has never lied to him before. This time is different from before.

Goat is very happy, believing he is going to become skilled enough to teach his friend, the dog, how to climb trees. Just after Cat jumps onto the tree, Goat also jumps behind Cat. However, Cat stands on the tree and looks at Goat, who jumps his heavy body over his own head. Goat's neck and horns break, and he is no longer able to stand up at this point. When cat sees that he said his head is too small to handle and support a heavy problem like that. Cat suggests that they call a doctor to take care of Goat. Cat jumps down from the tree and quickly runs away.

Five minutes later, Dog arrives and sees Goat lying on the ground. Dog notices blood on Goat's forehead and exclaims, "Oho! Oho! What happened?" Goat tries to respond, but he is unable to articulate his words clearly. Dog persists in asking until Goat can finally convey that he was attempting to climb from a big rock to a tree but had an accident and fell on his head. Goat's neck and horns are broken. Dog reassures Goat, saying that there is no need to worry because Dog is also a doctor and will take care of him.

Dog begins by lapping the blood off Goat's head. Once finished, Dog suggests moving Goat to a flat area where he can provide better care. Dog puts his mouth under Goat's neck, but Goat weakly protests, "Help! Help! Not now." Dog's actions remind Goat of what Cat had warned him about regarding Dog. However, it is too late for Goat to realize the truth. Goat reluctantly accepts that it is too late.

Dog transports Goat to a flat spot and declares that he will be the doctor for the day. Dog prepares to operate on Goat, stating that the procedure will take approximately two hours and assures Goat that he will be okay. Dog grabs Goat under the neck, and that marks the end for Goat. Dog, who hardly stays at his owner's house anymore, hides in the bushes until the last remnants of Goat are gone.

Goat had his one last chance to protect himself from the dog, but instead, he turned himself into a fool. He paid with his own life for his mistake and, in doing so, rejected true knowledge with his foolishness. Goat became a harsh teacher before dying. If you are afraid to call the devil by his name, then you are calling him your father, and you will be the first one for him to eat. Sometimes even two enemies can unite as allies without schedules and eliminate what poses a threat somehow, or at least have doubts.

Goat did not believe that the dog could be a problem for him and failed to see the danger of playing with fire, represented by Cat. His confusion about who to trust only secured that Goat should learn how to climb trees without the dog knowing. Goat did not keep the secret between him and Cat but rather allowed himself to teach the dog how to climb trees. These actions frustrated Cat, who was a bitter enemy of the dog. Cat considered Goat unfaithful and deceitful, trying to deceive and betray him. Fearful for his life, Cat decided to put Goat to the test, a trial by fire where the dog could easily find Goat and see him as a meal.

Today, neither the dog's nor the goat's offspring can do more than put their two front feet against a tree in an attempt to climb it. But true tree climbing can only be done by cats. Goat did not complete his education to be a good enough teacher to establish a school for the dog. Such an endeavor would never be successful for either Goat or the dog, as both remain at the same level of knowledge: two front feet higher than two back feet on the ground.

As for the owner of the goat, when he discovered that the dog had eaten the goat, he kept watch for any dog that might return for the remaining bones left behind. One fine evening, the dog returned, laying himself on the grass with a goat bone in his mouth.

When the owner of the goat saw the dog, he grabbed a rod and walked very slowly behind the dog. He hit the dog approximately three times before the dog was able to run away. The dog ran back to his owner's house but stayed away from everyone because he didn't want to go inside a cage that he considered a prison for him. The dog, being a wrongdoer, was afraid of being imprisoned.

The owner of the goat found out who owned the dog and went to him so he could be compensated for his goat. After meeting with the owner of the dog, he received compensation and agreed to it for his goat. Now, it was up to him to decide whether he would get another goat or not. As for the owner of the dog, he decided to catch the dog as soon as possible. He no longer put food outside the porch for the dog, hoping the dog would come closer so he could catch him.

The dog already knew what he had done, so he stayed far away from people. As he had told his former friend, the goat, humans were too mean and liked to put dogs in cages for too long. This time, he was determined not to go in a cage as his prison. When the dog was caught by the goat's owner, the cat was hiding on a tree, catching mice. When the cat saw the dog, he climbed the tree and hid himself. After the dog was beaten and ran away, the cat came back to the ground and enjoyed some mice.

The dog went somewhere and laid down with his tail between his legs. The cat said that the dog always put his tail behind his legs, which was why he always got beaten on his back. The cat said that when he got attacked, he carried his tail over his back so he wouldn't get hurt there and no one would be able to grab him by his tail. Maybe the cat was less brave than the dog because of that, making the dog more vulnerable.

Now, the dog didn't have a friend to go to, and he didn't have a secure place at his owner's house to stay. The dog, who always made his own challenges, wanted to challenge the cat to be his friend. For the first time, the dog entered the forest where the cat had his stronghold. The cat, who was lying on a branch, looked at the dog on the ground. The dog raised his head, looked at the cat, and said, "Hey, what's up neighbor?" The cat replied with a "Meow" and the dog said, "Hey, I'm tired." The cat didn't answer. The dog lay himself on the ground, usually when the dog was trying to catch the cat, he would be on all four feet if the cat climbed a tree. But this time, it seemed like the dog was trying to tell the cat that he didn't actually want to harm him. He lay down, putting all four feet flat on the ground, as if he was dead.

The cat, who was not always happy to receive the dog's company, stayed on the tree with a serious expression on his face.

He closed both his eyes, leaving only a tiny space to keep an eye on the dog on the ground.

While the cat was looking at the dog, the cat remembered a big festival that was going to take place on the island. The festival was going to last for a year. Transportations by airplane or ship was available for all the beasts attending the festival, but they required the beasts to have horns. The cat told the dog about the festival, and the dog thought it could be a good deal for him because he didn't have a regular place to establish himself. A festival where the dog could be around for more than a year was not something the dog wanted to miss out on. So, the dog said to the cat, "We should go to that festival."

The cat reminded the dog that he didn't have horns, and without horns, they wouldn't be allowed in. The dog said he preferred to swim and get there, but the cat pointed out that without horns, he would be denied entry. The dog insisted that they should go to the festival, maybe not wanting to get beaten all by himself this time. While they were thinking about how they could make it to the festival, the cat came up with an idea. He said to the dog, "We can buy some horns and seriously glue them over our heads and board the ship to get there."

The dog agreed, realizing that was what they should do to attend the festival. The cat suggested that before too many animals got on the ship, they needed to make sure they were both on board. The cat told the dog that he already had his horns, and the dog could go wherever he wanted to buy his own horns. The cat would be waiting for him. So, while the dog went to buy his horns, the cat went straight to the butcher shop. The cat made two trips to carry a pair of horns he needed for the festival. The cat now had a pair of long horns for himself that were even bigger than any buffalo horns.

As for the dog, himself a poor dog with plenty of scars on his back, he didn't have any money to buy buffalo horns. The dog went directly to where he had eaten the goat and found some horns for himself to make it to the island for the festival. Everything seemed fine to the eyes of the cat and dog, who were ready to travel to the island for a festivity that was going to last for more than a year. The dog glued the horns on pretty well, and now he looked just like a goat or a deer.

As for the cat, if you saw the horns, you might think of a buffalo. But when you paid close attention to the body, there was no comparison that could easily be made. The cat looked like an animal trying to carry a load much greater than himself. So, the dog couldn't make any comment about the cat because the cat didn't allow the dog to come close to him. The cat was the boss who chose for them to wear the horns so they could deceive the security guards. But the dog had to respect the social distance between himself and the cat because the cat never trusted the dog on anything.

As they approached the lane, the dog walked before the cat, and the very next would be the cat. This time, the cat didn't expect them to check his horns, but they had a rod to hit the horns to make sure they were real. Usually, they knew most of the beasts, and the security guard stood there with the rod in his hand while every animal passed by, starting from the largest to the smallest.

At the same time, the cat walked as if he were drunk because his horns were too big for him. His head went flush to the ground. Thanks to his short mouth and his sideways mustaches, the cat and dog were paying attention to everything. They could see all the animals boarding the ship without being checked. So far, no one has been sent back. Finally, they reached the dog. They said to the dog, "Go!" The dog hurriedly entered the ship. A security guard showed the dog where to sit, and the dog sat down, even though he became taller when he sat down.

That is not only a problem for the dog, so nobody sees that as a problem for the dog. Now the dog is watching to see the cat arrive as his counselor for their success. But unfortunately, they have never seen a beast like that before. The first security guard tries to let the cat go, so the second one says, "Let's check that one." The security guard then grabs the rod and hits the cat's horns, causing them to fall to the ground. The cat jumps over them and skips ahead while urging them to go ahead and check the one who was ahead of him. They hear what the cat said, but they are trying to catch the cat. However, the cat doesn't want to get hurt. The cat says, "Today is not a day to be afraid of water." The cat swam to land before they could catch him. They say nothing is lost and they let the cat go away. They go inside the ship to check the one who was walking before the cat.

Meanwhile, the cat, who is already on the ground and doesn't like to get wet, jumps over a wall to clean his body and enjoy the sunshine. What's up with the dog? When the security guards reach the area where the dog is sitting, the dog is already in the kitchen area eating food and licking up dishes. When the security guards find the dog in the kitchen, one of them says, "Come here!" The dog stands and looks as the security guard approaches and puts his hand behind the dog's neck just to check the dog's horns. The dog, who already knows what is going to happen to him, gets so mad that he bites the security guard. While that security guard is calling for backup, the dog is already on top of the ship and trying to run away. Unfortunately for the dog, one security guard grabs him by one of his back feet and hangs him in a way that the dog cannot bite anymore. They take off the dog's horns. This time, it's not only the back because the dog is hanging. Each time they strike the dog with the rod, the dog says, "No! No! No!" They continue to strike the dog with the rod until the dog stops fighting and they lay the dog down in sheer pain and weeping. Meanwhile, they discuss a way to put the dog in a cage. The dog jumps into the sea and starts swimming to the land, despite his injuries. He's trying hard, but the pain is so bad that he can't make it as fast as he wants. However, he's still fighting for his life. Finally, the dog reaches the shores and sets foot on the ground, using all four of his feet to run.

The dog did hear when the cat said, "Go check him out too." So, the dog swears to himself that it's not over. Despite the beating on his back and all over his body, the dog is determined to go to the cat. When the dog reaches the road and sees the wall where the cat is resting, the dog goes behind the wall and lies down in the shadow. While the cat is on top of the wall, the dog doesn't even know that the cat has already rested enough and the dog is still too tired to run fast. The cat knows that if the dog rests enough, the dog will regain his strength and pose a threat. The cat then jumps over the wall and speeds away. When the dog sees the cat running, he wakes up and starts running behind the cat. Two different things happen to the dog that don't happen to the cat. Eventually, the cat has already rested, but the dog hasn't rested yet. The cat didn't get beaten, but the dog got seriously beaten. The cat doesn't feel any pain, but the dog is in immense pain. This time, the pain is not only on his back but everywhere on his body. Due to all that, the cat has a greater chance of winning against the dog.

The cat and dog start running near the dock until they enter the city. The cat enters someone's gate, and the dog follows behind the cat. When the cat jumps over a private wall, the owner of the house hears the dog say to the cat, "Hoop Hoop, you better get down." The owner of the house goes over and closes the gate where the cat and dog entered. The dog doesn't know what is waiting for him. While the cat is over the wall, the dog lies behind the private wall, watching the cat and planning to make him pay for telling people his horns are fake. At that moment, the owner of the house pushes the privacy gate closed, just like the front gate. Now the dog is already in the cage, and when the owner sees him, the dog and cat try to run. The cat jumps the gate and escapes, but there is no exit for the dog to get out from the private wall.

Dog has become trapped in a private wall. The house owner is approaching to see what kind of dog is running after the cat. When he looks at the dog, he suspects some scars all over the dog's body. The house owner says to himself, "This is a dog who has been abused by somebody," and he calls animal shelters so they can come over and get that dog to a shelter and take care of him. When the animal shelter people arrive, they look at the dog and give him some food, and the dog eats. They also give the dog some water, which the dog is very happy to drink. Now they say to themselves, "This is a friendly dog who has been abused by a bad person." They try to pet the dog. "Ooh!" said the dog and he lay flat on the ground, shaking his tail. There's no way for them to believe that the dog might want to be skipped away from them. When they are approaching the vehicle, one of them grabs a cage to put the dog, so they can keep the dog in one place in the vehicle. From there, the dog runs away. They have no trace of the dog anymore. The first thing the dog does is try to catch the odor of the cat so he can discover where the cat is exactly. All that time, the cat is supposed to be going far enough not to be found by the dog. So eventually, what the problem is for the cat is a river that the cat encounters. The cat doesn't want to get wet so often, so the cat tries to find a bridge to cross on. The bridge over that river is very far away. You cannot find that bridge until you get to the main road of the city. The cat has never traveled on the city road. The cat always travels by the railroad, mainly by following the bush to avoid facing any enemies, like dogs especially. Finally, the cat enters the city after a long walk. What the cat doesn't know is that the dog, who has already eaten and drunk, is stringing himself to run faster than he did before. Also, the dog is not afraid of the water. The dog has already swum over the river by the time the cat makes it to the city.

Now the dog definitively lost control of the cat. The dog is in pursuit, making his way back to his hometown. As the cat turns behind the dog upon his arrival in the city, he passes by the butcher shop, not on the road, but runs across the butcher shop yard at high speed, non-stop. He does the same thing at the late goat yard and slows down upon reaching his owner's property.

The dog goes around as if he is still on duty and suddenly dashes towards the cat's stronghold. However, the cat hasn't arrived at his place yet. Now the dog is at the cat's property, but there is not a trace of the cat. The dog searches all over the place, hunting for the cat. Meanwhile, the cat heads directly to the goat owner's place, where he tries to catch his mice. The owner, who has seen the cat catching mice multiple times, is happy because he doesn't like the mice. He notices that the cat has lost some weight, so he goes inside his kitchen, grabs a piece of meat, and tries to give it to the cat. However, he doesn't fully trust the cat. The cat takes the meat and runs to the grass. While eating the meat slowly, ants start biting the cat for the meat. The cat takes his meat and jumps over the privacy wall to prevent the ants from attacking him. While on the wall, the cat eats what he can from the meat and drops the bone inside the privacy wall.

Now it's time to go home for the cat. He cleans his mouth with his tongue and heads home. However, the tribulation is not over because the dog is still around the cat's stronghold. As the cat approaches his gate, he suspects that the dog is there. The dog also sees the cat. The only chance for the cat is to grab a tree, climb up, and lay himself on a branch. From there, he looks at the dog on the ground, makes some noises, and constantly jumps with his two front feet at the bottom of the tree. After a long time of manifestation, the cat decides not to come down. The dog resigns and leaves the area. The dog forgets that the cat never had an agreement with him to eat him. The dog doesn't have a definite place to live right now.

While leaving the cat's stronghold, the dog pays a visit to the goat owner, even though he was beaten there. Who knows, maybe the dog will find a bone. The dog doesn't seem to stop, but he smells something. It must be a bone. The dog raises his nose to the sky and approaches the privacy wall where the cat left the bone. However, there is a gate that prevents the dog from getting inside to retrieve the bone. The dog keeps moving back and forth, raises his two front feet, and scratches the gate. He keeps pushing his head between the fence poles and the wall section.

When the owner of the house hears the noises, he steps outside to see what's going on. Soon, the door is open, and the dog, who has his front feet up between the wall and the fence poles, immediately jumps down to run away. Unfortunately for the dog, his head gets stuck between the fence poles and the block wall. The tribulations are not over for the dog either. He fights in vain to dash out. The owner of the house stands there for a while, looking at the dog, who is a non-stop fighter trying to get away, but he cannot make it. Every day cannot be the same. The man calls for animal rescue, and they come over to rescue the dog and put him under arrest. The dog was so enraged when he was stuck that they had to lock his body in a cage before they could remove him. Before his rescue, they also tie both his eyes with clothes so he cannot bite them. Now the dog is in a cage under arrest. His plan to eat the cat is almost unrealistic for him. A tone of misery curses every effort, unrighteous, deceptive, and unfaithful, especially to his owner. Now, dog carriers remind uncertainly that the dog might end up in captivity. But for certain, the dog may go to get his wounds diagnosed. After all, who knows how long the dog will last in that case.

So, peace for a cat who did not steal meat from the butcher shop. Peace for a cat who did not actually eat his friend, the goat. The cat did try to be his enemy's friend and partner with a lot of caution. Vigilant and intelligent. Make sure you know something that can guarantee you protection against your partner, enemy, and friend. An enemy does not bear another enemy, but a friend can become an enemy somehow. The dog dedicated himself to eating the cat, but the cat was a professional specialized in climbing trees. That profession was the only way to turn the untouchable dog's dream and words into an unrealistic proposition. The dog cannot accomplish his dream against the cat. Many people in the world use their minds and knowledge to say no to people who pretend they can harm them forever or force them to stay beneath them for the rest of their lives, even though they have been mistreated. When someone turns your path into darkness, it can be a weakness to apologize if you step on their path. When someone shadows your light, it is not good to apologize if you spray water over his heaven. Remember, when someone tells you they forgive you, they never said they forgot you. Take a lesson from what you have read, learn, and share with peace. Most of the time, you may think you have reached your destination, but you are not even close to where you want to be.

Who Taught the King How to Eat Egg

In antiquity, there was a king who saw an egg for the first time in his life. He wanted to definitively know how to eat the egg. He questioned everyone in his kingdom, but none of them came up with a good answer. Finally, the king sought public advice, and he decided to make a great festival where a major crowd could attend without any worries about disturbances. The deal is everyone who attends will be able to eat and drink whatever they choose. So, whoever shows the king how to eat the egg will become a millionaire. They will receive money, gold, diamonds, silver, houses, and everything else they might desire. They will miss nothing at all. They will be the strongest person before the king himself.

The day has come, and people from everywhere in the nation are coming just to attend and participate in that festival. Among them are those who believe they might be qualified for the deal and become the highest ones before the king.

People gather together in a big crowd, enjoying themselves. The king comes over among them and tells them that he knows there are some among them who know how to eat eggs. So, as you've already heard, whoever among you can come forward and show the king how to eat the egg will be the highest-ranking person before the king. The king asks them if they are ready, and they answer the king, saying, "Yes, we are ready for it." Among them, four people step forward and tell the king that they can answer his question. The king instructs his assistant to bring those people forward so they can prove their claim. The assistant brings the four people before the king.

The king asks them if they are sure about themselves, and they answer the king, saying that they are indeed sure. The king then tells them to prove themselves one after the other. The first person explains that to eat an egg, you have to cook it first. After the egg has been cooked, it is ready to eat. The king asks him if he is sure, and he answers yes. The king then asks the other three men if they agree with him, but the three other men say no. The king tells them to demonstrate their methods and says that they have eggs, water, a pan, and fire. They should go ahead and cook the egg to show that it is ready to eat. The men confidently answer the king, saying, "Indeed."

The first man begins his process. He takes the pan, puts some water in it, then takes the egg and places it in the pan with the water. Finally, he puts the pan on the fire and boils the egg until he believes it is cooked and ready to be eaten. When he takes the egg out of the pan, the man announces to everyone, especially the king, that the egg is ready to eat. The king asks the man if he is sure the egg is ready to eat, and the man confidently answers yes. The king then asks the other three men if they agree that the egg is ready to eat, and all three men answer no.

Now the king asks the first man if he himself can eat the egg. The man answers yes. The king expresses his happiness and tells the man that he is brave and believes in what he knows. He congratulates the man for his courage. The man listens to the king and says, "Yes, dear Majesty King." Perhaps the man believes he has won the case, but we will see further. Then the king tells the first man that because the other three men said the egg is not ready to eat, he is the only person who can prove that he is right. He can do that by eating the egg himself. The first man agrees with the king and takes the egg from the pan. He tries to knock the egg open, but everyone else objects and tells him not to do it. They say that if he has to knock the egg open, it proves that the egg is not ready to eat. They advise him to put it back in the pan. The king also agrees that the egg is not quite ready to eat.

Now the second man in line comes forward and says that in order to eat the egg, you must hatch it first. The king is impressed and says, "That looks like the truth." Then the king asks him if he is sure about it. The second man confidently responds, "Oh yes, dear Majesty King." The king then turns to the other two men and asks if it is true that when the egg is hatched, it will be ready to eat. The two men answer and say no. They believe that the egg, once boiled, hatched, and cleaned, is not yet ready to eat. The king wonders what is wrong with these two men who say that the egg is not ready to eat. "So, we will see," says the king.

The king tells the second man that he can see he is a very intelligent man based on what he said. However, because the other two men disagree with him, the king wants to see the second man prove to them and everyone else that what he said is true and authentic. Similar to the first man, the second man should try to eat the egg. The king asks him if he can do the same by attempting to eat the egg. The second man answers the king and says, "Yes, dear Majesty King." The king said to him, "Please do so." But before the second man gets the egg that is already hatched and cleaned, he opens a kitchen cabinet. Everybody objects and says, "No!" They argue that if the egg was truly ready to eat, he should not have to open the kitchen cabinet before eating it. What does a cabinet have to do with an egg that is ready to eat? This question is left unanswered. From that point it is not as easy as the second man thought it would be.

The king calls the third man in line and asks him if he knows for sure how to eat one egg. The third man answers the king and says that he must season the egg first with some salt, and then it will be ready to eat. The king asks him if he is sure about what he is saying. The third man confidently responds to the king, saying, "Yes, dear Majesty King." The king then addresses the fourth man and asks him if he is certain that what the third man said is true. The fourth man answers the king and says, "No, Majesty King."

Now the king tells the third man that what he is saying looks good and wonderful to him, and he honestly cannot determine why it cannot be true yet. So, because the fourth man opposes and claims that the third man is not telling the truth, the king wants the third man to demonstrate that what he is saying is true and correct by simply seasoning the egg with salt. This way, everyone can see that he is the one who proves to be right. The third man answers the king and says, "Yes, dear Majesty King." So, the third man opens the kitchen cabinet, takes some salt, seasons the egg all over, and says to everyone, "There it is, that is how to eat an egg." Everybody looks and sees the well-seasoned egg. They wonder what makes the fourth man say that the third man doesn't get it right.

Now the king asks for public comments, and most of them comment that the egg is well seasoned and ready to eat. The king then suggests that instead of telling one another who is right, they should prove it themselves by making demonstrations to help everyone see who is correct. Everyone says, "Indeed, Dear Majesty King". The third man and then the fourth man stand up to demonstrate their methods. The third man demonstrates that the egg is well seasoned and ready to eat. In the second place, the fourth man demonstrates that he is the one who is right by grabbing the egg, putting it in his mouth, and actually eating it. He shows that to eat something, you must put it in your mouth and eat it. The man who seasoned the egg only prepared it to be eaten but did not show how to eat the egg, as was the question asked by the king. Some people agree with this, while others contest it.

However, the king agrees with the fourth man and accepts him as the winner, the one who showed the king how to eat the egg. The king keeps his word and gives the promised rewards to the fourth man, who becomes the winner during the great festival. Everyone enjoys themselves, eating and drinking. After the festivities, they return to their own residences, except for the one who has become richer. There are many processes to prepare, but there is only one way to get ready. If you are not truly on the train, the train will go without you. Most of the time, you may be well-prepared, but if you are not ready, you will miss out.

The man who won all that wealth should share some with the other three men because they made great efforts. Even though they did not have the right answer, their contributions were important in the preparation of the egg. The king was searching for someone to show him how to eat the egg, not how to prepare it. Wherever lies exist, the truth is not too far away because lies cannot exist without the truth nearby. You can be sick and go to a doctor every day without getting better, whether you have cancer or any other disease. You may travel around the world and not find a good treatment. But believe that the cure for that disease, and any other diseases, is right at your doorstep. You are the one who ignored it. It could be a plant, and your neighbors know that the plant can cure the disease that afflicts you. However, you don't know your neighbor's knowledge, and your neighbor doesn't know that you are the one fighting that disease.

After all, who wants to believe in someone who hasn't attended medical school as someone who can cure a disease that even the best doctors cannot cure. That does happen sometimes. There was a woman living in a great nation on earth who had cancer. She would go to her doctor every week but never got cured or felt any better. One day, while traveling to a small country, she met a person selling the leaves of a plant. That person mentioned that the plant could specifically cure the type of cancer she had. She looked at the plant, which seemed common and easily available, so she didn't buy it. However, when she got home, she grabbed that plant from where she was living and gave it a try, as instructed by the person. To her surprise, she no longer felt the effects of the cancer. She visited a different doctor who confirmed that she no longer had cancer. Excited and happy, she took the plant to her doctor's office to show him what cured her. The doctor explained that many medications are made from plants, and it cannot be denied.

Imagine yourself thinking about the many people who are suffering from the same disease today and have that plant right at their front doors, yet they ignore it and continue to travel everywhere in desperate search for a solution. As for that woman, she is now happy because she has been cured of her cancer disease, something she did not expect. The only thing is that the person who cured her cannot be found anywhere yet. However, it has turned into a mercy for her.

You don't need anyone to tell you that if she has a friend today who is fighting the same cancer, she will help him out too. Her doctor will have at least a reduction in income from her, but she will have more time to enjoy life without pain and stress, without needing to consume medications more often than food. She takes a break until another event or age comes around.

Son Operates on Papa Doc's Client

A doctor was living in a town where not many people had big money to pay when they were sick. People always needed favors from the doctors and had no other sectors to help, neither them nor the doctors. Things were hard for all of them—the doctors and their clients. This doctor had only one client who was very rich and had a skin disease. The doctor knew that performing operations to remove the affected spots would provide a definitive cure. However, if the doctor left the spots untreated, the disease would remain with the patient forever.

So, the doctor advised his wealthy client to come to his office every week for skin cleaning, as it was the only existing solution to prevent the disease from worsening. Indeed, this continued over many years, and it was the only way the doctor could earn money to pay for his children's education. Eventually, one of his sons grew up and became a doctor as well. The father never explained anything about the special treatment for that particular client to his son.

As a young doctor, the son wanted to be good and honest with his clients. One day, when the father went on vacation, the young doctor was left in charge of the office. During that period, the client with the skin disease visited the doctor's office, expecting the doctor to clean his skin and let him go. Rather, today will be different for him. When the young doctor looked at his skin, he told the client he was going to operate on him because it was necessary. As for the client, he believed that the operations were necessary due to the worsening of his condition. He agreed to undergo the surgery immediately. The young doctor performed the operation, removing all the affected skin from the client's body. When it was time for the client to be discharged from the hospital, the father returned from his vacation and discovered that his son had cut out the diseased skin, the very skin that had funded his education from preschool to becoming a skilled doctor.

Today is for the hunter, tomorrow is for the prey. Every day is not the same, yesterday being for the doctor, but today is a day for the client to be free from a bad disease. The father called his son aside saying, "Ooh, my son, you cured that patient!" Dad went on to explain that the patient the son had cured was the only one who had put him where he is today and supports his brothers and sisters.

The son admits to his father that he was unaware of the significance of the client's role in their lives. On the other hand, the client, who had endured the disease from his youth to old age, now found himself liberated from its grip. It was a miraculous occurrence that he had not anticipated. A lifetime prisoner had been set free, no more weekly appointments for skin cleaning. He has a little more time to enjoy life without the disease that was supposed to be cured years ago. The great thing is that he will become old, but will not die with the same mindset, feeling as a loser all his life.

He not only defeats the disease but every reason that was blocking him from getting released from that disease. In that case, what is supposed to be the best: having money or not having money at all? Those who don't have any money cannot pay to cure their diseases; they must stay until they die. Those who have money also have another reason to hold onto it until they die. You just need knowledge of what's going on to make the most of your life and benefit from your rights. In the end, we can only see a patient free from his disease and a doctor with a reduction in money.

Next is a young doctor with honesty. Deception is not good at all, but when you are a righteous person, more people can trust you. That makes the young doctor trustworthy for all his clients without any doubt, especially after he performed the operation on the rich man with the skin disease. This client referred many good clients to him. Among them was another wealthy man who always wore short pants. Everyone in the city knew him well, and he despised thieves and looters.

A new man arrived in the city and bought a place to live, but he was already suspected of wrongdoing by most people. The rich man himself never trusted that man because he was often accused of stealing other people's property. Therefore, nobody absolutely had any trust in him. However, the rich man heard that the untrusted man had come to live in the city. As usual, he wore his short pants and took a walk around to satisfy his curiosity. What he did not know was that the untrusted man had a large female dog.

While walking slowly along the road, the rich man kept his eyes on the new property of the untrusted man. Unfortunately, the female dog spotted him and swiftly ran towards him, catching him by surprise. Immediately, he sees the dog and mistakenly thinks the dog will stop, but he was wrong. That female dog jumped on him, causing him to fall to the ground, and operated on him, maybe by mistake. The female dog put her mouth below his belly and bit his testicles, attempting to remove them. He was immediately seized and taken to the hospital, where the young doctor had to attend to him. When he fell, his pants were so short that the female dog had easy access to operate on him.

Despite the fact that the owner of the dog is a person nobody likes, he found a way to come here and live among them, and finally, his female dog operated on a rich man who didn't even want him to live among them. Now the dog missed the rich man's penis but got his testicles. He came close to losing his penis because of a dog that belongs to the wrong person, an individual whom no one trusts or considers. Thanks to a great doctor who took good care of the rich man, he proved to everyone that he is recovering well. After nine months, he even became the father of twin girls, showing that he hasn't been damaged as some had wondered. There is no doubt that he has recovered well and is now healthy.

The exact time when he was bitten by the female dog was not reported, whether it was at night or during the day. If it happened at night, more questions should be asked to the people who witnessed the event. However, the important point is that the man has recovered well, and there is no question about that. Curiosity can sometimes be punished, and in this case, the short pant man is being punished for his curiosity about the dog owner's property, resulting in him having to pay for a different operation.

After the incident, everyone agrees that if the man has already purchased a property, he has the right to build his house and live in it. As a result, the authorities of the city have enacted a law stating that anyone who owns a dog must build a wall around their property and have a sign that says "Beware of the dog." They are also advising whoever wears short pants to wear longer ones than the short man was wearing. At least a short pant that can reach their knees when going out, especially old men who are more vulnerable to accidents.

When the short pant man hears about the law, he reminds himself that this is not the first event to happen to him. He had previously fallen at a riverbank, breaking both of his legs. At that critical moment, he was taken to the same hospital where the young doctor took care of him for the dog bites. The rich man recalls similar events and wonders when he might truly die. He continues to express his hatred for those who live by stealing what hardworking people like him have earned, as well as those who are known as troublemakers.

What he hates most about them is that these stealers and trouble makers don't need any invitation. They are always the first to show up at your house, seeking food and drink without any invitation. No matter what kind of festival or celebration you have, they will show up. What annoys the rich man the most is their constant noise and impatience. They act as if they own everything and have the right to enter your private rooms and backyards. They want to invade every aspect of your property.

The rich man considers them worse than the dog that bit him. He believes they keep everything in mind and return overnight to take whatever they have seen. They come to your property and steal whatever you have when you least expect it. Because of this, the man in shorts talks to his family and tells them his plans. He will buy his own coffin and have them prepare his museum. That way, when he dies, his family members will not put him in a mug. Instead, they will immediately take him to his museum, which will be his final resting place forever.

By doing so, they can close the gates of the house and lock the doors, carrying on with their normal activities. They can continue with their daily routines as if nothing had happened. If the troublesome individuals come to their gate, they should not answer them.

The rich man did not only express his thoughts but also took action. He bought his own coffin and established his museum. However, he did not pass away anytime soon; he continued to live his life as normal for many years. His wife passed away before him, and he also witnessed the death of his first son. Nonetheless, he adhered to his plans until he grew very old. When he eventually closed his eyes, his children followed his instructions and carried out his wishes.

Some people commented that a man who was not poor should not be taken away so fast. Nevertheless, that was how he wanted it for himself. By making preparations in advance, he prevented his children from needing to spend time organizing things after his death. Since he had already prepared himself, there was no reason to delay his departure according to his wishes. Even though he was no longer alive, he did not want certain things to happen upon his passing. He did not want to go where they were going, and he did not want them to follow him where he was going. Thus, he chose to go to his grave without them. He desired peace for himself and wished the same for his children. His children would not face any reproach as they fulfilled their parent's requests regarding his remains after his death.

Life and death are a pair who side by side, some call this good luck and bad luck. The important point to understand is that you are not unlucky just because you will die one day. As we all know, everyone will eventually face death. Also, being a wealthy person does not automatically make you lucky. If you are a well-educated person, engaged in any endeavor to better your life, it requires hard work every day of your life; Shortening your sleep to make a better life for tomorrow than you even expected. When you consider all of this, you realize the significance of a beautiful dream, something you can call your own. However, it can be surprising how what people perceive as bad luck can occur. You find yourself looking from a distance, as a stranger, watching a wild beast come out from the wild and enter your place. It sits at your beautiful table in your wonderful dream home, eating your meal that you worked hard for. It enters your bedroom and turns it into its latrine. Powerless, you watch your dream turn into a restroom for a wild beast. Eventually, the beast leaves, raising its tail to the sky as it makes its ways back to the wild.

Now, compare for yourselves, a person who never had the chance to accumulate material wealth with a person who has a chance to accumulate material wealth, only to have it enjoyed by the wild beasts while he lay in miserable pain. Which one of them had bad luck?

A hardworking family can worry about misery and hunger. But, the lazy and thieves cast their eyes in the same direction, like locusts. In just one night, they can destroy what you have spent years building. They have no part in the anxieties of life. All they offer society is bitterness and wormwood as drinking waters.

A thief enters the home of a family and steals everything he desires. That same night, he violates the daughter of the family, taking not only their hard-earned possessions, but also leaving a scar that will never be erased from that family's memories. Especially for the young daughter, violated in her own bedroom overnight. Even if the thief is sentenced to prison for some time, many people believe he should never be released at all. Despite repeatedly finding himself in intense situations, he has never been definitively killed by someone until he became an old person. Each time someone hurts him, he plays dead, and when they leave, he makes his way out. But not every time can be the same. When he grows old and continues his wrongdoing, someone shoots him dead. This time, a bullet from a gun ends his life. Playing dead is not the deal, real death, that is the right deal.

That thief was the greatest thief in the city, having caused much harm to its people over a long period of time. What one person refuses to accomplish, another can accomplish very easily. That is why people travel to each other for their trades. If you are a doctor, you might seek the company of an architect to build a house for you. But when the architect falls ill, they must come to the doctor for treatment that they need. Whatever the degree of your abilities, you will never realize everything you want for yourself without the help of someone else.

The Senator's Family and the Mariner Man

At a time when wars eventually ravaged a nation, people needed to move from place to place to protect their lives. By chance, a senator who has fled for his life with his family encounters a young rural man who has never attended school. This young man is now the only available person who can help the senator and his family as a guide. Additionally, the young man is a mariner who owns a small boat often used to transport people between the mainland and the island, which is how he earns a living.

As things are getting worse, the senator believes it would be a good idea to take his family to the island for safety. He asks the young man to guide them to a port where they can find marine transportation to the island. To his great surprise, the young man reveals that he himself is a mariner and already has his own boat. The turbulence in the nation caused the senator and his family to have great experiences with all types of people. The family agrees to travel with the young mariner boy to the island.

Upon reaching the ship's port, a security guard approaches them. The mariner boy, who is unable to read or write, takes a little more time to handle the situation with the security guard, who is also new to the post. After everything is clarified, they are ready to depart. While they approach the boy's small boat and continue to converse, the senator asks the young man if he knows how to read. The young mariner replies, "No, honorable senator, I do not know how to read." In response, the senator remarks to the mariner boy that if he doesn't know how to read and write, he has lost three quarters of his life.

The mariner boy answers, "Yes, honorable senator." Then he begins to navigate his boat further and further into the sea until they reach the middle of the ocean. Suddenly, a violent wind emerges, capable of sweeping away any boat with its intense power. The senator and his family start trembling with anxiety, fearful for their lives. The senator asks the mariner man what they should do to save themselves. In response, the mariner man asks the senator if he knows how to swim. The senator replies that he does not know how to swim, to which the mariner boy remarks, "I don't know how to read and write, so I've lost three-quarters of my life. But you, not knowing how to swim, have lost your entire life." The senator remains silent as a baby, understanding that if you don't know how to read, you cannot have certain privileges at the office, but you can have a normal life. If you don't know how to swim, you cannot survive in the middle of the ocean without any safety.

The young man lives with only a quarter of his life, unaware of this fact, because in the area where he resides, there is no need to flee due to war. They live in peace, working together to ensure their survival. They are uncertain whether they need a better life because they have never desired to travel to a war-torn area for the sake of education and office jobs. They never had the intention to leave the peaceful place they know for an unknown destination.

As for the senator, he faced uproar where he was living, and encountered winds against him during his journey. During the trip, the wind tossed away everything they had on board, but the young mariner man did everything he could and finally brought them safely to the island. The senator and his family arrived on the shores of the island with only wet clothes, which was an unfortunate event. However, they have carried their lives as mercy. There were no reproaches except for an unexpected event. Now, since the senator and his family relied solely on the efforts of the mariner boy, they had to return to the mainland to replenish everything they had lost in the ocean. These were the supplies they were supposed to use on the island before returning. The event deprived them of those items, and upon setting foot on land, they resigned themselves and turned back as if they were returning from a war, having lost and escaped with their lives as spoils.

The boat was back on the ocean, and this time they were fortunate as there were no signs of any hurricanes. Finally, when they reached the mainland again, the senator had to restock for his family. He made up his mind and traveled back to his house with the family. Upon arriving at his stronghold, everyone was happy to be back home, but they knew it would only be temporary. Meanwhile, the first daughter of the family took her mother's credit card, as she had been given permission to use it. Now, she embarked on making strange and surprising expenses. They could never guess what she was going to buy, but she purchased engagement rings, clothes, and other items for her future husband. While her parents thought she was in town with friends at her grandparents' house, she had already traveled and taken her husband to a location for their wedding, staying at a very expensive hotel and paying with her mother's credit card. When the family was ready to leave town for another trip, they had to fetch her because they didn't want to leave her behind. They called her on the telephone, and she told them she had already packed her bag. Her parents only had to pick her up at the corner of the road near her grandparents' house.

They were not fully happy, but young people sometimes act funny or even crazy. They agreed to her request when her dad came to pick her up, but she asked them to wait for someone she was with. Dad asked who that person was, and she replied that she had her husband with her and asked them to wait for him. Mom exclaimed, "What!" They thought she was joking, but when they looked, they saw a young man approaching. Dad told his daughter that he didn't know she was married, and he refused to let the young man into the vehicle. He quickly dashed off and left him. She immediately rolled down the vehicle windows and started crying for help, making it seem like she was being kidnapped. People who heard her cries actually believed that the father was a kidnapper, and they quickly gathered around to help her. The parents raised their hands to show that they were not kidnapping the girl, emphasizing that she was their daughter. While they were explaining, she ran off to meet her husband, and everyone witnessed it in silence. The parents made their way out and left the girl with her husband. So, who was this young man she married and tried to surprise her parents with? Only time will reveal the answer.

When the rest of the family arrived in the rural area, they had difficulty finding the young man, the mariner boy who always guided them. They conducted some research in the area and were surprised to find out that their daughter had traveled there and met the mariner boy, who turned out to be the same boy she had married. This was the boy who had only experienced a quarter of his life and lost three-quarters because he didn't know how to read and write. Now he is the son-in-law of the honorable senator who had lost all his life because he didn't learn how to swim. It was a valuable lesson to learn how to approach a situation. Sometimes you can only be a complement. If he didn't know how to read, that's why they sought him for help. And that's why he needed them the most in his life. If they didn't know how to swim, that's the reason they needed him the most in their lives.

Where you want to go now, meet him halfway or wait for him to come to you. So, it's better to wait because you don't know which road they would take to get there. When you're running and don't know how to hide, there's no need to run at all because wherever you're going, they will walk slowly and eventually catch up to you.

It's similar to a dog that likes to run. The dog may run fast and pass you, but when it gets home, you'll find it easily, or it may come back to where you are. The senator, who had not yet found the boy to guide them, decided to go to the place they had rented before deciding to move to the island. After about a week, there was no sign of the young man. The family decided to return to their hometown for a few days to gather more supplies for themselves. During that time, they made efforts to get in touch with their daughter, who had been using her mother's credit card to pay for a hotel for herself and her husband. Now it was time for the new couple to come home because the mother had received a notice about the credit card and immediately canceled it, preventing any further charges. The new couple couldn't pay for their hotel or food, so it was definitely time to return. Although no one could discern what kind of atmosphere awaited the new couple.

Finally, the new couple arrived at the parents' house. The young man talked to the parents, but the daughter was too upset because her credit card had been canceled and she didn't want to talk to anyone. However, she talked with their food and drink as she was hungry. She remained upset with her parents, but happily ate their food. As for the young man, they offered him food, but he seemed afraid and refused to eat. He could refuse for now, but how long could he stay without food? It was his time to go to bed, and everybody entered their respective bedrooms. The new couple also entered their own bedroom, which used to be the daughter's room only.

People who ate well slept fast, while those who didn't eat at all couldn't sleep due to hunger. At midnight, all the lights were turned off, and the young man decided to make a trip to the kitchen to alleviate his inability to sleep. He found where they kept the food and couldn't resist due to his intense hunger. He went to the kitchen, ate some food, drank some juice, and even brought a piece of meat back to his wife. However, he made a terrible mistake when he mistakenly entered his in-laws' bedroom instead of his own. He went to his mother-in-law's ear and said, "The food is still hot, be careful." The mother-in-law woke up and smiled, thinking she was dreaming when she heard someone say, "Be careful, the food is still hot." But when she turned on the light, her heart broke. She saw the young man with the meat in his hand, and he was shocked and shook when he realized he had entered the wrong bedroom. The daughter, who saw the light turn on, grew suspicious and grabbed her husband's hand, leading him to their own bedroom. Everyone remained silent, no one said a word, but his hunger was erased. Perhaps shame was felt, but everyone had food in their bellies, allowing them to sleep better.

The night passed quickly, and a new day approached. While unstable conditions continue in the nation, they decided to forget about their past lives, as they couldn't change anything, and focus on building a brighter future. The whole family prepared for their next trip to the rural area, but this time, there was no need to wait at the corner of the road for anyone because everyone was already in the house. No one needed to call for help, so the parents didn't have to leave anyone behind. The trip went smoothly, and when they arrived in the suburban area, they stayed there for a few days before heading to the dream island they had in mind. Fortunately, this time there was just enough wind for a pleasant and safe trip to the island. The young mariner boy was no longer just an employee but a part of the family, a superhero who had saved them from the heavy wind last time. This might be why he became a member of the family. As they approached the island, they looked and saw how beautiful it was. They stayed there for some time, exploring everything. During this period, nobody wasted their time. They visited the beaches and enjoyed themselves to the fullest. Most importantly, even those who didn't know how to read and write started learning. And those who couldn't swim started learning how to swim. Right now, It was no longer about whether or not you could read or swim, but about being a family that could survive on land and in the ocean.

The family searched and found a beautiful place for themselves to live. They bought it and decided to leave the troubled city behind and start a peaceful life in this new area. The young man no longer had to wake up in the middle of the night to eat in the kitchen because he and his wife found their own place to live, separate from the rest of the family.

The couple now own their own lives. The wife is teaching her husband how to read and write, and the mariner man is teaching his wife how to swim. That way, no one will ever have difficulty identifying themselves at the security checkpoint, and no one has to be afraid of going to the sea. When one person helps the other, no one has to lose three-quarters of their life because they don't know how to read and write. Likewise, no one has to lose their entire life for not knowing how to swim.

Events are not a good reason for you to be lost. Eventually, there is no winner without events. Most of the time, when you travel on the road, you may be in a hurry. But if the road is curving or circling, if you know where you are going and truly want to reach your destination, you must follow every step of the road. Trying to enter a dead-end will only lead to a double mistake, causing you to go and come back, wasting a lot of time and missing out on opportunities.*

Do not follow the wrong while the wrong itself is following you too. Keep following the right and don't let the wrong catch you. If a darkness is on you, specifically it is because for you, specifically it is nighttime; lay yourselves down and wait for your own daylight, and you will shine. When the birds stop singing for you, it is simply because they are watching your step. Then follow your path with no excitement. When the power of the wind is too powerful for you, then rest yourselves as beautiful and wonderful butterflies and follow the wind where the possibility is greater for you. You should live with peace of mind and greater hope for a better and brighter future, the same as the young marine who did not fear to brave the sea for a brighter life.

*What you must do for yourselves, do so with all your strength. That is something you shall not regret. Now, the mariner man has formed a family, and he has to be more serious about his livelihood. Currently, he is making more trips with his boat and earning more money. In fact, he has made the choice to sell his small boat and buy a bigger one. That's what he's currently doing. Now, his boat is larger, and he also needs a pickup truck to make things easier for himself. Eventually, the mariner man is no longer just a boat captain but also a truck driver who knows how to read signs and navigate routes. So, he doesn't have to worry about traffic surveillance vehicles that can stop him for making traffic mistakes.

Back when he was only a mariner, he would often encounter a man carrying wood on his head while walking on the road. This man would often walk for miles with the wood on his head. Now, the mariner man has the choice to do a favor for that wood man when they meet again. While the mariner man and his wife are traveling on the road towards the dock where their boat is, they spot the wood man carrying wood on his head. The couple stops their pickup truck and offers him a ride, which he accepts with great pleasure. As they drive for about a quarter mile, they notice him in the back of the truck with the wood still on top of his head. Each time the truck hits a bump, the wood moves and jumps back onto his head, making him sweaty and exhausted.

They quickly stop the truck, run to him, and ask him why he's doing that to himself. They thought they were helping him, but now it seems like they're causing harm instead. The wood man answers and explains that they were merciful to him by giving him a ride, but he didn't want them to also carry his load. That's why he preferred to keep the wood on his own head. They tell him that it's not good and it can get you killed. They ask him to put the wood separately in the truck, so he can sit freely and not get hurt by the moving wood. Relieved, the wood man removes the wood from his head and thanks them for what they are doing for him. It was so good for him that he lives near the dock where the couple is going, and he is grateful to them.

They have to make a few more stops before reaching their destination, but that doesn't bother him. He just needs to rest a little whenever they stop. Eventually, they all get back on the road and finally make it to the town where he lives. Since he is the only one living in that area, he rarely finds any transportation to help him. He doesn't know anything about traveling in a vehicle. It's the first time he has ever been on a vehicle in his entire life. So, they have to do the same thing they did before, helping him get on the vehicle. At that time, they thought he was too tired to get on, but now they have to help him off the truck because his head is shaking a bit after the movement of the truck.

They need to hold him so that he doesn't fall to the ground. Before they can take him off the new truck, he suddenly gets sick and vomits all over the back of the truck. They take their time, put him down, and take him to the porch of his house where his wife gratefully waits for him. They all work together to remove the wood and then fetch water and bleach to clean the truck. Afterward, the couple goes to their boat at the dock while the wife of the wood man takes care of her husband, who is feeling disoriented from traveling on a vehicle for the first time. Throughout all the time the wood man traveled by foot, his wife never had to clean his pants right away. However, this time is different. It was a wonderful experience because the wood man traveled for the first time on a truck. So, it doesn't matter if his pants need cleaning, as long as he reaches his wife faster today, for the first time. She can give him some herbal medicine, food, and fresh water. After a good sleep, he will feel refreshed, and the world around him will be comfortable and stable.

As for the mariner man, he took his wife on a boat for a short ride over the ocean, and was teaching her how to navigate the boat, just as she taught him how to drive a vehicle. However, being on the ocean is not the same as being on land where she was born. She wants to learn, but it seems like she needs more practice on the ocean to become stable enough to handle a boat over the ocean. She starts feeling seasick like the wood man, and she's not strong enough to stand straight. So, they decide to return to land where the vehicle is parked. But on the way back, the wife vomits on the boat, reminding the man of the wood man's experience. However, this time it's not the wood man vomiting but his own wife on the new boat.

When they reach the land, the man quickly ties up his boat, realizing that there's no one there to help him with his wife. He can't handle everything alone, so he runs to the wood man's wife and asks for her help. She leaves her sick husband and rushes to the dock to assist the couple. This time they don't have to wait for the cleaning of the boat; that can be done later. They take the mariner man's wife to the wood man's house for first care. They help her change into clean clothes, take a bath, and provide her with some bush medicine, food, and water. After a good rest, the scrambling and discomfort should subside, and everything will become stable and comfortable. They are no longer on a truck or over the ocean. It's time to get back to normal.

It's important to understand that everyone can face challenging conditions at some point, regardless of their status, knowledge, or abilities. A superior power is beyond our control. Both the wood man and the mariner man's wife wake up in the same house, receiving treatment for similar diseases or comparable conditions, just like two patients in the same hospital not far from each other. Imagine what could have happened to the couple if they hadn't given a ride to the wood man or if they had been inhospitable when he was in trouble. We are too small to see beyond; we just have to be careful with our actions and our words, especially when mistakes occur. While this particular mistake may not happen to you, a worse one could. Great things are often forgotten, but the smallest things are never forgotten. They are like seeds in fertile soil. Over time, even overnight, with rain or dew drops, they will grow and bear fruit greater than you can ever imagine.

Experiences living together build a solid friendship, so the woodman never has to carry his wood over his head anymore. His friend, the mariner man, arranges with him that whenever he has his wood ready to pick up from the other dock where he always gets them from, he can let the mariner man know so he can just meet with the woodman there and get his wood on the boat and take it to the dock where the woodman is living.

From now on, each time the wood is coming, the woodman loads them right away on the ship, and his friend takes them to the next dock. If he gets tired, he just rests himself at the woodman's house. There is no difference; it is the same as being at his own home. The mariner man's family and the woodman's family are two perfect friends.

Man Steals the Prince's Wedding Clothes

Yet, some friends are truly appreciated, but not for everyone. Two men were friends while both living in the city. They would always entertain together, even when they were not invited. They would find a fake invitation to attend other people's festivals. At a time when a young prince was ready to get married, they both knew they would not be invited to the prince's marriage ceremony or the reception, where they were especially eager to go so they could eat, drink, and dance.

In order to be there, one must be invited and wear appropriate clothes that match the prince's attire. One of them found out where the prince's clothes were made and where they stored the suits for the people participating in the prince's wedding ceremony. So, overnight, he broke into that office and stole the prince's suit and some more clothes.

When they realized that someone had broken into the place and stolen the prince's clothes and other items, the police were called, and made a report of the incident. They began searching for whoever stole the prince's marriage clothes. However, the wedding could not be stopped just because of the clothes. It was a prince's wedding, after all. So, the wedding took place on the original date and time.

The man who stole the clothes never told his friend what he did. The two friends continued to trade ideas on how they could finally make it to the wedding. The one who stole the clothes said to his friend, "We must buy some clothes that look the same as the ones people who are going will wear." The other man asked, "Where should we find them?" The thief replied, "We can find them, but you know they are very expensive clothes. We also need to sacrifice some money. If you can find some money to give to me, we can get the clothes right away."

When the other friend heard that, he was so happy. He knew they could fake anything to do whatever they wanted. The thief reassured him, saying, "You don't have to worry about the high expense of the clothes. Just try your best, and after the reception, we'll return the clothes to where we purchased them. They will give us our money back, and that way, we can also replace the money right back where it was."

His friend agreed, saying, "This is a great idea." He immediately went to his bank and withdrew the money he had deposited to start building his house next month. He handed the money to his bad friend, who was going to betray him with his deceptive actions. After receiving the money, the bad man said, "Now we are ready to buy the clothes, as I promised."

A day later, he told his friend that he had already gone to the store and bought the clothes. He invited his friend to come over and see how beautiful the clothes looked. They said they shall be glad not to miss this occasion, as they usually do, and make it for real, with no doubt. So his friend, who couldn't wait to see his beautiful clothes that he'll wear to the Prince's marriage, went immediately to his friend's house with joy in his heart.

Both men got together and tried on their clothes and were delighted to see how they looked like princes. After that, the thief said to the other man, "The only thing we don't know yet is the song that people who lost their invitation cards must sing." His friend replied, "It is true. They must sing a song if they have lost their invitation card." The thief said to his friend, "Because you don't have the card, you need to sing the song. That is the only way they will believe you are a real invitee."

He looked at his poor friend, who became very sad upon hearing those words. He then returned to himself and said, "You don't have to worry at all. As you knew before, we'll make it." The thief said that between that day and the next, they would know the song perfectly well. His friend said, "Okay." Now he encouraged and strengthened himself to see what tomorrow would bring as good news.

Promises were apparently kept, and the bad friend came over and said to his friend, "Now we are cool, my friend. We have the song. Now we must wait for that date to come, and then we can just go and enjoy ourselves." Before that, we just need to rehearse that song, and then we are ready to go. The poor friend found this to be better news than ever in his entire lifetime.

The bad friend said that he had been trying to get the right information they needed, so by tomorrow, they would get together and practice that song. That way, when they got there, they would not have to worry about any problems at all. His friend said, "Okay. Now we are only one step away. We'll get that done tomorrow." Hearing that, the bad friend felt very comfortable. He knew he had not bought any clothes; he had stolen them and kept his friend's money in his pockets.

Do not let your money reach into your bad friend's hand. If that happens, they can create a serious event for you and keep your money forever in their pockets. Now, tomorrow is here, and it is also time to practice the beautiful song. Both friends get together to practice the song. The song's title is a question with the answer:

"Who stole the prince's married clothes?" And then tell them it's, "Me!" repeated three times.

It is a very short song, easy to remember after all those repetition practices. Both friends feel they are well-prepared for the song, meaning they are ready and waiting for that day to come. Both men day after day practice their song like an officer on duty. When the day arrives, they both say, "Well, that is finally the time we are going to enjoy ourselves. It is time for us to wear our beautiful clothes."

The bad friend keeps reminding his friend to keep the suit clean because they will take them back to the store to get their money back. All that is meant to deceive him and make him believe everything is going well. "The time for dressing is here!" Exclaimed the bad friend, "Because we must be there early so we don't miss anything at all." As they approach the entrance, the bad friend says to the other man, "As you know, we are not interested in the wedding ceremony, only the reception. We must hide ourselves so they don't see us until we get to the reception room." This is what both men agree to do when the ceremony is over.

Immediately, it will be time to eat, drink, and dance. At a wedding like this, they always prepare some people to sing at the receptions. One sings after the others. The bad man knows all that, so he tells his friend they are going to sit here before everybody else. Whenever they ask, "Who is the first to sing?" then his friend shall stand up and start singing. Then the thief will be the next to sing because they don't have any invitation cards.

The bad man deceives the other man between a person who is supposed to sing and him, who believes they are asking him to sing because he doesn't have an invitation. Unfortunately, when they say, "Who has the first song?" the poor man, who doesn't know the snare of his friend against him, raises his hand and comes over, immediately starting to sing his song.

When he starts singing, his bad friend runs away and leaves him, everyone listening to him sing his song. With a question, he starts, "Who stole the prince's marriage clothes?" telling them, "It is me!" Instantly, everyone pays attention and sees the prince's marriage clothes on that man. And, of course, the security puts him under arrest.

When he tried to explain the situation, he thought his bad friend was there to support him. Unfortunately, his friend has already abandoned him. Now he ends up in prison for stealing the prince's marriage clothes, where he himself declared with his own mouth that he is the one who stole the married clothes of the prince in his song. He is wearing the prince's clothes as proof of what he said is true. It is extremely difficult for anybody to make a case that the man is not the one who actually stole the clothes. The fool pays the price of being a friend to a wicked man. Then he has no other way out except where he is, in prison until he completes his sentence for stealing the prince's marriage clothes.

Now his bad friend is happy and enjoying himself with the money he did not work for. He continues to do wrong to other people. While the fool is in prison, his bad friend meets another man whom he befriends so he can always find a way to continue his bad business. He does whatever he can to present himself as a good person, even though he is very wrong. His new friend quickly believes and trusts him as a good friend, unaware that he is getting caught in the snare of a bad, venomous serpent.

He let that bad man come to his house very often, where they would eat and drink together. While the bad man retains in his mind everything good he can see in the house and makes plans for how he will carry out his scheme to disappear with them. For him, the man in prison is no longer a concern. He is now in the game for a different victim. After trying everything he can to steal what the man has in his house, he doesn't find a chance. He decides to spend a night in the house with his friend, and his friend accepts him.

Overnight, when the man who owns the house is sleeping, the bad man squeezes his neck and kills him, taking everything valuable he can carry with him. A few days later, the neighbors discover the man dead in his house. As for the killer, he is on the run, enjoying his wrongdoing, while they keep searching for who killed that man.

The first victim is released from prison. The bad man hears the news and then goes straight to the man's house, trying to convince him by saying he was trying to secure his release from prison. He claims his lawyer ate up his money, and he did not mean to do anything wrong to him. The fool remains a fool as he accepts the same thief in his house and lets him use him in the same ways as before.

Now the bad man tells the fool that there are so many festivals going on without them, and this weekend will be the greatest one they cannot miss. He insists they must go, even though the fool knows they are not invited. Then they must find ways to trick their way in. The bad man knows they are looking for him because he did kill a man. Now he tells the foolish man that he heard on the news that they are searching for a person who killed a man. He suggests that just to disturb the assistants at the festival's gate and gain entry without an invitation card, each one of them should say, "I am the one who killed a man!" This way, while they keep saying that, everybody will be disturbed, and they will enter the festival without any problem and get in the middle of the attending crowd. Eventually, they will not be able to find out who really said he is the one who killed the man. After that, they will enjoy themselves at the festival, eating, drinking, and dancing. Afterwards, they shall go home. Unfortunately, the fool man is still listening to his bad friend, and they both arrange to say, "I am the one who killed a man." The foolish man follows his bad friend's instructions and goes to the front.

As they approach the gate, the fool starts yelling and says, "I am the one who killed a man!" Many people at the festival ask him only one question: "Why did you kill a man?" The fool answers and says, "Because he made a wrong", just as the bad friend told him to answer. The moment the fool gives them that answer, his bad friend dashes out and abandons him for a second time in his life.

Now the fool man is wanted as the person they are looking for. The security puts him in custody until the police arrive and take him to a prison where he will wait for his judgment in the courtroom. That is the only way he may have someone understand his situation and describe his friend after he himself, with his own mouth, has been declared as the one who killed a man. Of course, that may never be the truth in the case of that fool man. Only a judge who always keeps in mind to verify records can shed a great light on the bad man and his friend's case.

When they take the fool to the court and after some arguments have been put on the table, the judge declares that, of course, they need to look for a different person they are interested in because when the man was killed at his home, that foolish man was in prison. Then he cannot be the true person who is the killer of that man; rather, he can be the good road and a real key to a good result of that issue.

Now it is the time to listen to the fool man who said his friend is the one who is the actor and author of his problems. The judge is carefully listening to the fool man and understands him. The judge takes a clear view of the matters and actually issues a mandate against the bad man to get him arrested without delay. The police immediately look for him and get him under arrest.

Indeed, the time is coming for the bad man to experience the food of prisons where he sent his friend twice to live. He was due to be in prison when he ran away twice and left his friend behind. Fortunately for him, this time they have let his friend go free after a short period because he was inside the prison when the bad man killed his new friend. But before they released him, they decided to give them some sort of punishment. They formed a big ball with some cotton and a different one with some lime rock. They instructed them to take the balls and carry them while walking from one city to the next city where they needed to be at a prison camp.

The bad man tried both balls and had a feeling that the lime rock was heavier than the cotton. When the guards gave them the alert to go, the bad man tried to grab the lighter one, but the guard had already switched the balls and put the heavy one in place of the light one. Now the game was changing for the bad man. He had to understand that he may be doing more wrong than his friend does while he carries the heavy load and the fool carries the light load. The bad man started saying something, but ears cannot hear exactly what he wants to say.

As they went far, the sun became tough on them. The man carrying the light load had a chance to walk faster than the man carrying the heavy load. Each time he found a shade, he stopped and waited for the man with the heavy load. The bad man with the heavy load had no chance to put it down and rest for a moment. Each time he approached the shade where the fool was resting, the fool started walking under his cotton balls and continued to go. So the bad man had to trail behind and kept complaining like a dog that got bitten by ants.

Now the bad man forgot what song to teach the fool so he could rule him out. After many miles of walking, they approached a river that they had to cross to make their way to the other side. Game seemed to change because the river was high. While crossing the river, they were essentially swimming with the balls. As a result, most of the lime rock was washed away, and the ball became smaller and very light. On the other hand, the cotton ball absorbed plenty of water, making the load more than double the weight of a lime rock ball.

Now was the time for the bad man to take a deep breath and pay attention to his fool friend under the heavy load of cotton. The sun continued to press hard on them. As they kept walking, the water continued to drop down and evaporate as clouds, providing some protection from the sun's rays for the fool man. Since they had a long way to go, the cotton ball gradually became lighter.

As for the bad man's load, the lime rock couldn't regain its weight. The bad man thought he was carrying a light and easy load, but when the water washed over his body, the chemical residue on his skin from the lime rock burned and cracked his skin, leaving it dried and shriveled. Now, the bad man experienced nothing but a bitter taste and sheer pain. Everything he had stolen was swept away, leaving him with a grip of anguish and scorching heat from the sun beating down on him while he was covered in the lime rock dust. No wonder today, wonder tomorrow.

Finally, when they reached the camp, the judge managed the case and released the fool man. As for the criminal who killed his new friend, he remained in prison for a longer time. As for the one he already killed, sadness and remorse resided in the heart of the one who isolated themself for one reason or another, but their ears were free from any reproach, critics, or even a premature death which could erase them before their time.

No one wants to walk in the darkness of the night, but they are waiting for the daylight so they can see clearly where they are going. Sometimes things need a little bit of time before a light can be shone on them. At that point in time, you can truly trust the proposition you receive, and you don't have to worry about the repercussions of reversals. You can always learn from what you are ignoring, but the fool cannot be cured. The poor and foolish man returns to his home, where he may get duped by a different wicked wrongdoer, but at least he may deserve to return to his home, and the prisoner deserves to stay in prison to serve his time for the wrong he caused to other people.

On his way back home, the fool man encounters two young men coming from a different city. They want to enter the big town to buy something they need for their artisanal business, but they are unsure about the road. They ask the fool man for directions. He looks at the four corners of the sky, and while he knows for sure the town is to the north, the main road or entrance may not be in that direction. Nonetheless, he tells them to go north, and they'll find the city. Of course, the city is to the north, but the starting point of the road is not in the north as he told them. Then he goes to his house, while the men head north. At a certain point, they realize they are not on the main road, but they are trying to take shortcuts over a mountain to reach the road that leads to the city.

After crossing a high mountain, the men face a major river they are unable to cross; it is a non-penetrable river. They are only able to follow the bank of the river to find a way to get to a bridge, which is the only way to reach the city. They stand by the shores of the non-penetrable river. They raise their eyes to the high mountain facing them and see two donkeys fighting each other from the top of the mountain. As they continue fighting, they slide down until both of them fall into the river pool. Instantly, a coyote emerges from under the water and attacks the donkeys, swimming among them. All three immediately disappear underwater. While they are fighting, one of the donkeys continues to walk backward while the other keeps pushing until they reach the river bank and lose ground. They try to swim to land, but there is no flat land available. If they enter the river from that spot, the only way to get out is by swimming far away, which is not easy at all. The two donkeys disappear, but the two young men continue to fight for a better life.

After a long time, they finally find a bridge to cross the river. Once they cross the river bridge, they walk for several miles before reaching the city for the first time in their lives. Now they are on their own in a great city. It's up to them to pay attention to themselves and understand that a big city never accepts newcomers without a little training. It can go both ways, but it will be their choice to navigate this new city. The men have traveled from far away on foot, and without a doubt, is it time for them to look for a place to rest and find something to eat. The two men don't know anything more than what they can see presently. Fortunately, they find a marketplace where many other people are sitting down. They both sit here and rest for some time until they feel more comfortable. While sitting, they open their bags and make sure they have everything with them.

They notice a pot with a cover and two handles, which they have carried their food in. They make up their minds and decide to go to a restaurant and ask them to fill their pot with food so they can eat. However, they took that pot from the family's house, and buying a pot like that would cost fifty dollars, which is not easy for their family. In that family, a pot like this is considered as valuable as gold. Only a trusted member of the family can use that pot, as dropping it on the ground could cause damage and degrade its value.

Eventually, the two young artisanal men end their pause, realizing it is time to find a restaurant that faces them. When they enter the restaurant, they ask to have their food in their own pot and show the server their pot. The server looks at the pot and says they can fill it for two. When the server says "two," they mean two dollars. However, the men, who do not belong to the city, believe the pot can only be filled for two quarters, which is half a dollar. Everyone had a different thought, and they were in agreement, which created confusion. The men said, "Okay, go ahead and fill the pot." The men thought they were going to pay half a dollar after they finished eating. However, the restaurant staff believed the men were going to pay them two dollars, which was the value of the food. But it was going to be different because in the area where those two men came from, food was less expensive. So, these men, who had no training about a big city like the one they are in, are now about to face a problem.

Indeed, the server at the restaurant placed the men's food on a table for them. They both sat down and ate their food. When they finished eating, they stood up and took out their money from their pockets, which amounted to half a dollar, and handed it to the cashier at the restaurant. The cashier thought they were joking and laughed at them, saying they needed to give him the money. The men replied, "You told us two quarters." Now the restaurant staff wanted two dollars. Imagine, two dollars for those two men was a big deal. They didn't have two dollars at the moment, not even to buy what they had traveled specifically to buy.

Now the restaurant staff decided to just take the pot, which probably cost as much as the food. The men had already eaten, so they knew it wouldn't end well for them if they didn't come back with that pot. They decided not to give up the pot to the restaurant. One person grabbed the pot by one handle, and one of the two young men grabbed the next handle. A struggle ensued until the part of the handle grabbed by the restaurant staff became loose, and the young man held onto the main part, only losing one handle of the pot.

Now, the two young men made a quick decision and ran away with the pot. The restaurant staff said, "We'll take the pot, or you pay for the food. If you fight now, you're going to get beaten." Both men ran away while a couple of people chased after them with batons in hand to give them a beating for the food they were unable to pay for. However, it was nighttime, and not everywhere was well-lit. Darkness fell. Fortunately for the young men, they noticed a wall where someone had put his donkey's saddle bag against the wall. The two men entered behind the donkey's saddle bag and lay down flat under the donkeys' belongings. The people who were chasing them ran past them.

They didn't know where to go, but they knew how to hide themselves. When the restaurant staff were no longer able to find them, they gave up and returned to the restaurant where they worked. As for the two young men, they continued to hide until early morning. At that time, when everybody else was going to the market, they followed the crowd and went to the market to buy what they had traveled to buy in the city.

Sometimes, if you must travel by yourself or with someone who has never traveled to that place before, you need to understand that there are great risks involved. By chance, they were the winners of that game, but the experience wasn't so sweet for them.

Unfortunately for the donkeys, who fought over the high mountain posed too great a danger. When the donkeys fell into the wrong river and encountered a coyote, they disappeared, and these men benefited from it. The two donkeys left behind their backpacks, which became life-saving equipment for the two young men. Sometimes, losses can benefit others.

If the donkeys had survived, who knows if that equipment would have been there when the two young men were running for their lives. Why did these two donkeys sacrifice their lives for the two men to stay alive? The donkeys had been there for so long, so why at that moment were they chosen to put themselves in such great danger from which they could never escape? Maybe the donkeys knew that place too well and knew not to fool around there. What happened underwater? Did the coyote eat the donkeys? The only certain thing is that if you don't belong to the river, if you end up there by accident, there's no easy way to get back on land anymore. In the end, the donkeys turned out to be a real mystery at the river, where no one is able to verify.

As for the men, they continued on their way to the place where they belonged. When they finally arrived home, their family was greatly surprised to see that the pot they had carried like gold was damaged. One handle of the pot had been removed, but the son of the family, along with his friend and partner, returned safely to the house. It was scary, but they returned without any problems. From now on, the outside friend decided to sell low-cost products, while the son of the family continued to sell high-cost products. Perhaps they were trying to avoid conflicts, just like the donkeys who carried the same types of backpack equipment. And one day, they may find themselves engaged in a fight that could cost them both their lives. Yet, they continue to conduct business together.

As everyone must know, better products lead to better business and more advantages. The son of the family gains more ground than the other friend. Nobody is hurt when everyone is satisfied with themselves. But it's time for a change of scenery because many people are talking about traveling overseas. The next country offers opportunities for a better life. At this point, the son of the family decides to go to a different country. This time, it's not a place he can walk to; he has to spend money if he wants to go for sure.

Now, the outside friend, who makes less money, may choose not to go. But his friend assures him that they are best friends and whenever he reaches where he is going, he'll help his friend to get there too. That way, they can still be together. Where he's at, his friend will be there soon. The outside friend must gather courage and leave himself behind, hoping that his friend will soon send for him. That expression means his friend will pay for his trip so he can join him in a better place.

But remember, many things can happen between two friends when they are in the same kind of business. Perhaps they are friends because they always have to travel together, especially when they are walking to faraway places. However, you should understand that you should not always depend on the other person. One day, you may have to continue on your own, while the other person may be on the next road not far from you but no longer on the same path as you. It can be sad, but when a friend has to start his own family, especially a friend who didn't inherit anything from his parents and has to work for everything his family and he needs, he cannot forget about his own family to take care of a friend who can handle his own yoke.

Some people may no longer worry about you because they are no longer involved in the same business as you. So, the outside friend is waiting and waiting, losing faith in his friend who promised to pay for his trip. He finds himself working at a restaurant, but who knows if he will end up taking someone else's pot when confusion arises and he doesn't have enough money to pay for the food. However, he may remember what happened with his friend who became a successful businessman, while he chose to work as a restaurant worker. He doesn't forget that he made the decision not to sell high-cost products. It's up to him to determine what he wants to be in life and not to please a friend at the expense of his own path. It's important to know where you can be when life gets tough.

There are two different situations at hand, just like a donkey carrying stones and another donkey carrying sponges. They are both called donkeys, but the circumstances are different. It's always better to prevent a problem rather than trying to fix it. A poor person can die under their own shack, and a fool can make a mistake that leads them to prison, but they may be released after a judgment. But, woe to those who in deceptive actions enjoy themselves! Their enjoyment may be for a short time, and they may soon find themselves imprisoned, not able to see the sun again anytime soon. You can cross a great ocean, but once you leave the shores, your wet clothes can freeze on you and potentially kill you if you don't know how to remove them off of you.

Little Man Billionaire Bad Neighbors

A man lived in a neighborhood where many suspected him to be poor. This led to most people avoiding him, as they believed he might come to their homes and ask for help. He was not a physically large man, but he was always working hard to take care of himself. One day, he unexpectedly comes face to face with a neighbor. He greets his neighbor with a hello, and the neighbor responds. The neighbor seems concerned and expresses a desire for him to visit his home sometime, as he might have something for him. The little man agrees and says he is available anytime. The little man doesn't want anything from them, and the neighbor knows that he is lying. The neighbor said it because he believes that the man may need his help to survive. After exchanging greetings, they each go their separate ways, and many times pass without them meeting again.

At a time when a little man was cleaning his backyard, he noticed a significant number of objects stacked on top of each other. They were too heavy for him to remove on his own. Curiously, they appeared to resemble gold as each spot he cleaned shone brightly. It seemed like there was something on top of them for protection, but over time, that covering had been destroyed, leaving behind the stable materials. The little man didn't know what to do, so he decided to talk to his neighbors about it.

He knocked on the first door, and when the owner opened it and saw the little man, he immediately told him he is leaving and doesn't have any time left, he'll see him later. The owner thought the poor man, as he considered him, is someone seeking a favor, so, the little man walked away and went to the neighbor who had promised to invite him to his house. However, seeing him, that neighbor chose to stay inside and didn't respond to the little man at his door. The neighbor believed that the little man was sure about his false promise to invite him to his house, and chose not to come outside to talk with the little man. Little man understood the neighbors' actions and he returned to his house and continued his work for the day, particularly cleaning up his yard.

One day, he tried very hard to remove a tiny scratch with a saw and decided to take it to a place where experts could confirm if it was real gold. About a week later, as the little man walked on the sidewalk towards the city, a man driving an expensive vehicle stopped and offered him a ride to the same destination. The little man accepted the ride. While on the road they both had a chance to get to know each other. The little man learned that the man who gave him a ride was a successful businessman with a kind heart.

The little man now has a chance to see if that businessman could help him determine the value of the sample he had brought. Once they arrived at the businessman's office, one of his employees conducted a test on the sample, and the result brought magnificent good news. The little man had unknowingly become a billionaire. The businessman may not disclose how much profit he makes from that business. However, he takes the little man with him in his vehicle for a trip to verify the exact amount of gold present. Upon reaching the backyard of the little man's house, the entrepreneur looks and warns him not to tell his neighbors about anything and that if he dares tell them, they will kill him and grab his gold. The businessman assures the little man that he will own a vehicle like his own and will be able to afford any desired house. He promises that the little man will never have to walk on foot again if he so chooses.

Although the little man knows he has money now, he realizes that counting it all would be an overwhelming task. The process begins immediately as the businessman follows all legal procedures, and the next day, they arrive with large trucks and a tractor. With this equipment, they efficiently extract the gold that had been hidden for a long time. The gold is then transported to the businessman's location, where it can be handled with care.

In addition to all this, the little man now owned a vehicle similar to the one the businessman had given him a ride in. Furthermore, the businessman took the little man to a bank and helped him open an account where large checks would be deposited. Thus, the once-apparent poor man yesterday, had become a billionaire overnight.

When the neighbors of the little man suspect that work has been done in his backyard and see an expensive vehicle parked in his garage, they assume that the poor man has sold his home to someone else. They think that when he went to their houses, he was trying to offer them his house for sale. Days and weeks pass, and their curiosity grows as they don't see the little man anymore. After all, who would search for a pedestrian inside an expensive vehicle? They might think that such behavior indicates a mental disorder. However, the neighbors decide to knock on his door to find out who their neighbor really is.

During the first and second attempts, the little man doesn't answer the door, but due to their persistence, he finally opens it one day. There is some confusion because the neighbors didn't expect to see the little man since they observed expensive vehicles and assumed they were going to meet someone else. Their initial fear of him subsides, and they start making short visits to ensure everything is fine. Although everything is fine, they will never know what they missed by not answering their doors when the little man was there last time to seek their advice about what he discovered in his backyard.

Currently, doubts persist among the neighbors about how the little man managed to achieve such success. However, the little man may choose not to reveal this information because they were never friendly or good neighbors to him. What belongs to you, if you want to give, is your idea, and if you don't want to give, you have the choice to give anything. There is no good reason to hide or deceive others. Not everyone can be on the same level; differences will always exist. The wind may last long in one area, but it will never stay in one area forever, it's bound to change direction. During a bad time or a good time, this will happen.

Instead of being contemptuous, the little man is no longer someone people hide from but someone they are interested in meeting. He has opened a place where people can seek help if they need it. They can also obtain loans from the little man's enterprises. People now want to meet the little man rather than run or hide when they see him. He doesn't seek more money in his life; he simply wants to help others. If you have to do so, it is better to make the choice to do this, as sometimes by giving you are also receiving, that way you can continue to give and help.   Giving and receiving go hand in hand, especially in a world where poor families and nations are hunted by misery, diseases, and death. Those three elements continue to hunt every second, night and day. Whenever you hear someone say they are miserable, people expect the partners of disease and death to follow. If they say you have a disease, you are closer, you only have one more step to the last partner, death, the last among the three partners. Misery, disease, death.

Most of the time, some intelligent individuals visit poor nations and families, making promises that don't become executed, and after some visits they become very rich. They often imitate the style of the miserable people and use it to make their riches. When your clothes are torn and full of holes due to poverty, you cannot afford to buy new ones, so you continue patching them up. After visiting, some people take pictures of you and invent new fashion models inspired by the clothes you wore. Rich or not, people are interested in buying these brands for many occasions. How much have the poor received for being the patron of the inventor? They are unaware they contributed to these inventions through their images, imitations, or copies by intelligent and smart individuals. They become part of a life that is not a movie theater but something to imitate.

In the neighborhood where the little man lived, a rich man invites all his wealthy neighbors to a festival exclusively for them. The poor who were not invited are not welcome at the festival. Just as the festival is about to begin and everything is prepared, two unfortunate people who were passing by notice the event and enter. When asked if they were invited, they try to explain their situation. The event organizers remove them from the seats they were trying to occupy and escort them behind the gate. When the rich guests are not showing up and it starts getting late, the owner of the house instructs the person in charge to find some people who are usually sitting by the marketplace, but they can't locate them. Frustrated, the owner orders the food to be taken to a nearby park where there are animals that can be fed.

However, upon reaching the park, they find that there are no more animals to receive the food. They return home and the owner directs them to a forest, saying that some life there needs to eat the food he worked hard for. As they enter the forest, they see a dozen pigs, and when they place the food on the ground, the wild pigs come and eat it. When they finished the food, the pigs followed the people who brought them the food all the way back home.

Now, wild pigs surround the house day and night, keeping the people living inside as prisoners who cannot get outside. The owner of the house decides to skips out with his family due to the pigs that have invaded his yard and are just walking over everything they have outside. The owner put two poor men behind the gate, hoping that the rich guests he had invited would come. However, the rich guests refuse to come over. Now he has enough guests as he might not want to go directly to his house. He recalls the advice of a longtime friend who warned him not to offer his good food to a pig. If he does so, when the pig is done eating that good food, it will immediately trample on you. Remember that if you must run from the rain, you also must be careful not to fall into a pool of water.

The two men who had traveled from afar find themselves without a place to stay. They search for work in order to earn enough money to pay for a place to live. In the meantime, they sleep in a local shelter where they have obtained permission to stay during the night. Each morning, they wake up and go to work. As the pigs force the rich man and his family out of their house, the family struggles to find the hotel they had reserved. They end up spending a night at the same shelter where the two poor men had stayed. The next day, they finally locate their hotel and leave the shelter. Although the family does not expect to encounter the two men again, they had spent one night cohabitating in the same shelter. This process takes about a week before the animals are finally arrested from the yard, clearing the yard allowed the family to return to their house that had been surrounded by the wild pigs. Those pigs look like they don't want a festivity for a short time but for a longer period of time. When they got arrested, they were apparently a little bit flat because the owner refused to give them any more food to eat. But they were happy; and as wild animals do, they tried to run away, but did not try to harm anybody.

The only thing is that the wild pigs didn't want to be the constant recipients of that kind of food every time. That's why they were following the man who brought them the food to eat. After all, the house owner may have come to understand that people whom you have never known for so long can sometimes be the best ones to invite for a short meal, if necessary. However, it's not often the rich who, despite being too busy and having all they desire, will want to associate with you just because you are rich too. You might think you are equal to them, but who knows if they like you or even wish to assist you in any way, especially sitting in your house and eating with you. Not too many people like to do that anywhere, but at least if they want to be honest with you, they would tell the truth and decline attending your festival. Sometimes, it's great to keep what you have and live in peace, while allowing everybody else to live with peace as well.

After all, there can be disgusting and decaying things under some white clothes that may appear pure but are actually harmful enough to poison future generations. This can be found in all social classes, categories, and grades of people. There should be no blame on a person who decides what to do with their own wealth. The real problem lies with those who focus on what others possess and refuse to work hard to eat their own bread rather than hope for something they do not own. Build your strength and work towards producing their own fruits.

There was a wealthy man who possessed vast amounts of land and other possessions. Many people believed that the man should give them some of his land or sell a portion to them. However, the man refused to share or sell any of his land. Just as it had been inherited from his parents, he intended to pass it down to his children. There is nothing wrong with that. While people fixed their mind on his wealth, they wasted their time when they could have been working to build their own wealth.

A different man tried to do something similar, but it was not much appreciated, likely because his opinions did not satisfy his children. He always told them to fight for themselves and provide for their own needs, as he would not give them anything or sell anything to assist them. His children took his words to heart and worked hard to build their own wealth. As the man grew older, his perspective began to change. It was good that he had encouraged his children to work hard and build their own wealth, but it was also important to provide some support and encouragement along the way. When the dad started aging and realized his children were no longer in desperate need of his wealth, he wanted to share everything with them. However, by that time, they were already wealthy themselves, just like their father.

Even if they accept or don't accept their father's wealth, it will still remain for them. But they tell their dad that he can keep his wealth because they are okay without it. The father agrees and says that if they don't want anything, he will sell his wealth and give them the money, but they refuse. So, the father puts his wealth up for sale, but nobody wants to buy anything. He didn't want to give or sell, and now that he offers, nobody is interested. The only positive thing is that his children understand that if their dad hadn't encouraged them to have a good understanding of how people acquire wealth, they themselves could have been people waiting for him to die just to sell his wealth for a few cents and then find some tobacco and smoke and be done with it all. He may have been a tough father, but he certainly cannot be criticized. Everyone can do something good with their own knowledge, and if what they are doing is good, then that's all that matters. Ultimately, they can find a good family with wonderful children and good parents.

A ship that docks on land with all its passengers does not arrive without any difficulties, such as violent winds, rising waves, and more. But it is a ship where the captain uses his knowledge and expertise to protect and save the lives of his passengers. Even if you make a mistake, you can still come out victorious if you don't give up. You just need to develop a positive mindset to gain the strength needed to determine whether you are on the wrong path or not. If you are, then take immediate action to get back on the right track. No matter how intellectually or materially successful you may be, unexpectedly, the storms or unexpected winds of life can throw you onto a path you never wanted or dreamt of in your life. Regardless of the conditions in which you live, whether it's normal or luxurious, expect that one day while on earth, you may find yourself in a cave with a disgusting animal that you never liked or even dreamt of encountering in your lifetime. If you can't tolerate tobacco, one day you might find yourself sharing a bed with a smoker. It's no wonder if you see a mouse taking charge of a lion and saying, "Come, I will show you how to live in a cave." And don't be afraid when you see a goat leading a cow and saying, "I'm going to put a rope around your neck and take you wherever I want, and you must eat what I give you and lie where I want you to lie."

One Day in the Wild; Mouse, Lion, and Spider

One day, a discussion took place among three creatures in the wild: a mouse, a spider, and a lion. They debated why the lion was considered the king of the wild. The mouse and spider questioned the lion's expertise, arguing that people only feared the lion and didn't pay attention to the true essence of the wild. They challenged the lion by stating that the same humans, who proclaim you as king, would eventually capture you and subject you to captivity. From that day you will know who is king of the wild. They believed that the true king of the wild would be someone whom humans couldn't easily enthrone.

The lion engaged in the discussion and disregarded the smaller creatures, considering them insignificant and too small to be worthy of his attention. However, one day, a human hunter set a snare made of nylon string in the area where the three creatures resided. The snare trapped the lion, leaving him unable to escape. The spider couldn't do anything for its neighbor, but the mouse approached the trapped lion and greeted him, saying, "Good Day, Oh Mighty King".

The lion closes both his eyes and does not answer the mouse. Usually, a mouse is too small to feed a lion, so the lion is not interested in eating a mouse. The mouse says, "Oh mighty king, if you cannot exercise your expertise to liberate yourself, let the mouse know, maybe the mouse can do something for you." The lion opened his eyes and looked at the mouse and laughed. The lion questions how a lesser creature like a mouse could liberate a mighty king lion. The mouse replies, asking the lion if he gives permission to the mouse to liberate him. The lion agrees and tells the mouse to perform his miracle. The mouse then asks the lion if he will agree that he is not the true king of the wild if the mouse liberates him. The lion remembers what the spider and mouse told him before about the true king being the one that humans cannot easily defeat. However, now the lion is no longer a mighty king but a prisoner who needs to count on someone's help before the human arrives. He has to decide very quickly.

The mouse takes action and uses his sharp teeth to cut the lines that are tied to the lion, finally liberating him from the snare. The lion puts his tail between his legs and retreats deeper into the jungle, where it may not be easy for humans to catch him. However, the lion's fear of humans makes it difficult for him to hunt for food, so he must settle for any small creature he can find on his path. Meanwhile, the mouse and the spider observe the situation. The spider, not happy with the mouse pretending to be the animal with the most expertise in the wild jungle. By precaution, each time the lion passes by, the mouse enters his small hole to avoid being eaten by the lion who needs food. The spider saw the mouse go in and out of his hole when the lion passed by. While the mouse is away looking for food, the spider blocks the entrance to the mouse's hole so that if the lion came around then the mouse would not be able to quickly get into the hole, and would be eaten. If this happened, the spider would be the most mighty, after the lion of course. When the mouse returns, he finds his holes blocked with webs by the spider. He tried to run with no success and the lion, who was nearby, grabbed the mouse and ate him. There was no agreement that the lion would spare the mouse's life after he saved him. The weak mouse had no power to defend himself against his friend-turned-enemy. The mouse is no more. He was eaten by the same lion whose life he saved, and revenge is not easy for his family.

Does the lion have to worry about the spider, or must the spider worry about the lion? Which one of them will not be easily defeated by humans? In another turn of events, the spider uses his abilities to build webs across the lion's shortcut to get to his stronghold, making it difficult for him to escape from humans who are trying to catch him. Unfortunately for the lion, a human is trying to hunt him and the way is blocked, the same as had happened to the mouse. His way was blocked and masked by all the webs that actually stuck him across the eyes and he suddenly could not run. This made it perfect for the human to grab him and take him into captivity. That eventual capture of the lion truly left the spider emerging as the winner and the true king of the wild.

The spider continues to put his webs all over the vegetation, to prove that he is the only king on the throne with his own strategies to defeat others who threaten his life or undermine his expertise in the wild. He became a merciless king with a bad attitude who wanted to keep his power. Any other creatures who want to inhabit the wild must comply, open an account, and share their account number with the spider. This allows the spider to track them wherever they go. Spider takes footprints, teeth prints, and DNA samples from every creature. If a caterpillar eats a leaf in the garden, the spider must inspect it to make sure the caterpillar doesn't eat too much young vegetation. Also, the spider wants to make sure the butterfly rests exactly where it's supposed to in the middle of his webs so that whenever the spider is hungry he can just add some more webs onto his prey and turn whoever it is into his meal for himself to eat.

Same as humans, today they have their own account numbers with only three words beginning with the sixth letters of the greater nation's alphabet language. Wherever you go, you must prove you have that account before you can gain access to anything. If you don't have it now, you must have it later. Spiders do the same as humans and say to them, "Before you can do anything or receive any help, you need to file a full application and open one account. Then you are okay with that, but if you don't have that, there is nothing we can do for you." Those three words are "file – for – finish." Alphabets f - f - f, numbers 6-6-6. If you are not file-for-finish with everything in your life, you will not buy and you will not sell anything. When you are filed-for-finish, you don't have to do anything more; they already have everything they need to finish up everything.

Just like the spider, when other creatures are trapped in its ribs, wherever they are, the spider can just pull the ribs or slide on the ribs and get that meal. It's the same for humans; wherever you are going, when they pull out your account, your DNA, your prints, which are filed for finish, those are the key that they will use to identify you. So, if you want to buy something, file-for-finish with your application before you can buy it. If you want to sell something, file-for-finish with your application before you can sell it. Whatever you want to do, just file-for-finish with that file-6-for-6-finish-6. That's it.

Beside every animal living on earth, there is an insect that is naturally born on trees but lives its life underground. Before their lives come to an end, they return to the earth, especially to the trees, to reproduce and lay eggs. These eggs then hatch, and after they leave, their offspring replace them, disappearing to return to a last trip back to the earth.

During this time, these insects, known as cicadas, who from the time they are born until the time they come back on the trees can be seventeen years. After all that time, they come back not only to lay eggs and have offspring but also to honor the nature of the place where they were born through their continuous song. Their music serves as a reminder to every other creature in the wild that they belong here, despite their long absence. They haven't forgotten their true home—the place where their parents were born and where they themselves were born.

The reality of humans who cannot live in the city, town, or country where they were born, and after returning to that place before they are deceased. That is not only happening to humans but also happens for most animals and even trees. Some fish are never born in deep waters; when they grow big, they go to live in deep waters. When they are sick or approaching death, they come back to the same area where they were born and finally die there. Some of them just pay a last visit to that place during the period they are in distress before they disappear or die somewhere while fighting for more time to live. As for the trees, from banana plants to sequoias, a lot of branches come back to the roots, and time after another time, that dead tree completely disappears.

As for humans, despite the honor and love they have for the place where they were born, some may not want to return while others may not be able to return for various reasons. However, sadness and remorse reside in their hearts until their last breath. One thing remains true: wherever you are, you are still on earth and will eventually return to the dust. Whether you are buried or cremated, the same word applies when someone remembers you and asks about you - they will say that you are dead. This applies to everyone who has passed away or disappeared before others' eyes.

A good season brings forth beautiful flowers that multiply happiness in the heart. However, just like flowers, happiness is temporary and can disappear in an instant due to bad news, a tragedy, or any event that shatters happiness forever. This fleeting nature of happiness applies not only to individual moments but also to human existence as a whole, influenced by age and health conditions. In the morning, you may feel good, but as the day progresses, you close your door and say goodbye to those dear to you. Happiness indeed exists, but only for a short period.

Many people can taste happiness, some more than others, but one event or the passage of time can erase that happiness. When your happiness is removed, for sure you will think it doesn't exist at all. But happiness exists temporarily, like a shadow of an object during the sunshine, like clouds over the sky, and like rain before thunder. Everything can disappear without a trace of its appearance. When happiness is gone, the human heart suddenly changes. Therefore, wise people do not honor a person actively on duty, as the human heart is constantly changing. What a shame to honor someone among many, only to later witness that same person's degradation and realize they are unworthy of honor. On the other hand, honoring a retired person is considered wise because they rest with their accomplishments, without any further continuity for themselves.

If a person accomplishes a great deal of good during a certain period, everyone is satisfied. However, if that person makes a mistake, all their previous good actions are overshadowed by that single error. It is important to understand that one wrong action can erase a trillion previous good deeds. In a moment, a human can undo all the good they worked hard to achieve. Often, people fail to notice when someone is striving to make improvements, but when that person makes a mistake, all eyes focus on that black spot.

If you ever wonder why not many people honor a living human, the answer is simple. Honoring a living person can lead to shame if that person makes a mistake and dishonors themselves before their life is over. Everything can appear wonderful for a human, but it is not advisable to believe in a stronghold, a place of true protection at any level one can imagine on earth.

Two Friends Travel, Do You See Any Car Coming?

There was a man living in a nice place who called it his stronghold - a gorgeous place for him to live. One morning, he decided to go out with a friend who was visiting him. They both got into a vehicle that he was driving. When they crossed the last gate of his house, he was unable to see the other side of the road. He asked his friend if he saw any cars coming, and his friend looked and saw a truck approaching. Because he specifically asked about cars, his friend replied that he didn't see any cars. As they crossed the road, the truck struck them and pushed them over. Perhaps he should have asked if his friend saw anything coming or any vehicles approaching. When he had the chance to question his friend about what happened, his friend apologized, explaining that he didn't ask if he saw any trucks, only if he saw any cars, and he didn't see any cars coming.

Some people might think he is a fool, and some might say he is stupid. Others might say it was a misunderstanding. Should he be more specific with everything he wants to say to his friend? Who knows, the only thing certain is that he blames his friend for denying the presence of any vehicle coming, while his friend complains that he did not ask about a truck, but only about a car. Then, he did not see a car.

Maybe when you are driving with your friend in your vehicle and you cannot see the other side of the road, you need to ask if they see anything coming, whether it might be an ant or a vehicle, just to prevent such accidents from happening again. If it is supposed to be a mystery, it can happen in many other ways where no one can explain why. Trusting somebody is always a risk, but it's important not to worry about it when it happens with someone you trust.

A family with several children from the beginning explains to them the kind of people they can trust as friends and the kind of people they should never consider as friends. They tell them that if they choose not to respect what their parents have said, if anything further happens, they will be on their own. The family takes their words seriously. However, the first daughter of that family does not listen, despite the warnings from her family. She continues to do whatever she feels like doing until she becomes pregnant by a young man whom her parents did not want her to be involved with. When that happens, she assumes that her parents will set aside their own words and marry her to that young man. However, her parents refuse and stand by their principles. They keep their own words, and if she is not willing to listen, she will be on her own. They are doing good, but they make a terrible mistake by minimizing the thinking that when a child becomes part of your enemy, that child also becomes your own enemy. Since they do not agree to marry that girl to the young man, they should have put her outside of their home because she is no longer just a child to them but also an enemy.

The parents do make that mistake and let that girl into their house. Finally, when the girl realizes that her parents will not marry her to the young man, she puts poison in her mother's food, killing her. A time of beginning, a time of change. This shows that you can trust someone now, but it is important to know that you might never have to trust that same person later for some reason. When that happens, you are the only person responsible for yourself. You need to be strong enough to build a wall between your life and your deadly enemy.

You are the one who must make your own judgment to see if your child, who disrespects the family principles you have raised them with, is still the same child you once knew. If your child has changed, it is up to you to exercise your own discernment and find out if they are a friend or an enemy from whom you want to keep a distance. It may not be easy, of course. But often, when you see someone with a disability, it is because a cancer was attacking a part of their body, such as a foot, an eye, a limb, or any other part. In order to protect the rest of their body, they had to remove that part. They may have lost a part of their body, but life continues for them. The same goes for distancing yourself from someone for a good cause. You must do so before it is too late for you. Never be too naive, as that can leave you lacking in protection.

A parent with many kids was telling them what they should and should not do. One day, a small kid sees his brothers and sisters doing something prohibited by their parents. This kid remembers what his parents told him and says that he will not partake in that activity. Not only is he afraid of punishment, but he also keeps in mind what his parents told him not to do. So, he calls his dad and explains what the other kids are doing. However, his dad does not take it too seriously. Eventually, this seemingly good kid watches his dad not taking it seriously and decides to join the rest of his brothers and sisters in doing the same thing as them.

That causes a great defeat for the parent, who is sad. But, if the parent had taken the disobedience more seriously, not only could the kid have prevented the rest of the children from engaging in that sad and horrible wrongdoing, but the parent could have also protected themselves and the entire family. It is even sadder for the kid who told his dad about what the other kids were trying to do, and his dad did nothing to protect him. The dad did not protect himself and failed to give the rest of the kids a well-deserved reminder. Now, a total chaos has ensued, and it is too late to repair anything at all. Unfortunate situations of that magnitude, or even worse, often occur not only within families but in every sector where hatred, jealousy, hypocrisy, and deception prevail among people, whether it be a group of people or an organization. When situations like these arise, malicious individuals are often the first to try to guide others towards their own objectives to achieve their goals.

But if anything is brought to light, two things are very important to understand: the serious damages that an irreparable mistake can cause and the credibility of the person who brings the truth to light. It is important to protect what needs to be protected, whether it is life or wealth. If you are the person in charge, you are responsible for analyzing the event and making the final decision, not relying on a friend or a neighbor. If you let others make decisions for you, especially if they are the masterminds behind a snare set for you, it can be detrimental to yourself. You should realize that by giving them control, you are also putting your life and the lives of those who protect you at risk. If you do nothing at all, they will eventually turn those who protect you into your enemies and qualify them to destroy you. You never want to act unwisely like a king who was betrayed by some people in his kingdom. When one of his guardians noticed what was going to happen, the king agreed to find out the truth and catch those responsible, just like capturing birds.

However, as a knowledgeable individual, if you recognize that you are an important person and if you see a snare being set for you, it is crucial for you to acquire knowledge about who set the snare, who sent them to set it, and why they decided to set a snare for you. As a king, no one else can tell you not to punish those who are trying to ensnare you like a wild animal.

Unfortunately for the king, who did not completely understand what it meant to have people hate, betray, and deceive him simultaneously, he was not acting as a serious king who truly wanted to punish and stop his enemies from crossing his path. He was naively listening to his enemies' deceptive words, as they were sent to dethrone him while concealing their true intentions. They assured him that these people posed no potential danger to him, guaranteeing him maximum protection and high security. They claimed that nothing at all could happen to him, and there was no reason for him to worry about any threats. They urged him to release these individuals, insisting that they were harmless.

Where in other parts of the world, a king would catch people who were scheming to kill him and remove him from his throne, and a neighbor, whosoever it should be, would stand up and declare that the king should order the release of those individuals, and the king obeyed and said, "Indeed" to the deceptive plotters and scheme against his own life. So the king didn't give himself a chance to think about his own life and the life of those who had alerted him to the scheme aimed at dethroning and killing him. The king was living with a clouded mind that made him believe his enemies were his best friends and the ones he could trust. With such thoughts in his mind, they used him as a puppet while continuing to destroy the nation. Eventually, they realized that they could no longer manipulate him like a tool, leading them to inflict even greater harm upon him, worse than that of a venomous serpent.

Eventually, when the guard notified the king about those who had schemed to kill him and seize the throne, the guard feared punishment if he was involved in that plan. However, when the king released the perpetrators, it gave the guard a sense that he wouldn't be punished for such a thing. He didn't want to miss out on the opportunity, as it seemed the king had taken no significant action. Everything appeared to proceed smoothly, as if nothing had happened. They easily manipulated the guard, making him a crucial figure in their plan to remove the king from his throne and assassinate him, with everyone involved directly or indirectly.

There is no doubt that if the king had kept those who had betrayed him in the first instance imprisoned and punished them as a true king should, his life could have taken a different turn. Instead, at the time they killed him, his life came to an end. If you are in a position of leadership, be wise. After considering various perspectives, you will be the one whom everyone must listen to. Whether you are the first in a family or part of a group, you can't blame others for the decisions made. You are the one who always has the final say in every matter. Your neighbors can say whatever they want, but it is up to you to understand that they have their own country to worry about. You are the one who is supposed to govern your own country. If you fail to understand this, you are surrendering and allowing them to rule your nation for you. Understand that as well. You become like a chicken to them, ready to be consumed whenever they desire. They build strong walls around you, so they don't have to lose you and you don't have to mix with the neighboring chickens. Stay within the walls. Whatever you produce, whether it's eggs or chicks, they come and manage it for their own profits. Sometimes, a predatory bird with its provocation can cause a mother bird enough stress to eat her own chicks and abandon the nest. Most of the time, when your enemies want to destroy you, they use the same strategy. They turn your own people against you, and they turn you against your own people, standing nearby, waiting for you to call them as mediators between all of you.

When you call upon them, their manipulation begins. Instead of offering you a sweet, enjoyable experience as you expected, they start manipulating and reshaping your mind, turning you against each other according to their desires, forever. Just like the bird that is stressed and sees her chicks as a cause of her own demise, leading her to kill them and leave the area. Your enemies can employ strategies to make you view your own children as your real enemies, and make them see you as their true enemy. They know that once this happens, your destruction is assured. They will destroy you, your roots, your children, your friends, family members, neighbors, or any other humans who are part of your life.

A truly poor family should be taken care of by those who are in charge of the family. If you fail to do so, others will take control of your family, whether it's another family or a group of people.

They will dictate how your family should be governed, even how you should live your lives. They will provide for your family according to the desires of their hearts, be it a good provision or a venomous serpent.

Similarly, in a relatively poor country, its people need to learn how to be self-reliant and work hard to meet their own needs. Those who are leading the nation must be smart enough to provide excellent leadership with strong character. If you fail to prove yourselves as good leaders who genuinely care for your own nation, it will suffer the consequences.

A different nation will take over your nation and pretend to provide you with whatever your nation needs to survive. In the meantime, they will use your own wealth and make you work for a piece of bread that is not enough for you to eat. This way, they can keep you as a slave and dependent on them to share that insufficient piece of bread among your children.

There are families who possess enough wealth for the family but live as the poorest because they call a neighbor to manage whatever they want to do. If the family cooks a meal, they must call the neighbor to share that meal among the family. So, what the neighbor often does is take the good portion for himself and his family and share whatever he does not currently want among the fool family. This not only happens at the family level but also among entire so-called poorest nations.

Smart people travel every day from wealthy nations to the poorest nations. What are their missions? To help, as they always say; but not true, as most of them enrich themselves with your riches while you and your family remain poor in a relatively poor country. Remember that there are zero poor nations on earth. In one nation, more people are living as poor because they never produce a good leader at all. Or whenever that nation produces a good leader, somebody else kills him, so they can continue to enrich themselves with the wealth of that nation.

Knowledge is the only key to remove a nation from poverty. That means a nation that is relatively poor is suffering from a poverty of knowledge, a lack of knowledge.

Whoever takes the lead as leaders is never the one who acquires enough wisdom and knowledge to produce anything good for a nation. If a family can cultivate a single farm with their knowledge, they find out what needs to be done to make their farm productive. A good leader should know exactly what to do to make a nation self-sufficient in many ways. After all, one brain can accomplish many things, but if thorns and thistles outnumber the hands, it can be impossible to cultivate the land in a fruitful manner.

The same applies to a nation. A few good plants can never thrive among a massive thicket of thorns and thistles. This also holds true for humans. A few individuals with positive views and different ideas from the wrongdoers will never prevail. If you know how to compete, such as running for a gold medal, you also know that you will be competing against another runner, and that runner will be competing against you. Would you order your running shoes from the people who are running against you? If you do such a thing, you would present yourself as a fool and depict yourself as a blind person wandering in the wilderness.

There was a person who had the privilege to observe many animals in a certain place. He witnessed a serpent searching for its food, and one of the preferred targets for serpents is birds. When the serpent approached a bird's nest where a mother bird was protecting her chicks, the serpent extended its tongue towards the bird. Instead of running away, the mother bird emitted a signal three times, and the serpent completely backed off from the nest. Sometimes, even those who present themselves as outlaws need a reminder of the existence of the law. This was a reminder to the serpent that it was crossing the boundaries of her territory.

But one thing is clear: no matter how small the power of the bird, she stood up for herself, her chicks, and her territory. The serpent recognized that it must respect the bird's territory. If the bird had trusted the serpent to defend her security, that day her life and the lives of her chicks could have ended as a meal for the serpent. The bird did not feel any burden on her back to be a strong protector of her territory.

A week later, the serpent embarked on a similar search for food. This time, before approaching that corner, it raised its head and extended its tongue for some time, then changed its direction. Not only the serpent, but that person also witnessed a large bird, comparable to an eagle, searching for food. This big bird was pursued from three directions by three different smaller birds who were fighting for their territories. First, a crow challenged the big bird, then a musician bird, and finally a hummingbird. Despite its size, the big bird was forced to leave their territories due to the authority exercised by these smaller birds. They protected and defended their territories, which belonged to them, and the predator had to depart without delay.

It is not only humans and animals that fight for territories, but plants also engage in territorial battles. If you have the chance to visit a forest, you can observe that some trees do not grow straight, causing significant issues for other trees. They engage in a struggle, intertwining with each other until some trees lose branches to liberate the territories of others. Although it results in some loss of life, they fight to free themselves from one another. If plants and animals do not want another life to rule over their territories, humans can do even better for themselves. They should strive to protect, secure, and manage what is important and recognize it as part of their responsibility for themselves and their territory. If a simple hummingbird knows how to protect and defend its territory, a human guided by intellect and intelligence should know much more and be much more proactive.

Predators should never be taken as reliable security. If someone allows that to happen, they do so for their own destruction. Many times, you need wisdom to discern certain things around you. For example, there is a spider that looks just like an ant. What does this spider do? It recognizes its vulnerability due to other creatures that can easily eat it. So, the spider abandons its own web and disguises itself as an ant, living inside the ant fortress.

Within the ant nest, the spider knows that the ants can be highly aggressive. If they were to discover that it is not an ant, it would face dire consequences. So, during the day the spider stays very quiet and when the night comes, the game changes. That is the time when the spider can feast on enough ants to sustain itself. It lives among the ants for its own security, while nourishing itself with the ants as food.

This spider is malicious and intelligent. The ants are never able to discern that it is not an ant. For the sake of fidelity, the spider's mate also joins it inside the ant fortress, continuing to deceive the ants by masquerading as ants themselves. Meanwhile, the ants are unaware that the spider is using them for protection against other creatures or predators, while also using them as a source of food. The ants provide the spider and its mate with a home and security, eliminating the need for the spider to worry about predators. In return, the ants unknowingly receive a deadly penalty, as the spider relies on them as a source of food. The ants work hard to protect themselves and diligently gather food, but they are unaware of the spider's true intentions.

If this can happen to ants, it serves as a powerful example for people, especially those in positions of power, like the king who was killed by his supposed security. Those surrounding the king were solely focused on matters that did not necessarily serve the king's interests or benefit the nation. They acted like hungry chickens seeing corn for the first time. They didn't even realize if they had a duty to ensure the security of the king's surroundings and protect those who needed maximum protection.

What they are doing is unprofessional, and their actions can be compared to foolishness. They cross their hands and call upon a neighbor to act on their behalf. When the neighbor arrives, they take advantage of the situation, as it is a kingdom and the house of a king. The neighbor would not leave that place empty-handed; every time they go back and forth, they carry with them many so-called tools to conduct investigations. However, the irony is that evidence is scattered everywhere, not just where the event occurred. Of course, when one is foolish, they fail to understand anything at all.

This neighbor carries away all the important possessions that belonged to the king's family, including money, gold, and more. For those who have acquired knowledge, if someone needs to enter a place with a specific mission, they should ensure that the mission begins specifically at the spot where the event took place and under the surveillance of the protectors or security of that place. This was not the case for those who lack discernment; they are deceived by numerous trips and bags that can never serve as evidence of those who killed the king. Instead, they become the means to acquire the wealth of the king's family.

After all, this is a harvest for the neighbors. If such situations occur in your nation every day, they would be pleased as it allows them to come and seize your wealth, leaving you in relative misery and foolishness. It is like a poor man who owns a property and has a cunning neighbor who suspects that the poor man has a hidden stash of gold underground in his backyard. The neighbor approaches the poor man and offers to help take care of his yard, stating that the poor man lacks the money to maintain it. The poor man, happy to have a neighbor willing to help, agrees and sees the neighbor as a savior, like dry land waiting for rain.

That vicious neighbor brings his tractor and trucks with him and removes all the gold. He has the poor man put them in his vehicles disguised as rocks and other objects that are not good for the land. Just after he grabs the last piece of gold, he turns away from the poor man and never comes back to fix anything for him.

Don't forget to take your own responsibility sometimes. It means refusing what someone promises to accomplish for you in one day. Take your time if possible and accomplish that in one year by yourself. At least you can call that the sweat of your forehead. Nobody can call you a hero for a gift you are receiving from someone or for what somebody else accomplishes for you. But they call you a hero only for what you accomplish by yourselves, or for your resistance which is part of your own activity.

A single person can be a curse for a family. A family can be a curse for a community, and then a leader can be a curse for a nation. Most of the time, it's not because they are doing anything wrong to anyone, but the way they let others abuse them. Whether you are a single person, a family, or a nation, whenever others abuse you, of course, you are the one who looks like a curse. You are the one who looks like the guilty one because you are the one who looks like a blind chicken among the serpents, with your head in the sky, waiting for a mercy that will never come for you, even for your descendants that will never be possible.

Truly, you can even be hurt in your own home by an animal, but the first one to blame is you. The real reason is that you either brought that animal into your home or through your negligence, you let that beast take advantage and enter your home. Unfortunately, you are paying the consequences of that.

At a place where many people were gathered for a reason, a paralyzed man was trying to exit his vehicle when another person approached him and asked if he needed help. The paralyzed man responded, saying, "When you have money, you have help." The person backed off and continued to observe as the paralyzed man managed to open his vehicle door and transfer onto his wheelchair.

Some people might prefer to simply say "no, thank you" rather than making a statement like "when you have money, you have help." However, whether you are paralyzed or not, whether you have money or not, you can still find ways to help yourself. The person who offered help walked away with a valuable lesson. Imagine if the poor man had refused the help of his neighbor. His gold would have remained in his backyard, and his yard would not have been damaged by deep holes. Perhaps in the future, even his grandchild could have benefited from the gold. But when he accepted the offer of the vicious neighbor who pretended to help him take care of his yard, everything went wrong. The gold was stolen by this neighbor.

Sometimes, you must not trust certain people, just like the crab who does not have good credit with many creatures, especially humans. If a human wants to rescue a crab, they need to make sure both claws are secure. If the claws are not properly secured, the crab will surely bite. If you see a crab with both claws tied and you try to release it, the first claw that you release will bite you. The crab does not care if you release the second claw or not. The crab does not accept any hypocrisy or any enemy trying to deceive it as a friend. Sometimes, the crab acknowledges that humans are trying to help, but it never accepts any free help from humans. If someone tries to touch the crab, it will bite them. The crab attaches one of its claws to the person's skin as a gift and quickly scurries away, never to be seen again. The crab acts out of self-preservation and does not need to remember any acts of kindness. If you touch the crab, you will be seriously bitten. This happens not because animals want to attack anyone, but because they naturally want to defend themselves and protect their territory. Therefore, when their lives are in danger, they are reacting in defense, just like many people do for themselves.

A man was walking along his pathway when he spotted a serpent. Another person alerted the man, saying that it was a venomous serpent. Dismissing the truth, the man downplayed the danger, believing it was just a harmless snake. However, if that venomous serpent were to enter his home and he failed to kill it or put it in a cage, he would be doing nothing to protect himself. If anything were to happen to him, it would be his own fault. Unfortunately, that venomous serpent made its way directly into the man's bedroom and fatally bit him. The man failed to realize that he alone was responsible for his own life.

You may think you have a million eyes watching over you and protecting you, but you are the only one who can guarantee your own safety. If you see danger and allow it to harm you just to please others or obey deceivers, they will deceive you like a serpent and bring you to ruin.

One day, a ruler of a nation was addressing his people but had difficulty pronouncing his team in the language of his nation. Instead, he repeatedly spoke in a different language and acknowledged that it was on his mind. He struggled to recall the words, and as a ruler, he admitted that he had another nation on his mind, which caused him to forget what he wanted to say. Speaking wisely, if a ruler has another nation on his mind that embarrasses him and prevents him from expressing himself to his own nation, it implies that he is ruling under the influence of that other nation.

A farmer had many chickens and tried to train them three times a day. His training focused on making the chickens stay quiet and sit down while he poured corn on the ground for them. He wanted them to wait for his command before approaching the food. Unfortunately, even after a year of daily training, not a single chicken obeyed the training.

A family with about a dozen members who always crossed their hands and waited for a neighbor to feed them with leftover food. Each time they received food from their neighbor, they appeared completely dependent and out of control, much like the chickens. They had no hopes for themselves and their minds were consumed by the neighbor's leftovers, which they relied on for survival. They refused to learn and understand that the reason they lacked what they needed was because they constantly crossed their hands and waited for their neighbor's leftover food.

Similarly, a nation had many good-looking, relatively intelligent individuals, including doctors, engineers, businessmen, politicians, religious leaders, and more. However, there were also many problems. This was because all of them were sons and daughters of a family that always depended on their neighbors for leftover food. Because of their education, they also prolonged their ability to cross their hands and wait on neighbors for food, that was not enough for them. Why not a bag of grain, even if it is expired bulgur? That is what it is for now.

After a full year of training, the chickens never obeyed the principle set by their owner. When they see corn, it becomes a question of death or eating the corn. Despite their education, these individuals all carry the sentiment of chickens, regardless of their role in the nation. If the possibility arises that a bag of expired grain might be taken away from them, they no longer make any effort to do better. If it means killing and destroying the entire nation to avoid losing that expired grain, they are ready to do just that. Without any remorse, for fear of losing a bag of grain, they transform themselves into weapons, worse than a cancer, gradually destroying one another. This is a compelling reason why they are sometimes referred to as more than just chickens. If a different ruler were to give them a name, they would truly deserve that name, as their actions align with those of real chickens.

When these individuals engage in conversations with people from other nations and claim to have been serving their nation for a long time, instead of saying they have been serving their nation, they say they have been working with others for so long. Their lack of knowledge is evident in their words. Yet, these individuals who pretend to represent their nation possess no greater power than domesticated animals. It is truly disheartening to witness that when night falls, if they go to bed early, a neighbor can come over and tell them it is too early and that they must wait until they receive a signal to go to bed. And when they wake up early in the morning, that same neighbor approaches them and tells them that they should have waited for a signal to leave their beds. Whenever this family tries to clean their home, whether it's the interior or exterior, the neighbor interferes and instructs them to wait until one of their own children comes to direct them on which trash to remove. This has become a routine for the family, who may own a home but do not even possess a moment of control over their own lives.

Someone else not only owns that family but also owns the family and whatever that family relatively owns. Certainly, that family becomes so afraid of their neighbor that when clothes are ready to be washed, they close their eyes in fear of their super neighbor's disapproval, whether it be for doing something without his advice or guidance. Even if they encounter a dangerous beast or insect in their home, they are not permitted to remove or kill it without the super neighbor's permission. The super neighbor is the only one they are allowed to call, and if they decide to keep that animal inside or outside their home, that's the end of the discussion. There are no further arguments. If something is important to them, they must take it away with them, as the relative owner of their possessions has the final say.

This family owns a vast piece of land and cultivates various edible plants and fruit-bearing trees every season. However, the super neighbor comes over and dictates what they should do with these plants and fruit trees, particularly those like potatoes, watermelons, and similar crops. If these plants encroach upon the super neighbor's property, the harvest will be claimed by the super neighbor, and the family is relieved of any worry regarding them. They are mandated to focus solely on the roots of these plants, ensuring their growth and productivity on the super neighbor's property. As for the fruit trees that produce good fruits every season, such as apple trees, mango trees, avocado trees, and more,

Effective immediately, the family is ordered to verify if any branches extend over the super neighbor's property. If the branches do cross over, the harvest will belong to the super neighbor, and the family is instructed to simply take good care of these trees to maintain their fruitfulness. As for the trees directly on the family's property, effective immediately, they are ordered to uproot all of them immediately because the fruits they bear are considered poisonous, and the family is deemed incapable of handling them. Imagine that the family plants and maintains the farm, yet they are not the ones who benefit from any harvest at all.

Do you know that this also happens between some nations? In certain nations, people live under the rules and orders of other nations. If a person becomes wealthy, they must immediately leave their own nation and move to the nation that rules over them. If you refuse initially, there will be a good reason later for you to leave, as they will subject you to persecution similar to what takes root in your own nation. If you definitively refuse to move, they can even go as far as killing you and finding a way to seize your wealth.

If you have a job in your own nation where you earn a lot of money, you must purchase a house in the ruling nation and relocate your family there, while you yourself must stay behind in your own nation, like a temporary stranger. Your bank account must be in the super nation as well. And when your children finish their education, they will not return to your own nation. You should never expect anything better for your own nation; everything is directed towards the ruling nation. You are uprooting every opportunity offered to you in your own nation, resigning yourself to a nomadic life under the rule of the ruling nation. You are forced to navigate between your own nation and the ruling nation, whether you see it or not, whether you understand it or not. They are turning you against yourself, just like a family uprooting their farm and abandoning all possibilities for themselves, their family, and their nation, all in favor of the ruling nation that dominates them.

Children take orders from their parents as part of their upbringing and education, but a parent should never take orders from an external person regarding the upbringing of their children. If that happens, you should know that the order may come from an enemy. When that happens, you are nothing more than a forest of rats sharing a border with a forest of snakes.

Your powers are worse than nonexistent. You are merely a tool for the benefit of the one who dominates you. If, for any reason, he wants to elevate himself by putting you on the edge of a ditch and ordering you to jump to your death, you must comply just to please your superior. Many so-called lesser individuals do this, while their nations lack those who can truly understand what is happening.

Certainly, if someone is killed by a disease, it is likely because that disease has already attacked one or more vital organs in their body. Similarly, before someone smart harms you, they implant in your mind the idea that whatever happens to you, you need not worry because you possess some invisible powerful force that will take care of your situation. With this idea in mind, you become vulnerable, and they easily exploit you like a pig, leaving you lying down, never to wake up again.

Among the animals that never harm humans or pose a threat to them are doves and pigeons, yet none of them fully trust humans. This means that if you don't have a good or wise reason to trust another person, you are solely responsible for your own safety, security, and protection. Even those who possess a tiny animal that can grow big should never see it as just a tiny animal once it grows in size. In the same way that animals don't trust other animals, humans themselves do not trust other humans. The underlying reason for this lack of trust, whether in humans or animals, is simply to protect their lives.

For instance, if you have a large snake in your home, at some point, that snake may want to eat you and will refuse to eat the food you offer, keeping its stomach empty to make room for you inside. You may find this hard to believe, but if you are the owner of a large snake, no matter how long you've had it, remember that terrible events can occur, and if you are involved, you will not be present to make any point. The lesson will be learned only by those who are observant.

Some people raise animals like goats and later consume them as meat. So, animals like snakes perceive things differently—if they are large enough, they can play smart with you and consume you as their food. Unfortunately, not only snakes can kill people. Many people mistakenly believe that a snake capable of eating a person must be larger than the person, but appearances can be deceiving, as snakes can swallow things that appear much larger than themselves.

Sometimes, people's actions are not much different from a snake attempting to devour someone. For example, a government official who seeks to harm an innocent man for personal matters. The officer approaches the man and steps on his foot, continuing to apply pressure. As the officer keeps his foot on the man's, the man turns his face away as if he feels nothing, and the officer, with his head held high, pretends not to notice. After a while, the man addresses the officer, saying, "Oh mighty chief, please forgive me for accidentally placing my foot under yours while I was walking. Could you do me a favor and lift your foot slightly so that I can free mine?" The officer responds, demanding to know the man's reason for placing his foot beneath his own while he was walking, claiming it is evidence of disrespect towards a chief. The officer then declares that today might be the man's time to put an end to his arrogance.

The man continues to present excuses and pleads that it is not his fault. However, both parties understand why this is happening. No matter how the man falls into the snare of that officer, it is not easy for him to escape with a favorable outcome. It brings satisfaction to the officer's heart. Sometimes, you do not seek confrontation, but someone else premeditated it and brought it to you as a snare, acting as a bird catcher. Unfortunately, you become the victim of them. Such events occur frequently when certain individuals like that officer abuse their power against others who may have had past conflicts with them or simply to assert their power to punish or even kill them as revenge for themselves or their friends.

The officer had in his mind that the man would act violently, then he could take advantage of the opportunity to shoot him as if he was being attacked. However, the man abandons his anger and uses his wisdom to protect his life. Ultimately, wisdom becomes his best weapon against the wrongdoer. The man proves himself to be wise, and perhaps the officer can learn a lesson from his actions. He faced a dangerous situation and an attack against him. A wise person is not only a blessing to their family but sometimes to the community, the nation, or even the world. On the other hand, a foolish person with any kind of power is a curse for those who know them. The consequences of their wrong actions will linger behind them like the morning fogs of winter long after they have been erased on earth.

A good man ascended to the throne as king of his nation. He was a respected individual who fostered a wonderful environment throughout his reign. During his time as king, the nation never participated in any wars with other nations, and his people lived in peace throughout his entire tenure. He also instructed his five sons on how to live better lives while they are on earth. In that part of the world, a person with any visible scars on their body is not allowed to participate in war. The king himself despised war, but no one can predict what will happen to the nation even after his time. They do not know if one of his sons will succeed him and whether that son will follow in his father's footsteps.

The only thing is, the current king does not like war, and he hopes that his sons will be the same. However, the king does not want his sons to go to war. At a certain age, all young men are mandated to register their names in case their nation becomes involved in a war. This ensures that every young person receives proper training for warfare. What could happen to prevent all five sons from going to war?

During the inspections, the inspectors will assess all the young people, and after the inspections are completed, they will determine who is qualified and who is not. Fortunately, their father didn't like war, and all five sons are deemed unqualified for war. What were the reasons for their disqualifications? There were some genuine reasons. The youngest son had cuts on his head from two different incidents while playing with his older sister. The older brother had a cut on his face from an object thrown by another young man while he was walking on a road. The second brother was cut on his face while running. The third son had his head injured by a schoolmate who threw a rock. And the fourth son, while playing with his friend, received a cut on his back. As a result, all five young men are unable to go to war, which no one had noticed prior to the inspections being completed by the inspectors. The king is also pleased with this news because he doesn't like war at all.

Hearing that, a good friend of the king says that the king's family and the king himself are blessed because he was not happy with the war, now his sons also will not be going to any war.

The king responds to his friend, stating that as a king, he doesn't want to call himself a blessing, nor his family or his nation to be a blessing. Whenever you hear someone call himself "a blessing", he simply means that they are the only powerful one on Earth, the one who is eternal. Whether it is a group, a nation, or a king, if the word "blessed" is used as a slogan, it means the one who is supposed to be eternal; the greatest one who every knee shall bow before. The entity possesses extreme power to make change, to create and destroy, as an absolute supreme authority.

The king says, as a king, he wants to see a smooth life for his nation, his family, and himself, not just only during his reign but for the future of his nation as well. The king emphasizes that the only thing he could never accept as a king is taking orders from any other individuals or nations. When he follows orders from others, he ceases to be a king with the power to protect his nation and becomes a mere servant executing their commands, whether they are in his favor or against him. A king should never obey in the manner of a child.

At the same time, the wise king describes certain principles for his sons that can also be very important for anyone who wants to run for a position in the kingdom. The king begins by stating that if, during your campaign, you fall to the ground without any reason other than the seat you are running for, there is no need to continue further. This means that you will not win that seat and you will be set back. It indicates that you may not have any future prospects for that role, whether it be king or any other important position in the kingdom.

During your campaign to be king, if you must meet with anyone to discuss your candidacy or engage in debates with someone else who wants to be king, whether in a private area, an office, or a public place, if a fly rests on you, especially on your face, forehead, or any visible spot on your body that others can see clearly, it means that you have missed the chance to be declared a winner of anything. It signifies that you will not achieve any victories in that campaign, whether it is securing the desired seat or ruling the kingdom.

If you are already a king and you fall during your activities within the nation, whether in the office or in public view, it may hinder the realization of your dream of being a good king. Anything can happen to halt that mission. In such situations, you must exercise your wisdom and take immediate action to protect and secure what is important.

The sons of the king understood the king's words and agreed with them. Years pass, the king grows old and eventually passes away, leaving his eldest son to succeed him. The eldest son promises the nation to rule as his father did and agrees to share power with his four brothers, which he does. They successfully govern the nation without major problems as they age.

When a person who is guided by wonderful principles has the possibility to rule a nation for a long period of time, many people acquire enough wisdom to keep up with many things, including family matters. Therefore, it is not easy to find any bad example as a man who divorces his wife just because, when the husband goes to the store, he puts the vegetables in one place, the meat in a different place, and other things elsewhere. But when his wife goes shopping, she puts the vegetables in a different place inside the refrigerator.

When the husband finds out that his wife never puts the vegetables in the same place on the shelf where he always puts them inside the refrigerator, he gets upset and decides to separate from his wife forever because she does not put the vegetables in the same spot where he himself puts them all the time. There is no scientific explanation to fully understand that action as a good reason for divorce because in a family, when doing things together, if one person insists on doing things a certain way, the other might not agree. After all, both people know that it is not a crime nor their priority in life.

Most men will go along with their wife in that case, just to make things easier for her rather than make it worse and destroy the family. The man chooses to make a foolish decision without any valid reasons. He classifies himself among the creators of problems. Imagine a person like that who later must tell his children the reason he got divorced. Now, if they believe that is a real reason for separation and divorce, one should ask themselves: how many times will these children go through divorce in their lives? It is not a good path to imitate, and too many children can become victims of such foolishness and senseless separation.

From the least to the greatest problems faced by humans, no one has yet found a code to resolve such issues. X and Y factors cannot be pre-analyzed to determine who will turn out to be a good person, and the world cannot rid itself of bad individuals. No parents should be cursed because of a child who was raised well but later becomes a creator of problems, a criminal. If it were possible to prevent this, no family would ever be blamed for having a bad offspring. Every family would be happy to have good children with the hope that their babies will remain the same and bring them joy until they pass away.

As the king who raised his sons on a good track, it is unfortunate that in this instance, nothing can bring lasting satisfaction. Good humans can only engage in a preventive war on a limited scale, trying to coexist with unresolved issues that they are unable to fully resolve.*

Contemplate the spring, enjoy the summer, see the moon closer to you, be like you are the first human who contemplates the sunshine. Fly your mind among the stars, see yourselves as the first guests to the galaxies. When you are on earth, be like a water frog sitting in the middle of a fresh source of water, enjoy your good time, and close your eyes before the bad time.

*Many things can be prevented, but they are not because these things serve the interests of others who present themselves as protectors. Somewhere in the world, if you are a pregnant woman who goes to the hospital, the first news you will hear is that you have anemia and will not be able to deliver your baby naturally as it is supposed to be. They will insist on performing an operation, claiming it is the only way to guarantee your life and your baby's. Some accept this as mandatory, while others seek different opinions and options. Surgery in a living body should only be considered in cases of emergency, and even then, it should be confirmed by multiple sources. It is not advisable to undergo surgery just to fulfill someone else's desires, leaving you with unnecessary and lasting pain in your body. Women are naturally meant to give birth without the need for incisions on their genitals or surgery to pull the baby out of their womb.

When you touch or wake a sleeping baby, the baby starts crying. This is because it is not always good to disturb a baby's sleep. Waking a baby naturally causes discomfort and pain throughout their body. It is not just the pain, but also the disruption of natural processes inside the baby's body. The same principle applies to the timing of labor and childbirth. It should not be done before the natural hour or minutes. Just like a baby butterfly must struggle to emerge from its cocoon, the process may be challenging but necessary for the butterfly's strength and development. If someone helps the baby butterfly by breaking the cocoon prematurely, it will not be able to fly and will eventually die. It is the same for a baby's birth. The birds also allow their eggs to hatch at the right time. If the hatching occurs before the exact time, the baby will not thrive and may not survive.

Animal females and human females do not need cuts on their genitals to aid in labor. When such interventions occur without a medical emergency, it is a needless pain inflicted on the body for no good reason. There is no significant difference between cutting to deliver a baby or cutting the genital area to assist in delivery. You should not be subjected to unnecessary pain during childbirth, which is meant to happen naturally. No one will inform you if your baby's progress is affected and the reasons behind it. You are the one responsible for protecting yourself and your baby. While it may not be possible to know everything, always pay attention to your concerns. Mental disorders, lack of intelligence, developmental delays, brain problems, circulatory issues, respiratory problems, and more can arise prematurely. Take care not to rush or get too tired at home.

Two boys went to school, and when they approached home, one of them was refused entry until the gate of his home. Instead, he decided to cross under a fence and ended up getting injured. The other boy walked all the way to the gate of his home and entered his parents' house safely. The boy who crossed under the fence and got wounded remained there by the fence. Although he managed to get inside the fence, his injuries slowed him down, and he had to call his parents for help. Meanwhile, the boy who made the longer walk to the gate was already home without any injuries or pain to his body.

When a woman gives birth naturally, everything that is meant to come out with the baby does so naturally. However, when someone performs a surgical intervention to extract the baby, sometimes they leave behind what was meant to come out, immediately creating a new emergency in your life. In such cases, the baby may also refuse to breastfeed, as if trying to convey that everything is unnatural and a bottle of milk is sufficient to satisfy their needs. Reality is the truth, like light dispelling darkness and freeing ignorance. When light shines, ignorance is liberated, and wisdom is gained.

Consider a person trying to kill cockroaches with a sweeping broom. The person may push the roaches away but not kill them, allowing the roaches to return and even crawl under the sweeping broom or even under the person's feet who is trying to kill them by believing they are secure. It may seem unimaginable if applied to humans, but do not deceive yourselves; such situations occur in the world we live in every day. Imagine someone trying to harm you at your home, and yet you call upon that very same person for help. If given the chance to escape, you run straight to the house of the person who was attempting to harm you, believing you will find assistance. People often focus only on the problem at hand without considering its underlying cause. Like the roaches, you are making it easier for them to destroy you.

During times of war, many people are forced to flee their own nations in search of a safer place to survive. Sometimes, however, the nation they choose as a refuge is the very one causing the problem, although they may not be aware of it. Rather than staying where you can see the physical danger, you choose the logical option of seeking protection elsewhere. However, sometimes the dangers you ignore can make you as vulnerable as a kite in the hands of children who can easily pull it back down to the ground, no matter how high it may fly in the sky. The only code a kid needs to bring a kite back to the ground while it soars in the sky is the string line attached to the kite, which the kid holds in their hand on the ground. By holding that code, the kid gains control over the kite. Similarly, if someone else gains control over you, they can do whatever they want with you. At that point, you cannot control your owner, and you lose control over your own life and become like a domesticated animal who does not worry for himself, but his owner takes care of him. The animal itself always does anything that doesn't exceed his power to protect his owner.

There were about seven big dogs who believed in their power to do whatever they were trained for when approaching each other. Each dog has the ability to understand the others. They sit down in their respective spots and observe each other. If there was only one powerful dog with six regular dogs, that powerful dog could engage in a fight and dominate the others. However, since all seven dogs are powerful, they respect each other's strength and continue to watch without attacking. It would be wonderful if every dog was equally big and powerful, but unfortunately, that's not the case. Some dogs must run before others to protect their lives because they are too small, don't have any training, and too dumb to be defensive, they become defenseless dogs.

These seven big dogs do not attack each other because none of them want to be wounded. On the other hand, when it comes to the smaller dogs, they often submit and close their eyes, enduring terrible punishments or even facing death sentences. Unfortunately, this not only happens in the dog kingdom but also occurs among humans on a much larger scale. Powerful people exert dominance over weaker ones. The greatest nations are against the lesser nations,

As for those who are rivals, they stand apart a great distance with no trust between them. Powerless nations face terrible punishments.

Those in power might say, "Yeah, these rebellious kids who don't want to listen to us, let's force them to do what we want." Their words become the only mandate, and if the weaker nations don't demonstrate their respect through actions, they must face the consequences of disobedience to the more powerful nations within a short delay of twenty-four hours, which might not be enough time for them to avoid the consequences of their disobedience to the great and super nations.

Three Sons of the King Choose Symbols

A king had three sons on Earth. When the king saw that his sons had grown big enough, he called them one by one and sat down with each of them. He questioned them about their choice for a durable and undefeatable logo or symbol if they were to become kings at some point in their lives.

The first son replied that he would choose a monkey's tail as his symbol. This son believed that a monkey with its tail would appear strong and durable, especially when the monkey draped its tail over its back. He saw this as a symbol that couldn't be easily defeated or destroyed. However, if it were you, you might not choose a monkey's tail, considering that monkeys can lose or shed their tails, just as a tree can cancel a branch when it's dry enough that the branch can fall to the ground. Nonetheless, the first son kept his word.

Next, the king called his second son and asked him if at a certain period in life he became king, what durable and undefeatable logo or symbol would he choose? The second son replied that he would choose a rooster, a quality cock as his symbol. He had witnessed a cockfight where a quality rooster fought and emerged victorious, which made him believe that a rooster was the most durable and undefeatable symbol. However, if it were you, you might not choose a rooster, as its strength may only be applicable in cockfights and not in other aspects of life.

Finally, the king turned to his third son and asked him, if at a certain period in life you would like to become a king what logo or symbol would you choose? The third son responded that he would choose a fish bone as his logo or symbol. He had heard people say that no one could throw away a fish bone, which convinced him that it was the most durable and undefeatable thing in life. However, if it were you, you might not choose a fish bone because it is a remnant of a dead fish. Who would want to be associated with death? This choice might be made only by ignoring the negative connotations of a bone.

As time passed, the king eventually passed away. Since the first son had chosen the monkey's tail as his symbol, he became the successor to the throne and was enthroned as the new king, replacing his father.

As a new king, like a young monkey with his strong tail, the young king started ruling with great energy and apparent perfection before the nation. Therefore, everyone had a formidable and reasonable interest in honoring that king and his kingdom's rule over the nation. For years, the people of the nation were very satisfied with the way the king ruled, and everywhere in the nation, people lived peacefully. There was nothing to be worried or afraid about. It was the best nation when it came to trust, peace, and security. People walked on the streets day and night without fear of being attacked by bad people. They could open their doors at any time without the word "insecurity" ever crossing their minds. Every resident believed in working hard to put food on their tables. All parents counted only on what they possessed to take care of their children, and the children counted on their parents, having confidence that their parents would never abandon them. Everybody respected each other. It was a sweet and peaceful nation ruled by an honorable king, with wonderful people living in it.

Many years passed, and then the king, who had not yet gotten married, chose a woman to be his wife. Before the eyes of the nation, the king chose the wrong woman to marry, a woman who could bring woes to the nation. Nevertheless, the king went ahead and married her. This woman caused the king to become the worst king the nation had ever seen. She squandered the wealth of the nation at every level and became as the commander in chief of the king. Everything took a negative turn along the king's path, igniting the anger of the nation against him. The people of the nation grew upset witnessing the events unfolding before them. Their anger escalated, and they decided to protest against the king, demanding that he relinquish his power to free the kingdom. However, the king refused to comply. Bitterly, the population did not give up; they continued to protest against the king, even as the situation worsened. At that point, the king told them they must not persist with their protests, as it would not make him abdicate the throne. He asserted that he would continue to rule the nation strongly, even stronger than a monkey's tail. If at a period in life the monkey tail ever quits him, that can be dangerous for the king while he did never know.

When an animal grows bigger, its tail also becomes stronger. Unfortunately, the same may not be true for the monkey. If a monkey loses its tail when it grows bigger, it means a loss of power for the king. If that is indeed the case, the king must lose his power just like the monkey loses its tail. Unfortunately, the king chose the wrong logo and symbol from the beginning. Soon after declaring himself stronger than a monkey's tail, the population continued to pursue him through protests, causing his popularity to decline in the nation. The situation escalated from exaggeration to degeneration, spreading protest and violence from one place to another.

The protesting turned to revolt and violence. As the nation grew hot, it became apparent to the king that the monkey would no longer live with its tail. Although it was never a desirable outcome for him, the king was forced to relinquish his rule, losing his throne and power. Now is the time for the population to calm down and cease their anger against him. The king lost his kingdom just as a monkey loses its tail. He was removed from power, and his sibling brother was chosen to replace him as the new king. The brother who will take his place is the one who has chosen the quality rooster as his logo and symbol.

As for the dethroned king, he had chosen the monkey's tail as his durable and undefeatable logo and symbol. Now, he fully understands that a monkey's tail can never be the most durable and undefeatable logo and symbol. Monkeys are not intelligent enough to be a symbol of responsibility or anything capable of defending themselves. Whether macaques, chimpanzees, or monkeys, it is a mistake to view their tails as symbols of durability and invincibility. These animals may not compare to others who possess knowledge of self-defense or protection against beasts like hyenas and lions. Some monkeys know how to grab a wooden object and use it to fight or kill each other. They may also know how to pick up a stone and use it to break open a bone to access the marrow inside. However, when they are attacked by a lion or another wild animal, they do not know what to do to help themselves.

So, choosing something like that as a symbol of durability and undefeatable was a great mistake for the first son of a king who became a king himself and lost his power because of his mistaken marriage. News for him to know is that he made a grave error, and that mistake cost him his throne. Now is the time for him to sit down and reflect on what the symbol of a quality rooster cock is going to mean for his brother, who replaced him on the throne as the king of the nation. The brother, who chose the symbol of a quality rooster cock as his emblem of durability and undefeatable, is now in power as the king. Following in his father's footsteps, he is utilizing his knowledge perfectly to begin his reign. The people were angry with his brother, so now is the time for him to prove to them that he has enough wisdom to unite them as one nation. And that is precisely what he is demonstrating—a great king who puts his people before himself and rules with respect and dignity, meeting most expectations of what a king should do for the benefit of his people.

Indeed, he is doing everything possible to prove himself as a deserving ruler. Embodying the symbol of a quality rooster cock, he strives to protect and provide security for his people. So far, everyone can agree that he is doing well. However, a quality rooster cock is not lazy; it wakes up early in the morning and alerts everyone else that it's time to wake up and go to work. The only problem is the cock may also be a domesticated bird. The females of that kind, hens or mothers of chickens, lay eggs that hatch into chicks. Some chicks grow up to be female hens, while others become males and gradually become rooster cocks. The females are called chickens. Can a quality rooster cock be chosen as a logo or symbol of durability and undefeatable? Not many people may agree and say yes.

Chickens and rooster cocks do know how to fly, but they are not particularly skilled at it. They also know how to run, but they are not exceptional runners. Those who own chickens and rooster cocks may choose to eat some when they need a quick meat. It's not only the owners who can eat them; other animals like snakes, mongooses, and even domestic cats sometimes attack and eat them. How about other birds from the sky? Even a hummingbird can frighten a rooster cock on the ground, flying strong as a big bird. Now, when it comes to an eagle, what chance does a rooster cock, with its vulnerable back, have against something descending from the sky? An eagle uses the sky to observe everything on the ground, and nothing escapes its attention.

So, the second son of the king chose the symbol of a quality rooster cock as his emblem of durability and undefeatable among wild reptiles, quadrupeds, and powerful birds in the wild. The future will determine whether this was a great idea to choose a rooster cock as a symbol of durability and undefeatable. Sometimes, hunters capture animals and later release them back into the wild. Due to this, some animals have been caught more than once. Undeniably, the king has a symbol of a rooster cock, which is also an animal. Therefore, some strangers mixed with malicious individuals who were close to the king, people who ruled the nation with the king, decided to remove him from his throne and take power for themselves. In this scenario, the external enemies played the role of the eagle, while the internal enemies played the role of the cats. Because the king had the symbol of a rooster cock, the cats relentlessly pursued the king on the ground, while the eagle swooped down from the sky and eventually seized the quality rooster cock, which is the king, from the cats, carrying him away to a different country. At this moment, the king was dethroned and rendered powerless. Now, the cats sat on the throne, while the eagle supervised them from above, believing they were in power.

When hunters catch something alive, they can choose to release it if they wish, or they can potentially cage it. In the case of the king, when he arrived in the next nation before setting foot on land, the eagle would assess whether the quality rooster cock was a mere rooster or something more. Perhaps the eagle himself respected that aspect of the symbol, the word "quality." You can easily defeat a regular rooster, but not a quality rooster cock. Therefore, the eagle would reserve the quality rooster cock for a different nation, just as a hunter might put what they catch in a cage. Even though the king was not on his throne, neither the cats nor the eagle truly held the kingdom firmly. Of course, one can win against or scare a quality rooster cock, but because it is not an ordinary rooster, one should never be overconfident in themselves as the ultimate victor without facing difficulties. Sometimes, a hunter may catch prey but fail to handle it as a personal gain.

After all, maintaining power becomes increasingly challenging. Finally, the quality rooster cock is brought back to his kingdom and reinstated on the throne. This happens with the strong support of his people, who dedicate themselves to the return of their king after a long struggle. The cats grow weak, and the eagle realizes that they need more allies to prevail completely. So, the king apparently prevails over the cat and the partner eagle, even though some of them are his own people who have turned themselves into the most vicious individuals in the entire world, influenced by external enemies. Eventually, the king seems to have prevailed, though this is only apparent. People in the nation always say that when an eagle misses its prey, it may look back to see if that moment could still be profitable for him. The eagle may continue its battle until it can secure a real prey, and whoever it is will ultimately become its victim. If it's a simple rooster, the hunt should be over. However, if it's a high-quality rooster with exceptional qualities, the word "quality" is hard to prevail against, of course. But if you truly want to be the last, then keep it that way.

So, immediately after the king sets foot on his land and is reenthroned as the king of his nation, he informs the cats and the eagle that he is not only a high-quality rooster but also a landslide. Now they have a bit more to ponder. After all, if it were you, you might not describe yourself as a landslide, because when a landslide occurs, both good and bad are swept away in the same direction. Everything must undergo mass destruction and cannot return to its previous state; that is clear and understandable.

In times of stress, an animal, whether human or non-human, might even kill and consume its own offspring. Humans often act under stress, not fully conscious of their actions until that stressful period subsides, which can be quite catastrophic before it concludes. As a human, it's not advisable to do things you don't want to do, because you must never forget that this is one of the most significant things your enemies expect from you as a real defeat.

Now, the high-quality rooster, reinforced by the avalanche of a landslide, engages in combat to push away those who have wronged him, especially the cats who harmed him previously. While these cats continue to multiply and establish disciples at every corner to strengthen their alliance with the eagle, the rooster's quality was reinstated on the throne through various agreements. If the hunters must release their prey, they will do so, learning how to recapture that prey whenever they wish to reclaim it for some reason. The same strategy was applied when the rooster's quality was restored to his domain. It was ensured that he left some areas open for them to enter freely and retrieve him at their discretion.

The hunters might miss their prey for a time, but they don't give up. The rooster is now back as a genuinely distinct king as a result of this disturbance. He faces the challenging task of trimming down the numerous enemies that have spread throughout his kingdom while he was temporarily out of power. Unfortunately, by acting this way, he has inadvertently multiplied the number of his enemies.

At this critical moment, the rooster becomes a real fighter, engaging in fierce battles day and night. Just imagine the multitude of problems that hold the nation hostage, and the people living here have to face numerous harsh situations in their daily lives. They must decide whether to stand by the king's side or choose a different path to apparently free themselves from these problems. With the symbol of the quality rooster cock and the landslide, tensions rise, and a second defeat looms. When there's a landslide, the cats can run over trees, but a rooster must fly away. If the rooster gets wet or refuses to fly away, don't forget that the cats are on the trees, and the eagle is flying in the sky with the ability to see everything on the ground. The eagle can easily swoop down and grab the rooster with its claws, carrying it away. This is currently the eagle's action against the rooster. However, due to the symbol of the quality rooster cock, they may take him away but are not allowed to harm him to the extent that is equivalent to a regular rooster. The law of the symbol's quality prohibits harm, and they can only satisfy themselves by punishing him as they see fit, but not by taking his life. He is a king who carries the symbol of the quality rooster cock. Yet, the eagle continues to fly with the rooster, eventually releasing him somewhere on Earth. So, the avalanche and the land slide with everything. The cats climb trees to stay alive, the rooster is removed by the eagle who cannot eat him, and now the quality rooster cock is no longer on the throne as the king. Instead, he is in a mental cage where the eagle has dumped him out.

Now is the time for him to reflect and understand that the symbol of the rooster cock quality he chose is not the most powerful, durable, and undefeatable symbol. A rooster cannot fight the animals on earth or in the sky. A quality rooster cock can only protect its own life when faced with another regular rooster. Now that the former king is far away, it is time for his younger brother, who chose the symbol of the bone fish as the most powerful, durable, and undefeatable symbol, to take his place. Is that symbol truly a good one for him? Only the future can prove its true meaning. The nation accepts him as their king after facing numerous challenges, as they are satisfied with the way he started ruling the nation. However, the cats are still present, and a simple bone will never scare them. Instead, the cats will be more than happy to lick a bone. The only time a bone can be dangerous for any life is when it becomes lodged in the throat, potentially leading to a serious death sentence. Despite this, the new king continues his work for the nation with great honor among most of the population. From the smallest to the greatest, he is doing his best for the nation so everyone can have a better life. He is accomplishing more for the nation than any previous king. Even though his enemies, who are the real cancer for the progress of the nation, continue to sow chaos in the nation. As the real cats can be the ferocious predators for the small creature, these human cats adamantly refuse to acknowledge anything beneficial for their own nation. They selfishly hoard everything good for themselves, using the poor as tools and shields to protect their interests. They stand against any project that could benefit others, dedicating themselves to the destruction and incineration of structures and other significant physical symbols representing the nation's interests.

Living as true animals, they harbor an insatiable desire for self-gain, disregarding the social well-being of others. They deny others access to electricity, roads, transportation, hospitals, communication, and employment opportunities. In the event of sickness, they insist on suffering in silence until death arrives. Their concern is only to place food on their own tables, neglecting the impoverished. Day and night, these cats lead their lives by harming the nation to further their personal interests. They persist in exploiting the poor, committing theft, violations, and robberies against individuals, homes, and banks. They have no qualms about killing as many people as they wish each day and using inflammatory language to provoke and incite disorder within the nation.

The king's sole and most significant misstep is that he was too moderate in his rule. His excessive kindness rendered him vulnerable. As a ruler, he weakened himself in the eyes of these adversaries by missing every opportunity to seize and confine them where they are supposed to be. Just like a parent who fails to discipline their children, only to have the children discipline them in return, the king's errors can be entirely explained by these cunning cats. These cats have their partner eagle in the sky. Whenever the eagle finishes its meal, it drops scraps and bones to the ground. The cats must then retrieve these leftovers, even though the eagle never discards anything of value for them. Nonetheless, they continue to maintain this peculiar partnership.

When these cats disturb others on the ground while they're on the move, the eagle can easily spot potential prey and swoop down to snatch it. After consuming its meal, the eagle leaves behind hard bones it cannot digest. These bones are left for the cats on the ground, who continue to salvage and play with them. Those who emulate cats should anticipate nothing more than a bone to play with. Perhaps, someday, they might even attempt to toss the bone, but if it lodges in their throats, the game could be their undoing. The eagle, however, remains wise, as his symbol is a reminder that he can see everywhere. He doesn't squander time since he identifies his prey before drawing closer to pounce. He doesn't persist in pursuing losses or even mistakes; he doesn't extend mercy to the cats who provide him with his prey. Sometimes, these cats themselves can become easy prey if not cautious.

Despite all this, the king remains focused on his goals for the nation and minimizes the harm caused by the wrongdoers and the wicked who are mean to him. Even with their visible schemes and snares against him, he has become the king, a good king. However, he lacks a true understanding of what we can call KST (King Self Training). He does not possess enough discernment to identify deceptive people, even if he suspects some of them. He has minimized them like they are nothing and can do no harm to him. Rather than casting them down himself, he lets them deceive him by keeping enemies close and pushing away real counselors and good friends until it's too late for him to act as a king. His logo and symbol, the fish bone, seen as powerful, durable, and unbeatable, reach a point of symbolic significance. While the king faces many enemies, he reminds them that he's like a fish bone that can become lodged in their throat. Of course, that can happen, but the king himself made a serious mistake by choosing a fish bone as a symbol of power, durability, and undefeatable because a bone is a remains of a cadaver. In order to be a bone stuck in a person's throat, you must die first. Strangely, the power to kill has been granted to the king's enemies.

Unfortunately, the beloved king of that nation has been killed by various enemies, including wild cats and eagles. In the middle of the wilderness, his body remains on the ground, like the remains of a meal. They are consuming the king. Is the king truly lodged in their throats? This understanding can only be reached through careful analysis of the reasons behind his assassination. This analysis might help comprehend whether the king's symbolic bone is truly stuck in someone's throat.

Most of the time, the animals that consume meat are not the same ones that eat the bone. Therefore, a bone can become lodged in the throat of someone who did not even kill him. However, if a bone is lodged in your throat, you should examine the cause. If they are gaining control over what they killed him for, they have essentially won his remains. Scientific reasoning may not be effective in such cases. However, if circumstances arise where they are unable to clearly demonstrate and prove their control over what they killed him for, or if they must face consequences, they are making a grave mistake for themselves. This mistake indicates that the bone is lodged in their throats. In order to feel like a winner, one should not be confined physically or mentally, nor should they hide. These conditions do not signify liberty, victory, or success. Instead, they signify self-destruction, destruction of others' lives, and the destruction of a nation. These conditions are curses for anyone involved, they are incurable cancers for the hearts of both present and future societies of that nation.

The real animals will always stay animals with no further changes. But, for the people who are acting like animals, sometimes it is good to think about your offspring. Suppose they don't want to be you, by heart, a person who has the same mentality as you. How will their children feel when they review their stories as their parents? How will their friends perceive them because of their association with you, with the deeds that shine upon them as records? A single water source can produce enough water to form many rivers, and each river can find its way to a different destination, yet ultimately, they all flow into the same ocean.

The three sons of the king each chose their own symbols. The first son, who had the symbol of the monkey tail, lost his strength when the eagle grabbed him and flew away to a different land. He remained there for a long time before being granted permission to return to his beloved land, just near his last days on earth. He may not have regretted being buried in his preferred country, the place of his birth and deep affection. As a former king, he enjoyed the heartwarming experience of returning to his land and witnessing many things before his passing, finding his eternal resting place in the dust. Before that, many of his old friends had the opportunity to see him one last time, just as he had the chance to bid them farewell in his final days. His grave mistake was the woman he chose to marry. The woman married the king to reign, but she never truly married the man the king was. It was like a woman marrying a man for his money, but not loving the man as a person. When that happens, expect your money to disappear like dust over ocean waves or dew evaporating on dry land. All the consequences will be yours because she will build her nest outside of you. When everything you possess is in the nest, you will be left alone as a human, while she transforms herself into a shark beneath the ocean. The regret and heartbreak will be yours forever. Ultimately, the first son of the former king concludes his reign over the beloved nation as a result of his error in choosing the wrong woman, who is ruining the nation. The people of the nation will never forget the kindness of that king, who ended up in a bad situation, not only due to his ill-fated marriage, but also because of the deception of wicked individuals who betrayed themselves by thinking they could deceive the nation alongside their king.

As for the second brother who chose the quality rooster as his symbol of power, durability, and undefeatability, he has a dual history as king. He was removed and restored as king for a second time, only to be removed once again. Was the symbol of the rooster and the avalanche landslide truly a fitting symbol for him? Upon analyzing everything, there seems to be a slight difference between a regular rooster and a quality rooster. Despite being the quality one, even during the second removal when the landslide was with him, his life was in danger, but he managed to preserve his own life. However, when it comes to defeat, he is defeated. He should never have chosen to be a rooster, whether it is a quality rooster or a regular one. There are too many predators on the ground and in the sky. He must beware of snakes and various quadrupeds, as well as numerous bird species in the sky. Not to mention the real enemies, even a hummingbird, a small bird that flies quickly, can be a threat to a rooster on the ground, whether it is a quality rooster or not. Among the notable adversaries are cats and many others. In the sky, a rooster will never forget about the eagle. Considering all of this, if you are going to choose a logo symbolizing power, durability, and undefeatability, selecting a monkey or a rooster, even a quality rooster, can be a mistake. The quality rooster may continue to live as a quality rooster, but in terms of power as a king, it is far away from him. The cats and the eagle are diminishing his power as a rooster, but he clings to his life as a spoil of his quality. Countless misery and poverty have been inflicted upon the people because of those wild beasts, especially the cats and their partner, the eagle.

As for the third son of the king, who chose the logo symbol of a fish bone, did he choose a wise symbol? Many people might say no because a bone is the remains of a cadaver. To be a bone, you must be dead, and after the flesh and skin decay, the bone remains as the only part of the body with no living entity. All of the above is definitely not appropriate for a symbol of power, durability, and undefeatability. While they may have the strength to do some good for the nation, they have all been defeated by these wicked wrongdoers who consistently prevail over the good. If a bone were to get stuck in someone's throat, that would be a very serious matter, but at least it is not a literal bone. Before you decide to cross a frozen ocean, make sure you are not carrying a crippling disease that could paralyze you, and make sure you have warm clothes waiting for you at the shores; otherwise, you may cross the ocean and finally die at the shores.

Two people were walking along a long road when it started raining. One person ran and entered his nearby house, while the other person also ran but did not have a house nearby to enter, then he continued to get wet. If you were in that situation, would you continue running without having a house to enter? Many people would say no, but I believe that if he decided to run, perhaps the exercise would keep him warm until he reached his house. Sometimes wise people do things that are suitable for their specific situation, even if others may not understand their views. If you are not in the same situation, it is better for you to do something different that aligns with your own circumstances. Many actions can be likened to a person traveling by boat over the ocean when a dangerous situation arises. In such a scenario, that person abandons the boat out of fear of what might happen. However, if that person is a skilled swimmer, he can swim until finally reaching the shores. Unfortunately, after reaching the shores, he can remain there and eventually freeze due to his wet clothes he was wearing.

Vehicle Maker Travels to the Planet Sun

Wrong ambitions push a person to build one vehicle that costs him more than a million dollars. Once everyone recognizes the project's merit, the person realizes that the vehicle does not have a switch to start it, the wheels are not mobile, and the engine was built with only one block with no access to anything inside. What a foolish move! Unable to get the vehicle moving on the road, he decided to do something different.

Well, he looks at the sun every morning and he sees the sun in the east position every time. He sees that the sun is continuing to move until it reaches the west. So he said to himself that he has already seen how he can make it to the sun. What he wants to do to get to the sun is start walking exactly in the afternoon and continue to walk all night. According to himself, he should be able to get to the east spot where the sun is the next morning. With that wrong imagination, he takes the road and continues his trip to find the planet sun in the east.

After the next morning, he is not even closer according to what he can see, but he doesn't quit. He said that when the sun goes to the west, by the time the sun gets back to the east, he himself is going to be closer to the sun. Day after day, the same thing is currently happening until he has no more provisions. Then he becomes weak because he is not eating enough food and drinking enough water. Now he decides to turn himself back to his town where he is living. He finally understands what it means to follow the sun. Many things people do are nothing more than following the sun.

On his way back from pursuing the sun, he meets a man whom he believes to be a good man, but rather than that, he is a very bad man. When he tells the bad man about his trip in vain to meet the sun, the bad man tells him that he has been to the sun before and he doesn't need that much time to get to the sun. But first, he should be a person with plenty of money. Secondly, he needs to know what direction to take. The bad man tells the sun pursuer that going to the east is a wrong idea. Instead of going to the east, he must go to the west and wait for the sun to reach him.

Now the sun pursuer believes the bad man and immediately endorses him as a good partner who can help him reach the planet sun. The bad man says to him that in order for him to see the sun and get into it, he must be a rich man with plenty of money. After an appointment is made for the two men to go to the planet sun, the bad man wants to know how much money the sun pursuer has in the bank. This will give him an idea if the sun is going to accept that man to enter its gate. Even though he is not allowed to pay anything on the planet sun, he must be rich in order to enter it.

Now the sun pursuer does not hesitate to tell the bad man how many billions he currently possesses. The bad man says to the sun pursuer that what they must do is go to the bank and combine their money in only one account. That way, they can see that they both have enough money to see the sun. Now the sun pursuer takes the bad man to the bank and puts his account under the name of the bad man. After all, the bad man takes the sun pursuer in the west direction and tells him that he is going to walk in that direction for about seven days. Then, when the sun comes from the east, the sun will meet him there, and he will see how marvelous that is going to be.

While the sun pursuer is happy to go west for the planet sun to meet him, he doesn't know that the bad man is running to the bank and trying to shift his billions to a different bank. This way, he can control that money with no interruptions. However, the bank workers were a little bit confused at the time when the sun pursuer was there at the bank with the bad man. Then the bank workers stop any activity in that account until further notice. Because more information must be received from the owner before the account can be freed. So, when the bad man goes back to the bank by himself, they are going to need much more information to process the transaction.

At this instant, the bad man, who is not able to furnish enough information for that account involving plenty of money, is unable to access his funds. Then the bank calls the security agent and they call the police, who come over and put the bad man under arrest until they can reach the owner of the account, which is the sun pursuer. For over two weeks, they are not able to find the owner of the account because he himself was on his trip to the west to meet the sun. During that period, the bad man sits in police custody as a jail where he is waiting for the sun pursuer to come over so the police can let him see the sun.

Now both men are thirsty for the sun. Because the bad man tried to steal money, he will never be able to follow the sun. The sun pursuer is going to the west for the sun to meet him, which will never happen. The big difference is that whenever the sun pursuer can get back, he will be at his house. So, as for the bad man, he will definitely have to go deeper in prison for what he did to the sun pursuer. He sent him to the west for the sun to meet him, and ran to the bank trying to steal his money. It is not an easy thing for the bad man.

After enduring plenty of misery in the west, the sun pursuer finally turns back to his house and starts looking for the bad man, who is now following the billions. So, pursuer of billions can tell him what mistake he made that prevented the sun from meeting him. However, he has not yet found the bad man whom he thought was a good man. After about a week, a police officer checks up to see if he is alive and learns that his friend was trying to steal his billions. By now, the police officer reports all the important information to the bank and to the authorities that they were searching for.

Since more than a week has passed after questioning the sun follower, he currently reports all the information to the police officers. He recounts how that happened and how much misery he faced because the pursuer of money misled him. After all, the pursuer of money, the bad man, has been removed from the detention jail and transferred to a real prison where he belongs. The pursuer of the sun is ignorant about the sun, but there is no law to punish ignorance if it does not violate any law. Even a dumb person cannot go to prison just because he is dumb, but only if that person does something wrong. Therefore, the authorities have no punishment for the pursuer of the sun but to help him out. He followed the sun and couldn't get into the planet sun, so he came back to his home peacefully. But as for the pursuer of money, that has a completely different significance because when you follow somebody else's money, you have more than one identity to prove. Not only that, you have more than one signature to be done on paper, with no mistake, to be approved, especially for a pursuer of money who is unknown to nobody. Nobody at the bank has ever met that face before, and he plays like he has billions of dollars in the bank. That much, and nobody even knows him. Where did he do his transactions in the past? How is it that he just won a lottery today?

If you want to follow the sun, do expect to see the sun behind at a certain time. If you want to travel with the river, do expect to make a one-way trip under the ocean where you'll be among the sharks. If you want to follow money that is not yours, do expect to find yourselves inside a safe place. Even if someone might call it a prison, that's because people always put money in a safe place like a six-sided unit. It can be the same way if that money is not yours; they will also put you in a safe place for your own protection. Even though some people may call that place a prison, you don't have to worry about it. When you don't want to work to earn it and instead want to steal it, someone must put you in a safe place just to protect those who have worked hard for it from you. That is what's happening to the bad man who followed the sun man's money. They have him in a prison where he doesn't have the opportunity to cause problems for other people's wealth. He is in a safe place where he cannot be out, for anyone who catches him stealing may also kill him at the same time. When you behave yourself in the right way as a good person, others can see you to a great extent that you may never imagine.

Worker Inherits Billionaire

A young man who was not rich but very respectful worked for some wealthy individuals. He never tried to steal or do anything that could jeopardize his reputation with them. His quality weighed heavily in their eyes, and when the head of the family decided to marry off their last daughter before they get old, they chose him as a suitable person to marry her in case they passed away. Now, imagine the young man who was a worker at that place has become the owner of it because he was honest to himself and to the other people. After the parents got old, both of them agreed to put him ahead in terms of their wealth, for the benefit of their last daughter. They were confident he would never deceive them or their daughter due to his established reputation among them. He was approved by them for the rest of their lives. He was a good soil, and the good seed sown in him grew and bore excellent fruits. The young man proved himself to be wise, deserving of such treatment. They treated him as a great man, and his kindness gained him wealth from the rich without spending money. He didn't end up in prison for stealing anything. Instead, he was rewarded for his good deeds. Sometimes, things depend on how you were brought up. If you had good parents who weren't afraid to hold you as a child and support you as a young person, not treating you as a baby all the time, and if you listened to your parents' principles, that would be awesome from the start and would last until the end. If you didn't listen, whether your parents were good or not, you would be a curse for yourself and for those who brought you into the world. It might seem like small matters, but they can lead to great depression in the end.

A little girl was born into a family where her parents always taught her how to keep her room clean to prevent insects like small creatures such as ants and roaches. Her parents emphasized the importance of eating and drinking only in designated areas such as the dining room or kitchen. However, she didn't fully understand or follow their advice. Time passed quickly, and she grew up, became an adult, had a good job, got married, started a family, and saved money in the bank for the future. Everything seemed to be going well as it should be, except for one thing: she neglected to heed her parents' teachings about keeping the house clean and not eating anywhere else but the designated areas. It's never too late to learn a valuable lesson, and she would be the one to remember that.

Unfortunately, the house of this young lady not only housed her family but also had some unwanted guests. These guests were invited by the family's habits of eating wherever they pleased inside the house. Among the many unwanted guests, the roaches were the most prominent. These roaches had infiltrated every nook and cranny, from the homes to the family's vehicles. One fateful night, as the young lady was sleeping, she was awoken by a pair of roaches who had recently tied the knot and were seeking a luxurious honeymoon destination. The couple found that opportunity by entering her ear canal and immediately engaging in their desired activities. Startled and terrified, she woke up in a frenzy, yelling for help. Her husband and other family members awoke to her distress, as she described the sensation of something moving inside her head or ear like a horse or a machine. In a panic, they called for an ambulance and rushed her to a renowned hospital.

Upon arrival, doctors and specialists examined her, and after a short while, they presented her family with a tray containing the culprits: the young roach couple who had entered her ear. Imagine how much pain was caused by these roaches inside the young woman's ear, in addition, a big medical bill. All of this was the consequence of not listening to her parents telling her not to eat and drink within the house, except at the dinner table or in the kitchen.

Now is the time for her to take responsibility for her expenses. Her parents no longer have to pay for her, and she must use her hard-earned money wisely. This way, she can understand the value of listening and trying to comprehend the advice given by her parents. Nobody wants to allow roaches, ants, or any other insects to enter and live inside their house. If it's possible to prevent them, one should take the necessary precautions. If prevention is not possible due to the living conditions, then it's important to be cautious and take steps to avoid unnecessary situations.

It's not as easy as it's supposed to be; some mistakes do happen frequently. However, everyone learns from the mistakes of others and becomes wise enough to lead a normal life. You can laugh at your own mistakes, and you can also laugh at someone else's mistakes, and others will do the same in return. There's no real difference – it's all one world with different human personalities. In the end, with many ideas and perspectives, humans remain humans without distinctions

In the hopes that children listen to their parents, it's important not to be lazy when it comes to keeping the house clean, especially their own rooms. This way, they won't end up paying a large medical bill after allowing newly married roaches to use their ears as a luxurious honeymoon destination. If that were to happen, it would seem like misusing money in the wrong way. The time taken to clean and maintain cleanliness in the living space is much less compared to the time spent working to pay off the medical bill and enduring the pain that follows. It's crucial to be responsible for oneself.

Some events are unpreventable accidents. For example, a boy was playing on his parents' back porch when suddenly he fell asleep on a chair. A minute later, he woke up crying and called for his mother, claiming that he had a horse running inside his ear. His mother rushed over, took the boy, and laid him down. She poured lukewarm water into his ear, and a single ant came out alive. The boy had mistaken the ant for a horse. Such events can occur at any time, especially with children. When people say "you are a child," it means you won't refrain from engaging in dangerous activities unless someone pays attention to you before an incident occurs. You may fall asleep without realizing it until your mother comes and carries you to bed, causing pain as your body is abruptly awakened. This is part of everyday life at that stage. When you skip that stage and fail to prevent certain events for yourself, others may view it as a bad habit or attitude.

Two Brothers are Outlaws

Two brothers were living in a great nation. One of them enjoys going on trips to other countries, even after getting married and having plenty of children. This doesn't matter to him. So, traveling itself is not a problem, but what can be a problem is what you want to do when you travel. Is what you feel like doing good for society? Is what you think you could do in violation of any laws or against your own well-being? If you don't know, just take a seat, sit down, and listen to your bad ways until you understand what is wrong, once and for all. During a good summer, one of the two brothers travels to a country where he wants to enjoy his wonderful summer. However, in that country, according to the law, if you are a married person, you must stay away from any other respectable young person. Scamming, lying, duping, or deceiving a young girl, you can go to prison for the rest of your life. Of course, that is what it is.

That young man should have been aware of the laws before, but he just thought it was something he could fake and walk away from without facing the consequences. When the outlaw man sees a beautiful young girl, he feels that she is the girl he wants for himself, even if he does remember that he is married in a different nation. He presents himself to the young girl as a person who is not yet married to any woman and tells her that he really wants to marry her soon because he has never been married before. The young girl asks him to meet her parents, which he does. When the parents of the young girl ask him about his parents, even though he knows his parents are already deceased, he tells them that his parents are alive and currently living in the same country where he resides with them. When the parents of the young girl ask him to present his parents to them, he calls his brother, and they scheme a plan for his brother to talk to them over the telephone and pretend to be the father. His brother assures them that his son has never been married before, and he will be more than happy to see his son make the choice to marry someone he loves. He stands with his son, supporting his desire to get married soon. After all that beautiful conversation, everything seems okay for that man, especially after his brother confirms that he is the father of his brother. Now the man is granted access to the girl's parents' house, but he is not true to himself. He only wants to take advantage of a beautiful young girl, seizing his opportunity to do so. After spending a significant amount of time at the young girl's parents' house, he leaves for the country where he lives. He feels like a big winner because he deceived a young girl and her parents, disrupted her life, and planted a scar in the hearts of the family.

As he departs for his home country, he leaves them with the hope that soon his parents and he will return for the marriage between the girl and him. They wait eagerly to see him come back with his parents for their daughter's wedding. However, time passes by, and the news is not sweet at all because they don't even receive a telephone call from that young man or his father. Whenever they try to make a call, they are unsuccessful, and no one answers. It takes a couple of months before they can be sure that the man was a scammer, already married, and has grandchildren. Now, you cannot imagine the bitterness of that family. They have no other course except to find a way to apprehend these scamming brothers who pretend to be good people. It takes many years until both men forget about what they did, and that family finds closure. It is many years after one brother made his trip to the country, without considering the death penalty for a married man violating a young girl. Suddenly, he is grabbed by law enforcement and taken straight to prison without a chance to contest. At that point in time, there is no news for his family, as they want to know where he is. After a week, the brother who pretended to be the father decides to make a trip as well, just to find out what happened to his brother. Unfortunately, he faces the same fate upon arrival.

Eventually, the two brothers begin to understand and believe in the law. Not only that but they also respect the law as they should. The only thing is, it is already too late for them because they will never ever see the sun again. They are imprisoned so deeply that the light of the sun cannot reach them. Chaos ensues, and when the wife of the violator man hears the news, she is immediately struck by a heart attack and dies suddenly at home. That helps them understand why some people always say, "Animals with tails don't cross fire." At that point, those who are considered animals do not even make it themselves. The wife, like a tail, catches the fire as well. It is a great lesson for everyone who believes they can go somewhere in the world where people don't know them and do whatever they want, mistreat others, and ultimately evade the real consequences of their wrongdoing.

The brother who presented himself as the father should have been the one to discourage the other brother from engaging in such actions. Rather than doing so, he contributed to helping his brother in that mist and shameless action. That error could have been prevented if there had been some self-respect and honor for others. Both men have families, wives, children, and grandchildren. But they are not wise enough to know that they should be a better source of strength for their families. What happened to them is not an accident; it is disorder and a lack of respect for others. Despite everything you may learn from your education, there are some parts of social education that you should receive from your own family. You cannot live without those parts. If you don't learn them from your parents, friends, or associations, you will eventually learn them from the city authorities when they finally put you in prison. If you still refuse to accept those lessons, they will be forced upon you. If you are finally unable to embrace this education, they will keep you in prison forever because it is not possible for you to live in society without those lessons. You may have never attended school, but you should have some social education to live as a human being. Otherwise, you may spend most of your life in prison, if not forever. That is exactly what has happened to these two brothers who are now going to prison forever. And you can imagine what their children, who still need parents to help them, will become in life. All of this has resulted from their unclean actions. Finally, friends and family must let go of their memories of them and focus on doing their best with their own children to prevent the repetition of such a horrible situation.

As the two brothers say their goodbyes to friends and family, each time they were involved in wrongdoing, they were only waiting for that day to leave without saying anything more. When it depends on you, of course, you should fight for your life. But when it does not depend on you, there is nothing you can do to protect yourself. When it does not depend on you, it means you grant others a priority over your own life, whether by breaking the law or trusting someone.

Visitors Trapped by Fire

A couple of people were visiting a valley between two different high mountains, with a river as a border that separated them. At this point, the two visitors were accountable for their own lives. While they were watching, they saw a terrible fire ignite seemingly out of nowhere, and the intensity of the fire was overwhelming. Each of them tried to run and find shelter by climbing a mountain they believed they could reach the top of. As they ran, they lost sight of each other.

At the pangs of the fire in the middle of the mountain, one of them sees that the fire has already spread to the four corners of the mountain. Eventually, the strong wind is pushing the fire from the bottom of the mountain to the left and to the right, surrounding them like a circle of fire. Feeling trapped, they believe it's time to stop and wait for the circle of fire to close in on them, risking their lives or falling into the hands of hostile people.

They decide to stop going up the mountain because there is more smoke rising over the top. The fire continues to burn on the sides, but at the bottom of the mountain, it burns a little slower. Now, they must decide which way is the best to try and escape, realizing that they don't have a tunnel underground for that. Over the sky would be easier, but there might not be a helicopter available in the area at that moment for that kind of event.

Maybe there was only enough time to run, not communicate, after all, both must rest themselves on the mountain while waiting for the fire to subside. At the border, the two people walk slowly enough to check and see if there is any spot for them to get past the fire without any injuries. That may never happen; it will take a lot more than you can imagine because the land has become hot. Even the rock is producing smoke and the trees are continuing to burn with live fire so they must wait. At least there is a good possibility for them to save their life than to be in a place with no hope as the two brothers who deceived the young girl. It's better they wait for the fire to be over, even if it takes a few days.

Thankfully, a good amount of rain overnight comes to the rescue of those two people sleeping underneath some tree branches. They were not panicked at this point because the intense fire had passed them and they just had to wait for the hotspots to cool down. They continue to walk along the fire border, looking for a safe way out. This time wasn't easy at all, they must pay attention to every path they take because the fire remaining on the ground is covered with rubble and tree ashes. They face challenges and detours, thorns, and thistles, but finally, they arrive back to the riverbank of the valley where they were at the time of the event.

The hunger for food was still lingering, but they knew they couldn't relax until they were sure they would make it safely. At that point, they needed to follow the river shores to find a possible crossing point. The river was not suitable for crossing on foot, so they had to use their judgment and follow the river as it flowed towards the sea. This was the wisest course of action to ensure a successful escape. They knew that if they reached the sea, any small fishing boat would be able to rescue them, guaranteeing their survival and their return to their respective towns.

After miles of walking through dangerous terrain, they finally reached the sea, where a fisherman with a small wooden boat helped them by taking them to the other side of the river, traveling along the sea. It was a wonderful moment for them as they were rescued and brought to the port, where the authorities took over to ensure their well-being and provide them with food, as they were very hungry. This was the most important part of their rescue from the valley mountain.

Fortunately, the two individuals returned safely to their families after being trapped in the mountain during the terrible fire. They may feel weak and possibly sick, but they must take care of themselves. The most important thing for them is that they were rescued and able to return home, giving them a renewed lease on life.

Beware, because sometimes your life can resemble a visitor trapped in the middle of an intense fire. You must endure numerous problems and exert great strength to finally escape after a long period of struggle. If this happens, you must visualize your rescue, no matter how long it may take. You must believe that you will make it out and stand on your own strength, deserving to live like everyone else. You may never imagine a reason for a prolonged period of bitterness, enduring various problems or circumstances of war. It could even be a family trouble, more complex than others might believe.

While trapped on the mountain, the two individuals slept under some tree branches to protect themselves, especially during rainfall. Though they sought protection from the rain, they knew it would help extinguish the fire. They had to be wise enough to identify hot areas and remnants of the fire. Their wisdom guided them from beginning to end, which is why they now bear no physical scars from the fire. They were rescued as strong survivors. If you find yourself in a similar situation, think twice before letting your emotions or a different event push you to expose your problems to someone who may leave a lasting scar on you, even after you've overcome the situation. The two individuals did not carry any scars because they relied primarily on themselves when no one else was there to help them.

Yes, sometimes you need assistance, but it's important to believe that you can help yourself without causing harm. Not many people may be willing to help you without leaving scars. When the two individuals reached the sea, a mariner came to their aid. Similarly, when you help yourself, the right kind of assistance will come to you. You should not be the one desperately seeking help when a situation arises. The help you need will be waiting for you at a door you passed by without knocking, and that help will recognize you and follow you.

The two individuals didn't even cross the river as they had hoped. And to leave the dangerous area they must follow the riverbank until they reach the seashore. Indeed, what you focus on can be a signal for your path, but it doesn't necessarily guarantee the comfort you desire. The remnants of the fire posed a potential danger to them as they wisely navigated through the rubble until they left the ashes behind. Whether it's a moment of darkness or what you consider to be the worst, a better period will erase the bad period. With caution, you need to beware of yourself, that way you should never be erased at the same time as the bad moment.

A situation can always affect you, but you should never let yourself become part of that situation. By dissociating yourself from it, you can navigate your way out. Don't mix with any bad situation, even if you find yourself caught up in it. The two individuals didn't become part of the fire or its ashes, which is why they were able to return home. Being apart from your situation is the best way to escape it. By proving and affirming to yourself that you are not a part of it, you can move forward towards a brighter path.

After the two individuals helped themselves reach the shores, a mariner came to their aid and took them where the authorities could provide them with some immediate assistance. If you believe in yourselves and help yourselves in various ways, others will be willing to help you as well. However, you can always go to a water source to draw water and do as you please. But a water source will not come to your house unless managed by extraordinary means of science.

Whatever problem you face, there is a solution somewhere, like a water source. You just need to understand the science behind obtaining it; otherwise, you won't be able to enjoy it like others do.

Pour some water onto the ground and follow its path if you think you're clever enough. Go where the water goes if you can, but if you can't, it means you lack the necessary knowledge. Water itself will not accompany you over the mountain; that requires scientific understanding. That's precisely why birds leave the branches and ground to find water.

If someone is allergic to dogs and you know this, you would never allow your dog near them because they dislike it. However, if you have a dog, don't harm it because of a friend. Your friend may eventually leave you, but your dog might choose to die for you, becoming your last friend if you find yourself abandoned by others due to poverty. Whether you believe it or not, rescuing yourself from a situation holds more value than being rescued by others.

A man found himself too weak to escape from a ditch in a canal. He saw another person nearby and believed that individual could lend him a hand to get out. He yelled for help multiple times, but the person turned away as if they hadn't heard anything. However, a different man who did hear his cries came to his aid and helped him out of the ditch. Thanks to this assistance, he avoided the ditch becoming his pit and the possibility of dying. In this situation, the only way he could help himself was by calling out for help, which he did. The person he initially thought could help him didn't respond, but someone else who was nearby came to his rescue.

Life is not something to give up on easily. Many people will fight until dust for their life, just like a man who gets bitten by a venomous snake. Despite the fear and panic that overwhelms him, he doesn't allow it to stop him from finding a way to prevent the venom from killing him. In a desperate attempt, he manages to swallow the snake to about eight inches before the ambulance arrives to help him. Whether his strategy was effective or not remains unknown, but at least he tried something to save himself. Whether it was to prevent his own death or to retaliate against the snake that bit him and caused him to lose control, the bite was undoubtedly painful because any form of pain is unpleasant.

In another instance, a man had a wart-like growth resembling a fungus on his finger. When he experienced intense pain, he used a gun and shot at the growth. However, the authorities put him in prison for doing what is illegal.

Imagine being in pain, but self-control is important to prevent you from violating the law. Making the wrong choice to end non-stop pain is not recommended by any law whatsoever. It is not wise to try to solve a problem in a way that involves harming oneself, such as shooting one's finger for any reason, as it will result in losing the finger permanently. It is not the right approach.

There was a man who injured his finger at the side of the fingernail, causing it to become unsightly like a fungus. It took a long time for the finger to return to normal, and it was painful during that period. However, after that time, he couldn't see any differences between that finger and the others. All his fingers looked the same. Imagine if he had chosen a senseless procedure, thinking it would be beneficial for himself. If you miss the road, you are not lost yet; just avoid taking any shortcuts when you're unsure where they will lead you. Exercise patience and follow a straight road until you reach your desired destination. Your time is valuable when you make progress, and it is wasted when you make no progress at all. Fight bravely and save your own soul from ruin; then you will be considered a hero.

Never believe that you will die in the mountains. There are always potential ways to bring you out, and it is not in vain to make every effort to survive. When your strength is diminished, think of it as your last chance to make a final effort to escape in your own way. People who do not know how to swim should avoid venturing too deep into the water, as they are aware of the danger of drowning. It is good to be cautious, but caution alone does not solve the problem or offer a better solution. The better solution is to learn how to swim and be cautious at the same time. By doing so, if you happen to find yourself in the water, you have a better chance of survival because you know how to get out of the water. While not everyone undergoes training for potential events, if such an event does occur, your knowledge and skills are what you are going to use to find a way out.

No one sets sail on the ocean without proper fishing equipment like a hook or a net. It simply doesn't happen. If, by some accident, you find yourself in a similar situation where you have no other option, what would you do to survive? It has happened before, even if you are unaware of it.

Two people were fishing when a storm intensely pushed them into the middle of the ocean with their small boat. The strong winds removed the guides they had to control the boat. Now, with nothing to steer it left or right, they didn't know if the ocean would take them to land or not. All they could see was the vast ocean and the heavens. For years, these two men involuntarily lived over the ocean. They had to keep their palms open in the water, and when a fish swam by, they caught it and ate it to survive. During rain, they tried to catch as much rainwater as they could for drinking. They lived with that knowledge over the ocean for years until one of them passed away. Then, finally, the ocean itself carried the other one back to land after years of this situation. Despite the wind sweeping out everything they had to help them survive, with their strength and knowledge, they did what they could to endure. One perished after years, but the other one returned to land to continue a life he fought hard for, carrying it as his trophy.

Sometimes, even if you live on land, your situation may not be different. If that's the case, remember that if someone can make it over the ocean and finally triumph, then why not you, living on land? No matter how tiny your possibilities may seem, if your eyes, heart, and mind work together, your brain will pave a path for your heart to lead you to a happier person. When your possibilities seem small, live as a tiny person, sleep as a tiny person, do everything as if you were tiny, especially your heart, mind, and brain. Eventually, you will grow like a small seed sown in perfect soil and produce many good things beyond your imagination.

Many things people fear about are immobile and will never come over to hurt them. However, you may be the one leaving your safe spot and hurting yourself on something, to them that means you are the one who hurt them, but they are never the one to hurt you. For example, a snake lived inside a stone cave with only a few openings to get out and find food. As the snake grew too big to get out of the cave, it only had enough space inside to survive. So, how would that snake currently find food to eat? You may be surprised that many other small creatures, such as rats, mice, lizards, and more, wandered inside, becoming food for the snake. Most Of the time they think they are looking for food. Instead of looking for food, they are going to be food, fed to the snake prisoner's obesity. Unfortunately, obesity can also happen to people. That's why it's essential to be wise in managing yourselves.

As for those creatures who approach the snake, if you were to ask if it's something they could avoid, "yes" may be the right answer. But sometimes, mere curiosity can make people look unwise, just like a mouse entering a serpent's cave. Some people swim without any safety measures among sharks in the ocean or swim in waters inhabited by crocodiles for no reason.

Once, a woman was visiting her friend who lived by a man-made lake. When the visitor saw an alligator by the lake, she wanted to approach it. However, the woman who lived there warned her not to, as she had seen the alligator catch a deer just a few days ago. Ignoring the warning, the lady questioned the alligator, saying, "Do I look like a deer?" While touching the alligator, then instantly, the alligator grabbed her and pulled her underwater. She quickly released herself, thinking she could escape while making a comment and moving slowly. Unfortunately, the alligator made a second trip and pulled her back underwater and killed her. She was not new on earth, nor to that country, more than that her friend told her not to do such things.

The big snake cannot get out of his cave, but many other creatures enter his cave so he can eat them as food. Sometimes, human actions are not different from animal actions. That lady did not return to life. Humans must use reasoning, not animals. Even though her friend said no to her, that was not enough. Sometimes, people who travel with kids tie them up to make sure they can hold that responsibility, so they tie themselves to their kids. They don't want the kids to go anywhere that could cause them troubles. If she had been tied up, maybe she would have lived longer than that unexpected dead period. As for the alligator, it just knows how to look for food, it has no reasoning to understand the importance of any life to each other. Hunters hunt animals and take them home to eat as food. Humans are also on the animal menu. That is why when a human finds himself at a wrong spot at a wrong time, they can be harmed by animals. Always be cautious in any dangerous spot in the world that allows curiosity, and if you take your family wherever you want whatever happens as wrong is what you should expect. A good driver will be more cautious with other people in his vehicle, that way he can prevent himself from any reproach the others could put on him for being negligent at the event something happens to any one of them. It is more important if you don't have anything to explain at all. Whenever you don't have the bad news, it is the good news, but when you don't have the news at all, it is a good time and a perfect moment.

Young Man Travels in the Village

A young man was living in a city not far from a village that didn't have a good reputation due to the attitude of the people living there. At a certain time, his vehicle broke down not far from the entrance of that village. Scared, he entered the village, thinking he could take a shortcut to get out faster. However, there was currently no outlet whatsoever in that village, with only a two-way in and out. The young man, who didn't know anything about the roads there, continued to wander from no outlet to no outlet, until he could no longer find the only existing way out. It became night, and he continued to walk through the village, encountering plenty of people at every corner. Each way he tried took him directly to a house, some being gambling houses, and some were houses for dancing and festivities. He never talked to anyone, but their stares made him feel scared. He spent almost a full night walking around. Eventually, he found himself facing a fence he couldn't cross. Others, like blocking walls and canals with water and rubble mixed with mud, made it difficult for him to find his way out after his multiple attempts. He encountered a man with his wife, someone he believed had passed away before because he had never seen him in the area where he lived. Seeing a familiar face gave him hope to find his way out. He thought a man who lived in that village should know how to get in and out, but when he approached the man, he realized how much it cost to enter a place where you don't know your way around. The man immediately starts thinking and puts both his hands on his head, indicating he had no idea how to help the young man. The man said he could only guarantee that they could walk together to the gate in the morning, but he had no memory of how to find the gate. The village had too many streets without names, making it too difficult to give directions to the right place. Now, the young man is worried about getting out of the village. He thought that anyone in the village is bad enough to kill him without giving him a chance to spend a night there. Now, it's up to him to decide whether he prefers to continue walking through the village while his life is in great danger or to stay at the house of someone he knows until morning. That way, they can guide him out to the gate.

Most of the time, people who have never been to jail or prison believe it's built only for thieves and big criminals. However, imagine you are traveling to a place where nobody knows you, and you lose your identity, whether someone else stole it or not. You cannot find your identity immediately, and you are in a situation that will last for more than one day. You are in a town where no one knows you. Where do you think the authorities will put you while they work to resolve the situation? Of course, they will put you in jail or prison, whatever they call it. If you don't want to sleep in jail or prison, you can continue to walk inside that place or room until they let you out, but that won't happen until your problem is resolved. You entered due to someone else's actions, and you will not get out by yourself. Someone must put you out. Although they may have to wait for your problem to be resolved, someone can guide you out but may not be able to explain how to do it until you get your identity back so they can identify you and set you free. The man in the village tells the young man that he can walk with him to the gate, but he must wait until morning, and he cannot explain how the young man can get out.

Morning time can be a period when you're able to get back your identity, which is your reason for being here. Then you will be let out. There was a well-known person with a good reputation who was also a public educator. One day, trouble occurred, and he was arrested by the authorities. He was supposed to spend a night in jail because the event happened at night. However, he declared to the authorities that he had never been to jail in his life, and if they dared to put him in jail, he would kill himself there. Many people could understand his feelings, but if an event happens, authorities must put someone in a place designed for anybody who becomes their guest until the trouble is cleared out. So, the guard said, "Yes, we are taking off all your clothes and putting you in here." They placed that person in the jail cell without his clothes, in a free empty room where he had nothing that he could use to harm himself. Of course, he didn't spend a complete night in jail, but by the time his people came to get him out, he was already in the room with nothing to wear.

Never put in your mind that prison is only for thieves and criminals, or that a hospital is for those who are not healthy, or that poverty is only for the lazy ones. What can take you there might be invisible to your eyes until you are there. It could be an accident or an event, an error of yourself or somebody else. Despite that, the result will not skip you because you are the one currently in the circle, whether it is excellent or a curse, sweet or bitter, it is your cup to drink. If you cannot prevent yourself from drinking from it, the only thing you must do is to prevent it from affecting your life forever.

Most of the time, the same road that good people walk during the daylight to do what is right is the same road that bad people own overnight in the darkness to do their bad actions. People sometimes say "wrong place at the wrong time," but it is also true to say "good place at the wrong time." Nobody goes to the hospital because hospitals are for those who are sick, and that can be true, but the hospital will never turn into a bad place. At your bad time, you will need to go to the hospital. You might say a prison is a bad place, but it is the only hotel built for thieves and criminals and for you too, when you make a mistake or when someone causes you to make a mistake. Therefore, the place itself is not bad or wrong, but the time you went there was the wrong time for you.

If you put a wild animal in a cage or a cave because that animal was not born in captivity, it will take some time before that animal can become tame and manageable for you. It's the same thing for a human who never got into prison. But there are many things to consider. Humans are mostly educated and understand what can happen, why things happen, and gain knowledge to know when and how to get out of a situation. If that possibility is not on the table, you have a reason to consider whether you are sitting on your own red line, or someone is sacrificing you, or putting you in the row of holocaust. That is undeniable. That is the real reason you should never minimize what humans can do as wrong to their resemblance. If you've never seen someone tie up his dog or another animal, and suddenly an event happens to that person and the animal unfortunately stays there to see itself perish gradually, second after second, you must believe that there are humans who perish every day in similar conditions because somebody wants them to die. A small kid sees his parents throw him high up and catch him back, which makes him believe his parents have no limits. He currently believes that even if he dies, his parents can bring him back to life. That is why parents must watch over their children because children are open to taking any kind of risk, believing their parents are there to protect them without a limit.

Because of some lack of knowledge, many people are following the graveyard and believe a friend will be able to rescue them if they fall in a pit. Unfortunately, your friend will not follow you to the graveyard to give you a hand and rescue you. A wise person will never enter a deep ocean with the mindset that his friend will rescue him, especially if they don't know how to swim. Like a village with only one entrance and one exit, many situations in life have only one way to get out or just one solution. Sometimes, a solution may not even depend largely on you. In such cases, you must understand that your problem may not be dependent on your effort to be resolved. Whether someone rescues you or guides you out of your problem, you just want to get out of it.

The young man was learning from his parents that the village was not the best place to go because of the bad residents, but by accident and error, the young man made his own experience. Even though it may be different, it's never good to try for the second time if you learned that it's a bad place.

A mosquito was telling his children not to approach humans, but if a human is sleeping, baby mosquitoes can draw something from the human just enough to fill themselves. One day, the baby mosquitoes were disobeying their parents and went to a human's habitat. When the human saw the baby mosquitoes, they opened their palms and each time the baby mosquito came closer, they clapped their hands together, slapping them to kill the baby mosquitoes. But instead, each time they clapped their palms, the baby mosquitoes flew a little bit higher, thinking that humans were greatly welcoming and applauding his visit. Now, the baby mosquito believes that his parents did not tell him the truth when they said that humans hate mosquitoes and that he should never go near them. Sometimes, when you really don't know, many bad actions can appear as excellent acclamation for you. Before your eyes, poison can appear as medication, and a snare can seem like a beautiful bed for you to rest. When someone curses your name, you will laugh and be happy, but when someone honors your name, you will be angry and mad. Because, like baby mosquitoes, you might not be able to discern anything in accordance with what you were taught by your parents, and your actions may suggest that you believe you are smarter than your parents, acquiring knowledge and experiences different from them. However, that same action may soon take you to a pit deeper than you can imagine.

Now, the baby mosquito is just waiting for some wind to fly on a one-way trip to visit his human friends, where he was honored and applauded by them. Yet, who can stop the baby mosquito from traveling to humans, where he can draw his flavor drink from them, and at the same time, they will honor him and applaud him? Now, the wind is happening, and the baby mosquito is flying away to the human habitat. When approaching the first human encounter, the baby mosquito tries to give him a kiss, but the person hears the voice of the baby mosquito and puts both his palms together and squashes the baby mosquito. With nothing to lose, the baby mosquito's ticket was purchased for a one-way trip to visit his human friend. What a loss for the baby mosquito, who did not listen to his parents about humans! The baby mosquito thought he was smarter than his parents, and that kind of thinking currently cost him his life.

Whether the parents lose a baby or not, the baby has their own life. The same applies to humans; a human can, of course, lose a child, but a child has their own life. After all, parents are always responsible for instructing their child and equipping their children with enough principles as best they can. If, at a certain time, they minimize those principles, they will face the consequences of that disobedience without you accounting for anything. If the kids lose their parents, it is a loss for them, but the life that is lost is the one that no longer exists.

This means that while parents can raise you as a child, you are the only one who currently lost your life. In some cases, parents are at fault. As an example, consider a family with six sons living together in one house. The father is an alcoholic. Right from the time the youngest son died suddenly, the examiner declared that the boy died from poisoning, and the parents claim that their son was poisoned by a neighbor who gave him some food. Now they have five sons in the house with them because they lost the last boy. A second time, the oldest son dies suddenly under the same circumstances. Who should be blamed as the real cause? The parents say somebody poisoned their sons. And of course, their sons are dying from poisoning. If so, why couldn't they stop them from eating the neighbor's food? The third time, another son falls to the street, and the parents accuse a different young man, saying he poisoned him. Fortunately for the accused young man, that son survives and is released after doctors find that he was drinking rum alcohol, which is not good for his system and causes his heart trouble. Now the young man who was accused must be released, and the young man who drank alcohol is warned not to drink it anymore.

Now it is easy to understand how the first death and the second death happened. Both were caused by alcohol, but their parents continued to say they were poisoned by the neighbors. The alcohol was a neighbor to them, but definitely not a human neighbor. Instead, it was some bottles of alcohol, which was rum of all kinds. That is not all; sometimes, people die due to alcohol consumption, but only time and events will tell the truth. Years later, the son who went to the hospital, this time falls on the street and dies immediately. His mother and the rest of his brothers, who are still living, declare that the son was poisoned by eating at a restaurant. However, neither the mother nor the brothers remember to mention that he drank alcohol, which could have been the cause of his death. The father had already gone down that same road. Not too long after that period, the other three brothers who were left behind also died, one after the other, leaving behind only one son from the original six sons of that family. All of them could have continued to live if they had been told by their parents not to drink alcohol and had listened when other people warned them against it.

The smallest brother who died first was a small boy, probably due to negligence on the part of his parents, who did not pay attention to where his father placed his bottle of alcohol. The boy drank some, and they mistakenly thought that a neighbor had poisoned him. This tragedy occurred when the baby boy was four to five years old, before both parents were deceased. Only one of the six sons is still alive.

Wrong people always blame someone else when the harvest they sow turns out bad. When parents refuse to see their child crying when they should cry, then they will make the parents cry, and they should know that a child can cry for fun, but older people cry for serious matters. Discipline the children for their own benefits, and maybe they won't make you cry. As for that family, burying five out of six sons before themselves as parents is not fun.

When the enemy, which is alcohol, sleeps in the house with these children, and your mind is focused on somebody else, that is a serious mistake for the family.

Unfortunately, you cannot undo the deaths of the children due to the negligence of their parents, who sometimes mixed alcohol with other drinks and put them on the table. The children had no idea about alcohol and didn't even know if the drink contained any alcohol in it. The kids were purely innocent but victims of the negligence and carelessness of their parents. You cannot do much for the past, but you can prepare for the future. You must not repeat the past and continue with principles that you need for yourselves and raise your child to the best of your ability to prevent any unnecessary events that can remove your joy forever. You don't have to worry about neighbors if you can keep your child under your control better than you do for your pet. Make sure you teach them how to stay within the limits of your property so that a neighbor will not worry about you and your kids. Learning how to stay in peace is truly important.

Neighborhood Cat

One day, a person sees a cat bathing itself with its tongue and asks the cat, "Why don't you use some water to make it easier for you?" The cat answers and says to him, "One of you humans dropped one of my grandparents in hot water. That is why they taught their offspring not to ever use water anymore." Imagine, because a cat fell into hot water, all cats in the world absolutely want to avoid putting themselves in water unless a human takes them there. For cats, because the water was hot and burned their old parents, water can be the same at all times. To prevent a repeat of that bad event, the cat prefers not to bathe itself with water. After all, the cat wins over other animals for keeping itself cleaner.

The big difference between a cat and other animals is that a cat does not need any water to keep itself clean. Humans must use water many times a day to keep themselves clean. If you try to be like cats, the parasites will eat your skin very fast and cause you itching and infection. All these can happen to you by neglecting to keep your hygiene and raise your risk of developing more diseases and finally being killed by parasites. If you refuse to use water to clean your skin and your clothes like a cat does, but not how a cat does, that will turn out bad for you. Use water many times a day to clean your house and your kitchen before roaches take over your kitchen.

A cat is burned in hot water whenever the cat sees fresh water, he thinks that is the same water. If a cat knows how to prevent a repeat of an error, people must do better. A person follows a road he did not know before and gets into a ditch where some other people must rescue him hours later. Would you ever follow a road if you don't know where that road is going to take you?

A family has a young girl who is about twenty years old. On a remarkable day, before the sun arises in the morning, that young girl tells her parents she is not feeling right. So, when the morning opens, the father catches bad news of a neighbor whose wife dies suddenly. He is going to help them, and the mother of that young girl has an appointment somewhere, so she is going. The twenty-year-old girl is abandoned at the house while she is very sick and passes away before both parents come back home. When they come back, they find their daughter dead in the house. If you have a family and you are a responsible person who understands that your priority is supposed to be your family, will you leave a member of your family sick without care and go somewhere to help someone else? Anybody with a good heart who witnesses that kind of situation will learn a lesson. As for you, if you ever get hurt by your error, you must learn from the cat burned in the hot water and then respect even fresh water. That should not repeat in your case. If anyone in your family, especially those who are under your responsibility, has a situation that should be your priority before you should see anything else. If you lose some money from your pocket, after some time you will forget about that money. But losing a daughter in that circumstance, that scar will never erase from the heart of a real human. The blame of your own conscience will be too burdensome for you to carry anywhere far in life. It is the same as cutting the head of a young tree to stop it from growing anymore. Now you have a life reduced to a bad example. If an event like that is repeated in a community, that will never be a great thing, not only for a community but also for the entire population. Do not minimize what the cat does about the water; what happens to him today would not be the same to happen to you tomorrow. Don't let the same enemy beat you twice.

A woman was leaving a newborn baby alone to carry medication to a neighbor who was sick. By the time she comes back, her house is catching fire, and her newborn baby is burned to death in the house. People must never leave a baby alone in the house to go somewhere else. But when a situation like this happens, whether negligence may play a part in that, everyone else must take a lesson like the cat does, that way you can prevent that from repeating on you. When a severe accident like that happens, the one who has the most pain is the same one who is carrying the most blame for his errors. The greatest solution is to keep in mind all the principles you need to prevent yourselves from that kind of situation. If you are supposed to carry your baby with you, that is what you must do. Don't take any risks as a chance. You cannot repair a destructive error, and you must answer questions from others forever, whether you feel low or high. Even those who made some greater mistakes than what you eventually make will question you, and you must answer them. Cats don't have to answer any questions; they prevent that from happening to them.

A cat was living in a neighborhood, and that cat always visited a family who routinely put some food for the cat in the backyard every day. The cat made his own schedule to visit the family's backyard every day after sunrise. However, for about a week, the family couldn't put out any food for the cat because a member of the family was sick and at the hospital. After several days, the cat didn't find any more food in the backyard. So, the cat decided to come closer to a window to satisfy his curiosity about what was happening. By coincidence, someone inside the house was crying because the person at the hospital had passed away. The cat heard the news and said to himself… "Cat don't have any head to carry that kind of box that humans use to bury their dead. Whenever you hear a human crying like this, that means another human has died. Now, before they ask cat to carry that deceased person to the graveyard, cat must find a place to hide himself very deep. After the burial service, cat will come over to help them by crying and saying, 'Cat sees your pain and is feeling the pain too! Cat is sorry! Cat is sorry! Cat is sorry! Now, Cat wants some food! Please, people, more food!'"

If you have a cat, then you know that if you have someone die, you must tell the cat he will not be the one to bury the deceased. That way, the cat might not hide until after the burial services. In the world, many people are playing cat games with others. You can hear the words, "If only they were knowledgeable of your situation." Believe it or not, most of them are hiding behind your problems, and after enjoying themselves with what they cause you, they come over with a clean deceptive appearance.

As for the cat, everybody can see that a cat cannot carry a casket to a museum or a graveyard because dogs steal all the cat's food, and the cat doesn't have enough to sell to make money to pay for a funeral. Besides, the cat already has too many problems in his head, and he doesn't want to hear people crying for his help to bury their dead. The cat requests a festival of contests where a big competition is going to take place to find out which animal is the cleanest. From the start, the dog says he is the animal who is going to win the big prize, the cat says he believes he can win, the goat says he will win the prize very easily, and the pig says that those animals who don't even want to see water cannot win him for the cleanest. There are four animals among every animal that believes they can win the big prize. So, time will tell the truth. The competition is taking place in a large park where varieties of animals are welcome.

There is a second competition for those who can prove they are tough enough to rule the wild. But every beast is going to be put to a trial while they are not even known. For example, at the four corners just before you can get to the park, there are some pools of water and some expired meat they placed there as a test to see which animals are going to bathe in the clean pool water and which ones are going to take a bath in the dirty mud pool water, and which animals are going to put their noses or tongues on or even eat the expired meat.

For sure, the cat will not be any of those because the cat doesn't want to meet with a dog where people are not present to separate a fight. The cat says he already knows; if he stops there, he might remove the dog's face with only one slap. He doesn't want to do that and get in trouble with security, so he won't stop outside until he reaches where the humans are. So, the cat runs straight to the park. The dog was worried behind when approaching the four corners. There were two dogs in the front row, both dogs raising their noses to the sky and taking in the smell of something. Both dogs then skip to the side of the road and see some expired meat, which they won't have enough time to deal with because the competition time is near, just a few minutes away. So, both dogs roll their bodies over the expired meat as if they were taking a bath. The dogs think they are doing better when they get back. Unfortunately for the dogs, the security sees them and stops them from there and reports them inside to the judges of the contest competitions, where they proclaim and declare that the cat is already the winner over the dog. Without any contestation, the dog is lost, and the cat is the winner, which means the cat is the cleanest animal, according to what the dogs have done during the trip, proving that the dog is not a clean animal at all, despite some good actions the dog sometimes does, especially towards humans. But at this time, the dog cannot win against the cat for the cleanest.

Dogs have been put outside for not being social enough to be among a society of humans. Now the cat, who doesn't like to hear the noise of the festival and has already prevailed over the dog, climbs over a flat roof and watches the rest of the activity for that competition.

Now, the second great opportunity is for the pig and the goat. So, time will prove the truth between the goat and the pig. If you want to guess, maybe you can win, but just wait and see who is going to win. The goat and pig are in a competition to see which one is the cleanest animal, so now they are approaching the four corners with the pools. There is a clean pool and a dirty mud pool, as well as some expired meat in view of the pig and the goat. The pig says he is the one who will win because the goat is not friends with water, but pig, whatever water has more aggregates, should be the pig's favorite bath. If that strategy can validly win the pig over the goat in that contest, only the judges might say that.

Now, at the four corners, the goat jumps straight over because he doesn't want to touch the water he sees by the corner. When approaching, the pig starts by putting his nose at the side of a pool, as if he is laboring, and that was at the clean pool. But a few seconds later, the pig shifts over to the mud pool and lies flat on his stomach, rolling over in it. Now, the pig gets out and heads straight to the park where he is stopped by security, who tells the pig he is too dirty to make it inside where the clean animals are. The pig starts to understand he is not clean and shakes his head, saying, "Ron! Ron! Ron!" While the pig is saying that, the dog is lying behind a tree not far from the road and steps out immediately to ask the pig, "Who dares to call 'Ron! Ron! Ron!'?" A big fight opens between the pig and the two dogs who are so upset because they lost the competition. Now the pig is also a loser, but the dogs just want to win a part to satisfy their anger. The dogs receive some cuts from the pig, but the pig is seriously wounded by the two dogs. Some animal hunters were in the wild when they heard the voice of the pig and the dogs, so they approached and captured the pig, taking it with them. Both dogs run away. There is nothing over the cat and goat, who are in the park receiving their winning prizes and gold medals. The cat and the goat are enjoying themselves with the others who are going to continue the competition. Some of them are for aggressiveness to dominate the wild.

While the competition is happening, a complaint has been filed for a couple of dogs who are hiding behind the gate of the park, the losers' dogs. They are turning back and waiting for the cat and goat to attack them for the prizes they are winning, but these dogs have been put outside. Now, security calls the animal arrest, and before the festival is over, the animal arrest controls these dogs and puts them under arrest. This time, the dogs are taken to captivity inside cages, and there are no more chances any time soon to take vengeance against the cat and goat for their winning prizes.

As for the pig, only the hunters know what the pig has turned into. Dogs are taken to captivity for their bad actions against the winners of the competition.

Now, a different competition is happening between a big animal who has a great reputation, the lion, and a simple ant. Some say an ant is just an insect and cannot compete with an animal and win in that competition. The competition is to determine truly, without any detour, who is the most influential and respectful beast in the wild. You may be surprised to see that the competition is between a lion and an ant. The lion said he cannot understand why the ant wants to enter a competition with a king like him. The lion says it will take him no more than a second to step on the ant and eliminate it completely. As for the ant, it declares that it believes it can win the lion in just a few seconds. Who among these two animals at this instance is right about its confidence to win that competition for real? The time arrives for everyone to see who is currently going to be the big winner of that marvelous competition.

The organizer put the ant and the lion in a very small area together where all attendees are watching to see what will happen between the two. It looks like the lion forgets about the ant a little bit and quietly lies down, while the ant, who was on the ground, makes its way to the corner of the lion's eye and gives the lion a couple of bites. At this point, the lion wakes up and rapidly wraps his eye with his paw. While doing that, the lion's claws scratch the corner of his eye, and the lion immediately feels a difficulty to see. He leaves that area and asks for help because he is scratching his eye and has become a little bit blind.

The judges ask the lion what made him scratch his eye. The lion answers and says he believes he was bitten by the ant. The judges ask the lion if he is sure that happened to him. The lion replies and says yes, he is sure that it happened to him. And the judges take his word and ask the lion if he now knows he is the loser of the competition. The lion says no because he had not yet met with the ant. The judges say to the lion, "That is why you were there, to meet with the ant and to prove you are the most dominant animal in the wild." Now the lion bitterly regrets his situation and is discouraged about what happened to him. The only thing is, whether the lion is confused or not, there is no messiness between loss and win. With his tail so low and his face down, the lion walks outside as a big loser, and the ant prevails over the lion. This time, the lion does not know how to win against the ant in that competition. Each time the lion faces the ant in the wild, the lion is the one to run away for his life, despite the lion being smart enough to eat the elephant. The ant, as an insect, is beating the lion for real. The ant becomes untouchable in the wild as the most dominant beast, and every other beast must bend down their back and follow their knees to the ground. The ant becomes the wisest in the wild and also the most respectful. No other animal or insect wants to face the ant if they don't really want to be an irreparable victim. So, the ant proclaims victory over the lion, who pretends to eliminate the ant in a few seconds, unfortunately not even knowing when he was defeated by the ant. If you naturally don't know if you are lost, you will not know how to win. A mighty one should never accept to compete with a lesser one; it looks like you are lying on the ground like the lion did, believing you are agreeing, and by your error, the leader is taking your title of greatest, and you will become a shame for yourselves among everybody else.

At a certain time, big people eat at a table; if some food falls on the floor, that food must be taken to the trash. At that festival event where all kinds of animals are present, the king of animals in the wild, who carries the name lion, is lost in that competition. The ant is unafraid for his life to do what he is supposed to do to adopt a big name despite his physically small appearance but wise enough to defeat a mighty lion. After all, the ant is declared the winner of the competition to find out who is the most dominant in the wild kingdom. The ant is the winner, despite its name "insect." Whoever attended that event, including the judges, learned a great lesson for themselves by seeing the ant win against the lion in that competition. All three competitions of that festival are out with winners and losers, followed by some events where losers get upset and try to create some troubles for the winners. Some of them do not return to the same places where they are from. The pig is going with the hunters, and the worst troublemakers, the dogs, are taken to captivity in cages.

Among the winners, the cat, who beat the dog, takes his trophy and goes to enjoy himself. Goat, who defeated the pig, takes his trophy and goes to enjoy himself. In the last game, Ant grabs his trophy and goes to enjoy himself. Physically big or small, the winners are great among the attendees. Their physical bodies do not stop them from winning. Some may be physically small, but they are wise enough to win big.

Among the losers, only the lion has a chance to return safely to his fortress where he lives. The dog is no longer free, even though dogs may never win in a fight against the lion. But as many of you know, dogs never estimate any dangers when they want to fight. They might die a few minutes later after the fight, but if they must kill, they will kill if they can and die later. If they must capture, they don't really need to know in advance. As for the lion, he is going peacefully with his tail low behind his legs and his face bowed down while he steps outside of the festival park. As everybody knows, this is the lion that they proclaim as the king of animals in the wild, so they still have a lot of respect for him despite his loss to the ant.

Now, the competition is over, and there are many things to consider. If you want to be like a cat, many people may want you at their place because you live with peace and prevent unwanted creatures from entering their spaces. Cats are adorable for that. If you are considering a dog, despite their many bad ways and attitudes, some people love dogs for their loyalty and serious commitment to protecting and defending their owner until death. Dogs remain worthy friends forever. Whatever dogs do, if it's not severe, they will not kill the dog, even though the dog might remain in captivity forever.

If you consider a pig, no one might encourage you at all to try that competition. Whether the pig wins or loses, the pig will finally be the loser, as you know that the pig will never win for real. If a pig gets involved in a fight, they may not take the pig to the hospital after the fight; instead, the pig might be taken to a butcher shop. If captured by a hunter, believe that the pig might be fried anytime soon. People say that pig is not clean, but when people clean the pig, it will taste good and be a good meal for the clean people. Like the pig that was attacked by two dogs behind the gate of the festival park, the hunter gave that pig a good clean bath for its last time. It won't return to where it came from. Pig doesn't like to travel with humans because they will stop it from taking a bath whenever it can find the opportunity.

When the pig puts mud over its body, that protects and prevents it from dying due to the heat of the sun. Whoever is not happy to see that criticizes the pig. Now, if you consider a goat, that's better. Goats win for their beautiful, clean bodies, even though goats don't like to take baths. Their natural bodies match their attitude, as they don't want to get close to any mud that can get them dirty. Like cats, goats clean their bodies with their tongues. A goat can win, but never let go into the wild without a farmer's control. Goats win today, but tomorrow the farmer might make big money with the goat, or the butcher will turn the goat into what people want the most at the marketplace, the meat market. Therefore, even if they apparently win, goats will later be losers when taken to the butcher shop.

The goat is different from other animals who want human food. If a human bites a piece of food, the goat will not eat the rest of it. Goats don't like humans to breathe or speak close to them. They are afraid of the smell of human nose or mouth and will never use a brush. Goats don't like dealing with water either, but if a human spits somewhere or sneezes, the goat will not eat there and will run away immediately. They are allergic to the human breath and the odor of human mouths.

Interestingly, goats like fire even more than dogs. If there is a fire, and the goat doesn't have enough sun or if it starts to rain, the goat will prefer to stay close to the fire instead of getting wet. Goats are also attracted to beautiful grass if they can find it. In terms of cleanliness and beauty, goats are considered winners over pigs, even though neither goats nor pigs may end up at the butcher shop all the time.

Now, if you consider a lion, that's not bad. Even when a lion is defeated, it will never be an easy prey for others. When it is considered lost, it will go with peace because it likes peace. Whether the lion wins or loses, it will return to its habitat with no fear, and its title as the king of big animals will stay with it among the creatures where it lives. The lion lost the contest to an ant, but no other beast can dare proclaim a complete victory over him. The lion must respect the ant and the ant's family and their territory. Ants are winners like a king. A lion can either die in a fight or due to old age, in captivity, or free in the wild.

If you are considering the ant, just put in mind that any other small creature can eat the ant, but at the same time, none of them can stop and fight the ant without being defeated and running away. The ant fights, kills, and eats any existing life, whether big or little. So, ants are the most feared and respected creatures, even when their appearance and the name "insect" do not imply anything big. Any other creature that sees an ant will run away from it. Ants make their wise reputation as hard workers, strong fighters, and supporters of their queen and protector of their colony stronghold. They never give up and are highly respected by greater or lesser beings. There are many ways you can be wise like an ant, and that will be great. But if you are as small as an ant, you can enter many places like the ant does. But be careful; even a sparrow can throw you into its throat, which is not good.

Many privileges can be offered to anyone who wants them, but do not be surprised to see that so many others refuse those privileges as they mean nothing at all. An ant can be at so many great places, of course, but walking on the ground for anyone else to step on is not great; it is a completely different matter. But ants are the greatest example for the lazy people, they are hardworking and wise enough to know when a hurricane is near. Before the hurricane arrives, they have already stored plenty of food in their nest or caves and sealed the entrance door. After the water is over, the ants open back their homes. Ants build their nests in a way that rainwater cannot disturb them, and even fire cannot easily kill them inside the nest if the fire is not strong enough to render the earth hot enough to kill them. Ants not only beat the lion but also win over many people who call themselves human, although they do not behave humanely, especially in the way they manage their families.

There is a man whom every other person in his city calls a great man. That man has enough food to share with many others. He has almost forty women and more than one hundred kids and grandkids. He owns many villages, but the way he builds those living places means nothing at all. When it rains, kids and women are about to face tons of misery; sometimes houses fall over them, and neighbors must come over to unstrap them from the rubble. The only better life for them is a sunny day. More than that, if a kid or a woman is sick, the only chance that sick person has is to stay laid down until they die. The man will have some friends take the deceased to a cemetery and bury the body. And immediately forget about everything. The worst are the children when a woman dies and leaves them behind with the man, who will not take care of them. They will follow their own mothers to the graveyards, and that man only wants some kids who are already big enough to work for his other women. But when sick, the sick one must die quickly, then go to the graveyard, and then everything can be better for them. If a woman becomes sick during that time, he is too busy to go where she is abandoned. If there are any survivors, it is by luck or the favor of a super neighbor. That tyrant who everyone else is afraid of is not comparable to an ant. But a father crab, if a father crab doesn't take care of his baby, when strangers do something bad to his kids, it looks like they are doing him a favor. All he wants is the women. But when they are sick, things turn out to be different; if a kid is sick, that has no importance to him. Hunger is not so sweet; most of the women are trying to be somewhere they can afford some food to feed their children when they can have some. But they are not premeditating what kind of person that man can be as a father for their kids and what kind of protection he can provide them.

Sometimes, if you do not enter the river, you will never know how deep it is, and then to enter, you must know how to swim to get out; otherwise, you will be considered dead and swept away by the water. When a parent who was everything to the kids deceases, more misery is added to the world because misery itself does not exist without a body, which is a person. When someone becomes misery now, misery does exist, but when that one person who is misery dies, the misery disappears until someone else becomes miserable again. That is why people don't worry about a miserable one because they are currently afraid of misery. If you are a miserable person, don't be surprised to see many people you have known before, when they see you now, they will hide themselves because they are afraid of misery. From then, you must understand people don't need you anymore in life. The only entity that never refuses anyone is that entity they call death. Wherever you are, whether rich, poor, or miserable, death will not refuse you; it will accompany you when no one else will, and when life has refused you, death will take you.

Abortion of Child

The ant's power can always justify where the human superpowers disappear. When all help is over, when all pretended protections are freed from the views. Those who are killing their resemblance by words and by physical actions are always ignoring the greater good of a kind heart for the whole world, including themselves and their offspring, who can be the most beneficiary.

A tree can exclude a small branch for a reason, and that tree remains formidable. But when someone is destroying a branch of a tree, that tree's life is reduced, and the tree becomes stressed. That stressed tree will die because it will remain under stress for the rest of its reduced life. There are similar situations that often happen to some people, whether you understand it or not, that is the pure truth that cannot be erased by mind or opinion diversity.

The same problem that happens to the tree also happens to a woman who is having an abortion, removing and killing a baby in her womb, inside her belly. Any woman who does that immediately has depression and stress for the rest of her life. Based on the circumstances of life, some might live for a long time, but for those facing many difficulties, different kinds of depression can shorten some lives at any time when stress rises to a high point.

A tree may not have reasoning, but the life progression can be stopped due to the gravity of stress. A person can reason and have some insight that can always remind him about any past thing. What you are doing, whether it is good or bad, will follow your path. When at a certain time you slow down, your actions will surpass you, and at that time, you might be scared and depressed enough to die.

During the rainy season, a friend of yours may encourage you to buy a horse because grass is everywhere on the land, and you don't need protection from rain, wind, or sun for a horse. It's a happy and good time. But during the dry season, you will not see your friend helping you nourish your horse. Your friend will stand so far away from you and say he was seeing that for you, as if you were a fool who doesn't know what to do. It's up to you to hear and understand why the pigeon calls the chicken "cousin."

Honestly, some people encourage you to do certain things because they have a great interest in it. When chickens have corn, pigeons call them cousins. When the corn is over, chickens must stay on the ground, and the pigeons fly high in the sky, resting on a high castle and paying attention to the chickens on the ground. The pigeon laughs and says, "Chicken thought the pigeon was a cousin to him." The pigeon laughs and says, "Come where I am now." When the sun goes down, the pigeon becomes hungry again, and at that time, the pigeon knows his cousin, the chicken, has some corn he can swallow before going to sleep. Everything they want to do for you is because they want to help you. That is only to your own interest, so why should that not be done for free too?

Okay, be aware of what you are supposed to do and what you should refuse to do, or think twice before you do it. There might be something you will regret later in your life. Stand the trial in your own interest, not only destroy yourself for the profit of your convincing person. As for those persons who do abortions of kids, who could be the only ones to help them tomorrow, not only are they destroying the kids' lives, but they are also losing that help from the kids, and they are planting in their own bodies an eternal problem that will take them to a graveyard prematurely, which is horrible for them.

You are afraid of somebody and not afraid of doing what is worst; you must think twice before you do anything bad because of somebody else in life. The greatest error a person can make in his life is an error of being afraid of others. There is a plant in the garden somewhere in the world, it is an "obey" plant. That plant can crawl over rocks and sand like sweet potatoes' branches. If you come close to that plant and talk and tell the plant to die, that plant will play like it dies for real, and every leaf will immediately fold and hang, balancing like everything is over for them. If you don't tell, you can just touch that plant, and all the leaves will appear dead. If you don't know that plant before, you might think the plant is dead for sure. But when you come back next time, you will find it alive. Then, if you do the same, that plant will obey you and die for you. Every branch will fall flat to the ground, every leaf will fall as if dried and rest on the ground. Many people call this plant a "shaming plant," as it obeys anybody, but when you leave, that plant has the ability to get back to its normal life. The big difference you can find between that plant and a human is the ability that plant possesses to get back to itself without any damage. A person doesn't have the ability to repair a mistake without paying serious consequences. So, a person cannot and should not obey every word they hear, not because someone went to the sky, he has an obligation to know about the stars, and not because he did not go to the middle of the ocean, he doesn't know how to swim.

Most of the time, when a good talker talks, everyone laughs, but everybody knows that they are just trying to make him happy, and they are not going to imitate him. Sometimes a simple smile can reduce a long conversation that is not important. A smile sometimes prevents arguments that can cause major problems, like that plant, which is a simple plant but has the ability to fake its death to prevent any confrontation. Humans should listen to everything and execute only what is right, what has the best interest and must not have any repercussions as a bad side effect or bad at all. Something might not be true as a person pretends it, but it might not be harmful to anyone, or it does a few good things that are better than anything else that is wrong and dangerous.

War Solution Miracle Paradise

Two countries that share the same border engage in a non-stop war for a very long time. People are displaced all over with no mercy, at a certain time a man who was granted a chance to talk to both parties goes ahead and tells the same word to both parties. After all, both parties agree with him, and they cease fire and restore great peace for both nations who were destroyed by the long-time nonsense war. That strategy he used was not true, but because it was not a bad idea, it became a perfect strategy to protect many people from death and used as bridges for those who are fleeing the nations because of the war to get back. What did that person say to their leaders to make them stop the war? He says to everyone, "There is going to be a miracle between the two nations, and that will happen by the border between your two nations. The leader who is more worthy will be the one who rules both countries." So, to be the worthiest leader, you must stop the war and build a park for your nation close to the border and continue to maintain that park really clean because in that park, a tree will grow. When that tree arises, both countries will become a paradise, and that paradise must be ruled by only one person. So, between the two leaders, whoever does better during this period will be the one who is qualified to rule both nations as one nation.

Both kings want to be the worthiest one to rule both nations as one nation. Now they have stopped the war immediately and currently engage themselves in building the two most beautiful parks you can never imagine. After each king completes his park, now everyone who is passing by says that country looks like a paradise. Both kings cannot wait for a tree to arise in his park and for him to rule both nations as one. In the meantime, people in both nations live with a wonderful peace among themselves. What a beautiful moment for two different parks face to face, not far from the border, waiting for the peaceable people who want to relax themselves a little bit while they memorize the harsh moments they left behind them. That is clear evidence that they are currently in a paradise compared to the past of both nations.

But their kings are waiting for the miracle to come, so their jealousy and thirst for power can be resolved once for all. If you are the one who caused the problems, you must believe in something, whether it is true or false, but it appears to be a good deal for everyone who was facing the thirst of the bad situations. Each king wants to do a million good actions per day so he can be the most qualified to rule both nations as one nation. From hostility to perfection, imagine what can change a human heart completely from the worst for something really good. This time is for something good, for the kings know they have a reason to stop the war. But for the people of the nations, they are only feeling a super release from the weight the war imposed on them. So, everyone tries to find a paradise in the sky, but an ordinary man establishes a paradise between two nations who did not want to stop the war, which was destroying both nations. Time passes by, and as for their kings, they are both getting old and never see themselves as rulers for both nations. But they have a great time hearing everyone say these countries, which were destroyed by wars, are now tasting a moment of paradise. That gives them great insight to strengthen themselves more and more until they both die. Both nations remain in peace thanks to a great person who put a plan of paradise and park miracle in the minds of both kings.

From the kings to the nations, by the time these kings are getting old, they are passing their secret to the people of the nations. That way, they can continue to wait for that paradise to be established. So, now everybody wants to live with peace without doing anything wrong. That way, they can evidently maintain that peace they benefit from and guarantee a perfect hope for the miracle paradise to come. Even though they might never see that miracle, rather than live a harsh life among a destructive war, they are now living with peace. As dreaming of war is a curse, many people in the world think hope makes living better. These two countries hope one day that miracle can be possible because they have skipped the war to a durable peace among them.

The reality is, if you believe in something, the action of everything is dependent on you. If that something is bad, your actions will be bad actions, whether what you believe is true or false. If you believe in something good, your actions will be good actions, whether what you believe in is true or false. The plan of a miracle paradise worked well in favor of these countries, from the interest of the kings to the interest of the people of the nations. For the generations to come, they will keep it as a serious principle to follow, like an engagement for them to keep up to date with the two nations and live well. That is what it means for them and what it will be for their offspring after them, like something normal in life, and that is a perfect way where nothing has ever been better.

If only those kings had known that the plan wasn't real for themselves, no one can ever imagine what they could have done. But despite the untruth, as they were expected, it works for everyone living in these nations. They could never ask for anything better. After all, these kings were making a lot of wars in the past. So, thanks to that man who made the miracle plan for paradise, both kings are currently at peace as two great kings. After these kings died, the two following kings who succeeded them followed the same procedures to eventually see a miracle happen and one of them was the most qualified to rule both nations. That plan was invented by only one man to stop the former kings from destroying both nations with war. It became a covenant to keep both nations in peace for as long as people who are from the kingdoms of both nations live with it for the benefits of both nations.

In the darkness, without a bed to rest and sleep, people are sleeping while they are existing, whether standing up, sitting down, or lying on the ground. If you are in a state of silence, everyone is in silence. Therefore, if your nation is not at war, other people can always say you are at peace. On the other hand, if your nation is at war, you might hear people say you are at war, even if you, as an individual, never go to war. That is why the solution for the two countries was so important to the people of both nations, where their young generations might never face the same situation but only must learn about the history of the past situations. That is the best way they can make their own efforts so they will not be swept back to that bitter pit that swallowed so much of their parents in the past.

Boy Story

A boy had two hens, they were young chickens. A big brother threw a rock that eventually killed one of the young chickens. The other hen stayed by herself. Another bad day, an eagle flying dived from the sky and grabbed the other young chicken and ate her. Now the young boy lost both his chickens. So, between the two destroyers, which one is to blame? Not too many people might want to blame the eagle because the eagle is just looking for his food, then he grabs whatever he can find at that instant. As for the big brother, can he justify his reason to throw a rock at that hen and kill her? Only he himself knows what is inside his heart. As for the young boy, he is the only one who is suffering the double loss and annoyance. Now, it's not so sweet anymore for the boy to continue to have chickens. So, the boy decided to buy himself a pair of goats.

The boy feels better with his two goats, which he takes care of every day before school and after school. Unfortunately, one day, the boy's big sister was running, and one of the goats was surprised and got so scared that the goat jumped to his death accidentally. Now the boy has only one goat for him to take care of before and after school. Another event suddenly happened when one morning the boy realized the only goat left disappeared from his place. That goat had been stolen by somebody and never came back because the goat was already killed and eaten by those bad stealers who grabbed the goat. For the second time, the boy must suffer a different double loss of his two goats. This time, it appears to be an accident in the case of his sister. As for the stealers, they are doing something bad they should not do. Bad or better moments, the boy is growing, while the problems are navigating around, the boy is growing bigger.

After those losses, the boy tries something that is apparently not visible to people's eyes and decides to invest his money. Then he becomes an entrepreneur and opens his bank accounts with his small sister's name on every account, as a person he trusted. The boy thought there is nothing to be afraid of to put his small sister's name on his accounts. The small sister, who was already a gang member, while it appears difficult for the brother to know anything about that. She schemes with her gang partners and fakes ways to steal everything, including all the money from the banks, and turns every account empty. What horrible actions!

That looks very ugly, but sometimes it's hard to understand what can hide behind anything that is not visible to your eyes to view it. If you can learn from what happens to anyone you know, that can help you to prevent many dangerous situations. It is not because of them or so, but the reality is a point to understand and keep in mind. If a road is a no outlet, just do not enter it. If you feel like your brothers and your sisters are not in your way of life, don't say they are your brothers and sisters, then you must trust them.. If you continue to see it that way, when it is too late, you will not be able to do anything with your life, if by chance you are skipping with your breath of life as gain.

The boy has had no luck with any of those brothers and sisters. The first loss was caused by a big brother, the second loss happened because of an animal, the third one was an accident by a sister, and the fourth one was the action of theft. You may ask, why should the fifth horrible action be done by a small sister? Maybe because the boy loves them, but people you know as your enemy are not often the ones to harm you for what you have, as your wealth will not stay for them. But your brothers and sisters are the real ones for you to pay attention to.

If you are among those who are jealous of everything you do, they can destroy your activities and even harm you. They can catch you like a fool while you try to help them. That is why so many of you are victims because it's hard to believe your own brothers and sisters can be your worst enemies, especially when you are the only one trying to help them. After you die, whoever witnesses it will learn a lesson for themselves not to end up the same way too. If you die, everything will belong to them, and they can waste everything faster than you want them to.

Sometimes, it's people outside the family who control their life and encourage them by force to do such bad things, but most of the time, people are born with bad ways that develop and grow in their minds, directing them to become what they want to be. Some of those bad behaviors can be detected by a good parent. Sometimes, when parents detect that bad attitude in a child, good parents often fight those bad ways to help the child. Some parents win because they take that case seriously in advance and understand the seriousness of it. However, some parents give up, and their kids unfortunately become criminals.

Believe it, every wise person can tell you that if they want, they can just watch your small children's actions and tell you if your children need special attention to prevent them from becoming criminals. Unfortunately, nobody is going to tell you that, whether they see it or not. Maybe a rare good friend may tell you to be careful with that kid because they want him to behave well. That's why sometimes a good friend might tell you that a kid is a kid you need to pay more attention to. Nobody wants you to say they can predict what your kids are going to be. Most of the time, you hear a wise friend say to you that is a kid you can count on. If that person has any intelligence to understand what is good, don't you think that person can understand what is wrong also? Sometimes, the father wants to correct the problem in the child, but the mom opposes. Sometimes, the mom wants to fix the problems, but the dad opposes. Too late is when the river has already sprayed over the land. Some people who know how to raise good kids can put food in the same plate for more than one kid and see which kid needs more attention. This kind of approach is serious, and any weak parent will never survive with a kid from that.

You must be serious if you have a belt because your kids must not be crooked because of the times you refused to use that belt on them. If you do so, you are a weak parent, and even the kids sometimes understand that their bad ways are the result of the parental weakness in disciplining them. Parents who are supposed to discipline them but fail to do their work. Sometimes, it is good to separate the rotten orange from the good one. If somebody doesn't want to be good, you need to avoid the good ones from going the same way with them. Avoid them from participating in the same entertainment, avoid some conversations together, and much more. If you have a feeling that someone can grab you before you enter the mud, you need to avoid entering it. If you do enter, you will be washed before you sit, and if you refuse to be washed, that is not in my power.

As for the boy, who is no longer a small boy but has been deceived by a deceptive sister, even though life is short, sometimes you cannot prevent mistakes, especially when they involve a person you had trusted. Robbery and fraud are the strongholds of the wicked. But a free person, with honesty and wisdom, enjoys the fresh air of truth. Life continues for those who are constant and believe they can work hard to survive until everything is over for them on earth. Indeed, they contribute to making life on earth beautiful.

A tree produces so many fruits, and some people come and pick every single fruit without leaving even one. Because they carried all the fruits, many people think the tree will follow them so it can continue to produce fruits, but they never see that tree move from its spot. Nevertheless, those people are the ones who, at each season, continue to come back to the tree to harvest more fruits. The reality is not about how much you can carry, but how much you can produce for yourselves and others who look up to you. People who eat more are not necessarily the ones who work harder, as some may not work at all and still consume the hardworking people's food. These same individuals may also wish for the hardworking people to die so they can seize everything at once and create misery and theft, as abundant as the sands on the shore. They never sleep at night and only rest during the daytime when security is at its lowest, that is when they strike to destroy the wealth of hardworking people.

Like a tree that produces fruits every four seasons throughout the year, hardworking people can produce enough for themselves and to share with those in need. In a country with many cities, each city is large enough to secure the needs of its inhabitants. The people must know how to cultivate the land. They must know how to plant grains and other nutritious crops to survive. They should produce enough food and learn how to harvest and store these harvests for themselves, securing their sustenance until the next season arrives.

The country comprises more than one hundred ninety active cities, and from the beginning, it wasn't perfect for the people in every city. However, the people in each city must make their best efforts to put food on their tables. With this in mind, many cities engage in competition to become the best city which is currently not dependent on the other cities to feed themselves. So, there are some that cities trail behind, either unwilling or slow to learn how to become self-reliant. Instead, they travel to other cities to seek help, leaving their families behind. This has become a routine and a kind of market for them, and some never return to their respective cities. Now, they must work day and night for the people of other cities to survive, abandoning their own families in the process. When the head of the family doesn't come back to take care of his family, this kind of attitude has plunged these cities into deep difficulties and miseries day by day. While the other cities may want to help, they must first view things properly. With more than one hundred ninety cities, if only a few face misunderstandings, what stops them from learning from others? They travel to many other cities, where they should, of course, see how people work hard to render their cities prosperous for all of them who are living there. The same spirit they cultivate to stay in other cities should motivate their minds to find a way to establish a solid foundation for their own cities so they can produce and harvest what they cultivate themselves.

Mother Hen with Her Chicks

A mother of chicken was sleeping somewhere on the ground with her chicks when they were small. After more than a week old, she starts training her chicks to sleep on the trees. Before the time to sleep, she is going with them to a low tree to give them some training in accordance with the way they are going to sleep on the trees every night.

From the first night, one chick stays at the ground and cannot get onto the tree. She has sixteen chicks all together because one is not able to fly onto the tree, she flies back down and calls her fifteen chicks to come back to the ground, and she turns back with them to the place where they are sleeping every night. The next night arrives when she flies on the tree, she walks at every part of the tree that way the chicks must not fly too far away from where they currently are at the ground when she calls them to come over.

Now the chicks must fight their competition to reach their mothers; at last, the same chick stays at the ground and cannot make it. That is the second time, so before it's too dark, the mother heads back down from the tree and calls all the other chicks to come back down, and they are heading back to their place on the ground. The third night arrives, the mother of chicks is back to the tree before it's too dark for them to see the way to go. This time might not be the same somehow to every chick. When the mother arrives with her chicks at the tree, she is doing the same process: flying a short way, then making some walk. When she is currently at the spot where she wants them to be, she calls them to come up, fly up, or however they can.

So, for the third time, when she calls, the same fifteen chicks can reach their mothers, but the sixteenth one, which is the same one who failed to make it two times before, is failing again for a total of three times. So, the mother does not get back down for that chick anymore. Worst for that chick, he must return by himself in the dark to find his ground habitat after his mother gives him a final notice he understands the truth; his mom will not go back to the ground this time.

Then you might be surprised what happens on the fourth night. That chick was the first chick to get on the tree, maybe he was eating too much; this time he has lost some weight overnight when he stays only by himself. At a certain time, those cities will be able to do something good for themselves if the other cities let them fight for their own help. Sometimes it is good to say we did that way to help you, next time you too you must do that way to help yourselves. Things to understand, most of the people don't even want you to know how to put food on your own table because when you don't know how to gain food for yourselves, of course, you must come over doing what pleases them; then they can give you a little food each time. That is why year after year the same cities have some of the worst situations.

What do the other cities do? If every city was the same at the beginning, what makes it so impossible for some few to make any progress at all? To live in a city like that, you must know how to survive with what you are producing on your own farm. If you choose to skip your city to work for the others, you must know your family will also be slaves to the city you are a slave to. If you choose to make a farm for yourself to take care of your family, tomorrow your children will continue your projects as a wonderful trace to solidify your city. Whoever lives at the house of a friend might grant a favor of a corner for his child, but whoever builds a house to live with his children gives more sleep to his eyes, and his heart will never fail and be stronger as getting old.

In a country with more than one hundred ninety cities, where everyone has enough land to cultivate, there are no questions about trade, professions, nor specialties. If one or more cities fail to cultivate his own land to survive, and year after year the same city is the one who is searching for help from the other cities. Are the other cities profiting off that lack of their handyman to keep them as slaves? Or is it the city cannot produce anyone at all who can acquire enough knowledge to lead the city to a level where the people can see and understand what can resolve their longtime troubles is for themselves to put their hand at the land and cultivate enough for themselves. And put in mind a day in life, they might be able to help some others. No one might never need anything from you, but if you currently have enough for you, that means you don't have to view the other cities as a supper paradise for you and your family. If they have land, then you have land also, if they can build a paradise, you must be able to build a paradise too.

What you can view in the other cities, the others must view some similar in your own city as well. You cannot continue to be as the late born in the family where your big brothers and sisters are not protecting you, they are grabbing the whole wealth for themselves and dropping you in misery. You cannot be as a person who is let down nor abandoned by the others, but you are among and parts of many cities who existed at the same time in a nation. That is the way mystery is fulfilled under your eyes when your brain and your heart are not ready to explain what you are seeing or reading. Generation after generation, the conditions of the same cities remain the worst, sometimes the other people who are coming from the other cities with special missions to help them with some food, which is good, but some others might say good help coming from the heart should include instructions about how those people in the city supposed to put their hands at the ground and plant enough grains who can produce an abundant harvest for the people in the city. There are people in the city who don't know how to share nor put food on the table for their own family. Whenever the family has food ready to eat, whether meal, breakfast, or dinner, the biggest children put their hands on the whole food and grab the food very fast, and the smallest kids who are weak stay hungry at all the time. The big brothers and big sisters don't worry about the lesser ones; things are sweet for the greatest and bitter for the little ones.

That bad attitude is adopted by every generation in the city. The other cities do understand that each family must have a head who is controlling and directing the rest of the family. If a person is supposed to be the head of a family but fails to do what is right as a leader of a family, and you are counting on your neighbors or strangers to control your family for you, believe it or not, in some cases, your children might never be enough to sit by the other people's animal domestics. Most of the time when you are counting on the others' help, you will never have an appetite to help yourselves, and the others will never help you to a level where they will lose the powers they have on you as a slack person and on your tails.

Only the strongest ones can skip the high walls. A fish who makes a wrong jump from the sea falls into a boat. Instantly the fish can no longer be able to breathe, so someone gets some water and pours it onto the fish, and the fish starts breathing again. Next, that person takes the fish by his tail and his jaw and rests that fish in the water while holding his tail only. The fish plays seriously dead, but when that person releases the fish for good, the fish skips over as fast as he can with high speed.

Sometimes people even need to skip fast to rescue from being condemned as slaves of the others who pretend to be helping but look for their own interest. There is more than one road ahead, never steps to the same path outside. When you don't know how to swim, throw a rope to your friend who is in the waters by accident, and keep in mind you are a person who doesn't know how to swim; never let the waves grab you because of your trust in a friend who knows how to swim. In the locker room, put your items in a safe place where your own hands can reach at all times, whether you are happy or not happy at all.

Those who currently do not possess a signal to wake them up when sleeping, those persons always wake up on time because they are dependent on themselves to wake up on time. But people who count on others to help them have one excuse for each mistake they cause in their lives. A chick was left on the ground for one night by his mother because he did not make enough of his own strength to get on the tree. So, the following night, that chick is the first one to get on the tree.

A real person who makes mistakes only needs to face his trial to put some sense in his mind and understand if a person crosses a river, it is not a miracle but a result of learning how to swim. If you want to do the same thing, before you even try, you must consent to learn how to swim. If a city has enough food, it is the result of good workers; if a family is doing well, that is the result of the good leadership of the family head manager. If a country altogether is going smoothly, that is the result of some good leaders who are accepted to be guided by only one leader who is chosen to be the guidance of a real nation.

The earth we are living on is the only planet we can know as the planet where life is possible because the earth maintains its possible distant atmosphere between the other planets and continues its routine non-stop speed, rotation, and turn, which are resulting in the possibility of life on earth. If the planet sun is not burning, every life on earth is because both planets are keeping their positions perfectly between each other. Everything is in order that renders life possible on earth. If any life is refused to be in order, that life will be as a dewdrop and disappear at the rising of the sun to make place for the others to grow up. If that is a nation, a city, or a territory, that will continue for as long as you refuse to understand that you must be in order. That is the only way you can have a sweet and able life, whether individually or collectively as a nation or territory.

Whenever you are against yourselves, you are unprotected and will be ruined to dust. Then as dust, you will not be able to stand on your own. Whatever your category, you must be in order to match your current resemblance to those around you. If you want to visit a garden of flowers, there you can have a great chance to admire many wonderful and multicolored flowers. None of these flowers pretend to be a tree nor minimize the others as they are grass. There is no superior tree among them; they are all flowers. Humans can be different by reasoning, having some different views, and living differently. For example, in a real nation where many people are poor, the rich ones try to live as a clan, where their children have been taught not to participate with the other poor children. The rich have the great privilege to send their child to a school they want. But the poor children never have a chance at all to attend school. Therefore, rich parents don't want their children to even talk to the poor children. While the rich child sits down at a school they prefer to attend, then the poor children who don't have a chance to attend school stay at home or where they are living.

While they don't have anything to do, they are trying to find a way to enjoy themselves while they are living. What they are doing is that they find some objects that they can use to make some music, whether that can be a soda can or some plastic gallons, bottles, broken pans, and plates. The poor kids are training themselves to play music. Such an appetite for music takes them far ahead in music, for them to teach themselves how to become great and honorable musicians. The most important thing the rich parents forget is that their children are going to like the entertainment and music. When the rich kids see the poor kids playing their music, they want to learn how to play music and they like to dance as well. So, how can you put a fence between the poor child and the rich child who already sees their own interest in the poor children? Now for sure, some of the poor kids who want to know how to read and write have a great chance to trade with the rich kids who want to learn how to play the music. Instead of what the rich children learn from their parents, which is not to entertain with the poor children, they become friends and share some interests, and that makes a good balance between them all.

Unhappy and wealthy do not mean a natural cancer permanently nor criminal, the same way a poor can turn to a bad person, a rich also can turn to a bad person. That is dependent on what kind of seeds you sow in your heart, mind, or spirit. With the help of each and the other children who did not know how to read and write, now know how to read and write, then children who did not know how to play music are becoming great musicians. Thanks to the spirits of children who learn what is better in life, then the clan problems are resolved in that nation. Whether you are a single person or a group of people, even a territory or a nation, if you are weak enough to be considered as a dispersed one, you just have to stop looking at what other people do as a miracle to you. Instead, rather than seeing them as a miracle, sit down and reason in your mind about a good way for yourselves to make a road the others will be happy to walk.

You can produce in your mind something they can see as the birds in the sky see a tree that produces abundant seeds for them to eat, and that will be your own interest. Currently, people are unable to see in the darkness. If you really don't have anything to shine a bright light on, do not mind seeing the other people stepping on you by believing you are an object for them to rest on whenever they meet you between their paths. If a bird in the sky is not interested in a tree that is not giving fruits for them to eat, then people will never stop at a wilderness rather than a restaurant or a marketplace. Both categories the children are promoting the nation and help their parents to understand more about what you need to avoid and what you must not avoid. Rather than avoid a person just because that person is less fortunate or wealthy than you are, it can be much better if you help them to reach a level where you are more comfortable with. As the young people who share and trade knowledge between themselves, they become equal as a single beautiful item. But it's important to resemble varieties who unite themselves together.

Even the small animals sometimes unite themselves to make some beautiful music. The cicadas can be about three thousand and four hundred species worldwide, some periodical, some annual, and some emerge every two to five years. The difference between annual cicadas and periodical cicadas is the amount of time spent feeding as nymphs underground. Annual cicadas spend two years eating underground, and the adults emerge every two years for mating. Then, periodical cicadas eat and grow underground for thirteen or seventeen years, depending on the species. Despite the different sizes, all of them are united and make some beautiful music. Unity can result in good fruits as beauty and comfort. Disunity can cause ugliness and discomfort, misery and destruction.

A blind person with his good heart sings about colors and beauty; deaf ears and mute of tongue describes their enjoyment by signs and drawing some activity signals their happiness. Who grants the privileges to see, to hear, and to talk? If that is you, for sure you can also grant them privileges to do whatever they want without those privileges. A paralyzed person shoots a cry of joy to prove his sentiment for the better future; that also proves sometimes things may not be easy, but with good courage and strength, you can get where you want to be, no matter how strong the wall and how high it is on your path.

A crab who unfortunately lost his claws and all his legs and the crab stays laid in the mud until his legs and both claws grow back. Of course, sometimes you don't have any choices; you must wait as one who wishes to see a miracle to come at any time for him. But you should be the one to know your situation because you are the one who guides your life. If you know you are facing a no outlet currently, you should stop and make your mind for a good path to your destination. Any error in life can turn you into a crab without legs or claws, an error of another person or a person who just meant to harm you for any reason that pleases him. At that point, you have nothing more you can do except lay down in the mud, which is your only way to survive until your legs and claws come back naturally. One way or the other, your situation will end. A crab can lay in the mud and be nourished by the mud, but when a person finds himself in a situation like this, that person must live inside the situation honestly until everything is over. Whenever you are dependent on others to do anything for you or to give you something to eat or favor of a place to live, frankly, a crab without legs and claws is more than you because that crab will have its legs and claws grow back at a certain time, but for a human who is harmed by another one, it will be hard to get back on your feet, even though it all depends on the gravity of what your enemy has done against you or to you directly by trying to destroy you forever. That can be worse for you if you are ready to depend on your enemies to overthrow the snare they have put in your way.

Someone can be happy to see you resign from life as a wounded bird who is resigning his life and isolating himself in a pit, waiting for his last breath to expire. Happy are those who want to see your wrong in everything. When you stand as an avocado tree on the top of a rocky mountain, every single fruit you produce must hurt a rock and destroy it to pieces and feed the wild beasts. Whoever agrees to bind their knee before the wrongdoer and do the same as them can sleep in honey and wake up without a single ant bite. There will be no annoying for them while you agree to let them daunt you, your life can go smooth, apparently for a short time period. But when you are not agreeing to bind your knees before the wrongdoer, every second in your life will be a ton of bugs and misery caused by the wicked wrongdoer who is trying to destroy you. Do not mind seeing people who are trying to kill you every day in your life eating your own bread while you are hungry for a piece of bread. A piece of the rope stops travelers; your possibility and your capacity are not depending on your size nor your clan but only on your knowledge. Nobody must tell the ants about deluges nor heavy rains before these happen; they are all together secure themselves.

Your enemies understand the importance of being united; that is why when they want to destroy you, the very first thing they do is to disunite you, devise you as soon as possible, and make you enter to kill each other, each one of you mistaking the other as a piece of rope to travel. There, none of you is able to go anywhere. Unfortunately, you are mistaking each other, by letting them make you see each other as the real enemies. Your lack of enough knowledge to see each other as a piece of rope to take or help you to go wherever you want to go, that is already a serious cancer that is there to destroy the whole world, a nation after another without a different weapon. The more you are begging, the greater your poverty; the more you are working with good sense, the greater is your chance to win the idea of those who want to put you down as a beggar for your entire life. Sometimes it is good to know a bird flying tree after tree to look for his food, but not because he has wings to fly. A bird who finds his food where he lives may never fly from trees after tree. If you don't have a good reason for that, don't do anything just because someone else did it. No bird flies without getting tired, no human travels without expenses, and physically gets tired. A source of water may not retire easily, but a dewdrop source of water pauses after each redraw the water from its curve.

A better life is not often resided in one place after the other. A gallon of water is not the source of water; a gallon can be empty and may not be refilled. There is no guarantee about what you can hunt in the wild. Sometimes it is important to make a fraction by turning one to four pieces and growing each of them as one. Even though you can find someone or a friend to help you, never absolutely count on the others to resolve a situation for you; always count on your own powers. Whether you are an ordinary person or a group of people, even a nation, you should never put your mind on others to help you. Instead of continuing to receive from others, you must be the one to put yourselves on the line to help others.

From one person to one nation in the world, who, for some reason, continues to put their eyes on others to help them, that creates chaotic disaster, troubles, and misery. If you categorically refuse to take care of the place you are living, first you will have some bugs as your guests; later, you will have some other animals who are looking for the bugs as food for them. Mice, rats, snakes, and more will all be your guests. That is not limited to a household; if a nation always wants help from others, that is for sure you are inviting those who want to harm you and take whatever your nation possesses as wealth. Yes, instead of helping, they will harm your nation and take what you already possess. You will never see another animal grab his baby and look for a predator territory to live with his baby, but humans believe they are the smartest, but sometimes unfortunately, as roaches, humans enter under their predators' feet and believe they are fully secure.

Planet Earth Shared Between Humans and Other Animals

In a grand world where everything is shared between animals and humans, there is a great portion for each kind of animal, including the sea, marine animals, land animals, and animals in the sky. There is a great park that belongs to the dove family, surrounded by a great river and a wonderful lake where many species of fish, especially the mullet, live. A time has arrived when so many doves are disappearing every day, not only the doves but also the mullet fishes are disappearing by great numbers per day in the waters, especially in the lake where there are many trees. Sometimes people see the remaining birds on the ground, but after a few minutes, they disappear. The same thing happens in the case of the fish; when they find the remains, after less than one hour, everything is gone, nowhere to be found. For so long, so many doves, mullet fish, and other species of fishes and birds are disappearing. Then the leaders of the animals meet this time to talk about the situation, and they decide to hire some investigators to find out what is happening exactly to the rest of the animals.

A meeting takes place where they are choosing some investigators; among those investigators they choose, there are some respective authorities, such as the honorable hawk, honorable osprey, honorable and majestic eagle, and an independent investigator, the untouchable snake. And for the disappearance of the remaining, they hire investigator Heavy Black Costume, Honorable Majesty Vulture, Inspector Cadavers.

Now, Vulture, as an investigator of the remaining cadavers, is responsible for finding who removed the remaining cadavers of the birds and fishes. Vulture gives his point to the press every month and says he is closer to a good result in his investigation. When he finds whoever it is, he will bring them to justice. Every month, Vulture gets closer to a good result, finding and bringing the guilty inside where they are supposed to be. Imagine that Vulture is the one who is responsible for the disappearance of the cadavers. It is true, Vulture is the one who is currently eating the remains of the dead animals. Then that same Vulture is the one they hired to investigate the disappearance of the rest of the remaining cadavers. What a good job for Vulture! Whenever he wants to eat a cadaver, he can do that without any interruption because he has the right to be there at any time he wants to do his job of investigating.

When can Vulture come over with a real result? Every time they have a meeting with Vulture, he says to them, hopes are there because he has some suspects. Sometimes Crow is the main suspect, and at other times, Vulture has questioned Pelican, who may be a suspect. Vulture sends arrest orders against Hummingbird and Sparrow on the disappearance of the cadavers. Vulture says without a doubt these two, Hummingbird and Sparrow, have something to do with that case. They both must face justice. The poor innocents who cannot defend themselves are the ones to grab just to put a veil of darkness between the eyes of the others to make them believe Vulture is currently working hard on that case and, in the end, will find the real one he is looking for.

Currently, who among the birds knows Vulture is the one who is truly removing the rest of the dead animals? These animals don't have access to any justice, and be careful of what can happen to them if they are falsely accused of any matter regarding these big birds. They are big; when they do something wrong, they are also the ones who get paid to conduct investigations; then, they have enough powers to do and undo. They are untouchable and well prepared for anything. Where you see one, there are so many more. They are well-trained in the sky for the ground. But if they do hire Vulture as an investigator for the rest of the cadavers that are disappearing, who are killing and eating the birds and fishes in the first place?

Hawk, Osprey, Eagle, and Snake were the main investigators who were hired to shine light over who is responsible for those crimes. The Dove family, a very quiet family living in that very nice environment, turns into a graveyard where every single day many doves are disappearing, and the fishes in the lake, rivers, and ocean around them. The investigators promise to find out who the killers are, and the small animal's community is confident that these investigators have enough capacity to bring whoever is responsible to justice, instead of Vulture, who gives his point to the press every month. Hawk, Osprey, Eagle, and Snake give their reports every seven days;

they are detaining Owl as a suspect. They invited Falcon to come over before their palace of justice to say what he knows about these crimes. Snakes send requests to the judges for them to issue a mandate to get Cat, Mongoose, and Honey Badger under arrest as the key suspect. Hawk even put Pigeon under arrest as a bird who has something to do with the death of the other birds and eats them out. Eagle, as for him, Chicken is the main suspect; every day, Eagle puts some Chicken under arrest as the bird who eats Dove and the fishes, especially the Mullet fish in the lake. While these activities are going on, doves and fishes are continuing to disappear more than ever every day.

The big mistake of the small family of birds is that they are hiring the same enemies who are killing and eating the animals as investigators. While they pretend to investigate, they are continuing to kill, eat, and drop the rest at the ground for vultures to eat. There are some confusions between what Snake threw and what the big bird eats; even though the big birds always leave a remaining for vulture, and Snake never leaves anything at all, the family of the small birds and fishes are continuing to wait for an answer they will never obtain from those investigators who are in charge and responsible for the crimes. Rather than let the others find out that they are the criminals, they prefer to arrest and condemn as many innocents who cannot defend themselves. Indeed, some kinds of animals have no mercy from their predators who depend on them to nourish themselves. That is true for the animal's kingdom. So, don't be excited or surprised to know that on planet Earth, some people act as the predators who can kill others for some reason. And at the same time, they are the ones who get paid to shine light over the killers. To say it right, the criminals are hired to look for themselves. If they thought you may be the one who knows what they are doing, without a doubt, you will be the next victim if you are not hiding yourself and staying quiet. They must be sure you cannot pose a threat to reveal their wrong actions.

Greater good is good when it has to do with something in favor of the others, but when it happens as a destruction for the lower grades, who can become strong tomorrow, it is absurd for the people who have to face that, even for the world of the smallest who is empty of powers, like some doves and fishes who are so vulnerable under the powers of eagles, hawks, ospreys, snakes, and more. Every second in life, they will continue to die, and the powerful ones always say they are continuing to investigate, and they condemn what is happening. What's happening is already condemned. Whoever did it doesn't have to be found and punished anymore, whether it is your kids, your doctors, your lawyers, even if it is supposed to be your leaders or your king in his kingdom. The search is continuing to find those who are responsible for these crimes, and the result will be forever to find anyone to be responsible.

The talk can be hot until another important one will be killed again, and the last one will be forgotten to his dust. The bird's family was choosing the wrong investigators; the human family also chose the wrong investigators. The professors are writing on the board, and the professors erase what they have written on the board so nobody must read what they were writing. They have powers from themselves to do and undo and isolate what they want without interruption. If they are doing something they don't want to be suspected of, they can just grab anybody else and say to the public that they are the one who is responsible. And for sure, that person will never grant freedom as a pretend favor or mercy despite never knowing anything and being not guilty; that person will be there forever as the wrong person to stand for any penalties.

Parents who have more than one kid sometimes blame one for what the others do; that is a confusion that is not valued much. But when someone must go through a long period of disturbance, where his life can be destroyed for what another person has done, where he did never know, that is horrible. Those victims are often put at the front row just to be a windshield for the real criminals who are too powerful to be punished for wrong actions. For years, Snake can continue to nourish himself by eating birds and definitely forget about the existence of the Eagle who is flying over in the sky. Suddenly, Eagle flies lower and grabs the Snake and currently puts an end to his life as Snake. Same as people, for several decades, a powerful person can continue to kill the other people and multiply his powers against the others who are around him. Don't be surprised to see a great power grab him as an Eagle grabbing a Snake and put an end to his life. A Snake has nothing to worry about when swallowing a bird. After all, the Snakes know where the birds live; Snake is powerful and often counts on his venoms to kill his prey and to defend himself in case he should be attacked by any others. But seriously, Snake was forgetting about Mongooses, Honey Badgers, and Eagles. Those powerful foes are no friends to him, who are immunized against his mass destruction venomous arms.

Humans also abuse their powers against others, especially against the weaker ones. The only good thing is that a superpower is always hiding behind who can catch any greater power by surprise. That makes life resemble a war where the lesser must always surrender to the greatest. That is true sometimes between vegetables, animals, and reasonable ones who are human. It doesn't matter who you are or what you think you are. If a human resembling you is in power and wants to abuse his power, step on your foot, then you will be the one to bend down to your knees to beg him for forgiveness. That way, you might run with your breath of life as you skip a wild beast attack. Sometimes, animals must run from humans to protect their lives. Sometimes, too, humans must run from certain animals just to protect their life. As for the vegetation, they accept whatever comes from humans or wild animals, even though trees sometimes act strangely and even compete with each other. A young man who is taking a mission to go over a big mountain has to do so after his great effort which has taken him years to accomplish.

When the young man arrives at the top of the mountain, he encounters a ram animal who tries to beat him. Then he instantly grabs the two horns of that ram who is continuing to push the young man until the lower ground of the mountain as a total defeat for the young man. Sometimes, what you accomplish with your strength over many years can be destroyed on a bad day for you by your enemies, especially by those you respect or fear. It is not good to hold the hands of the enemy and let him take you where he wants so he can get you defeated at any moment. The young man did not understand the horns of the ram are his weapons he uses against him. Holding those weapons without doing anything else reinforces the power of that ram against himself; which costs his defeat so quickly, as the ram wanted it to be effective. Now the young man has to take it as the way it is and start over with that lesson in his mind; he must not lose the same way again at a different period.

Climbing over a mountain can mean everything you have done in your life, to be just what you are today, and everything that you possess in your current life. Pushing you back to the lower ground means that you can suffer a total loss of everything and start over as a child who doesn't even know yet what he wants to be in life. Do not let yourselves be weak enough for someone to push you from the top of everything you already have until the bottom of your life. Most people take more than half of their life to achieve a better way for themselves to live; to get back at a very start to this point of progress means for them a perishable life. If that is a disease or an accident, these are unpreventable, and everyone is subject to those kinds of events, especially humans, animals, vegetables, and even lands that are often disturbed during hurricanes, landslides, or any natural catastrophe. In these cases, yesterday was very good, today is good so far, and do not panic if you hear bad news tomorrow, nor if an event happens to you. The news you are listening to all of your days are some events that often happen to others; do not mind, one day they might listen to some news from you or from your loved ones or your neighbors. That can be sad, but currently, no one can minimize that. For instance, when you are extremely in a degree where you are the only one speaking and thinking with a sad mind with that pain in your heart, you are a depressed person who every unfractured and inexperienced one really wants to take as a joke and wants to laugh at, just to enjoy themselves.*

When half of the planet Earth is plunged into deep darkness, then the other half contemplates the light of the sun. Whenever you enjoy yourselves, a best friend of yours sits down in a corner of life with a sad and depressed heart. When your heart becomes sad, and you are alone, a best friend of yours is enjoying himself and even thinking about you. That is one of the ways ants, as small as they can be, prove to be wiser than humans in many ways. Ants are more united and less private to each other from birth until the end of life. Never should one suffer or die because of the absence of the others.

A Friend Offends His Friend
and Both Have Regrets

* **A** man always offends a friend whom he considered as his best friend. At a certain time, his friend refused to visit him and prevented him from entering where he is living. After some time, when a serious dark moment happens in his life, he continues to make some serious efforts to contact his friend with no good result. His friend did not answer his calls and didn't even read his messages. Months later, his friend learns that he has already passed away. You can imagine how he was feeling while he was going to die and knowing he would never see his friend anymore and talk to him anymore. And his friend never knew what was in the messages he was sending to him. That was, of course, a bad moment for him before he passed away, but that is also a harsh and sad moment for the one who is left behind while approaching closer and closer to his last day of life.

Errors and mistakes are easy to make, but the results are not so sweet at all, especially when you do not have a valid reason to justify them. The book you have inside your mind is a book you are going to read the most of it in your bad days, and when you get older and cannot repair anything, at that period you will continue to read constantly every error and every mistake you have made in your life. Your sadness will continue to multiply and grow bigger, greater, and greatest until you expire when the last breath is dashed out from the body and leaves you truly dead.

Even though that is not going to happen to everybody at the same level, it is important for each human, like you, to understand the impact that might have on the rest of your life. Nobody wants to live with a little freedom and, after all, be a slave to their bad ways. A group of people who were slaves to a different nation after many years of slavery decided not to be slaves anymore, so they revolted against that kind of slavery. They started causing great troubles, refusing to do the work they used to do day and night. They were fighting; all they wanted was to be free.

Now the owners of the slaves decided to make a deal with them. First, the slaves did not understand that their owners would never make a deal that is in favor of the slaves. Second, the slaves didn't know that people who possess nothing as wealth cannot be free for real. If anybody tells you about freedom, that can only be a relative freedom. That is why someone might tell you, "Work is freedom." While the group were slaves, their owners were responsible for their food and shelter. The owners always gave them enough food to keep them strong to work for the owners. They provided restrooms for them to use in emergencies and took baths at the owners' schedules.

Now the slaves want to be free, and their owners said to them, "You will be free. We will set you free, but we want to continue to help you with whatever you want. So, if you please, you can work for us, and then we'll pay you for whatever work you have done for us. Whoever doesn't want to work will not be forced to work. We only want to be good with you, that is why we ask you to work for your money, and we promise to pay you good money. We don't want to take away your freedom; enjoy your freedom." The slaves are very happy they fought for liberty, and they finally received their freedom and liberty from their owners. Now, they are free, a free group of people. They are just waiting to see if people who possess nothing as wealth can be free for real.

Indeed, just after the slaves have been set free, they immediately realize that they are in need of a place to sleep, food to eat every day, clothes to wear, education for themselves and their children, payment for doctors when going to the hospital, and even for communications, electricity, and water. More and more things they are going to pay for are waiting ahead for them. If the slaves want to survive, they must recall the words of the owners, "If you please, you can work for us." Yet, the slaves are employees, and their owners become employers. Your employers are going to find out how much your expenses are for every day, so they can determine how much to pay you. If your employers, your former owners, find out your expenses are four cents per day, they will pay you two cents per day. Then they will make sure they are paying you a wage that can only cover two cents of your four cents' expenses. That way you can see a good reason for you to do some extra work like overtime. After all, you are still in need of more money to complete your four cents' expenses.

Now, whatever you cannot pay on time stays in your mind as an absolute cancer that ruins your soul. Now the free slaves, or relatively free slaves, realize that they are still slaves, whether it is voluntary, obligatory, or mandatory. They can't change it to "work is freedom" or "liberty." You can take it as you want too. But if you really want to be free, do not take a deal for you to dash out empty-handed. With empty hands, you are worse than any real slave. Empty hands are hands free without liberty nor freedom. Whenever you are hungry, a piece of bread is too much to purchase your liberty and take you back to being a slave again. When your family is in need of something and you know you cannot provide that for them, then you will find out that you are not free for good.

The owners of the slaves knew that, of course. Other than that, they would prefer to die before they should let the slaves be free. That is about them, how about us today? Are we on a different path? If so, good for us. If not, maybe we are in the same basket. But for sure, there are some people out there who have something in their hands. These people may be different because the empty-handed people are the only category who cannot be free and feel free. Some are fighting hard to learn a trade, some have already become professionals enough to be set free. There are tricks sometimes, those who skip the slave's row are forced to keep the others who are behind as slaves. They must not look at someone and say to that person, "We want you to be a slave," but people who are not enabled to reach their needs, they surrender themselves as slaves by strengthening themselves to fulfill their needs within their minds. They may do it for some time, then when they reach their goal, they will take a deep breath and rest themselves and enjoy it with their family. In that case, some win, and some others do not win. Because nobody wants to lose a fight, each time you are not the winner, you can continue your fight until you feel that you are a winner, even though you don't have to be equal to any others to be considered a winner, but depending on the level crossed you were at before, that can tell whether you made enough progress or not.

An eagle has the ability to build a big nest, then an engineer bird builds a small nest, but only a major hurricane can tell which nest is more secure and built for maximum protection. Next time when the slaves want to be free, they are making a deal for themselves to go with what belongs to them because hands-free are not soul-free. Sometimes it is reasonable to think that a lime or lemon can be ripe and even change color, but will never change its thirst despite its maturity and changing colors. A slave-keeper may never want to be a slave, and it may not be easy for a slave to feel free while under his owner's power.

A family finds a wild mother cat with her three small babies, and then they disturb the mother and grab one of the babies. That small baby cat is trying to be furious, but he is too small to help himself get free from the family. They keep that little cat in the house with them until he feels his life is not in danger and finally accepts to be friends with the family. They feed that little cat with milk and everything he likes. That little cat starts growing big, and sometimes they release him. He plays by hunting lizards, like his parents taught him. The family believes that the small cat who has become big is going to stay with them forever. But at a time they did not expect, the cat's family comes closer to the human family's house and collects back their son. Brothers and sisters reunite, and they all step into the wild. Even though that little cat, who has become a very big cat, always remembers the human family, he always prefers to stay with his parents. Whenever he remembers them, he comes close to the house and meows for as much as he wants during some minutes. He does that often after the sun is over. Each time he yells, they always remember him. The only thing that is true is that the cat still wants the family's food, but he refuses to come closer to them anymore. That way, they may not put him in captivity; he doesn't want to be in a cage anymore.

When he comes by and continues to talk for like three minutes, he may be trying to tell them he is hungry and still wants his supper from them. When he was with them, he never got hungry; they were treating him well, so he doesn't forget the kind of love they had for him. But despite that, he needs to respect his family's principle to stay with them in the wild as a wild cat because they were not happy at the time when humans caught him and took him to captivity. The lesson that the family learned from that cat helped them live through a harsh situation later when they had a neighbor who was different from them. The cat always comes over sometimes after sunset and meows for a few minutes. Now, they have a neighbor who always plays some music after sunset, and that family has never lived like this before. So now, for them to be comfortable, they must take that music noise as the voice of the cat who is continuing to yell at them for some food, or just to say hello to them before they go to sleep. Of course, they received their training from the cat for their future neighbor's attitude. Indeed, they schedule themselves with the neighbor's music and live with the situation like there was no problem at all for annoying them.

Of course, a wise person analyzes every aspect of a situation and finds a good lesson for them rather than getting upset to a point where your life can be at jeopardy. One government officer wants to kill a man for his own purpose, attacking the man in many kinds of ways so that he can get him upset, that way an argument can happen for him to kill the man, and that man never proves himself hurt enough to get involved in an argument with him. Finally, the officer retreats as a predator, and life continues for everyone. Sometimes a formidable defense can be done with just silence. Be wise and at each time a good or bad situation faces you, find a way to make it resemble a smooth and nice wind to refresh your ears at summertime.

That man freed the cat and put his anger in the cage, and the officer didn't know that part. His wrong plan against the man did not prevail at all. The lack of wisdom can cost a free slave to get back voluntarily to be a slave for a second time, like a man who was so poor, he must beg for food or some money to buy food. On a good day for him, he then finds a treasure that raises him to a multimillionaire. Because he spent a lot of time begging others, he knows most of them, he always begs at the same street corner. When he begs, some people give him only some change, some give him a good amount of money, some others just give him some food for him to eat. He was always happy with whatever they were giving him. That was the way he made his living during that period.

The day he becomes a multimillionaire, he immediately changes his point of view. Rather than seeing these people as a great step that directed him until he gets where he's at now, he thought they were assaulting him and mocking him by giving him little food and a few dollars. His bad point of view will soon divert himself into a terrible chaos. Currently, he says to himself they were rich and gave him a few dollars, now he's going to start giving them each some few thousand dollars. That way, they can see he is not currently the same as them, who were giving to him too small an amount of cash money. What the multimillionaire is doing; he is following his heart every day, he draws enough cash money and stands at the same corner. This time, if you are thinking about a person you're going to give a few dollars or some food, then you will be surprised to see the beggar man. It is the man today who wants to offer you some thousands of dollars or even more. The beggar multimillionaire does not know a dollar every day can ruin his pocket, who is not a source of money. Then many thousand dollars can make a million dollars, and a million dollars can make a millionaire. The worst is that the beggar was not wise enough to understand that when they say he is a multimillionaire, his million has a limit. If he spends that money too fast, he will be empty of money. The beggar thought that when a person is a millionaire, that person can never run out of money. The beggar who became a multimillionaire is continuing to show his former givers how large they were supposed to be. Generous to himself and the others, a good deal for them today. Tomorrow, they may share a small portion of that with him again.

Unfortunately, after some months, the multimillionaire goes to the bank to redraw some thousands of dollars. To his great surprise, he hears them saying to him he doesn't have any money in his account, and he currently owes a little overdraft and some fees. What a kind of surprise for the multimillionaire with a large heart! The multimillionaire who was faster than a bird working hard to build his nest to share his money is now back on the street to ask for help as revenge for those who offended him with their small amounts of money. He wants to prove how generous he is by giving his million to others, and now he finds himself back on the street for his third time.

The first time as a beggar, the second time as a multimillionaire who wanted to prove how much he could give, and the third time as a beggar without any choice, back to his duty. Now he is happier to see some people still want to help him. Now he has his chance to understand that when people give a little, whenever it becomes many, it can do great things. As much as you can have, if you continue to remove without control and not replace anything, you are not far from the pit of poverty and deception of foolishness. Greater is to give than to receive. If you don't give just to make others see you are the one who can give more than others, and whatever you receive, that does not belong to you, whether it's small or big, you should be happy with that. And when you are free from a harsh situation, that is not a reason to turn back your mind and think the small things they shared with you were an offense to you. In that case, no one can tell the real science that can turn an adult person just like a kid who is not making his grade for many years until the professor decides to shrink him back to the first grade, that way he can understand how to learn and make progress at school.

The beggar multimillionaire is learning his lesson this time. He only spends a few years begging on the street. This time, it's not because he finds a treasure, but because he is viewing life differently. He is learning how to manage what people give him, and he makes his way out to support himself. Currently, when he finds it possible for him to help another person, he does that like everybody else. He doesn't give them a million dollars, but enough for them to also find bread for the day, and both should be satisfied. He is learning from his mistake and becoming a person wise enough to live a normal life like every wise person who knew him before. He is learning how to appreciate and respect what he receives from others and believes he can share these with others who are in need.

Indeed, the wind is changing direction for real. He is growing what he has received for the year legally, and after years later, he becomes once again a very rich person. He did pay for his disgraceful mistake. He learns that he should never minimize the help he received from others at a time when he was in need. The good understanding is that this help was concretized as a strong bridge for him to stand and cross the ocean of misery and slavery. The good lesson is for everyone, wherever you make an error and whatever it is costing you, try to learn a lesson from it. Then you can sell it to yourselves and feel comfortable enough as you make everything back. Use it as an investment that you did to win, not to lose anything.

Two Ugliest People You Pay to See in the World

Two ugly men were living in a city, and they were so ugly that everyone who saw them would stop and look at them. Anyone who had a chance to see them before was trying to find out where they could see them, as everyone was talking about those two men. One of them always got mad because he seriously didn't like people looking at him whenever he went out. So, he decided to leave that city for a different one, hoping to have a break from people constantly following him just to look at him. When he left the city where he was known, he felt happy and thought everything was over. Little did he know that things would get worse as every person living in his new city wanted to see him too. He eventually faced even more people paying him curiosity.

Finally, that man wanted to go back to his former city, which made him more popular among the people. He didn't take long and turned back to his original city to meet with the other ugly man. Few days later, the one who never ran away sat down with him, and they tried to plan where they could find a way to stop people from annoying them. After they visited an uncle for some help and advice, the uncle agreed to help them by being their manager while they practiced to become comedians. The news spread like smoke, and at their first event, they sold tickets for several million dollars. Not only because people wanted to hear the comedians, but they also wanted to see those two men specifically.

To their surprise, those men talked and laughed. Each time they saw them before, they always looked as if they were mad. Now, they were the ones inviting people. They talked and laughed, and each time they had an event, the tickets were sold out. They opened a slot for those who didn't have a chance at the last event to be the first one at the following event. Everyone was thirsty to see the comedians they were paying money to see, and they were very much happy with what they were enjoying. The comedians acquired money like a miracle, turning their bitter moments into sweet honey for them. Good comedians and a good manager made everything go smoothly. Last time when you saw them, you were not allowed to laugh, and now they were personally inviting you to a large place where they gave you a comfortable seat for you to sit down, look at them, listen to their talks, and laugh as much as you can without interruption from anyone. You don't have to worry about anyone telling you that you are against the law if you laugh.

It may take a long time to turn over a burden you are carrying, but you can turn it over if you really want to do so. You may not throw away the stones because you cannot eat them. You can build a beautiful place for you to live with the stones instead of throwing them away. You must find the right way for anything you must face in life. There were many things different between the two ugly men. One was mad enough to quit his city where he was living, but the other one did not quit his city. The madness could occupy his entire life until he shall die very quickly, but the one who did not get mad worked his mind and found a wonderful way for them to turn the situation into real fun where everyone could be happy.

Most of the time, it is hard to understand and accept other people's curiosity about you, but truly, the people who are curious about you do so because they believe you are different from them. They don't want to hurt you at all, even though you may feel that way. Both ugly men listened to each other to facilitate their business together and become billionaires. They were not only billionaires of money but also billionaires of ugliness, as other people thought. They were the ugliest people you could find on planet Earth, but when they practiced comedy, their ugliness could no longer affect them in any wrong ways as people viewed it. Instead, they turned into the most super fun for everyone. Wherever people lived, when they heard about them, they came over to attend their events, see them, and be happy. Excitingly, people couldn't wait for the next event to come, and tickets were always sold out. Some people had to wait for the next event to attend because of the many people who purchased tickets. Now, instead of a man getting mad when other people look at him, it is the people who get mad when they are cramped for the next event. Yes, it is really appreciated to see it like this. If you want to see them, pay them some money, see them, and feel happy. The two ugly men themselves will be satisfied with their fortune, which is what they are receiving as gains for their comedians' activity.

If a person eventually becomes unconscious and lies over a road, many vehicles can go over and not hurt them. But if you deliberately lay yourself over the road, the very first vehicle passing by can hurt you to your death. The comedians were naturally ugly, and their ugliness was not fake. That is why they were so successful, even more than any longtime comedian who was smart and an expert as a big celebrity. The good lesson is for everyone who must deal with others. If you feel you are upside down, then turn around and make it look better and feel better. If you are swimming involuntarily with your clothes on, don't let the wet clothes drown you while on the land. It's up to you to find a way to remove your wet clothes and dry them out for the good time.

It can be sad if you die inside the waters, but it will be even sadder to see you drown on the ground with wet clothes. When you travel a long distance, you must not worry about the beautiful bed you have at home. Do what is necessary to render your trip a good and successful one for yourself. The more cautious you are, the better it can be. But remember that wicked people always appear as good people because they are really preparing to do what is wrong. And don't forget, currently, wrong people are punished only thirty-seven percent of the time, and the innocent are punished ninety-seven percent of the time. Only three percent of the innocent are not punished, but only one percent finds justice. Innocents are not given bribes to have what they deserve where honesty is not sown to harvest. Innocents are for the most part painted with the red and black colors, while the wrong is painted with the white color.

An honest man sees a thief breaking into the house of his neighbor and stealing some objects. When he tries to confront the thief, the thief drops everything on the ground and runs away. Then the neighbor goes to the nearest police and reports the thief, giving some descriptions to help them identify the thief, so the police can easily find him. What the thief also does is go to the authorities and report that he saw that neighbor breaking into the house. Now it happens to be a dispute between the good man and the real thief.

A thief is a thief, and the person who is concerned can catch that thief at any other moment, but for now, the man they know they will not get any more, is the one they want currently. Then, they release the thief and keep the good man in prison so that some money can be given or paid to set him free. The good man says to them he didn't have enough water for him to drink, now they are forcing him to find water for him to take a bath, so he tried to help his neighbor, but that turned out to be a pain for himself. The judges render the judgment in favor of the thief for their own reasons, but the other neighbors who were witnesses of the situation step in and have them pursue the real thief. After all, they make him leave that community for him to return to the city where he lived before he came to live in that city. Maybe that neighbor should have just called the police and reported the thief to prevent himself from getting too involved in that matter. It's sad to see the thief walking away, and the good person must sleep in prison, but sometimes the mistake happens from the start. The first thing is that the neighbor did not have a police identity, because of that, he should call the police for help in any serious matter. In that case, he just had to call the authorities and report what is important to be reported, and the authorities are the ones to execute their job. The second thing is that the neighbor is not the real owner of the home. With that in mind, the thief can accuse him just to defend himself so he can run away unpunished for what he did.

As for everybody else who says something, most of them blame the neighbor as a person who believes he was an authority and even ask who placed him as an authority for him to confront a thief. His family members also blame him, but he is a person who doesn't want to see any thief come to his community to steal and break any houses. Of course, the entire community knows him as he is a good man. Even though he didn't do that with a recommendation from the authorities, but a stealer stays a stealer, and an honest man stays an honest man. A man whose community will always want to help so they live with more confidence that they are surrounded by good neighbors. They are making sure that some warnings have been put in place to prevent that kind of thief from ever setting foot in that neighborhood. For the rest of his life, if anyone meets him there, they have the right to act against him. In the case of that man with the thief, the man just didn't do it the way he was supposed to do it, but they were able to understand that matter. Therefore, sometimes it is important to do things in accordance with the law.

So, whenever you want to buy shoes for yourself, don't buy anything too big nor too small. Just buy something you'll be able to wear anytime you want. You may see a very beautiful shoe, and it's wonderful to buy, but if that shoe is too big, you will have difficulty walking with it, and if the shoe is too small, your feet will not fit into it properly, and that will cost you serious problems without a doubt. A similar case happened like that man's case, but only a little different, where a man who had an ambition to become a chief was involved. That man caught a thief who broke into a shop overnight. Currently, he put the thief under arrest with some of the things that the thief was stealing in the shop. But he acted foolishly, where he took the thief to his own house instead of calling the authorities or taking the thief to the police station. Worse than that, he allowed that thief to leave the things he was stealing at his house because it was nighttime and granted the thief permission to go to sleep at his house for him to come back the next day, so he could take him to the police.

When the next day arrived, the thief was not present. Now he decided to go to where that thief was living to grab him and put that thief under arrest at his own house as a thief he caught overnight and granted him permission to go sleep in his house for him to come back the next morning, and the thief did not obey to come back. Now it happens to be a dispute where the real authority of the police is going to take part. When the real police arrive, that thief denies stealing anything. The thief says he did not break any shop, and his neighbors saw the man come to his house to arrest him while he was sitting down at his place where he lives. Then the things he was stealing are at the man's house right now. The good man looks more like a thief rather than the real thief who declares the man is coming to his own house to accuse him of stealing and assaulting him. Imagine the neighbors of the thief seeing when the dispute started. They did not see him leave his house that day, and the good man did not have a single witness, only himself with the thief. That looks a little bit crazy for that man who wants to act as a chief but doesn't know the right way to exercise the law.

Somebody must be responsible for the broken shop, but the way it appears now, they cannot handcuff the thief. If they cannot handcuff the thief, they still have to look for those things that were lost. And for sure, wherever they find them, if it's at a person's house, that person will be the one to be questioned and, in the end, may be taking responsibility and be punished for the stealing of the items that were lost. Currently, the things are found at the good man's house, where nobody can ever believe him when he declares he caught a thief and had let him go to sleep at his house. Who are you? Are you a chief? Who grabbed you as a chief? Can a real chief send a thief to sleep at his house or in jail? So, if you thought you were a chief and did send the thief to sleep at his house instead of sending him to jail, now you are the one who will go to jail currently for several counts against the law.

Despite that, the thief wants significant compensation for that accusation against him. If that is a private person, that person will be the only one to compensate the lucky thief. Yet, if you don't know the law, can you be a chief? Surely no, you cannot be a chief if you don't know the law. Can you appoint yourself as a chief without the permission of the other chiefs? No, you cannot be a chief without the permission or recommendations of the other chiefs. The man who has in his mind that he is an active chief is paying for his own mistake and ignorance of what he's supposed to know. Despite the doubt about whether he was the one who broke into the shop, they have no other choice for him because the stolen items were found at his home, and his dispute with the other man cannot prove that the other man is the real thief of these things. So a good man is the one they find more proof for him to be responsible for the loss of the shop items and be punished for them according to the law.

Now, rather than a title of chief, it happens to be the title of thief who broke into a shop and carried some items to his house. Of course, he is getting upset, but he is the one who put himself in trouble with his own mistake. That man who thought he didn't have enough water to drink right now is forced to find water for him to take a bath, then a serious bath because he is not only having to deal with the stealing and breaking of a shop, but he must deal with the authority for his action by acting like an active chief, and he is not. Other than that, he currently must pay the lucky thief for his accusation. Lucky and happy, the real thief is prevailing over the good man who was thirsty for the power of chief without the knowledge of the law and isn't even wise enough to make a good judgment on himself.

A wrong ambition takes that man to prison where he must deal with the same sentence as a thief, then like a thief for stealing, even though he did not mean to be a stealer. Whatever is wrong doesn't have a measure, whenever you decide to take a wrong way, it is a wrong way. You do not know how far that will take you and how much consequence that will have, and how much that can affect your life. And what that may cost others who are going to deal with your mistake. So, it can be too late for the one who is already a victim of their own error, but everyone else who can have a chance to visualize the situation can draw a good lesson for themselves and share it with anyone who wants to listen and learn from that. Jealousy of what others accomplish should never come to your mind. You must learn as much as you can because your knowledge is your protection in life on Earth. Never try to just jump on anything when that is required for a person like you in accordance with a specific knowledge, where you can absolutely be sure of yourself as a person who can produce good and excellent results to satisfy everyone. You must not expect any error where absolute reproach can follow you forever.

A family has two young children, and that family currently wants both children to go to school and learn how to read and write, then have a chance to learn a profession for them to lead a better life. But after both children finished their high school education, one of them already learned and knows certain things to survive life. That same one opens himself to learn a better trade or profession. As for the other child, he always believes learning something will take him too long. All he wants is to find a job to make some money fast. There is nothing wrong with that if you can work and make some money for yourself. But before being granted the work to make that money, they will ask you what kind of job you can do. You may say anything because you did not learn anything, but most of the time, they will not find anything to hire you. If, by chance, they hire you to do anything, they will pay you anything too. As for the child who is disciplining himself to learn a profession, he is doing very well. But the one who doesn't have enough patience to learn a profession, there is a big difference. Of course, everyone cannot be the same nor at the same level, but no real person wants to live at the bottom level where the chance was at your hand to be at a better level. The time you lost or wasted is nowhere to be found anymore; that is why the lazy boy never reaches the true level of his dream. In order to get it, you are the one to look for it. But if you just watch and think without any effort, absolutely you will not get there if you did not inherit that from someone. The important point is that if you want to get there, you must make an active path at the beginning.

As two men who decided to go to a different city by walking, one of them wants to run to get there as fast as he can. But the other man wants to walk normally to get to the city. Then the two men depart, and the man who is running passes the one who is currently walking for miles. At a certain point, he gets so tired that he must lay himself on the side of the road until the man who is walking reaches over to switch hands so he can stand back to continue the trip. They both enter the city together at the same time. You simply need to be wise enough to make it so you don't have to ruin yourself over time while you don't even know if you are doing so.

Two Young Girls Become Registered Nurses

Two young ladies want to become registered nurses. They have both decided to go to school and learn what is necessary for them to succeed. A lot of effort is needed for them to discipline themselves enough to study whatever they need to become registered nurses. The interesting thing is that they both become registered nurses, accomplishing their dream. That was their dream, and they both succeeded. But that is not all; one of them decided to work eight to twelve hours per day, while the other one decided to work sixteen to twenty-four hours a day. The one who works eight to twelve hours a day is always doing well, but the one who works sixteen to twenty-four hours a day has lost her balance of health because she doesn't make enough space for herself to rest and get back strong. So, one of the two ladies leaves enough time for her to cultivate what is most important for her, which is her health, contributing to her success.

Unfortunately, the other one sees it differently, which is not profitable for her health at this point. Everything in life must have a balance that must be respected; if anyone goes over the balance, they will pay a serious consequence for that. It is the same way when you are hungry; you cannot overeat the food or eat a certain quantity of food to delay the amount of time you will get hungry again. That way, you can take a longer time to eat again. It is similar; you cannot continue to push yourself without the balance of rest when your body needs it. Whether you want to continue what you decided to do or not, if your body needs to rest, and you refuse to rest, your body will inevitably put your mind on a different track. Regrettably, sometimes when you force your soul to work overtime, that can cause you to spend all your reserve of energy and money to get back to normal, and sometimes you may never get that chance anymore. It is more important to grab the first opportunity to make sure you are not making that kind of mistake that can erase all your years of labor in just a second and prevent you from enjoying many other things in life.

If you are the one to do it, do so in a good manner; give your body the source of energy and time to regenerate so you can continue the next day without any interruption. The title of the hardest workers on this planet Earth, which is the ants, also finds time to rest and gain more energy to continue working. Objects like a motor can stop when running out of gasoline and later run if someone replaces the gasoline in it. But if a human heart stops under pressure, a simple rest cannot restore anything; you may have more chances to stay in silence than to come back to life.

Most of the time, when you are looking for more, you end up losing what you already have. Sometimes even those who are looking for a better life lose their lives; we have seen that in the case of reasonable humans and in the case of all kinds of animals living on Earth. That happens because not all eyes see everything at the same level, and everyone can be happy at a comfortable level. The entire Earth can be considered at three visible levels: one we can view as high, a second as flat, and a third we call deep. On the other side of the mirror, we can see the sky, then we can see the land and the ocean. If the three are never at the same level, that may be done for a good reason. If, at a time, you can visualize anything joining the three all together, something will not skip anything without making a story, even though you are the last one to see that. By the way, don't forget the name of that book if the meaning of anything skips your mind; refer to the name of that book.

A three-way wind can float and not skip any tree at all, whether it be a tall tree, a middle tree, a low tree, or a small tree. There is a matter you can skip only if you are not yet born to life at all. When your parents are not able to answer your questions, they can either tell you something to occupy your mind while they are thinking about what to tell you or respond with a resemblance of a tree. When the one who is piloting doesn't know what road to take and currently doesn't want you to notice that you are not in good hands, that can be the worst situation ever seen. If a child sees his mother crying, that child may lose hope in her, and that can retard the child's growth. If a woman sees her husband crying, she might lose her strength and assurance in him. The tallest brothers see what is coming but do not allow them to tell the smallest brothers. That way, they will not disturb them; they fix it before they can see it. When they cannot fix it, one has a chance to skip it.

The ocean is there; maybe it is not possible to cross it at that point in time, but the captain doesn't want to accept defeat and tells people that they must build a stronger boat to cross the ocean over. Okay, now we are ready; let's try. The first one is sinking; the captain said that is happening because while building the boat, the ocean has turned greater. Now we just need to build the greatest boat to face not only the ocean but also its waves and the current. Not too long after that, the third boat is ready to hit the ocean again, unfortunately, the third boat sinks again. So, what happened to the captain?

Now listen, said the captain. From the first time, we knew we had only the ocean as the matter. Then, just after we prepared for the ocean as usual, the ocean turned out to be greater than it was. Of course, at the second time, a current interrupted the boat from crossing the ocean. This time, we have the ocean, the current, and also a serious wind. Now we have a triple matter that is very serious to face. So, for a fourth try, we can do that, and that may never be the end of what we must do. We understand that everyone is concerned and has questions for the captain and wants to hear what the captain must say. They all want to hear the good news from the captain, and the captain himself, even if he knows an immediate solution may not be possible for him at this point, to declare the truth is rendering him invalid, where everybody wants someone to believe in. They want to hear the captain say to them that they are ready to cross the ocean without any difficulty. At this instance, a simple presence of the captain gives great hope to the passengers. If the captain does not abandon them, even if it takes forever in his process to find a way out, everyone will consider him a hero, where no one else can step over and do the best; he will remain the only one to count on when so many lives are at risk of perishing, and people are wondering about answers and solutions. Where everyone is at the same risk, there is no reason to look for anyone to blame. If the captain pushes the wrong button and causes a serious mistake, no other eyes are open enough to visualize anything about that.*

With the hope of enjoying tomorrow, today we can engage in a fight of a lifetime, even though all generations may be far away from anything. Then, enjoying the early morning and seeing snow hiding the sun before it arises and shines for everyone. Before midday, it happens to be the end of most hopes. A life in dangerous combat becomes currently the gain for so many souls who never see and enjoy the sun nor a good afternoon. With so many hopes in the heart, they are dreaming day by day, and that hope is only the suitable light for a good path in the mind and heart. Hope makes a living. Wish it, and hope it. Have it in your mind and heart, you can continue day after day until you might close your eyes and return to your silent moment where you don't have to remind, recall, or memorize anything. The best moment for those under the heavy load of eternal fight they cannot win.

*Be strong and always understand that there are some people who live on earth, and even their merits will not accept them without misery and deception. Those people, in order for their remains to rest in the grave, must wear misery and deception as their uniform to enter the gate of the graveyard. Never mind, because the others did better, than they were less, but that is the way it is supposed to be. It doesn't matter how much effort you make or not; if that is supposed to be you, then it will be yours to bear just the way it is.

To heaven, you can raise your eyes and see so many stars; some are big, some are small, and others are so small that your eyes can barely see them from earth. Some are greatest, and anyone can see them from earth. Some people believe the big stars are brighter than the small ones; yes, that is what we can see, despite that, compared to the sizes, they are all bright enough. And for the most part, always at their respective limit.

As for humans, some may be more successful than others, but sometimes the one who is more successful may not be the one who makes more effort or works harder. There is no comparison between those who must work with their hands and those who not only work with their hands but with knowledge, heart, and brain. For professionals with high-skill professions, among them, there are so many differences because of the different environments and situations in which they are living. That can mean many things and greatly affect them. Understand that situation, and you can carry the same identity but not at the same level. Sometimes, it is normal, not only among humans but also between wild animals and trees.

You must contemplate and enjoy the effort you make with your own strength to get where you are. A young person was born in a poor family. That young person saw a necessity for him to find a better way to live. There were a couple of people who were very rich and currently had no kids. That couple agreed to accept the young person to help them with some work they had to do at home, and in return, they would help him with some money for him to have a better way to survive.

After some time, the couple was very pleased with the attitude of the young person, and they offered him a place to live with them. Imagine that the couple had no kids, so the young person became like an excellent kid for them. Whatever road you are appointed to, if it is not illegal or against any law, you will not deserve any reproach from anybody.

That couple, who were not young anymore, saw nothing more than a good favor in having such a kind person to help them as they were getting old. Little by little, the couple switched everything they owned to the name of that young person from the poor family. The couple became good parents to him, and he stayed as a good kid for them. They helped him form his own family as their own child. Years went by, and people who did not know them before could never understand if that young person was not born as a real kid to the couple.

When it was time for them to no longer appreciate life as it was when they were young, they didn't just lie down and die, but they made sure that no other persons shall come over and disturb that young person and his family. The couple showed that they counted on him for the rest of their lives, and he would be the one to take them to their final resting place forever. He himself considered their kid forever. They had established him over everything they owned, and he became the owner of everything. Promises were kept when the couple got old and died, one after the other. The young person took to heart his responsibility to satisfy what he had accepted as a mandate to put them to rest at their last places peacefully, just as they had protected him and his family from disturbance by others.

After the couple's remains had been put to rest, the young person and his family inherited their parents' adoptive wealth and became rich. Everything depends on the road you are approaching and the quality of person you want to be. When life appears not the way you expect it to be, that is the time you need to review yourselves.

A child will never grow up without the help of a grown person. A small tree planted in the middle of a dry land where no other trees exist currently will not grow. If you want to be anything tomorrow, today you must be under the shadows of good and straight principles, with the power of somebody to supervise you. However, the more you care, the greater you can be on your own. You are the owner of everything you care for because you are the one who cares for them. That young person at a time believed he was working for someone to make some money to survive, but it was not so simple. Everything depended on how he dealt with his assignments and his attitude towards others. His good attitude held a value for a long ladder to climb a superior relationship as a kid and parents- an eternity value that came from a good heart and good faith between them. With his good qualities, he became the one to inherit the wealth of the couple as a super kid who never betrayed nor deceived his parents until they died.

How long should he work to acquire that wealth? Forever. That will never be a dream for an ordinary person without a high education and profession in this world. A good attitude is worth more than what money can buy.

When you fall under your enemies' powers, your merits are not less than a life condemnation with hard work. If your enemies establish themselves as judges over your soul, you can have a real reason to regret your existing life. But as everyone is born with intellect, which can help them become intellectual, if that intellect develops and you become intelligent, then you must bend your back to a narrow spot if you must switch out and go ahead to a further shelter for better and sure protection of your soul.

It is important to verify the seed you are sowing to see if it is good enough for you to have a good harvest. If it is not good enough in your own eyes, it may not be enough for others at all. Truly, sometimes those who sow some perfect seeds are harvesting something good even when the soil is not so fertile. Sometimes you can rebuke bad with good, whether it's attitude or serious action against yourself. The baton you have in your hand is what you use to protect yourself against bad dogs. Your good kind of attitude can always prevail over your enemies. By the time they must think of why you don't act the same as them, then you will find enough time to dash out. Don't let go of what you have at hand until you replace it with a better one.

At a time when a boat was sinking in the ocean, a person who had a writing pen in his hand kept the pen while swimming over the ocean. Because his swimming took him so long before he could make it to land, he had cramps so many times. Then, he used that pen to sting his veins in a way he could release from the cramp and continue his swimming until he made it to the ground. You may think the mission of that pen is over, but not at all. When he got to the land, his tongue became too heavy for him to talk, and then he used that pen to write and let people know what happened to him so they could help him get to safety and receive the treatment he needed to reestablish his health. More than twice, that pen was used as a savior for him, from writing what he wanted on paper to sting his own skin when he was cramping in the ocean, to the time when he currently reached the ground where humans and certain other animals are more comfortable. That is enough to help you understand the reason why you should never let go of what you currently have in your hand until you replace it with a different but even better one.

Among the things that a person will never forget in their lifetime, eventually, that pen can be one of them, remarkably true for himself. In so many cases, it may never be a simple pen, but it can be any other subject that can contribute to you as a guarantee of protection or any kind of help authentic for you and probably not only yourself but your friend. You don't have to be like a man who was walking in a forest. When his former parents used to walk in the forest, they always had two objects at hand: one was a piece of metal that could make a great noise, and a second piece of iron to beat the large one as a drum to make some great noise. The parents taught that man to always carry them while walking in the forest, but after his parents passed away, he no longer carried those instruments with him when walking in the forest, and then he paid a serious consequence for that mistake. The reason for those instruments was because of so many wild beasts in the forest, like lions, bears, and more. So, each time they encountered a wild beast or more, they would slap together those pieces of metal, and these animals, who were afraid of that kind of noise, would run far away to avoid hearing the noise. At the same time, the animal didn't have any chance to attack anyone who made the noise. As for that person who definitely abandoned the strategy of his parents, in a day he did not expect, while he made his way through the forest with no fear, suddenly some wild animals approached him, and at that time, he did not have his arms, which were supposed to be two pieces of iron and metal. At this point, he survived by chance and miracle but not definitively without injuries.

If that person did not abandon the strategy of his wise parents, he could have prevented his problems with what he learned from them for his own protection. The same goes for the person who kept the pen; if that man was supposed to abandon his parents' strategy, he should have something better to protect himself, which may not always be something to make noise but anything serious that is true, like a map you need to use to go on a trip. If you minimize what is in that map while you are traveling, you may never get to the place where you want to be. It is the same if you are rejecting the good counsel of your parents; you may not do well as you expect in life.

You can replace a long road by a shortcut, but never by a dead end or a no outlet. Among what you are drinking, there are two things that nothing else can replace: number one is your mother's milk, and number two is the water most of you are drinking every day. Whatever the time and technique can offer, changes and replacements are good, but there are many things to consider unchangeable and not to modify for certain. Don't block your original long way before you are sure that you have a real shortcut.

Young Lady Displaced

A young lady was born into a rich family where everything was going well for her, but while a war caused some unstable conditions in her nation, she had been displaced to a different nation where there is zero communication with her parents and friends. Now she has to be everything for herself. Then she is a person who doesn't make friends easily and always refuses other people's help. At this instance, everything she had is already over, and she is refusing the help of others. Now life is not so sweet at all for her, day after day, things become harder and harder. A day arrives where she decides to end her life because she doesn't have any more money to buy food, she can no longer pay for her shelter, she cannot pay for any transportation to go anywhere, and she has no job to make any money to pay for anything. When other people who look at her as a person in need approach her and try to help her, she is refusing their help. She goes to a river border with it in her mind that she is going to kill herself to avoid more misery and suffering. When she eventually arrives at the river border, the first thing that grabs her attention is a kind of great ball. She tries to see what that ball is, meanwhile, she was thirsty, so she drinks some water and pours some over her face to wash her face. That way, she can see what that ball exactly is. So when she pays closer attention, she finds out that the ball is many ants who want to cross the river and cannot cross the river individually, but they are forming a great ball together. The river waves are pushing them while she continues to look. At a quarter-mile to a lower spot, the ants arrive at the other side of the river. As she continues to look, the ants form a long chain while they are walking away and leaving the side of the river.

Why do small creatures like ants cross a river looking for food and a better place to live? While you are looking for many answers, the greatest lesson is for the young girl to understand that sometimes she may not be the one to give to others but the one to receive from them. A major part of that lesson is to understand the importance of collectivity and doing certain things together, even just to survive. She should accept the help of others until things can be changed for her. One person can be weak, but more than one can be strong.

After observing the ants, she has forgotten about killing herself and tried walking back to town. While on the road, she meets some friends who have also been displaced and re-established themselves. They are helping her and give her some comfort and advice, which she does accept. Taking the step to accept their help keeps her more comfortable with them, and not too long after that period, she has reunited with her parents, and life has returned to normal for her. A winter of life can be caused by any means, but that should never be the end of the current life. A bridge is not the end of the road, and nut after nut makes the cane stronger. Now she sees and understands why so many people are different from others, but all remain the same as people, and if many ants can come together to help each other survive, humans can come together to help each other survive a harsh period.

Life continues for her and her family, thanks to the great example of the creatures named ants, who always accept the help of each other. Sometimes even the one who receives help is not so happy, only because they are not able to help themselves the way they want, but they currently don't have any choices, and that is the way for them to survive, so they must take it as a step to take them to their destinations. A person who never depended on others for anything at all, now, for some reason, has to turn to someone else for a piece of bread. That has a lot to think about, so if you are not crossed, you can be the weakest person ever. The best is the one who crosses with strong courage.

A group of hunters pursued a lion for more than seventeen times in three years and never caught that lion nor hurt him at all. While trying to hunt that lion out, any event can put you down in life before your time, but it is a simple game that means you can continue to win until your own time arrives, and you lay down and pass away peacefully as the hero of your time. A second of death erases a full life of enjoyment, just as a second of sadness puts a dark pit over a full memory of enjoyment and paints darkness over every rose in the wonderful hope garden for the future. As a second of darkness erases multi million years of light, a million bad actions in the past trail behind a good action in the present, but only one present bad action erases a million good actions done in the past.

When you say good morning, open your eyes as a sign of your presence with all your heart. Then, when you say goodbye, close your eyes as a sign of courage. Always remember something that may happen in your life or in somebody else's life. It may happen to be the one you do not like and even hate, it is the one who loves you the most, and the one you are loving with all your heart and soul that can be the one who hates you the most. The most perfection resides in what you can see from far away, as you look at the planet Earth from the sky in the airplane. The mind can be as perfect as the heart is, so nevertheless the eyes might see a great different history which is the truth.*

Enjoy all your perfect moments with your good strength, and be exempt from any moment of darkness in a person's heart with your own knowledge, and even your enemy will continue to memorize you and meditate at your untouchable passage, unforgettable forever. If you help the people you encounter to always have a beautiful smile on their face, that is the best of you. While they are living on earth, the most enjoyable moment they know is when they are breathing the fresh air. Despite all that, they do not complain about anything because complaining does nothing more than worsen a harsh moment in life.

*Some people are even afraid to do anything or go anywhere because whatever they do and wherever they go, there is someone who attacks or even hurts them, whether it can be physical or verbal.

If they are helping someone, the person they are helping may pay them with a bitter heart in return. If someone promises to help them, it might be a snare just to trap them and do something wrong to them.

If you have never witnessed anything similar, you may never believe it, but surely that exists in many cases for some others. Some people create actions that are not pleasant at all to make fun of people they don't even know or don't want to live in peace. They find pleasure in seeing others in discomfort.

Whenever those people are eating ice cream, they want to see the other eat toothpaste; that way, they can be happy and make fun for themselves. Now, when they are eating cheese, they will be content to see someone they don't like eating a piece of soap as if it were cheese. When that happens, they will be happy enough to ask how it tastes, whether it is sweet or bitter. Then they make fun for themselves, and the victims, themselves like perishing animals in a mud pit, just must believe a moment of unconsciousness can be the better moment for them to be. For instance, a man may call another one and invite him to drink. At the table, he puts some alcoholic drinks for him, while he himself drinks some non-alcoholic drinks. He wants to prove that he cannot get drunk even if drinking a lot, and at the same time, make the other person drunk with an alcoholic drink. Then he can go ahead and make fun of him with the one he believes is a good friend for him.

If you are not too sure what kind of friend you have, just beware of what can happen to you, especially when new friends invite you. If you don't have a good reason to go, remember you can always buy your own drink and food. Not too many people have to be eating and drinking with you to be your friend. If you don't have a good reason and are unsure about who you are dealing with, be cautious.

A woman who wants to make fun of her friend puts a hard cheese among some soap. She grabs the hard cheese and asks her friend to grab some to eat also. While eating the hard cheese, her friend eats the soap. Currently, it is just like doing something wrong to a baby, and she is doing so just to make fun. Some people do such things to make the other person feel sad or humiliated somehow. Sometimes, those who do such things think they are wise, but such actions can never be the actions of a wise person. It is like a blind person trying to guide those who are walking in the darkness. A blind person may need a guide, but when night arrives, there is much difference for a person who is not blind to walk in the darkness.

If it is a serious darkness where you cannot find any light at all, you need to beware and not follow a blind person who may try to guide you. In times of uncertainty, where you cannot identify the faces, try to identify the voices, so a blind person may not try to guide you into a wrong path in your life.

You may say, "Well, that will never happen to me, and a friend cannot make me eat soap for cheese or toothpaste for ice cream." But how many times have your own friends made you do something they will never do themselves? How many times have you declared with your own mouth that your friend made you do something you didn't mean to do? If you realize that is true, you need to beware of being influenced negatively because if your friend would not do it themselves and they make you do it, then, they are making you eat soap while they are eating cheese, and make you eat toothpaste for ice cream while they are enjoying real ice cream. Now they are drinking a good non-alcohol drink, and they are giving you some alcoholic drinks for you to get drunk. As a result, you are doing every undesirable thing you never wanted to do before.

Never let your false friends push you to do any regrettable things that can put you down in life. Instead of false friends, it is better to follow your principles as guidance for yourself because even friends with good hearts sometimes may have no knowledge of the wrong course they lead you to. More than that, some of your friends may be mean enough to put you on the wrong track just to become superior to you. The first heart that enjoys your defeat is a friend. Be a light for yourself and be responsible for your own actions. You must deal with your own conscience if things go wrong, and take courage to pay or repair your own mistakes if you can.

A mother is trying to breastfeed a baby who is not her own baby. That baby makes a test with his nose and by his actions says to the mother, "You are not my mother. Thank you for your help, but I will not drink your milk." Sometimes you must know how to discern right and wrong in the way of life and make what is best for yourselves.

Two Young Men Running for a Pretty Girl

Two young men were running for a beautiful girl; one of them was a lot wealthier than the other. But the parents of that young girl were preferring the man who is less wealthy because they thought the less wealthy man can be more responsible than the wealthier man. Meaning that the wealthier man may not care for the girl, as they care for their daughter. They were not only looking for a rich person, but a person they can be comfortable with, that is true. But the girl will go soon in the path of the wealthier man. How will that happen? So, the wealthy man who sees the parents of that girl does not prefer him over the other man, so he tells the other man, "My friend, we want to show the other men over here we are the best. When the weekend arrives, we are going to make a festival not far from the house of that girl. That way they can see who we are exactly."

So, both men agree to make a festival, and the wealthy man makes sure the other man consumes enough alcoholic drink where he may not be able to control himself. And when that happens, he says to him, "Let's go to the house of the girl." The less fortunate man, who is already drunk, is the one they preferred for the girl. Now, after his so-called friend guides him to enter the gate, he dashes out and leaves him here. What happened? That man is so drunk he currently doesn't know what to say, he doesn't know where he is at. Then he does something wrong, very unappreciated. They didn't know what was happening, so they put him outside.

After that day when he gets back to normal, he becomes so ashamed and has no more courage to go back to the house of that girl anymore. Then the fortunate wealthy man grabs the spoil. The less wealthy man was not only less of materials or money but less of knowledge and wisdom. Then he lost his battle for the beautiful girl who loved him, where he is not prepared to defend himself against the malicious so-called friend who schemed the snare against him.

Then he drinks the alcoholic cup his competitor gives him to drink and defeats him for the pretty girl. After his unintentional bad action, he is morally destroyed and becomes too weak to stand before the girl and her parents. His false friend eats the cheese and gives him a soap for him to eat as cheese, the other man eats the ice cream and gives him the toothpaste to eat as ice cream. Sometimes your kind of relationship with someone can make you trust him completely. If that can be just for a simple reason, if that reason is over, you will not have that friend anymore. Sometimes it is good to know a person who climbs a tree for its fruits will go back down after harvesting the fruits.

Imagine if it were you who chose a friend who made you drunk just to degrade you enough so he could grab what was at your hands. Can you blame him or yourselves? After all, did that man used to be his friend before? If not, why did he agree to make a festival together with that man? Did he know that man is competing with him for the girl? Should that man be happier than himself to see the parents prefer him as less fortunate over himself? If he should not be happier as a defeat, he should never be the one to make a festival for you to enjoy yourselves. The malicious eats ice cream, the fool eats toothpaste for the ice cream. Most of the time when someone wants to steal what you possess, he puts you to a test to see if you are wise enough to tie him out. If he feels you are not strong, he just makes you give that away to him instead of taking it as a real thief.

If you have a feeling someone is trying to steal what you have, don't even listen to his talks, always make your path greater than his path. That ladder is very tall; each item is found at a different level, each kind in a different manner. From a person to his resemblances, and territory to nations. If you betray someone who is important for you, not only for yourselves but for a nation or for the world, those who view your actions will see you as a person who is deceiving himself without proper knowledge. You are the unwise who eats the soap in place of cheese and eats toothpaste for ice cream and drinks pure alcohol and rum for a non-alcohol drink.

A man was receiving plenty of money and has a lot of proposals of what he is going to receive if he betrays and kills a very important person. Of course, he can kill that person, but he just ignores when he kills someone, he is a criminal who cannot be at any important place if there is a good reason for that. As a criminal, you cannot talk to a good person at any moment if there is not a special reason for that. And you cannot be free. How would you enjoy that money? These things they propose to give to you, how would you receive them? Even with the money they already give you, they know exactly you are going to give that money back to them via some other sources when you are trying to shield or be free from the trap of greed, selfishness, and criminality. You will add what you had to it just to breathe some more hours before they can just forget about you in your bitter cup as a fool. You will never sit down together anymore with the one who pays you money to do such wrong actions.

Fools don't take time to act and don't ask questions even to themselves about how things may turn for them or their surroundings. It happens as a fool who leaves his home to sleep in the jungles with rats and venomous serpents. As a plate of food given away for a load of mud who cannot eat nor use it as anything good at all. The man makes his action; he accepts the promises and takes the money and betrays and kills the important person. That doesn't take him long to see he can no longer stay at his house with his family, and he is no longer a free person with a lot of possibilities. Now a rat can be seen anywhere, as for him, at this time, if only he was a rat, he could be happy.

He was a tool used for a certain thing. After it is used, they must put that tool to a safe place so that nobody else who is important will be injured by that tool. Of course, after he has done killing an important person like that for them, they must make sure they are keeping him in a safe place with the maximum security that way he may not get money from someone else and come over to do the same action on them too. Small tools like machetes, picas, and knives can be used at a farm to plant vegetables. After that, they must put them in a safe spot just to prevent any injury from them. That man let them use him as a tool to kill and believe they are going to let him be a free and rich person around them.

They sharpen you as a machete to cut anything they want to cut; now your missions are over you must be retired inside between four walls with a top on it that way you must not cut anybody else. Your better food where you are right now is some rust, no more meat for you to cut, no more vegetables for you to plant. Not everyone of those kinds is put in safe places, some of them are turned to dust before opening the mouth, because when they have a feeling that what they were thinking turned out to be different for them they may tell the truth. On that bridge, whoever gives them toothpaste for ice cream can stop them before they are told who hired them to commit a crime and become criminals. That man destroys what he had, which was a good person, and destroys himself as a person who can be a good tool for himself in some good manner. And if he has a family, that family must be living as cicadas before they rise from the underground where they spend most of their life.

Deception, misleading, and betrayal; these actions always have a big repercussion on the shameless person who always commits those actions. The same as a small seed planted in good soil can grow big and give so many fruits, the same way those who are put in their mind to execute those actions will never stop producing the wrong ideas until they guide themselves to a dark pit where they will not be able to get out anymore. The apparent winner is the one who wants them to be involved in greed and selfishness as the result of many disasters. It can be sad to have ears and always deaf or play deaf for self-destruction. Have a nose and never be able to smell the good odor. Have eyes and never be able to see clearly what is the right or the wrong way.

You cannot always have a believer in mind; whatever they are presenting you, that is exactly what you were waiting for and hoping for. All the birds eat at the same tree, but they are flying in many directions to different habitats. If you let anyone use you to do what they want to do as wrong and personal actions, then you are the one who will pay the bad price. Every bird at a certain time must go back, whether on a branch or to a nest. If you are the one who gets drunk, you will be the only one to forget where your branch or your nest can be. At that point, you will not be let out to cause any dangers to the others. They will put you somewhere, and the one who was getting you drunk for his own purposes can be the first one to isolate you for his own protection.

Make sure you can identify soap and cheese, and what is ice cream and toothpaste, then what is non-alcoholic drink and alcoholic drink. That means to identify malicious friends and their wrong intentions to use you as tools to execute their wrong ideas. You don't want to look like people in a poor village where a rich man is coming over here and sees their miseries and the rich man decides to build enough houses for everybody. When that rich man started building, they were very happy. Not too long after that, some of them start receiving some beautiful apartments for them to live in. Everyone is happy because that rich man opened a place for them in that village where each one can collect enough food for every month, then the families are happy.

So, things start going smoothly for that village. Years go by; the people in that village are no longer going outside the village to work for their neighbors for food anymore. And the neighbors learn about the projects, they are coming over, they look, and see for themselves what the rich man accomplishes for those poor village people. After visiting the village, they see what the rich man realized for the poor. They become so jealous, and that jealousy is pushing them to meet with those who don't have the sense to understand what is bad nor good.

They say to them, "You guys have been working for us for a long time; you always have food to eat, and we let you build your own place to live. Now if you accept to live in that rich man's house, it is the same as if you are living with him at his own home, and he can come over at any time to put you out of those houses. What you must do is to use fire and burn these houses and make a plan so you can kill that man, so he might not take over your village. Then we'll give you whatever you need to make these actions. As you know, we have been good friends for a long time. We cannot sit here and let that happen to you."

Unfortunately, the poor and dumb fools don't have the sense to reason for themselves to see that they were only leaving the village to work for their neighbors just for some food. Not enough for their children to eat, and they must do it at all times in their life until they die. They never have a chance to build any house; their neighbors did never help them to build any place to live at all. Why should they destroy what they have for free, and kill the man who made that good for them? That question was never asked because they met with a group of fools who cannot identify soap and cheese, toothpaste and ice cream, alcohol and non-alcoholic drink.

One venomous serpent carries enough venom to kill so many people. These fools, with their brainwashed, start their wrong activities burning houses until they are killing the rich man and continuing to burn and destroy the houses he built for them. Even though most of the people in the village don't want to see that happen and do not enjoy seeing those actions, they have no control of what's going on in the village day and night. Some people lost what they possessed; for some others, they even lost their lives inside the houses.

A wise person always takes some time to think about right and wrong, but the fool is content with less than an oz of alcoholic drink to destroy a million lives that includes himself who weighs nothing good. When most of the people who live in the village believe they've crossed a terrible ocean and they are going to thank the mercy of a good man, unfortunately, the venomous serpents they had among them drag them deeper into slavery with no choices. Where they are going to be condemned to an activity work force for a piece of bread, which is not enough to feed their children, that way they must continue actively working.

The same way a venomous serpent often poses a danger for any other life around, that is the same way the people who can compare to venomous serpents are always active and always want to lead ahead, but nothing good can be expected from them other than demonstrations of intelligence and ability to jump and skip over to create a nightmare for those who are around them. Their words are enough to cause a million accidents per day and destroy more than a million trees per second and put fire over more than half of the world in one hour of sixty minutes.

After the fool does the assassination of the rich man who was helping them, it doesn't take a long period of time for them to find themselves back in pure misery, where they are constantly accusing and blaming each other for that horrible action that is causing so much loss of lives and materials.

Right now, the neighbors are reducing their breads to half a piece instead of one piece. Whoever in the past received one piece when they worked for it, now they will no longer receive one piece but half a piece. Those who used to work for half a piece are no longer able to be there at all. What a regrettable action! The fool always regrets and must regret after their wrong actions when they are not yet dead as a result of their own bad actions of malice, threat, and often betraying themselves by believing they are doing a good action. After all, the neighbors who hired them to kill the man who was there to help them and build houses for them, these neighbors are too far in their offices, nowhere to be found. Those kinds don't have ears to listen to the fool crying behind them.

Truly, anybody can be poor, but one category will never skip poverty: those who are fools. Being associated with them can cause some serious dangers for any existing. What not to minimize is that a fool always wants to rule and dominate the others, easily deceiving them to betray the important one just for the false promises that cannot help them after that accomplishment. A snake can identify its tail and its head, but those who are fools cannot identify what belongs to them nor what can protect them or what they must protect for their own profits.

A snake knows when to sleep under a rock and when to sleep on the rock. Fools always believe they are at peace even when a fire starts at their own house. If the neighbors say to them, "Put fire at your house, and only the bugs will be burned, and you with your belongings will be saved and safe." The fool will go ahead and put the fire, and later, when they have lost their strength by crying for help, the neighbors will be too far away, and the next day, they may negotiate on something so they can give you some cereal as help.

Now the neighbors are back with a different face, with a questionnaire for you to answer questions before anything else may be promised. Not only questions, but a lot of undesirable actions may be on the table to be addressed before another proposal can offer hope for living. Yes, hope makes living possible; take patience, be hopeful, and you will achieve something if you are not yet deceased before the time arrives. As you might expect, another event will happen again before the previous one can be over, and then the process continues. One daylight, or half of a day; if you are not dead, you exist. If you are existing, you can witness the sunrise or the earth turning over. People say 'sunset,' and that may be true, but when the planet Earth turns to the other side, Earth itself may block the sunlight from the side that is not facing the sun. Truth be told, if it rises, it can also set, but if it arrives, it can also depart.

After a real act of foolishness, the foolish one doesn't care about night or daytime. Most of them prefer not to be there at all. Every case may never be the same, but just as you see people put all kinds of food on the table to nourish themselves, it's the same way that every bad action can take anyone to the same place in life. Think twice each time you must face a certain situation. If you think you want to make a different name for yourself, because those who are weak, those who don't care about anything, will do whatever they can to make you the same as they are themselves. Not everyone in the row is meant to be there; sometimes they are not the real ones or the right ones. Sometimes it's the wrong place with the wrong ones. Sometimes you become a victim for some reason. Crazy can be cured, but there is no cure for a fool.

A wrong neighbor is so jealous of a family that he schemes a plan with the children of the family. He subdues them to make them kill their own parents. That wrong neighbor washes the brains of the children and promises them that he will be everything for them, telling them their parents don't want their freedom, but he is the one who will set them free and give them whatever they desire in life. Then, after the children become drunk with that kind of brainwash, they no longer cultivate any love for their parents and do what the malicious neighbor wants them to accomplish against themselves. That neighbor deceives the children and makes them act as the real wrongdoers, and all that bad neighbor wants is to destroy the family.

Unfortunately, the kids believe they will be free and happy without their parents because they don't have enough sense to understand that the neighbor is a malicious demon who wants to put them in a pit with their parents. They put all their minds in that bad neighbor. Not too long after the tragic events, the neighbor tells them he cannot take them to his family because he is afraid they may do the same thing to him and his family. Now, the victims' kids fall to the street and beg for food to survive, with their consciences too burdensome for them to carry. Whoever knows what happened sees them as horrible children. Most of the time, children are too vulnerable and don't have enough strength to resist certain malicious snares.

The only way to prevent those is to understand that your friend has nothing much to do with your kids. Your friend is your friend, but not a friend to your kids. That means if your friend has anything to do with your kids, you must be the first for him to address, and in your absence, your kids may never be present to your friend. If your friend has a conversation with your children, honestly, you have the responsibility to know the nature of that conversation, and you should never let your kids out of your own supervision when you are among others, whether you call them friends or not. You will never know who can provoke jealousy against your family. Your enemies cannot poison you, but just your friend can do that, directly or through your own child who doesn't have knowledge of what they are doing until after they take the wrong path.

A drunk person has no control over what he can do, and that is no different for a person who continues to multiply bad ideas against others. At a certain time, that will turn into a real disaster for anyone he can contact directly or in any other ways. As for the kid, parents always want their kids to consume something good. It is the same way for their hearts; parents need to make sure that their kids do not consume any bad ideas from what they listen to from others, especially from malicious people who can destroy your kids with simple words, just like small seeds sown in fertile soil that will not take long for those seeds to sprout and grow enough to produce a lot for many. Imagine if those seeds were bad; that is not what you hope for your kids.

Remember, this not only happens in the kids' kingdom but in many ranges. Sometimes, it's important to live like a serpent; when you believe you are going to find a serpent under the rock, that serpent is on the rock at the point where you did not prepare to meet the serpent there. That serpent has a great chance to flee or even harm you by surprise. The serpent knows the importance of its head and its tail, so it doesn't leave them behind when it is sleeping; it puts them in the middle of itself for its own protection. That should be the same thing for good parents; you must put your kids under your supervision at all times. That is protection for your children and you.

You can be betrayed and killed by the most trusted friend of yours, the one you share half of your loaf of bread with; it is the same one who wants to have your whole loaf. The person who gains possession of your bread might be a trusted friend, but they will be the one who gets you killed. Never minimize the fact that if a thief doesn't know you and thinks you have no knowledge of them, they may grab your bread and leave you with your life. However, those who know you will get you killed before they grab your bread. This can happen at every level of wickedness; they won't worry about your life, no matter how important you are to them or to others. They only want to destroy you so that no one might mention your name higher than theirs.

Just like a predator bird that doesn't worry about how many eggs or chicks the victim might leave in the nest, and how much it reduces the population of that bird, those who are malicious are only worried about what to eat when they are hungry and what to feed their chicks. As for the animals, they are only doing what they need to feed their chicks and themselves. But humans kill because of jealousy; if a person is ahead of them, that can be a big cause for them to plot your death, so they can have a door open to jump over. Even though most of the time they end up in a one-way situation with serious dangers waiting for them, it may happen many times, but it's not enough to make changes. Don't be surprised because thistles and thorns remain the same at all times; they never change regardless of the season or the kind of soil they are in.

You must be prepared and careful of where you currently are and who is around you, what to do and not to do, what to say and not to say, who to embrace and who to stay away from. This way, the thorns will not be your seat, and the thistles cannot be your dress. In a landslide area, the wise don't sleep under the rock but on the rock; that is the only way to survive the landslide. As for the unwise, they make deep rock a stronghold for them, and when the landslide happens, they are not able to save their lives. But the wise, who were on the rock, can either skip or just watch the event passing by around them.

When you encounter a wild animal, you must be cautious and keep your distance, but when you must deal with bad people, you need to be wise because bad people can kill you, and others might come and say you killed yourself or committed suicide. It is much better, as you can do with the animal, to keep your distance if you can. However, sometimes you must deal with people every day in life, and that's when you need to be wise. When others can bring and carry things, then you don't have too much control over people. The more you might believe in a new technique to protect yourself, the faster others can kill you. While you might think there are some techniques that might scare them off, you are the only one who can watch over yourself. Every other person can be paralyzed just to get you killed, and this can happen from humans, just like a river that can be turned away from its original course to accomplish a mission good for some and worst for others.

That is why a mother tells her son that his two eyes in his head are his bodyguards. Honor people but don't trust people, don't put your faith in people too much when you are not completely paralyzed. Do the most for yourself, be the most for yourself if it is necessary to do so; that can be the best way to exercise your wisdom against any snares you may never know about. Expose your help, but not yourself to them when they scheme against you and do not prevail. Then they will consider themselves lost, and you will continue to prevail over them each time you refuse to let them give you toothpaste for ice cream, soap for cheese, and rum alcohol for non-alcoholic drink. When you are instructing your family and everyone who wants to listen how to prevent themselves from being victims of those predators who can remove and destroy all important persons and materials around you and leave you as a blind person who can never see, who always needs someone to guide them, leave you as a deaf ear who can never hear anything at all, as a mute tongue who can never talk. That way, you will not seek anything good and cannot follow any real path as a human who cannot fully depend on others' help for an eternity.

A real mother with a lot of patience is continually helping her newborn, knowing that one day her child will grow and will not be completely dependent on her for everything. They may even help the mother at a certain point in life. That means a person cannot be dependent solely on others, except in some special cases. Those who are helping you can never be your enemies; therefore, even when you become rich or better, you should never minimize those who were helping you in the past, whatever kind of help you received was appropriate for the time that you were in need of it.

Man Abandons His Friend and Counselor

Two young people were born in a country with valleys and plains. There were rivers in the valleys between two mountains with many sources of water, torrents, and ravines joining the river. One of them was born into a family that others called a rich family or better people. Because they were friends, the one born into the fortunate family was a counselor for the other one. Everything he wanted to do, he asked his friend, and the friend always helped him out. This continued for many years, meaning many help for the one who was in need.

At a certain time, the man who was born into a less privileged family started making some progress for himself. At that point, he looked at his counselor and friend, whom he believed hadn't made enough wealthy progress to be his friend and counselor. He no longer needed the counselor's advice and started acting like a great person. Of course, that is what his friend and counselor had hoped for him when he was helping him with good advice. However, his friend didn't see it that way. He believed that a little material wealth could make him the greatest, but he forgot that if not with the knowledge of his counselor and friend, he wouldn't have achieved that level of success.

Time goes by, everybody lives with peace, so materials can disappear, but the knowledge you acquire will not leave you while you are in good health. That is why people must understand wisdom is a stronghold, meaning protection. When friends meet, everything is fine. However, if a friend no longer believes in some instances, a friend cannot be a counselor for him anymore. For him, if that friend had enough knowledge, he can be materially rich. That is the way he thought, but that is not the point of view of the other friend.

One day, by coincidence or by traveling at the same time, both friends are crossing the river and reaching the other side of the country. Not too far away, they hear some kind of noise, and they both look back to see a great tornado actively destroying the area they came from. At that point, both men were there, but indeed, each one must make a decision for himself whether to go back or not. While the wise one stops to think about what to do, the other man is running back so he can probably save his materials. There was so much wind and so much water; the river was not a safe place for a person to cross at that moment. If anyone was in the middle of that river, things could be very serious. The man who only worries about his wealth behind him takes no time to consider any advice about whether it is safe to go back or not. All he can think about is crossing the river and getting back to his house so he can protect his wealth while the tornado is not yet over.

His friend and former counselor had no chance to talk to him before he ran back, and he himself didn't want to hear anyone telling him what he didn't want to hear. He attempted to cross the river and was immediately swept away by the current and strong wind, rendering him unconscious. Fortunately, some people were there and immediately took him to the hospital, where they took care of him and released him after about a week so he could go back to his house.

After that event, he remembered his friend was there and didn't go back into the active tornado area. Now he had a chance to understand that if he had talked to his friend before deciding to cross the river, that wouldn't have happened to him. His friend and counselor would never have let him try to cross the river. Now he not only lost his house and wealth or materials, but he also had to pay plenty of money for the care he received at the hospital. Additionally, he lost a bag in the river that contained a lot of cash he was going to deposit in a bank not far from where he made his decision to head back because of the active tornado in his city, where he lost his home.

After these losses, he realized that the most valuable thing he should have acquired was knowledge to protect his life and the discernment of what is most possible in his life. A tree can produce many fruits, but a tree will never produce the one who planted it. If you want to go south and you are taking the north direction, you will never get to your destination. If his counselor had given him some wrong advice, he would never have reached the level where he believed he could get rich. So when he believed he had become great enough to abandon his friend's advice, he led himself down the wrong path in his life.

Now, after losing what he had, he realized that he needed some help. However, the smart man did not lose his knowledge in that tornado; he still possessed his ability to discern the better way to survive. If the eggs' basket does not abandon the chicken, don't forget to throw some corn on the ground; that way, the chicken can continue to produce eggs. That man believed he would never need his friend anymore, but after the tornado event, he knew for sure that he needed someone to advise him in some way to get back on track.

This time, would a lesser counselor agree to advise the greatest man? Only the future can tell what is in the heart. A wild animal can live in a house or in captivity, but a wild animal can kill itself if you take it into captivity without good care or some special protections. Similarly, a person who was once rich, after becoming poor, may see the world disappearing with them due to the loss of material possessions they considered their wealth. Of course, if they eat and drink, they will not die, but in their minds, there are so many unexplained situations that create many mental disorders.

Despite this, everyone else who never became rich is comfortable where they are. Maybe for the poor, it's not surprising because not many people believe that if they become rich, they will have a better life. That might not always be true in every case. Some, if they become rich, will die at the same time or too soon. Some will see that their riches disappear. It's fortunate if you don't disappear before your wealth does. For many, it can be easier to catch by hand an eel in a river or catch a murray in the ocean than to keep their inherited wealth or the wealth gained by luck or chance.

To manage anything, you first need training. Unfortunately, not everyone knows how to manage so many things in life. Often people try things that later turn out to be the worst for them.

A man has his beautiful stronghold on land he inherited from his parents. On that land, he has a water source. The running waters from that source form a ravine near his land, and this ravine diverts into a river not far from his property. One day, the man decides to prevent the water from going anywhere but staying at its source. How can he do that? He decides to create a canal in a circular shape that can return to the main water source.

After he completes his canal, he opens the last section so the water can enter the canal. This is what he has done. Because he made the canal in a circular shape around his property, when he opens the canal's last section, the water continues to follow this circular path. Finding no way to divert, overnight the water creates a lake on his land. Then, with the help of heavy rain early in the morning, the man finds himself in the middle of a lake, with everything submerged.

Now is the time for him to see how much water he has accumulated and how much water he doesn't need. Now, he has a chance to understand why a water source, while running, can form a ravine, and further, that ravine can become a torrent, then a river, or even flow into other rivers until it reaches the ocean. This man, who doesn't want to live forever as a crab or a two-foot fish, undoes his canal and lets the water find its way down to the river. Perhaps he wanted to achieve something great, but he lacked the knowledge to accomplish it.

Naturally, the water was there, and the man had nothing to lose, whether the water constantly flowed away or created a lake. The only thing is, certain things you believe you own, cannot respect the order of private property; they will switch out and go wherever they want. Water is one of them. You may claim to own the source of water, but you cannot stop it from flowing away and crossing into other people's property. You may have the privilege of the mine, but you cannot control the water as if it will obey you unless you possess specialized scientific knowledge to control it for a limited time.

A farmer may try to keep the water mostly for himself, but if he does so, that can cost him his productions. Sometimes, country neighbors may try to stop a river from shifting to the other neighbors, but most of the time, that can be in vain. The real thing is to take what you need and let nature pursue its course for the benefit of others. You cannot stop the rain from going where it wants to go, and you cannot prevent the sun from shining where your heart is not desired. That cannot be private to you, and it will not obey your orders.

Where humans can decide to betray one another, nature cannot and will never do that. Imagine a man who always goes under a mango tree to pick some mangoes. One day, he goes and doesn't find any mango fruits. Maybe the season for mangoes is over. At this point, the man looks around and sees some thistles at the base of that mango tree. He goes back to his vehicle, returns with his tools, and uses them to remove those thistles from the mango tree's roots. This makes it easier for the tree to produce more fruits.

The man understands that the mango tree doesn't have any fruits to offer him today. However, this is not a reason for him to cut down the mango tree. Instead, he offers the tree some help as encouragement. How long have you been receiving from others? If you have nothing to give at the moment, that's not a problem. But it's always better when you're the one giving rather than receiving all the time. One appropriate word of encouragement is worth more than a fortress.

Man Casts Net to Survive

A man was living in a city where the ocean was not far from his home. That man had to cast his net every day to catch some fish for him and his family to survive. One day, he was catching plenty of fish, and now he needed someone to help him bring these fish to the marketplace so he could sell them for some money. Each time he went fishing, there were two men who always sat on the side of the road, and he always gave them some fish. So, when he needed help with his fishes, he approached them and asked if they would be comfortable joining him on his fishing trip. One of them agreed, but the other one did not. The fishing man was happy to take the one guy with him every day to the ocean with his net, as they were doing it for a living. He was no longer by himself, and having a partner allowed them to catch more fish in the fastest way so they could go to the market at the right time. This partnership allowed them to make a good amount of money every day, which was appreciated by the man who used to sit by the road every day, doing something he did not enjoy. Thanks to his fishing friend, he became a free man who could support himself and no longer had to beg for food from others.

As for the man who had refused to join them in fishing, he continued to beg on the side of the road and did not work to become self-sufficient like his friend. He chose to stay on the road rather than work to become free from being a beggar. Meanwhile, the two fishing men wasted no time in buying whatever they needed to make their fishing activities easier and faster. They even built a small store to sell their fishes. The new fishing partner learned how to be a great fisherman, thanks to the chance given to him by the fishing man, and they both became good partners, making enough money to live a good life like everybody else. There's a valuable lesson here for the lazy man who refused to work. Laziness is a form of negligence that keeps a person enslaved to inaction and leads to a dead end in life. Being lazy does not take a person anywhere good; instead, it causes them to be a disaster in life. A lazy mind can lay you down at a dead end of life where only what you want to put in your mouth can occupy your mind at all times, which is not good for a person who is physically capable to sit down and put mind to the others to supply their needs.

Sometimes people ask for help, but you can benefit the most from offering that help. For instance, imagine the man who used to sit on the side of the road receiving fish from the fishing man. Now, they are two good partners who know how to catch fish and share them. Even the former friend, who was not happy to join the great fishing man to become a great fisherman himself, now benefits from their partnership. Taking action like this is like refusing to leave an internal camp and saying goodbye to the cause. If this refusal leads to discouragement, a person may never want to ask for help or even eat anything. Waking someone up from their sleep may require knocking many times before they wake up, and although this can be relative, unfortunately, not many people want to offer more than one opportunity, especially when many others are waiting for that offer. If you miss the first chance, you may no longer qualify for anything in this part.

A young person was moving from one town to another. Among the new people he met were two young men who did not have any jobs and were not in school. They were always at home. Currently, the new man is encouraging them by saying, "While you are not working and the school in this town is free, let's take the chance and spend some time at the school. Probably that can be a good path for us to the possibility of learning a trade for a better way in life." One of them agreed and followed this path for about a week before he quit. The other one did not make it because he found a job the following week.

As for the man who decided to quit school, he never found a job, and he refused to spend his time at school. This continued for a long time. The new man who followed school had a chance to get a degree, learn a better profession, and become a person who can discern right from wrong. He could also help himself and those in need. As for the man who refused to learn a profession, he continued to be jobless from a young age until his retirement. He was known as someone content to live this way.

Whether you cannot find a job or you are never qualified to get one, others will see you as a remarkable person, like a lazy one and a parasite who wants to live at the expense of somebody else. Turning a deaf ear to good advice is a direct refusal of a good proposition, like a free life and a good opportunity to become a person who can help themselves and not rely on others for their daily living.

The most a person can do for you is to show you a road out of the wilderness and darkness, freeing you from dependence on others. This way, you can extend a helping hand to those who genuinely need your support to survive.

Sometimes it is more important to even refuse a plate of good food while you are hungry and listen to wise talk, because a simple word can redraw you from a pit of darkness. If you have a good memory, the best time to remember who was teaching you to swim is after you have been swept away by the current of the river, and you swim back out by yourselves. At that moment, you may take a moment to ask yourself, suppose you did not accept learning how to swim. That is a good question because if you did not accept learning how to swim, you will never be there to ask yourself that question either, because at the time you were swept away, every memory of what you can produce by yourselves should be over with you at the bottom of many waters.

A person who is refused a good idea by another person and pays the price of it does not often remember it. Every person who is taking the wrong road by refusing the advice of someone after their defeats, they prefer not to see the face of that person anymore. That is the gate where only one of the two enemies can enter; if the bad one enters, the right one will not enter, because the wrong are afraid to meet with the truth. If you tell someone not to do something, and he does it and gets punished, make sure if you see that person you go to the other way, sometimes people can feel like they are punished twice when they have to face a person who knows their error, especially a person who was trying to prevent them from that snare when they had refused to take the right path for their own protection.

Alarm Security Bird

Someone can tell you to beware of a danger, but they cannot guide your life, you are the only person to make sure you secure your life in the right way. As the alarmed bird who rings his alarm to notice the other birds of the presence of the predator, at the same time that bird puts himself in a safe place, that way he must not be the victim of the predator. That bird is not only letting the other birds know the presence of the predator, but he lets them know when the predator is leaving the territory, that way they can feel safe and free. If only humans could have that high security! Unfortunately, human security gets paid, and most are not honest. That security bird may not get paid any money but gets the trust and respect of the other birds for his honesty. He is a volunteer who puts himself at the service of the community birds.

If you have any chicken or some other birds, you may already know the security birds. Whenever he is alarming, all the other birds go in hiding until he puts the safety alarm out for them to be free. No bird can ignore that signal. Immediately they hear that alarm, they must hide themselves instantly. If one bird makes a mistake and is not hiding, probably that bird will be the one to pay his life for that mistake. Every other bird, big or small, respects that security bird, whenever he puts the alarm, all birds obey him. Do you know why every other bird always obeys the signal of the security birds? And why are humans not too serious about the others' human alarm?

So, imagine that the bird is a volunteer who wants to protect the others, this is a bird who doesn't know anything about glory, and this is a bird who doesn't have anything to do with a paycheck, and will never be interested in getting pay for anything, a bird who doesn't know anything about dishonesty, a bird who doesn't know anything about deception, a bird who has no reason to betray, a bird who is smart enough to discern if he betrays a bird today, the next day when the predator cannot find a meal, he will be the meal for him. That bird doesn't have a feeling for any other bird to adore him and venerate him for anything he does, and that is not considering doing anything for the other birds, but he just views his mission to be accomplished in their favors. That bird doesn't feel like he wants comfort and retirement where the others must be grateful to him, whether as a hero or anything greater, not even a savior. That bird never changes his plumage to disturb any other bird for a personal reason or to please a greater bird or predators. That bird spends all his life with one kind, the nest, if destroyed by an event, that bird builds another nest as the first one. That bird never builds multiple nests to rent or sell with the other birds, this is a bird who finds his food today by himself and finds his food tomorrow by himself.

So those multiple reasons make it safe for all the other birds to love him and respect his order at all times because he has no reason to lie or do any false alarm to betray them. If a bird can find that much respect and confidence among the other birds, what about humans? So, humans can protect humans and let them know a lot of things, among all of them is a hurricane when a hurricane is on his path. Everyone can be grateful to hear the news and much more detail about what to do to protect yourselves. But human is not so absorbing of every alarm of the others because humans have some weakness who can push them to exaggerate or falsely managing certain thing they may have to share as alarm of protections for the others, certain people even can create some tracts or railroad of events to disturb others for personal reasons causing so many ideas, it make it so difficult for the true human alarm to be taken as serious as their supposed to be, even though some of the many are seriously supportive. The people who are working so hard with all their strength to provide with their sincerity and severity what the others hope from them take it as seriously as possible, Those are many of the ones who are concerned can also confuse and pay the price for not being obedient to such a serious alarm.

If the bird can be honest, humans maybe can be honest too. If the bird can be trusted, maybe humans can be trusted too. Before the clock and particularly watches were branded and available for many people, birds like roosters were so important for the people. Because most of the roosters crow to indicate a precise time, especially at night time. Each time a rooster crowed, that indicated a time important for the people at the night, and the rooster would remain silent until the morning time when all farmers and travelers were waiting to hear when the first rooster would crow for them to wake up, because the roosters were trustworthy in helping people know how to do their schedules. Some wanted to wake up at the first rooster's crow, depending on the distance they were going to travel. Some other people wanted to wake up at the second rooster's crow, and some others wanted to wake up at the third rooster's crow. Some who were not going anywhere waited until they could see the light of the day. Each time the roosters started to crow, that meant one exact time hour; then after some minutes, all roosters remained silent until the next important hour. Some roosters crowed at supper time or dinner hour after the sun was over the earth. And they would crow again until midnight. After midnight, it would be at the hour of four o'clock in the morning, then next would be at six o'clock, and they would continue to make war with the lazy people until they finally woke up. Because of that kind of loyalty, there was a conversation meeting about a festival they wanted to make to honor the roosters.

When that conversation was taking place, a dog was lying down under a bench and listening to the conversation. When the dog heard the word "favorite meal," he thought it must be meat. The dog listened to the festival's schedules and the place where the festival would be. Even though the dog was not invited, he made his plan to be there in advance so he could own the place and make sure he could eat enough meat. The dog was happy because he knew roosters don't eat as fast as himself, and the roosters might be a little afraid of him when he grabs the meat, he will be the super dog at the festival. The dog took three days to prepare himself before the festival, during which he found nothing to eat. He stayed there, waiting for the festival to enjoy a lot of meat. However, when the day arrived, all the roosters came with their families, crowing beautiful songs. Musicians played various instruments, including drums with beef skin covers, creating beautiful music for the roosters. It was a grand festival for the roosters and their hens, chickens, and chicks.

When it was time to savor the food. The dog heard a voice that said to bring the food over. The dog is very happy because he hasn't eaten anything in three days and became so weak just waiting to be compensated with a lot of meat. The dog switched himself under a table from the bench and stopped behind the drum made with beef skins. He cannot wait to see them put some meat where he can reach so he can start eating and build back his powers. However, rather than meat, everybody brought baskets filled with dried corn and threw the corn all over the place. All the chicks, hens, chickens, and roosters began enjoying the corn, while the dog sniffed at the corn but couldn't eat any. The dog, who had not eaten anything for more than three days, was disappointed. He had hoped for a meat feast but found nothing but dried corn. Now, the dog knew that his favorite food was meat, while the roosters' favorite food was dried corn. The festival turned out to be a disappointment for the dog, as he couldn't eat the corn. The roosters, on the other hand, enjoyed the festival with their families. Maybe the roosters were happy to see the dog there, providing protection from cats, but unfortunately, the dog couldn't enjoy the corn. In fact, he was so weak that he couldn't even make his way back to where he lived. While standing there, watching the roosters enjoying themselves, the dog began sniffing the drums made with beef skins, thinking they smelled good enough to eat. The dog started gnawing on the drums, but a musician saw him and struck him over his back many times with a baton. The dog, weak and in pain, cried out, and someone called animal control. When they arrived, they thought the dog might be aggressive, so they put a needle in his back that put him to sleep with anesthesia and then took him away in a cage.

After taking care of the dog, he was taken into captivity. When he woke up from anesthesia, the dog found himself in captivity. The meat feast he had anticipated turned out to be nothing more than dried corn, and he was now weak and in captivity. The dog realized that he had made a wrong decision driven by his love for meat and the festival. Even though he was not invited, he wanted to be the first to attend. Now, the dog must stay private and under control to prevent him from disturbing anyone with his belief in his loyalty and faithfulness. He must wait for his own time to prove his merit. As for now, the roosters and their families are the ones who benefit from the festival, and the roosters may be happy to see the dog there, providing protection from cats. Unfortunately, the dog cannot eat the dried corn, and the festival was not appropriate for him. As for the roosters, everything was great, and they deserved the festival, as they started well, with no reproach, never deceiving anyone, and not betraying anyone at all. They executed their missions without any criticism.

About humans, can humans deceive other humans? Can a human be so dishonest as to betray another human? If so, to whom do you do a good action? Beasts or humans? The planet Earth will bear witness to good or bad actions. Today, not too many people may know about roosters, especially with the existence of clocks and watches, but they still crow wherever they are, whether you understand them or not. They fulfill their mission perfectly, and most of the time, you may ignore certain things in life that often depend on the area where you were born. As you know, where they have the greatest, they ignore the lesser, but they are still there, waiting in case we need them. Maybe it's good to know that chickens, especially roosters, not only serve as food but also help with time control for overnight activities and are great fighters with lazy people who don't want to wake up early in the morning. Each time the roosters continue to crow, the lazy people also continue to change sides on their bed. If the roosters crow ten times, the lazy person turns on his bed ten times too. The roosters continue to put their beak on the lazy and make them war until they can quit the bed and go to work.

Roosters are not only making war with the lazy people but also with some other animals who want to eat them, including cockerels, chicken chicks, and even other roosters. In the sky, there are many predators, and on the ground, there are also many animals eyeing rooster families as their favorite meal. Therefore, roosters have to be strong enough to fight off these predators. From the sky, there are eagles, hawks, and more, closely observing the roosters on the ground. The first thing they notice is the roosters' comb on their heads, which they believe to be a serious weapon due to its red and sharp appearance, resembling a dangerous weapon. These sky predators are genuinely afraid of this weapon, along with the roosters' wattles, which are also seen as formidable. Notably, the sky predators are more afraid of the roosters' combs and wattles than their spurs. However, they attempt to communicate with the roosters to persuade them to destroy these perceived weapons, which are considered as potential tools of mass destruction against other animals.

Despite repeated efforts, roosters steadfastly refuse to disarm themselves. Even eagles suggest that ground mammals advise roosters to get rid of these weapons, but the roosters remain adamant. On the ground, there are cats, snakes, mongooses, and even dogs that sometimes attack roosters where they've had a taste of their spurs. However, these animals cannot clearly see the nature of the roosters' spurs, which they carry to defend their territory. They are telling roosters that these spurs are capable of destroying the entire population of animals, making them a threat to the environment. According to them, carrying such weapons that could devastate the environment is a violation of the rights of birds and mammals. Consequently, the roosters must comply with the law, not just for their own benefit, but for the well-being of all mammals, including birds and roosters' families.

For many years, there have been attempts to deceive roosters into presenting themselves as defenseless so that they can be eaten along with their families. However, these efforts have been unsuccessful. Critics have even called the roosters crazy because they refuse to disarm themselves. Yet, these critics fear the roosters' combs and wattles more than their spurs. Clearly, demonstrations are more powerful than actual combat. The roosters' combs and wattles are so red and sharp that they are no joke for those who do not know how to deal with these weapons. It's like a situation where a man challenges another man holding a weapon and then asks him to disarm. You might find this amusing or think the man who puts down his weapon is foolish for letting others take it and overpower him. This scenario doesn't just occur between individuals; it happens among groups and nations. Both small and large nations may ask others to disarm, and the naive ones are often deceived and defeated before they can find an alternative way to resist.

As for the roosters, they adamantly reject the predators' demands to disarm, and they even argue that humans should be cautious when approaching them to avoid getting injured. Roosters are prone to becoming aggressive and are not known for their politeness towards other creatures. If you own roosters, they'll recognize you as their owner and come to you for their needs like food and water. However, they may not always obey the laws meant to prevent them from using their spurs. Someone may try to train them to be more dangerous, but not to be friendly to enemies, especially on their own territories. Roosters do not worry about the status of others; if a territory belongs to them, they will fight to the death and not easily flee from their own land. Roosters are faithful to crowing on time, warning the lazy to wake up, and they protect their families and territories, never giving up without a fight.

Not many humans run from a problem and abandon their family with their good knowledge. But that happens very often, even though they don't understand what they are doing. On the other hand, a rooster never does so. Some people don't live long after returning to their own story; remorse and regret often happen to the people who left behind a family in a bad situation or meant to be. They are not helpful for the family, and after so many years where life no longer offers anything for them, that is the time when the moment arrives for them to meet a member of the family who decided to tell them about the misery the rest of the family experienced due to their absence. Sometimes it is better to die together like ants rather than abandon each other forever or until the wintertime of life. That apparently looks like a curse that throws a shear pain incurable. Bad news might not taste good, especially if it happens to be your errors.

A serpent knows what his tail means to him; whenever he is resting somewhere, he puts his tail in the middle of himself. So, before a decision can be made in this case, make sure you understand that when you are far away from the sun, you will not feel the heat of the sun. If many clouds are in the sky, you will not feel nor see the sun. Being far away from a family can fade your love for a family who is waiting for you, like a dry land waiting for some waters. If the roosters are doing better, we can compare them while we are comparing, we might find a different way to beat our problems instead of saying, "Wait on the rock; we'll be back." If then before we are able to come back, it is all really too late. Sometimes don't say, "Wait"; you are going to look for transportation, but it is best to say, "Let's walk slowly until we find transportation." Together, the wind might be blocked away and cause no serious damage that cannot be repaired at all.

As the roosters' crow on time, try to be serious and not deceptive; take to heart your words as a covenant that cannot cause any weeping and gnashing of teeth, to you, your family, or someone else. That can prevent you from any curse of resting your load on somebody else's shoulders. Most of the time when you use your own strength to reach your path, everybody can view you as a wise person who is responsible and engaged in constructing yourself. May your weakness turn into a heavy weapon for you to defend your path. When you are not dependent on other people, they always see you as a strong person, even when you are facing the worst moment in life. A rooster never tells his predators or enemies that his comb is a soft comb that is not a real weapon to cause injuries to them. A rooster never tells them that his wattles are not capable enough to make them afraid of him. A dog runs a group of lions on his territory, and the lions simply know the territory belongs to the dog and imagine somebody else may be behind them. They are running and quit the territory of the dog because it belongs to the dog. A good life belongs to you; whatever the subject that may try to isolate you from seeing the good time you have, it is your responsibility to fight that in a proper manner and clear your path. A pedestrian might never have a vehicle at his possession, but he can know enough about shortcuts to arrive at his destination even close to a driver who takes a straight road.

Fish and Crab Racing

A regular fish was engaging with a crab while they were bidding to see which one of them is more capable in life. They decided to start at the ocean. From the start, everyone can see clearly that a crab cannot beat a fish in the sea. A crab cannot even come close to one percent of the fish's speed when diving. The crab agrees to his big loss and is beaten by the fish, but the crab is not agreeing to quit the bid. He wants to be complete. When they terminate at the ocean, they now switch to the river. When facing the river, the crab doesn't even know if he belongs to the water. In only a minute, a fish can cover a mile, and the crab cannot even make one percent of that distance. After many tries, no one needs to tell the crab that he cannot win anything. Then that is not a race he can even dream of winning at any time. The crab says they have two more stages to go, and he will not give up in the middle of the race. When they are complete, he will agree to his loss, and the fish might grab his winning prize for sure.

Effectively, the race is now leaving the river and heading up to a torrent of waters. At that torrent for the third time, the crab doesn't even make a signal of progress. The torrent has a lot of pool waters. When they get to the pool, the fish only jumps over to another pool of water. The crab must run as fast as he can at the side of each pool and sometimes under the pools. During these times, the fish has already jumped over many pools of water. Now, the fish is very happy because he currently has only one stage to get the prize over the crab, who is not able to perform as well in the waters compared to the fish.

Time is running fast. The crab and fish spend one week at each game, and they have four weeks to complete all four games. The ocean game is over, the river game is over, and the torrent game is now over. During these times, these were just simple exercises for the fish who was a little impatient with the crab, who takes a whole week to do what the fish can do in one hour. Now both must be patient for the last game's time to arrive.

While the time is approaching near, fish and crab are preparing themselves to the special place where the last event is going to take place, which is a ravine. Now it is the time, but sometimes the ravine doesn't have a lot of water except when a lot of rain happens. So right now, crab and fish are getting into the first pool of waters to the ravine, but fish must stay here in that pool waiting for the rains so the ravine can get enough water for him to run away and skip the crab. Meanwhile, the crab is starting to walk away and climb rocks by rocks, crossing pool after pool.

During that period of time rain is happening, but not enough to connect all the pools together for fish to run away. That game was set for a week, and that week is complete where the crab makes his path at the destination and fish is still waiting for more rain to come over. Fish, who is not able to make his way out, spent a lot of time at only one pool before that ravine received enough rains for its pools to connect together for the fish to find his way out. Crab was declared the winner because no one was hired to rescue the fish from the pool. Fish was waiting naturally for the right time to get back to his destination point. Currently, fish understands crab is the winner. The most capable at every season and moment. Fish is the loser, then crab is the winner of the big competition race.

So, the chance to win is not always at the side of the fastest one but sometimes more with the one who is capable of enduring some unexpected events. Sometimes a driver must know when to abandon his vehicle to run by foot. The fish doesn't mind about the eight feet plus the crab possesses, but a fish's fins cannot beat a crab at the dried spot. A crab can cross a dry area and even live here for sometime. That possibility makes the crab far more resilient than a fish can be. Even humans who resemble each other, there are many things one can do and the others cannot do, especially when it comes to the one who learns certain things the others are not familiar with, like a senator who did not learn how to swim.

Reality is a person may not know how to do certain things but has a normal life, instead of certain things you currently don't know for sure. Let's say you are a person who currently doesn't know how to swim, and you eventually get to the middle of the ocean with no one to help you get out, that is for sure you don't have enough hope for a quarter of your life, that means you might lose your life. Yet somehow you can be the lowest one; in the other way, you can be the highest one. You must be a specialist who can study the fish and the crab in order to know how much faster a fish can travel than a crab. But in the event, the crab can make his way out, and the fish is stuck off behind, watching his energies sitting down here with him and let the crab win him a race.

Water can make it possible for the fish to go wherever he wants, but in case the water currents are running out, a fish might stay in a pool of water or be at risk for survival. Where do the waters always go? Maybe they travel around, evaporate and come back as rain. Even if the rain never falls over the river and ocean, if the water falls over the mountains, the river and the ocean will benefit from the waters, and the mountains and the ravine will be the first areas to be in need of water. Because of that, the fish finds it easier for him to live in a river or in the ocean. For the fish, the ocean and rivers can represent great things, as for many people, the big and developing countries can represent great things. In that, a great developing country can represent the ocean where all the great fishes prefer to live their life while some of the lesser ones are living at the rivers. For so many, they prefer to make their lives between traveling from the sea to the rivers then from rivers to the seas. Then the crab often does not travel too far but can either among the categories who live at the sea or the categories who live their life at the sweet waters and any suitable land with some sources of waters.

If the big ocean can represent the great nations, the ravine and the other sources of waters can represent the small nations under development, if the ocean and rivers represent something greater than the ravine lesser. What about the fish and crab? Many people know persons who live in the suburb area or rural areas where most people are working, maybe in the farms. Those people do not benefit much in a developing country. Whether they know about a developing country or not, what they are harvesting at the farms does not stay there; somehow their harvest travels to the big nations.

It is the same way as you see the waters fall at the mountain and ravine, but they are always the first to need more water. The ones who cultivate and harvest the products can be the first ones to be hurt by hunger if for some reason a season or more is not so productive for them. Why is that happening to themselves? That happens because when the products arrive in the big and developing places, they do not use them the same way as the producers. They have ways of techniques to conserve, preserve, and transform the long-lasting products and export. Unfortunately, the small areas under development cannot do that. Most of what they harvest perishes sometimes after harvesting at the farms.

All those who can compare to the crab who can live wherever they are, are always happy to continue their routines among them. If a doctor arises, that doctor can no longer live here in this area; the doctor must move to a place where the doctor can have enough clients to make some money. The good reason is that people do not often go to the hospital. Most of them know how to make some medicine for themselves. The other thing is there are not enough possibilities for a doctor to use his technology in favor of many people, so that doctor must move to a place where things can be possible to practice medicine.

When that happens, you can see it as the waters coming from the source after ravines and rivers. The waters divert to the ocean, like a fish that was born in the ravine pool water but after some rain that fish finds enough water to skip from the pool to the river and from the river to the ocean.

If an important professional arises in this area, that professional must leave for a bigger place. At this point, you can see that each time a person goes to a great place or a different nation to learn something good, it will not benefit the original small place or city where that person was born because they will not see a benefit in returning to the original area. That means after learning how to be a good professional, that person is no longer a crab who can live anywhere, but a fish who needs a large space to run, whether it be a river or the sea of the ocean. They cannot practice medicine or any other profession in the farming areas. Of course, they must move to the city, a big town, or stay in a great country. At this point, the ravine is there to taste the waters and send them to the sea via the grand rivers.

Underdeveloped countries can only see their sons and daughters progress in different areas because the possibility does not lie in their homes, the areas where they were born. If they are sent to learn anything good, they are not cultivating the good ideas to come back and practice what they have learned with the intention of helping where they were born. There is no one to blame; the only thing everyone must take to heart is that if enough efforts are not made, sons and daughters might leave their hometowns to go outside looking for a comfort they will never acquire. Every great person may stand together and say they are going to help others, but before any help is given, they already know how long it will take for that help to reach them at one hundred percent. Moreover, it ends up being less than a quarter of what they have collected in the name of the recipient.

The waters may not return to their sources, but they are going to the big ocean via the rivers. All the hard work happens in rural areas to generate money, but you must put your foot in the mud to walk on any so-called road to reach where you want to go. Most of the valuable materials you see in a nearby city come from the hard work of rural or suburban areas. All the big houses you can see belong to someone who deals with the people from those areas, who often neglect them despite those areas remaining their wonderful money-making machine.

If you go to small nations where plenty of money has been donated to help and you see no changes have been made, switch back to the nearby big nations and find out how much wealth those who are responsible possess there. This means that the sand drains the water in the name of soil and sends the waters to the ocean. You are the crab who always needs a place to hide, but a fish might not stay in one small area because a fish has enough water to swim fast and possesses the pelvic fins' possibility or swim bladder they are born with, which provides a great advantage for them in rivers and the ocean. A crab often doesn't need water to travel short distances, but a fish needs plenty of water to traverse ravines, where every path must have abundant waters. This could be a reason why fish might be rare to find in any ravine, unlike in rivers and the sea.

If you want doctors, you must be in the town. If you want anything related to an office or technology, it has to do with a city or town. Whether you mind or not about the science cycle or recycling, the truth remains true, but the way the water is running is the way your eyes currently perceive it to go. The way your money is spent is the way it can be stored or utilized differently. Where you make purchases are the places where you spend your money. Whatever you must do, remember that the lesser will be in life to achieve their missions and the greatest will be in life to achieve their missions. However, no missions can be possible without the help of the other.

The sharks and whales are not found in small waters; they thrive in big waters. Sometimes when people say "big," they are not referring to physical size but to capacity and possessions of money and materials, essentially physical wealth. Just as a palm might never disperse the bamboo because of its greatness, each of them has an important role in their range of considerations. The fish can win a race against the crab in the sea, and then the crab can win against the fish in a race at the ravine. This can be the same in every aspect of life.

Many things can be found in the marketplace among the varieties, some of which are the food we eat every day. Most of us don't take the time to ask who cultivates this food and how it arrives at the market. If you work in an office, you must know how to use computers; of course, you might know it better. However, if you were to compete in a different trade, someone else might beat you in that race. After all, you know how to help them with what you know, and they know how to help you with what they know.

A crab can live better in low water, and a fish might enjoy the high water. Even though some sea crabs show differences in deep waters, it's not enough to compare with the original fish in the ocean in terms of moving quickly from place to place. The only real reason a crab can win against a fish in a race is that in the sea, crabs move slowly compared to fish. However, the crab is able to make its way out before the time runs out. On the other hand, when on land or in a place like a dry ravine, the crab manages it well. But for the fish, while it fares well in the sea and river, when in a place where the waters are not abundant, the fish gets stuck and cannot make its way out until a significant amount of water comes to its rescue.

In that case, the crab is well equipped to win the race, and the fish agrees to be the loser. After all, crabs and fish both contribute to the proper flow of the waters. Farmers hold a lot of importance in the world, especially for people living in areas where they cannot cultivate anything for food production. Thanks to the farmers, wherever you are, you can find some food to eat. We agree that when a son or daughter becomes a doctor, they must move to a town. But when we're sick, we'll find them wherever they are so we can receive the treatment or cure we deserve. Not only doctors, but many other trades can push you to move from one place to another. Often, this happens in the case of those living in underdeveloped countries. Fortunately, for developing countries, everything can be so close that you don't have to make long trips to resolve every little thing.

At this point, no one needs to live like a fish waiting for heavy rains to come so they can skip from one pool of water to another, making their way to the river or ocean. In some areas, many young people are waiting just to learn a trade that can support them, much like waters support a fish as it moves toward a better place, thinking it can be for them.

Three farmers living close to the farm where they work, one day decide to go to a jungle where they can find a lot of crabs in the wetland areas. Long before these farmers came to live in that area, there were some rich people living there. These people had plenty of gold and diamonds. Some of those who did not die before leaving the area buried much gold and diamond underground just a little while before they departed.

Meanwhile, a family with so many big pieces of gold and diamond that they couldn't carry with them where they were going, decided to bury the gold and diamonds somewhere in the jungle so that if at any moment they return at the need of this wealth, they can find them where they are underground. That time never arrived and their wealth had stayed underground where no one had knowledge about that. The wealth was buried in materials that could not rust or be destroyed. Each bag of gold and diamond was placed with two full bags of heavy stones and iron on top. This process continued for each half bag of gold and diamond, meaning that beneath two bags of iron and heavy stones, there was a half bag of pure gold and pure diamond, marked with a sign of bronze. Then, at each bag of iron and heavy stone they put the sign of gold and diamond.

The wealth stayed underground with rust-free chains that last a lifetime, about a foot underground. Movement started happening in the soil over many years. The discovery of one of the spots happened when the farmers were searching for crabs in the jungle. As they continued their search, one of them noticed a piece of chain. Upon trying to pull it, the chain was stuck very strongly underground. The man followed the chain until he reached the first bag, which was iron. Although he didn't know what was in the bag, he suspected it might be a treasure. He called his two partners to help, and together, they pulled out three bags from the pit: two full bags and a half bag. They now understood they had found something valuable, instead of the crabs they found some wealth or treasure.

The men decided to carry these bags to their houses. As each person had his own home, this became the moment to identify honesty and deception among them. They had to decide where to store the treasures until they could find an expert to evaluate them. The two last men tried to deceive the first man who found the treasure. Each of them wanted to take a full bag to his own house, leaving the man who found the treasure with the half bag for himself. They believed they had pure gold and pure diamond, while the other man had only a half bag of bronze. Imagine the kind of dishonest and deceptive people the last two men are.

The three men went to a big town to consult experts in weight and the valuation of gold and diamond. They wanted to get information and be knowledgeable about how much money they will get for their bags. As for the two last men, they already know they are going to be much richer than the first man who found the treasure, because the two men believe they have pure gold and pure diamonds and the other man has only a half bag of bronze.

Right after consulting those buyers, they are making a plan to go with the first man to sell his bronze so they can be sure that everything will be right for themselves. The two men ask the man who found the treasures for all three of them to enter the town to sell the half bag with him first. After that, they can all three go back to sell the other two big bags. The man agrees.

On a good morning, the three men head to the town, especially to the office of the dealer they prefer to make a deal with. The dealer will not pay billions in cash; that money must be put into one account that must be opened right away. Now, the two men who know they are going to take the other two big bags of pure gold ask the first man to put his name only on that half bag bronze account. In their minds, they are going to make two different accounts, one for each of them. The first man agrees and puts that account in his name only.

At this point, the dealer must talk to him privately in his office to tell him everything about the deal and how many billions he will receive for his pure gold and pure diamond, the two wicked partners believe who is bronze. After everything has been set and sailed, the dealers tell the man to keep his mouth closed about his millions until he can make himself more secure so nobody can be jealous of him and might kill him for the money. So far, only the first man, with the dealers who currently know he is a billionaire. As for the two partners, they don't even ask the first man if he knows how much money he's going to get in his account because they didn't get the price for bronze. They already know for sure his half bag of bronze cannot mean anything compared to a big bag of pure gold and diamond.

So, the two men who are trying to deceive the man who found the treasures arrange themselves to go into town without notifying the other man so they can be the most billionaires who never existed in their nation. So comfortable with themselves, there is no rush to anything so they don't want the first man to ask them anything; they are distancing themselves from him. That means everybody has a bag, everything has been shared; then no one needs to know anything about anyone. That's why they didn't ask him anything when selling the half bag.

Great for the first man; holiday season arrives, all the businesses are closed. The two men must wait in town until after the holiday to sell their gold. So happy they are while enjoying themselves in a city nearby. A man makes a meeting on the street, where he speaks through a megaphone, saying to the people if you want to be rich, you need to share everything you have with the poor; you need to sell everything you have and separate everything among the poor. These two men are so wicked; they both know they are going to get rich in only a couple of days. Then they raise their hands and say to the man with the megaphone, "Yes, we want to do that right now so the poor can have a better life. We want to give you everything we have, then you are the one to share it with the poor." When the man hears that, he quickly approaches them, takes every piece of information he needs from them to grab whatever they have, and on the first day of the week, he takes them to the place where everything can be notarized and makes them both sign every piece of paper he needs to be the real owner of everything those two men had in their name, and every little thing he can carry, leaving them with nothing at all to survive. Meanwhile, they are not worried about that because they thought they were billionaires by stealing gold and diamonds from the other partner.

During that time, the real billionaire, who is the first man who found the treasures, has already sold everything he possesses in that area and left without notifying his two bad partners. Yet, they are both giving out everything they had without his knowledge, so now nobody has knowledge of what the others are doing.

As for the two men who thought they would be the greatest billionaires in the next few days, they are currently living at the favor of the man they are giving everything to. In their mind, in the next few days after selling their gold, they will not go back to that place anymore. This way, the first man must not see them to ask them any questions about the two big bags of gold and diamond. If so, we'll see that and good luck for them both.

The next day arrives, and both men, who have already arranged themselves to enter the big town to sell their gold as the wishing to say goodbye to their farms they owned for so long, enter the town. They go straight to the dealer's office where they have arranged to sell their gold and diamond. Unfortunately, when the dealers take them into the office and open the sealed treasures, the first one is revealed to be a bag of stones and irons. What is the hope for the second bag? When opened, it's revealed to be a bag of irons and heavy stones. The only question they can ask is if those stones can be precious enough to make money. The answer is no. Some regular stones can be found on the ground everywhere. At this point, the dealers, who have clients waiting for them, cannot waste any time for people who grab bags of rocks and irons and bring them to the dealer's office. The two men are ordered to grab their trash and leave immediately; they are not allowed to remain inside the dealer's property.

Now, what does it look like for these two men who want to use a restroom and cannot find one, carrying two big and heavy bags they cannot leave on the street as they could get arrested and sent to jail. They don't have any money to pay for transportation. Moreover, the luxury hotel where they planned to stay until they purchase their stronghold in town is right ahead of them, but they cannot enter that hotel; mainly, they look like blind people, but they cannot stay there. Whatever the case, they must leave now.

The two men are currently not at their farms where waters are free, food is free, and sleeping in the house is free. The two aborted billionaires by mind, must ask some poor people for them to find some water to drink. They must ask the poor, so they might not die hungry. About where to sleep? Now is not the time to even think about sleeping yet. The two farmers are going to walk night and day, trying to get back to the area where they are coming from. Overnight, when nobody can see, they quit their bags on the side of the road. From that time, they are turned to be lighter and released from their loads. Fatigue of walking and begging to survive, the return from the trip, is not everything. When the two men finally arrive at the farms not far from their homes, some other people are not permitting them to enter their farms. Those people declare they have just purchased these farms, and these two stealers are coming over and trying to steal things from their farms. The man with the megaphone, the man they gave everything they had, is the man who has already sold everything to some other people. The two men thought they were going to find that same man at their wealthy houses and farms, but unfortunately, both houses are already occupied by some other people. Everything has already changed; all locks have been changed to the new locks. When knocking at the doors, someone else answers the doors with some different appearances they were not expecting.

After everything turned bad for the two partners, where their own properties cannot accept them, what is left to be done? They are now thinking about their partner who found the treasures. So, why not go to him now? That is what they want to do—go to their first partner and find some lies to tell him. He is a good man; he will accept them to stay with him, and he has plenty for his half bag; he will help. That is what they are imagining. After talking and reasoning among themselves, they both decide to go where their partner is living. Both men cannot wait to make it to the house of the billionaire with a half bag of gold and diamond. So, they can get relief from their current misery.

Unfortunately for them, that partner has sold the entire wealth he had in that area and moved to a different place, where they don't know. When they reach his former door, it appears the same thing as for their own homes—someone else answers the door and declares not to have any knowledge of the person they ask for. The first partner has already sold his wealth in that area and moved to the next town. His two deceptive partners cannot see him anymore. They thought to be smarter and more deceptive than they are, deceiving themselves and hurting themselves.

Now, both men want to meet with the man to whom they were giving all their wealth, including houses and land at the place they were living. But that man also cannot be reached. They have given him all the titles of the wealth, and he has already sold everything to some other people. Now, they are not only tasting the fruits of deception and dishonesty, but they are currently enjoying themselves night and day with the fruits of these actions.

If the three partners had stayed together and taken all three bags to the dealers and tried to sell them together, all three men should be billionaires at this point. But two of them were chosen to deceive the one who found the treasures. Now, they are putting themselves on the trail of paying the big heavy prices for stealing the big heavy bags of stones and irons for gold and diamond. And for not being loyal to themselves, they treated the good partner as a criminal because he found the treasures and called them to share together.

Yet they gave him the half bag of bronze, and they took for themselves two bags of pure gold and diamond.

Currently, that action clearly reveals that the one who found the treasures is a loyal person, a person with an excellent heart, and he doesn't even worry about the others' two big bags of gold and diamond. Then he gets enough for himself to live with his family; he just sees for himself that those two partners are some partners he does need to take his distances with. So now he might not yet know any story of them; even themselves do not yet know any story of himself. If at a time they should know what happened, the partner with the half bag of gold and diamond will understand the importance of his decision to leave that area. As for the two bad partners, nobody might tell what a bad person can cultivate instantly in his mind.

A loyal man is faithful with himself and keeps for himself what the dealer told him as good advice. He was told not to tell anyone about what he is going to do and about what he is currently doing; that is going well for him. The bad former partners don't even know where to find him anymore. That means each time anyone can think about them, you can say, "Peace for the one who is separated from the other two partners and poor partners for the two deceptive men." Now the two partners become beggars. Everyone who sees them says, "There are the poor partners, they were plotting and scamming to steal together, then they are turning themselves to be poor together."

As for the real man, he is running with his family like a fish that was stuck in a ravine pool. Soon he finds enough water to run; he runs to a river or to the ocean, a loss for the others because they are not able to find him anymore. Yet, a different life happens between the two men and the partner who found the treasures while looking for crabs in the forest. One of them is turned into a real billionaire, and the other two have turned themselves to be two real poor. Everyone can draw a serious lesson from those three former farmers and partners.

If you are climbing a tree, when you get to the top of the tree and then you want to continue to go much higher, that is impossible. Or you might jump off the tree to nothing. As a result, you will pay the law of weight and fall on the ground. There you might learn how to respect the law of your weight. That means if you want to be too high, of course, you will be too low. And if you try to spit into the sky, your spit will fall on the edge of your nose.

The three men were there in the forest looking for crabs, but not for gold. Finding the gold should be considered as good luck for them. And before that, they were not considered as people who cannot provide for themselves. If they were content to live that way, that means there was nothing unpleasant for them in that area, and they had no intentions to leave that area. Happy is the man who leaves without regret, even though he did not have in his mind to quit his farm area for a different town. The worst is for the two bad men who gave away their wealth and hit the street begging for food. Imagine those two people who don't even have a reason to sell their wealth are just giving them away and turning themselves on the street as some poor who did never have anything at all.

After some years of misery on the street, those men are trying to make a way for themselves to go to a courthouse or anywhere else where people with the law might help them get back their wealth. But wherever they are trying, that turns impossible because the certificates have been signed for the properties to be owned by the person who sells them, then they have the titles. The only thing is the man who received the properties is himself in a prison currently for misleading people, taking their properties, and selling them right away to other people, so the judges have put him in prison but are unable to defeat any title that has been signed legally. Therefore, the wealth cannot recover for the people who signed the title or any certificate for him to become owner of the properties, because if he currently owns the properties, he can also sell these properties if he decides to do so. That man has been put in prison for his role in convincing people to give him their wealth for him to share with the poor so they can get richest, and he always guides them to a place where they can sign titles and the other documents he needs to be the legal owner of the wealth as a person who is going to share that wealth with the poor people. Then he is guilty because he does not share anything at all with the poor people. As soon as he gets some wealth from anybody, he then sells that wealth right away.

As for those two men, they just learned that he is in prison, but nothing can be done to help them because he had the right to sell, and those who are buying are receiving the right documents as purchasers, in accordance with the law of the nation. Judges can grab what that man possesses in vain or steal from the others, but cannot repossess anything for the one who signed the legal documents of giving away and did not report any kidnapping during and after the time everything was done to completion. So, the two men are condemned to the street as poor for their involvement in trying to steal two big bags of gold and diamond. And the megaphone man who was telling them to give their wealth or share their wealth with the poor so that they can get richer and grab their wealth from them illegally is himself condemned in a prison for his way of misleading people to take their wealth. If you want to get to the wealthiest spot, you might have to take a straight road. If at any time you take a crooked road then the legal ways come against you, that crooked road may turn out to be the longest road, you never know. Two mountains might not easily meet together, but two people can always meet together even after years of an event or any accidents.

Yet, at a time of release from prison, the megaphone man doesn't have any place to go as his house because everything he owns was seized by the authorities, so the megaphone man must be on the street. The two men who gave him their wealth are also on the street; those three might have a great chance to meet somewhere on the street. That does not take very long, for sure. One day the two men who gave to be poor, meet their counselor, the megaphone man who has received to sell and become poor.

When the three men meet on the street, the megaphone man tries to defend himself by saying he thanked them for their gift to him, but he gave that wealth to somebody else. If they are in need the same way they were giving that wealth to turn poor, someone might give to them enough for themselves to turn poor. Then he was not telling them to give to get rich, but he was telling them to give so they can be poor. And as you can see, he himself gave to become poor. Now, all three of us are on the street after we gave to become poor.

As for the partners, the two bad partners lost a good partner they did not deserve who became a billionaire with the half a bag of gold and diamonds. So now they are well-founded because these three men are all bad people. But all three of them are paying the big prices for their wrongdoing against the other people who trusted them. At this point, all the rotting oranges have been put into the same bag as some heavy stones and irons, for the two bad partners to carry into the town where they are trying to sell them for pure gold and pure diamond.

Those three new partners who are trying to be rich by their deceptive and dishonest actions have in their minds that they are going to be rich. Instead of being rich or billionaires forever, they are going to be poor forever. They were trying to grab from the others, so the truth's greatest have disarmed them legally and put their back flat to the sand where some weeping and gnashing of teeth are truly waiting for them. Their reproaches are on themselves, then they become curses for themselves and for anyone who might want to be part of them. Good lessons are for anyone who might have anything to do with others as a partner or leader. It's up to you to choose the right ways to run your horse so that you might never carry your head down before anyone in your path, whether you are wealthy or not wealthy.

There are too many errors that can never be repaired, then the worst always appears as nothing at all until the worst reveals the worst and puts someone on their back and not able to stand anymore. Not only that, if the two bad partners had done as the good partner who sold his gold before he sold his other wealth, they would never be poor. But their deceptive actions blinded them, and their craziness of becoming billionaires by deceiving their partner blanked their minds, and they had no way to currently think about what they can or should not have done at the first part. They tried to eat their meal before preparing it. Then they become private from the good taste of that food.

If they had waited until they sold the gold when the bags turned out not to be gold and diamond as they thought, they still could have had the chance to get back their wealth because their wealth belonged to them, and nobody else should have come over here to ask them anything. But that was not in their minds; they believed they were original fish who were born in the ocean, then they would run and leave the crabs behind them. But the crab won the race where they are both stuck in a pool for the reason of the lack of water. As for those two men, even the reserve of their waters has been drained away, and they are never receiving any water at all for them to run away. They are currently turning out to be like some fish who are making excessive speed and run them to the ground where they are not able to get back to any point of water. Every hope for a life disappears, not even a miracle might be at the table for them. The important reality to understand is most of the wrongs you do will turn against you. A human can always have a small head and a big body size, no matter how big that body is, he can never be the one to control the head. That big body will stay at his spot to be in accordance with the whole body because the head belongs where he is.

Snake Conflicts

A conflict occurred in the community of the snakes between the head of the snake, his middle, and his tail. During that conflict, each part of the snake decided whether the head of the snake would continue to govern the body all the time, or sometimes the middle section would govern the rest of the body, or if the tail could conduct the body. After all, the three parts met together to make the right decisions. One expert suggested that because the head always conducts the whole body, it is good to let those other parts of the snake try for a certain period, then if everything is going well, yet a better change can be made. With that suggestion, they agreed to let that happen.

At that time, the rattlesnake was the first snake to ride his body with the middle part ahead of his head and his tail. The rattlesnake carried the middle section of his body ahead to his front, then his head and his tail were at the spot where his middle section was supposed to be. So far, the middle of the rattlesnake didn't make any mistakes, then they tried a different serpent. But that serpent must be carried by his tail, which will be at the spot where his head is supposed to be to be considered a serpent guided by his tail. Meanwhile, because the rattlesnake carried his tail at the spot where his middle section was supposed to be, and that is almost the same way he carries his head, they mandated the rattlesnake to also carry a bell so that he can protect himself and other creatures from getting too close to him.

Each time the rattlesnake sees another creature, he must ring his bell to let them know that the rattlesnake is closer than he sees his head. That can remain as a safety precaution for them both. So, the snake community agreed to let the rattlesnake carry that rattle while accepting him as a snake who can use the middle section of the body as a head wherever he wants to go, but he needs to be vigilant to have his chance to ring that rattle each time another creature is approaching him.

Today, the rattlesnake may still carry his rattle, but if you have any knowledge of that kind of snake, when you see one of them, find out to see if that snake is carrying the rattle he was mandated to carry at all times. By the way, never go too close to one of them, even though he might let you know if you are too close to him by ringing his bell to alert you to the danger. As for the other serpent who wants to use his tail as the section to go ahead of him, the community of the snake did not approve of him because he only uses his tail as a stand for him when under attack, but not for him to govern himself away nor travel. Therefore, that serpent is not approved.

In order to let every snake ride in a different way than the head, the community of the snake must find at least three kinds of snakes who can ride different ways at the test, which is not found. Then the community of the snake fails to pass that grade. Because of that, every snake must continue to ride ahead with their head up to the front. So, those who received the training keep a little sign to prove they were in a procedure to make a change even though they failed to do so. For example, the rattlesnake, who was the most intelligent at the training, still remembers the most and is granted legal right to carry his rattle and govern his middle section, looking to the front like he is walking to his side.

As for the reptile like the cobra who gets to the second row, even though the cobra tries to stand on his tail when he is under attack, his head is always up, he is not governed by his tail. When under attack, the cobra tries to prove he knows something more than what he looks like by playing like he's going to stand on his tail, then he runs away. But the reality is sometimes you cannot operate without the right training. Powers cannot touch any knowledge because knowledge is the strength that governs the powers. Yet, the cobra is intelligent but not approved as a serpent who can walk with his tail ahead of himself. From animals to humans, whoever has a lack in the test to win can become a lot in physical powers.

Just after the cobra is not approved to walk with his tail before his head, the cobra engages himself in self-training where he cannot add anything to his knowledge to make him do anything acceptable. But cobra becomes a physical power among the serpents, and his power becomes so great that cobra has the ability to swallow any other snake who dares to believe to stand in his path, as for attacking him, that might never be a dream for the other snakes. Therefore, cobra carries the title of king.

Of course, the cobra is trying to stand on his tail and play like he can fly and have enough muscle and strength to swell, if any others know how to swell also. As for cobra, he not only swells but also knows how to make his neck look large enough to frighten the others. Another snake can stay on the ground, but a cobra can stand on his tail. When the others see him, they know the king is there. That is a question if they can have a chance to run or to hide where no chance can be possible to win the cobra. Most of the other snakes prefer not to run. If, by chance, the king is moving in the other direction, yet a life dream can be renewed.

The king wears protection of a deadly venomous weapon of the other snakes, which his system immunization against the venom of the other serpents gives him the most power he needs to kill and swallow the others. As a king, no other animal can come over and stop him in that category as a snake. Of course, not as a snake to put a cobra on his knees or beat him and win out.

After all the search to find the way to stop and prevent the crises of objects running over the snakes' tails, the snake community is not able to find a way for the snakes not to leave their tails behind them. That is not working at the level they want it to be. Still, snakes are continuing to stop because of some objects, other animals and humans who sometimes press on the snake's tail behind it. Because of their tails, snakes never crossfire, but other lives continue to grab their tails and cause them a lot of trouble. When snakes are sleeping because of the fear of these enemies, snakes must put their tails in the middle of themselves and put their heads also as hiding for the protection of themselves.

King cobra might not worry much about the other snakes, but, as everybody can tell, a king always has enemies that can be for any wealth or territory where other animals believe they own, and the king himself continues to rule over certain other snakes those creatures also want and consider as their wealth. The king is continuing to steal. Each time the other animals eat, they are leaving some on the ground for the poor animals or those who become too old to catch anything. But the king cobra never leaves anything for the poor animals who cannot catch anything; therefore, so many complaints have been compiled for the king.

However, it is not so easy to find a court that can accept to make a judgment against the king cobra. At a time rattlesnakes go to the mongoose's territory to complain about the king cobra. But the rattlesnake never came back. Even piton rock goes to the honey badger's courthouse for king cobra, and the piton rock does not come back. So, whatever the king cobra does, he is a king. But the eagle in the sky can see very clearly at the ground. Whenever the eagles are hungry, the king cobra must hide so hard to prevent a judgment against himself.

As cobras always swallow the other kinds of snakes and leave no trace of them, when honey badgers, eagles, and mongooses eat, they are leaving some for the other animals on the ground. So, one day, the king cobra leaves his kids behind, and the king and his wife cross the limits, entering the eagle's plain near honey badgers and mongoose territories.

While crossing the limits to enter the eagle's plain, unfortunately, an eagle was in the sky surveilling the trespassing. Seeing the pair of cobras, the eagle flies down to put them under arrest. While the eagle puts its claws on the back of the queen cobra, the king runs straight to the mongooses' areas looking for help and protection. Unfortunately, mongoose was mandated to put the king cobra under arrest at any time he can find the king cobra. Now the event is not in favor of the cobra family; the couple, king and wife, are arrested at the same time and will not return to their territory where their kids were left with the hope of seeing their parents back.

Both cobras are trying very hard to resist the arrest, but they were not enough to stop the strategies of eagle and mongoose to put them under arrest for what they are doing by violating the law of no trespassing of the eagle's plain and entering the mongoose's area. So, both cobras will not have a chance to return to where they were living because a life sentence is applicable to any other creatures found guilty at the eagle court. The same law is also applicable to the court of the mongooses and some other animals.

With that law in mind, the eagle has decided to give the female cobra a death penalty by eating the cobra. After the eagle's belly is full, then the eagle leaves some of the cobra for the other animals, as he always did, and that portion is left as proof the cobra is no longer alive but over. As for the king cobra, he is at the mongoose's direction, who always condemns the cobras for a death penalty. So, the judgment at this point is not taking a long time to be done, as you already know, a king will not condemn without a fight. But a king cobra, king of the snakes, cannot violate the law of no trespassing of the mongooses' property and stay without being punished. The mongoose law for a cobra is the same as the law of the eagle, death penalty if found guilty. And as it is when mongooses put a cobra under arrest, the case is automatically guilty, and a judgment will be done immediately where the cobra will be put to a death row and be executed for its violation by entering the mongooses' territory.

Yet the cobra is executed and immediately eaten as lunch at the palace of mongooses. During the arrest of the cobra by the mongooses, the cobra sprays some of his venomous poison over the mongooses. Then mongooses say the rest of that cobra family must pay for that horrible mistake of the cobra's attempt to kill mongooses. If the mongooses were not immunized against the cobra's venomous poison, by now, the cobra can be the cause of many mongooses' deaths.

The kids of the cobras, who take the chances to look for their parents, find the remains of the deceased left behind by the eagle, making them believe for sure that their dad and mom are not alive anymore. They are in immediate high alert, ready to put themselves in a safe place where eagles from the sky may not be able to see them easily, as that can be the only good chance for them to survive the eagle attack from the sky to them on the ground.

Whether the nonstop research of eagles, mongooses, and honey badgers, the cobra's kids grow big enough to form their own family, keeping the stronghold of their parents, even though sometimes they are continually lost—certain of them who are victims of the eagles, mongooses, honey badgers, and some others.

As for the cobras, they never quit from swallowing some other animals, especially the birds and some snakes. When it comes to the chicks, the chicken must protest only against these enemies. Whenever chickens protest against enemies, if humans are listening to their voices, whether snakes or eagles, that predator must run away with his mind behind himself before a human acts against him, especially mongooses who have the case in a country where some people who cultivate pineapples brought mongooses from a different country to stop the rats from destroying their pineapples. Then mongooses quit the pineapple farms and go to the chicken farm and attack the chickens in the farms.

At this period, they see mongooses as the only creature who can destroy the rats in the pineapple farms. But they minimized what mongooses can cause if leaving the pineapple farms. Instead of killing and eating some rats, mongooses are sprayed all over, attacking the chicken farms. Then mongooses say, "You are humans, you believe completely you are more intelligent than mongooses are. You are eating everything that tastes good in your mouth; you are eating all kinds of fruits. But you also eat meat." And mongooses say, "Mongooses don't even know at one hundred percent if some humans don't eat mongooses, and humans believe with all their hearts mongooses are going to stay on the pineapple plants forever, eating only the rats. No! No! that will not happen;

mongooses are going to leave the pineapple farms and switch to the chicken farms. Attack, kill, and eat the chicken very often."

Now humans begin not to see mongooses with only one eye but with both eyes. Instead of only attacking the rats, mongooses also attack the chicken farms. At this point, whether humans betray themselves or mongooses betray them, the only good thing is that humans must not pay mongooses anymore for that contract of eating rats at the pineapple farms because humans are getting upset with mongooses.

But mongooses tell humans, "A mongoose might not look as faithful as you thought a mongoose is supposed to be, but a mongoose can be loyal to people. Let's sit down and negotiate a deal." Now tell mongooses, before mongooses were here in your country, were there no other creatures eating your chicken? Humans are getting so mad; they are answering while making plans in their minds to kill mongoose for their chicken mongooses are eating. So, they humans are answering to mongoose and say only one creature is currently eating a lot more chicken than you mongooses are eating now: the snakes.

Mongooses say to humans, "We are mongooses; you are humans. The mongooses will compensate you by destroying all the snakes who are eating your chicken. Beginning from now, no chicken will be eaten by the snakes anymore, so you must not worry when mongooses eat a few because mongooses will be destroying every snake who is continually eating your chicken at all times. If you are not agreeing, tell mongooses if you can find a better deal than that. Whether you put your dogs behind mongooses when mongooses try to eat a chicken, but mongooses destroy your rats and your snakes who try to eat your fruits and your chicken. What can you find better? Even though it's not so easy for a human to find mongooses at all times, so reasonably if mongooses were there to destroy mice and rats, mongooses attack the chicken, but at least mongooses reduce the snakes who were the greatest danger for the chicken farms.

The owners of the chicken farms must ease themselves with mongooses because one against three, that is much better—no more rats and mice in plenty, and the snakes are reduced seriously. That is a good deal between humans and mongooses. So, mongooses still must be careful about themselves when they must face humans in the farms. Run and hide can be the best option for mongooses. Some farmers might say indeed, mongooses did not belong to that country; the other people should not bring them here. Yet, the mongooses are not welcome because that did not happen before to see the mongooses eat their chicken. That may be true, but everything belongs to one place, which is the planet earth. Even though humans possessed greater knowledge and power, coexistence necessitated negotiation and compromise.

Birds and Human Families

Some birds were born in a garden. After the birds are big enough to help themselves, their parents fly to a different country and currently don't see them anymore. Then a couple of young birds who are always together are considered married and build a nest for themselves. The female lays some eggs, then before the eggs hatch, the birds must spend nights and days incubating the eggs until their newborn completely hatches and is ready to help themselves.

During that period, both birds were there encouraging each other, but when the kids were born, there was not enough space in the nest for the father. Now the father must lodge on a branch to guard the rest of the family. But one day, the male signals the mother that he will fly far and will not return anytime soon. Now the mother must take care of the chicks by herself and help them understand how to live as a single mother bird.

As for the father, he flies to a different country. When the male bird arrives in the other country, there are so many other birds in the garden where he chooses to stay. Time after time, the male bird may have reminders of his family in his mind but not enough to guide him back to the family. He stays there for so long and eventually has a different partner whom the bird gets married to. Actually, the first family is considered an abandoned family. Currently any comfort or security from the bird must be the new family or new wife. Years go by, the bird is no longer young, and the chicks are young enough to help themselves and even form their own family. But that mother who continues to stay as a single mother always in the garden with her children singing together and eating together, they are always together. She, as the mother bird, proves herself a good mother, a model to be followed by the other mother birds. When all the kids got married, she was the only parent there for them each time, one after the other. After all, she has no reproach for raising the chicks by herself as an excellent mother. At this point, the only regret she carries in her heart is that she is not able to tell the kids, "There is your father, the father who never came back," so the chicks never have the chance yet to see their father. As you know, when the kids see other kids have a father, no matter how well the mother is taking care of them, they will continue to question you as the mother about their father.

Whenever they have a different mind or think differently, they also have different questions to ask you as their mother. Most of the time, they are agreeing to be satisfied with only a great mother, but the holes in their hearts cannot be full without the one and the only one who can fill it. No one can tell what the mother herself must deal with every time in her heart by not seeing her partner, the only partner that she ever had in her entire life. Most of the time, she only wants to look at the kids as her gifts for her love she has for that partner, but she doesn't feel like she can do enough to make the chicks understand her. As a mother who raises their kids by herself, she doesn't want them to discover her sadness for her partner who is their father, as they never see him at all.

At a good time, she decides to rebound her strength and fly in the same direction. Despite the chicks getting big, she is giving them a signal that she will fly away far and might not see them for a while. The chicks get the signal from their mom and feel that they are going to miss their mom for some time or even forever, as they never know their dad. The brave mom, as a bird who can fly, follows the signal her husband had given her since many years ago. She continues with the mindset that everything will be good for her. Yet, after some days of travel, she finally arrives in that country and, for sure, she is resting at a tree in the same garden where her partner is. No longer young as she was in the passing years, but she has the same voice and still remembers her song she did always sing for him. At the tree where she is, she starts singing. Then the male still recognizes that song and becomes so panicked and confused after listening for a little time. The male then answers the voice, and currently, that female remains silent. After the male continues to sing and doesn't hear the voice anymore, the male then becomes more and more panicked. Meanwhile, the female who already heard the voice of the male and is sure he is still living then she is kept quiet and rests from her long trip she has accomplished. When the male doesn't hear the female voice anymore, the male flies to the next section of the garden searching for her. Fortunately, when resting on a tree where the voice was, both birds have seen each other, and the male starts singing and dancing as he used to do in the past. But the female plays like she does not recognize his song and dance.

If so, the male cannot approach the female closer. For the male to come closer to the female, the female must approve of his voice and dance. If the female approves, that means she remembers him as the real partner. If not, the male must accept the denial of the dance and sing to prove himself as the real partner. As for the female, she remembers him, but she tries to act differently. After many rounds of singing and dancing, the female sings and proves she remembers him but doesn't give him a signal to approach her. This continues for over a week. Then, the female bird shows signs of stress and sadness, indicating that she will fly back to her chicks. If the male is concerned, he should do the same—fly after her to the country where they were living before. If the male successfully completes this trip, then the female will agree that he is the real partner and husband she has been waiting for. The male gets the signal and assures her that he will fly behind her to the country where their chicks are. This happens—the mother bird flies back to her country where her children are. The male takes a few days to end his relationships with the other birds and flies back to the country where his family resides. He is warmly welcomed back into the family with love and respect. The bird family is happy to have all their members together in one place for the first time. What a strong mother!

After many years of absence in the family, with her strength, she brings back a father the kids were asking for all the time. She is not only comfortable with herself but with her children. Now she can be confident that her kids must not keep any doubt in their minds about their father. Yet each one of them can have a chance to talk to him, where he himself must face his own heartbreak and comfort the children. Mom grows them up by herself, then they continue to ask her for their dad. Of course, she knows the kids have a dad and they deserve a dad. That is why she accomplishes the dream and makes a long trip to a different nation, mainly to prove to the kids that everything she was telling them was true with all her knowledge. *

*"*Now, my dear children, there is your dad. And you, my friend, my partner, and husband, you are my trophy of my long trip to get you back to my children. Will we continue on our same path of life to be there for our children? Whether they are already big, but our hearts will continue to be renewed second after second, especially when we have the chance to see our kids. They are all doing fine and continue to be a reflection of us. Your absence was painful to me as well as to the children. When I feel the pain, I just look at the children like you were there, present in my life, and I always want them to look at me and each of them as mom and dad. I always say to the one who constantly asks me for his dad to look at his brother who looks just like dad was. Just to embellish my pain I do feel. Today, I am not only the winner, but we are the winners. My courage was not in vain, then your courage was not in vain. Now it is the good time for us to continue to be an excellent model of family for our chicks and for the other birds who are part of this garden we are also a part of since we were born before our parents were going to rest somewhere in death, maybe one by one. If I must go today, I will feel like I'm going to rest in peace because the children have nothing anymore to reproach me. Now they are so confident that I was true as a real mother for them. I was loyal and faithful to them, and that is what a good life means to me and you and our children as well."**

*After all, the bird's family sometimes travels together to the same country where the male bird had flown before. Because the kids are big and can support themselves, mom and dad don't need to worry when deciding to spend more time in that country. This provides the opportunity for the rest of the family to also fly to that country whenever they want. All birds are free to fly whenever they want and stay if they wish. Whenever the error happens, it does not get addressed properly which makes an irreparable error, instead you must turn it around into something greater that can be helpful for everyone, whether small or big. Imagine what it means for a mother bird to raise her chicks among so many predators, and yet none of them have perished under the claws of those predators. This is truly excellent, and any reasonable person should consider this and ask themselves if they could make that trip and land at the real destination port.

If only life were not so short, and time could give a second chance to those making mistakes in life to erase their errors and start over. Perhaps they should learn and fulfill the requirements necessary to please everyone who sees them as curses to the world. Sometimes animals follow people just for food, but often people look at animals because certain among them set great examples that can help people in life.

Most of the time, people already know a lot of things, but witnessing even animals trying to do something good can motivate them to take things more seriously, especially regarding what must be done. A juvenile chick is abandoned while entering a forest searching for food. Unfortunately, that chick becomes lost from the chicken family to which it belongs and finds no food for itself. The worst day for him in the forest, where he is lost, is the same day the rest of the family satisfies themselves with a lot of corn.

But the journey of that chick can be seen as an effort to help itself. The only thing is that it wasn't his luck at that point to find food in the forest without the experience of a parent who knows that, in the forest chickens and chicks cannot find corn. In order to eat in the forest, chicks must know how to use their claws to harvest insects in the soil by removing some old leaves from the ground. Being a wild chick for a couple of days and rejoining the rest of the chicken family is great for that chick, but the experience to survive is not always specific; it always depends on the current situation you are going to face.

A young man who has gotten married and his wife becomes pregnant, leaves his wife at home and moves to a neighboring country in search of a better life. Snakes never cross fire because they always remember their tails trailing behind who can catch fire and burn to the snake's loss. It's wise to choose the right timing for everything in life. Otherwise, your decision could happen at the wrong period of life, and that error might not be easy to repair or might never be able to be repaired at all.

The young man arrives in the other country, finding things not as sweet as he had thought. Days and months fly by rapidly, especially when you're on foot, trying to match the pace of motor vehicles. Your time behind will continue to triple before you like a hail from the sky. Eventually, the young man encounters many challenges and he doesn't have enough strength to control his new life. He loses sight of the reason he had come to this other country.

As for the wife he left behind, she continues to care for the baby and tries not to put their misery in a basket, so nobody might count them and put a number on that basket. After tons of misery and deception, she continues the hard fight to take care of her baby and herself. Every day can be a good day for that lady and her baby after it's over, leaving them a life to begin a different day.

As years go by, the baby becomes a child who can contribute through work to help his mother and himself. The good fight continues until the child learns a profession and finds a job and makes enough money. Misery and multiple other problems are afraid and troubles start running away. The path ahead for the mother starts to shine with a light, and her eyes begin to witness positive changes in her life.

Now, it is time to remember how many troubles she went through to get here. Currently, mom and baby have a chance to see and know the difference between day and night. You need to know that some people are living with so many problems they are not ready to worry about day or night; every minute is the same for them.

When age starts to happen, that guy who was young and left behind a young pregnant wife is back to his country where their welcome was there for him. This time he is going to meet not a pregnant wife but his family. Imagine what it can be like for that young man who is no longer so young and did not have a chance to do what a wife expected from him. Now, both of them, plus the baby, will be sitting face to face where each one is going to listen to what the voice of the other is going to say to him. That might never be sweet; it is bitter and heartbreaking at a time when the family is at the house. Of course, the baby is no longer a baby, but sometimes, parents always say, "my baby" or "my kids." Other people might not see them as kids, but parents always say "my kids," whether they are big. Parents want to hear only especially good news about them, as some babies who are dear to them.

This time, the father is at a spot to know how his family was doing without him anyway. So, whether with tears in the eyes or not, the wife must tell that father what she crossed to get there on that road. As you might know, it is not sweet, but someone must drink it. Nothing tastes sweet; not only does it taste bitter, but the way it can feel and hurt. After all, you cannot refuse to listen, and the others cannot refuse to tell. So, before the wife is getting to the middle of the story, the husband unfortunately hurt by a stroke and gets a heart attack; then, they must call an ambulance and take him to the hospital where the situation becomes worse for them. A wrong decision can have long term bad effects to every person's concern—family and more.

When it is possible, be like the snakes—wherever you must go, then have your tail behind you; that is the only way they can call you a snake who is worried about his tail. Most of the time, when someone wants to remove a strong object, he just removes it piece by piece. That means one piece cannot be so strong. It is the same thing if you lead a family or so; think twice before you make your decision, especially when it comes to sharing even for a short period. You might just think it's going to be a short period of time, but you never know what is hiding further for sure. It can be something not many people want to accept. People who don't have a good interest in you can't always make good propositions for you because they already know exactly what's going to happen at the very first hour of the absence of the important one in the family.

Do not try to be the one who is more worried and more of a victim because when you are worried the most, you can be the most to be a victim. Of course, it is good to worry, but you need to be careful about that. Indeed, be worried and be careful at the same time because even a predator always tries to scare prey. That way he can get him easier or get one who is protected by the others who are getting distressed and disturbed. Then, everything can become easier for the predator. It is important to know a real problem can be a real predator for a good family or even a single person or a couple. Whatsoever, people need to be intelligent and have the ability to review their minds to see if their decision can be good support for you or if it can be good for your dear loved ones. Then, be able to analyze how to prevent a problem that can waste your time and might never be able to be resolved.

Be the one who is properly fit to make the right decision on the right path to go further where a road must be straight to you. Because most of the time, it must be you but not what you are running for. Your presence can mean a lot more than your richest dreams, which may not always be found at any times of need.

Two Partners are Casting Their Net

Two friends were living in a town where many people don't have a job to make a good living. Because they were living close to the shores of the sea, these two men put together and purchased a cast net for them to catch fish. Since they have that net, they have become fishing men, making a living every day for their families and themselves.

One day, different from every other day, when another man was in his boat on the sea, he was also a fishing man who encountered a very big fish. He tried to catch that fish, but after hurting the fish, he thought he could take it in his boat. However, he failed to do that because the fish was more powerful than he expected. Finally, he had to give up and release the fish so he could take control of his boat and prevent it from sinking underwater. After releasing the fish, he continued his fishing by catching some smaller fish. The big fish, which was hurt, did not feel comfortable enough at the high level of water. Therefore, the fish surrendered to the shores and lay in the sand not far from the ground where the two men with the net always passed at the sea before and after fishing.

That day, as they were passing by on their way back home, they saw the big fish laying in the low waters, continuing to float its tail. The men saw that it was a very big fish, not the kind they could cast their net on. If they put the net on that fish, they might never be able to get it to the ground and would lose their net. They both knew that, but they couldn't walk away and leave that fish. They continued to multiply ideas in their minds about what to do to grab that big fish. At this point, they completely forgot about their everyday living without that big fish and the time it might take to get a fish that big on land, just the two of them.

The two men made the wrong decision. They put their net and their fish on a place near the shores and entered the water, believing they could probably grab that fish by the tail and drag it to the shore until they could pull it out of the water. That is what they were trying to do, but it was not only what they had thought. When grabbing a part of the fish's tail, unfortunately, the fish made a very strong move, the water waves became much higher, and both men found themselves far away, fighting with the sea's current to reach the ground.

Now, it was not a big fish to catch, but the two men's lives were in danger — either the men in the water or the big fish out of the water. Eventually, the fish did not get out of the water, but the two men were in the water. After more than one hour of swimming and fighting with the sea current, a small boat encountered the men and grabbed them. This was a significant help for the two men who were close to a real disappearance in the ocean.

Taunting a big fish and abandoning their net and fish they already had led to the loss of everything. Now it was already dark, and the men who had the boat just did them a big favor by carrying them to the city dock. There, they had to explain to the city authorities how they ended up in the water. They spent all night at the station explaining the entire story to the authorities so they could make a record for them.

The fishing men, who were so close to their house with a net and fishes, arrived the next day at their house without a net and fishes. Now, it was time to think and put to mind the value of that net they had and the satisfaction they were supposed to have with the fish they caught. Indeed, the two men returned to the place where the net and the fish had been put and found no trace of anything — neither fishes nor the net. About the big fish, they didn't want to hear about it anymore.

But the other people who were always at the sea where the two men always fished together, called these two men "big fish men" just after hearing that story. So, the only good thing about them, both of them know how to swim in the water, so they will not lose all their life. Honestly, now they are going to need somebody's help to survive until life might offer them a different chance to be on their own.

Most of the time, the way you fall down is the way you wake up. So, both men head to the dock every day and head to the fishing section. There, they find other fishermen who need their help to fish in the sea. That is the way these two men are living at this moment. Day after day, both partners remain faithful to the person who hires them to help with fishing. Currently, the men are no longer fishing in the low water with a net but in a boat over deep water. This is the way big fishes live, and that was the way the big fish took them before they were rescued by the other fisherman who took them to the dock.

Days go by, months and years pass, and both men are always loyal and faithful to their boss who hired them during a very harsh period of life. Even though the two men probably have the possibility to buy a net now, they prefer to stay where they are currently because they have nothing to complain about. They are satisfied with that job that helps them a lot with their families, and they are not willing to make mistakes twice.

After many years of fishing, the owner of the boat decides to retire from fishing, and these two men are still a little bit younger than him. He decides to leave the business to those two men who now become owners of the business. Both partners now own the fish business they were hired for so long after losing their net with their fishes. That event happened to them at the sea, but they understand they made a terrible error they don't want to repeat in the future. They become strong enough to put themselves in a position where they can make a living for themselves and their families. So, becoming the owners of that business compensates them for being loyal and faithful at all times to the owner who hired them for the business.

They learn a lesson about how much you should respect what you already possess for yourselves and never put what you have in a non-secure place to leave it abandoned while you are trying to gain something greater. What you have is what you must secure before you run after anything else. If you are not currently winning, you might always get back to your spot without interruption. After all, it is better to understand what is rendered possible or not. That way, you must not continue to waste your precious time for bad results.

It is not good to sacrifice a net for a fish you are not certain you can catch because with a net you can always catch a fish for sure. But the risk of a fish you cannot get will never buy you a net. As for the two men who were partners in fishing, they restored themselves after losing the net and fishes by joining a man who had a boat. Indeed, they were loyal and faithful, and then they became owners of a fish business, living in peace with their families in the city where they are living at all times of their life.

One year later, a war happens in a neighboring country. At that time, many other people must leave their places to form some migrants who shift to different nations. When situations like that happen in a nation, the poor are always left behind because they are not able to pay for some expensive trips organized by the rich people for the rich, like themselves, who want to be in a safe and secure place until the unstable situation might be over.

When the migrants arrive, there are so many of them, and those who have enough money to do whatever they want, like when they were at home, always have entertainment every weekend. So, even though war has happened in their country, they have chances to escape, and they have the possibility of money. So, why not entertain themselves? There is a man who sees all those new people in town, and he tries to find out how he can steal some money from them. He keeps watching them, sees where they are going to the stores, and tries to be friendly, appearing as a good person. He always says hello to them and talks to them sometimes, and the new people also like to have someone to talk with.

After that bad man talks to many new people, he realizes that they are much more interested in entertainment. So, he schemes an idea of false entertainment in the name of a popular comedian by the name of "nothing." He presents himself as an agent who is selling tickets to people to go see "nothing," the most popular comedian in the country. The new people become so happy, each one of them buys a ticket, and everyone pays for the ticket. On each ticket, the bad man writes that the ticket is paid to see "nothing." That means if you are seeing nothing, then you must be satisfied at this point.

The sellers are free from any reproach or complaint by any manner, and the sellers are not accountable. The loyalty of the sellers is to make sure that you see nothing, and everyone who purchases the tickets signs and gets his ticket, waiting for the date of the event to go to the stadium. The address on the ticket indicates where the stadium is, the biggest stadium in the country.

A lot of money has been made by selling a lot of tickets. After the tickets are sold out, that man makes sure that no one is left behind without a ticket to see nothing. Say as much as you want, but see nothing. These people are new to the country; they don't know what "see nothing" means. As for the name, many people have funny names, and celebrities and any diva always carry a nickname that sometimes can make them more popular to their fans. So, the time is coming soon, and the bad man is already finding a place to put all this money — the multimillion dollars he grabbed by selling his fake tickets. If you are one of them who bought the ticket to see nothing, then a blind person might soon ask you why you are seeing nothing while you can see from your eyes.

Not far from when that day is there, everybody grabs their ticket and heads to the biggest and most luxurious stadium to see "nothing," the most popular comedian of the nation by the name of nothing, as the ticket seller was telling them. Now, everyone is at the stadium in the capital of the nation. All the high security for that stadium, who see that many people they have never seen before, are approaching that stadium. At the gate, everyone presents their ticket to the security of the gate, proving that they are coming to attend the event of the master comedian, nothing, the most popular comedian of the nation. So, the security guards at the gate become very confused and let everyone get to the yard of the stadium despite all the stadium doors being closed.

The time arrives, and the only question you currently hear people asking each other is, "Do you see him?" The only answer is, "We are seeing nothing." Everybody continues to walk around the building and try to look inside but sees nothing. The security guard calls his superintendents. When they arrive, they ask them what they are here for. They answer and say they are here to see nothing. The superintendents are confused and find it hard to understand and believe what they are saying — that they are here to see nothing. So, if they are here to see nothing, then leave them alone. When they are satisfied with seeing nothing, they can just leave.

Two hours after the program was supposed to start, there was nobody at the stadium. Then everybody decides to leave the stadium to go back to their houses. Many talk, many ideas, maybe they are at the wrong place, maybe the date is wrong. But the only bad thing is the agent who was selling the tickets is nowhere to be found at any time after the tickets were sold out. What is the problem?

So, the agent was a bad man who came over and made his own idea to rob the new strangers and take their money and go into hiding to a different place where they might not find him easily. A man who is not working now collects plenty of millions of dollars very easily and may never let anyone catch him so easily too. Now, the new people who tried to start a way to get the authority of the nation to know what happened to them and how they may be able to get back their money. The money is big but collected from many people. That's going to take a lot of time to get that in order for all these people and to get the complaint registered for everyone.

When finally the authority tries to hear some of the plaintiffs, they ask them to show the original ticket they purchased. They give the tickets to the authorities, but the tickets state that they were purchased to see nothing. So, if they are seeing nothing, then they should be satisfied, and nothing must be done. The authority asks them what they saw when they got to that place. They answer and say they have seen nothing. The authority replies by asking, "Did you see anything?" They answer and say, "We have seen nothing." For the third time, the authority asks them, "Did you see anything?" They answer, "We've seen nothing." So, you had paid to see nothing, you went over and saw nothing. What more do you want?

Maybe they are at a moment of misunderstanding because they are new to the country and currently don't speak the language of that nation. The bad man is taking advantage of that situation to rob them. Now they are in need of someone who can interpret to explain what happened, so the authorities and everybody else can also understand what was happening. That is what they are doing now. They are hiring someone who can explain the situation. It takes a little while, but as soon as the authorities get to understand the matter, then the bad man will be tracked down, arrested, and brought to justice for falsifying the title of a comedian to collect money from the people who are new in the nation. The name of a comedian who never existed for real. Eventually, they are paying to see nothing, but according to the law, it is illegal to do those bad actions to other people. That is not only robbery but also many other charges can be filed against that bad individual who is breaking the laws by doing such things. Justice must be done to them accordingly, even though the people were paying to see nothing.

So, what does that mean for anyone who does not completely understand? That means you need an interpreter who understands to help you. If the strangers completely understood what "nothing" really means, they would never lose their money by paying the wrong people for the tickets for them to go see nothing, and nothing is what currently does not exist anywhere to be seen. So, only the authority of that nation can eventually stop those bad individuals from doing wrong to others.

As for the man who is taking the strangers' money by selling them the tickets to see nothing as a comedian who did not exist, after taking that many millions of dollars from the new persons, he is leaving his own country to live in a different country so that the police of his country who are looking for him currently must not find him. When he arrives in his new country, he takes someone to guide him to where he wants to go. At a time when entering a town, that is also the time for them to go to a place where they can find a restaurant so they can eat. In that town, whenever you go to a restaurant, you must bring with you your own plate to eat and your own cup to drink. That is the way they are currently doing it because they changed the policy. Now, no one must eat off a plate that another person has eaten from before. Because of that, the guide asks the new millionaire to give him some money to buy a cup for him to drink and a plate for him to eat.

The fugitive millionaire, currently faced with a new language he does not completely understand, hears the guide ask him for money to buy a cup to drink and a plate for him to eat. However, he believes the cup is exactly what he is going to drink, and the plate is also a food he is going to eat in his mouth. Before going to the restaurant, they stop at a shop to buy a cup and plate for him to drink and eat. Afterward, they go to the restaurant, where everybody must sit at a separate spot. Upon entering the restaurant, each person has their own plate to go ahead and order their own food.

When the new millionaire arrives in his small room, it is the time he is supposed to pass his plate and cup to a server so the server can bring them back with his orders. However, the new millionaire is not doing so. Instead, he tries to drink the cup and eat the plate. The server watches him bite his plate many times, trying to bite it with his teeth and attempting to swallow it. The same goes for his cup—pushing the cup into his mouth and trying to swallow it.

The server calls the manager, and when the manager and the server observe this, they believe the new millionaire is a crazy person who got into the restaurant. They call a security guard to ask him to leave, but the new millionaire does not understand what the guard is trying to tell him. He believes there is a police officer who has come to get him for the money he took from people by selling them fake tickets to go see the non-existent comedian "nothing." Getting frightened, he tries to run, not knowing the area, and cannot run far enough. They call the police of that area along with the security guard and catch the man. They take him to a police post where they can get someone to translate for him because his identity shows he does not belong to that nation.

After the search, they find out where the man is coming from, and when they communicate with the authority of his nation, it turns out to be a good search for a fugitive—the man the authority is looking for. So, the wicked man knows how to run, but he doesn't know how to hide. The wrong millionaire, with his millions of dollars, cannot escape what he has never seen before and learn what that means. When you don't know, you are about to ignore everything you don't know. The new people who were strangers to his nation did not know what "nothing" means, but today the bad man himself doesn't know what a plate to eat and a cup to drink means. He knows how to run but did not learn how to hide himself.

If you don't know how to hide, whatever the million miles you are running in advance, they will catch you wherever you are on earth. In the end, the bad man has been sent back to his nation where he must pay back all the money he stole from the strangers who are immigrants in his native country. No one knows how many days or months the bad man spent in the millionaire's row before he got to prison, but for certain, he was a millionaire while vacationing in hiding.

Now the strangers know what "nothing" means, and the bad man also knows what a cup to drink means and what a plate to eat means. He also knows what the plate is and what it is made for. You can always hear people say they are buying a cup to drink, but don't listen to them. Never try to drink the cup itself; only drink what you can pour into the cup, like water or juices. Also, when they say buy a plate to eat, even if you are there and they buy that plate for you to eat, don't believe them. Don't try to eat that plate. Instead of eating it, put your food on that plate and eat your food, leaving the plate for the next time you might use it when you want to put your food in it and eat the food.

The greatest experience of the bad man is that at the time he was a prisoner in the foreign country, he had the chance to see other prisoners drink with a cup and eat on a plate. Now, if he finds a cup, he will know what to do with it, and if they give him a plate, he will not try to eat it. Instead, he will use it to put his food and eat his food only, not the plate. This way, nobody needs to write "do not eat" on the cup and plate because of him.

After the bad millionaire spent many years in prison, he realized that if he were out of prison working for himself, he could make enough money to have a good life. But trying to get what he did not work for led him only to the bad sport of his life.

The great thing is, sometimes the authorities can take time to make him understand what he's supposed to be doing, even though most of the time it can be late. But the bad is paid for the bad actions, and there is nothing wrong with that. Never abuse the good time to go where you are not supposed to go, while you are going to walk back, and the good time can carry you like wind. Later, the return can take a period you underestimated, and during that sweet moment, your holes might already be filled with someone they estimate to weigh more than you and have better feet than you were.

You are important when nobody else can do any better than you. That is what most of the people say when it comes to a job, but that part cannot play a role in a family because family is always important. You only need to keep straight and not let any wrong wind take you where you do not belong and where the rest of the family did not expect you to be. Truly, after years in prison, the bad man is released from prison and turns himself into a better person—a man who was punished for what he did wrong and changed himself into a person who wants to work and eat with the sweat of his forehead.

The King's Dream

A king dreamed about a world in the universe ruled by more than five kings. Currently, he rules over a nation that governs other nations with less capacity to face the bigger nations. These larger nations often engage in wars, and the one standing strongest to the last moment becomes the most powerful to rule over the others. This king is considered ahead of every other king, although sometimes it is hard to see a big difference between him and the other three powerful nations in that world. Due to this similarity, these four nations not only press on the weaker nations, preventing them from finding ways to become powerful but also a ferocious race to prevent each other from ruling over as the greatest.

The one considered the most powerful is not willing to fall behind, and the other three compete not only to take over each other but also to reach the very top where everyone else can be under and see him as the most powerful. In the king's dream, he sees some animals like snakes and dogs. In that world, there are four powerful nations, and the king sees two big snakes and two big dogs. The four animals become partners, but the two dogs always try to kill the snakes whenever they see them. A fight happens, and the snakes must stay in their cave where the dogs cannot reach them to avoid getting killed. The only good time for the two snakes to be out is at night when the two dogs are a bit tired or when the dogs are fighting for some meat bones.

In the king's dream, the dogs are not only against the snakes but also against each other, and the snakes are against each other. One snake, driven by hunger in his cave when the two dogs block him from getting outside to look for food, eventually gets so hungry that he goes out and swallows the other snake. Now, only one snake remains, so the dogs don't kill that snake directly but by stopping them from getting food, one of them eats the other. The king continues to watch in his dream and sees the dogs open a fight against each other until both dogs become too tired to stand, lying on the ground like they are dead. At that time, the other snake, hungry and angry because the dogs were blocking him from finding any food for many days, sees the dogs on the ground as dead and swallows both dogs on the same day.

The king is continuing to look in his dream and sees that after swallowing both dogs, the snake becomes too heavy to make his way out. The king watches as three little boys coming from school see the big snake trying to cross the road. However, only his head and tail can move; the middle portion of the snake cannot move because the body is too heavy. The three little boys, seeing the snake struggling, roll a big rock over the snake's head, and the snake dies. That snake, which both dogs caused to eat the other snake, is now eating both dogs as enemies. Imagine how much effort the dogs make to eat the snakes, so finally, one of the snakes is the one to eat both dogs.

Indeed, the king is continuing to look and see the snake after swallowing both dogs. He becomes too heavy to make his way out. As the king watches, three little boys come from school. They see the big snake attempting to cross the road, but only his head and tail can move. The middle portion of the snake cannot move because the body is too heavy to run away fast. The three little boys put their strength together and roll a big rock over the snake's head, and the snake dies.

That is the dream of the king. It's up to the king to know if that dream currently has anything to do with him as a king who believes in himself as a ruler ahead of every other king in that world. Whatever the greatness of an animal when it dies, the lesser animals might eat its remains, especially small insects like flies and ants. As for these animals, sometimes unusual things happen, and finally, some small boys are killing the last one who is thought to be the one who will win the last victory, where he will sit as one with zero enemies who can defeat him. So, the king has enough to think about regarding the three boys.

When the king finally wakes up from his bed, he continues to think about his dream until he becomes afraid of himself as a king in power who rules over a great nation. First of all, the king doesn't want to consider himself as a beast or even compare himself to one of what he sees. Indeed, none of them had a real victory at the end. If so, it must be the boys. Reasonably that cannot be because the boys are three, and they were small. For those reasons, they are not a match for the king. Now the king needs to find out, a snake and a dog, which one he considers as the most powerful. And you might not forget, the snakes were so careful with the dogs all the time, and the dogs were always causing the snakes to do what the snakes didn't want to do, like stay in their cave for days without seeing the sunlight. That can be true evidence the dogs were somehow more powerful than the snakes and ruled over the snakes' kingdom with their kind of actions and rules; they caused the kingdom of the snakes to crush each other. That can be proven when one snake was locked in his cave by the dog's actions, staying in that cave until he got so hungry and angry, as a result, he swallowed the other snake.

Right now, it appears that the dogs are getting closer to winning the snakes because there is only one snake staying behind, endlessly powerful. Currently, you should see it as a game lost for the snake's kingdom. But that does not mean anything good for the dogs who are continuing to fight among themselves for the meat and especially for the bones of the meat. At a specific time, you must identify when it is too late to make any changes in the attitude of the dogs. A fight without a break is happening. Of course, that should have an impact on everyone involved who can apparently win until every expert and everybody else can see the bad result of the war or fight because in a real war, no country can be the real winner. The dogs are continuing their fight until one bad moment happens to them. They get so tired, and they both lie on the ground, thinking it's going to be the same as before. So, this time, the hungry and angry second snake in the row is getting out and finds the dogs as dead. It takes that real chance to swallow both dogs without a single bite by them, powerful radical dogs. Both powerful partner dogs who were the most powerful king fall in just one time. Now there are no more super kings, no more time to compete. The competitions are over without any notice or signal.

When the big trees start falling, then the smallest trees might have a chance to grow. So, after these big kings are no more, it is the time to ask about those small kingdoms that are lesser and too little to be mentioned on the list of the powerful kings. If an old man gets drunk and lies on the ground, a little child can forget where his mom always takes him when he must go to pee and currently believes an ear can be that spot if found on the ground. So, something similar is happening to the great snake after that huge victory. Unexpectedly, his hunger and anger both disappear at a single moment. Then after dances, the drums become too heavy to carry. Just after that victory, the great snake who becomes the most powerful king in the world gets drunk with his spoils, and some kids come over and touch his ears to see if these ears might be used as places where moms tell them to go when it's time to pee. So, who are these kids? They are coming from those small kingdoms. Now they are crushing the head of the only big and powerful nation and currently in the race as the ones who are using their strengths to erase these former powerful kings of the nation's ahead of that world. If you can imagine the dream of the king and consider what a serpent can cause, even prudent but venomous for most of them. As for the dogs, that error can only happen when fighting for meat and bones among themselves. So, everybody knows that a dog will never give up alive when it must be for his territory or things adopted as the wealth of his owner. After all, only humans can rule over them even though sometimes it is not without some tragedies.

After those kings understood that they might be defeated, and the lesser ones might be at a time to take the lead, they engaged themselves in big wars. At this point, some of them interrupted the others in many ways that caused them to become more aggressive than they were before. By the means of those situations, everything in their path is not safe and can be destroyed, like the snake who swallows a snake like itself, and the biggest ones engage to destroy each other—a kind of action that puts everyone engaged in that action vulnerable to the loss of life.

Before the disappearance of the kingdoms, comparing them to the snakes and dogs, the king sees they were conducting many wars over the world. The poor, especially the immigrants, become the markets for many identities like some so-called authorities, scams, thieves, and more. Every identity takes the ride of unstable conditions of a different nation to make their stronghold or fortune while the migrants continue to live like a home depot where everybody who runs out of what they always want to use at home can come and get what they currently need. That means if the immigrants have something like money, the work for that money is already counted among the budgets of some entities.

For some specific reason, most of them might spend a long period of time as slaves with the voluntary title. As you might understand, if you continue to put water in a gallon from the top, and someone else continues to draw the water from the bottom of that gallon by putting a hole at the bottom of that gallon, you will never end up putting water in that gallon. For sure, it is like a moment when everybody must go to the marketplace to buy a lot of things they need. At that same time, the workers at the market are continuing to add products but never being able to fill any spot at that market because each time they add something, the buyers are already standing there waiting to buy it.

At this point, the refugees or immigrants are not only at wars where they are from but also at wars where they are. They must work at every time they can breathe, and if not working for a day, then stress takes over their minds because somebody else is controlling what they are working for. Whether they are working for money or not, what they must pay will not reduce. They must pay to identify them, they must pay to be there in the world, they must pay to renew their life, and they must pay to exist. Then they must pay for their payment to be accepted, and they must pay to get paid for the work they have done, and pay to be slaves. So, whoever believes they are not slaves uses themselves as slaves just to keep the others as slaves. In conclusion, you find self-slaves ruling over voluntary slaves.

Indeed, self-slaves rule over voluntary slaves because voluntary slaves are those who always want to find legal ways to resolve their problems. With that determination, they accept any kind of work just to fight the harsh situations. Some of them must face heavy and destructive loads that someone else weighs on them. As many of them know, in times of war in most nations where people enter for protection, there are some other people, even among the authorities, who take advantage of that problem to abuse others. That often happens in cases where those people are in need of help, whether to make them a little more free and comfortable with less stress.*

*In a garden where many flowers are largely open to show how much beauty the area can be, where their blossoms are abundant and awesome, where many varieties of birds from the sky adore and render their majestic songs for the glory of beauty, where the human eyes cannot skip without curiosity and a communication between the brain and the heart with a mind of mystery. Despite that when you are looking closely at the garden, you'll find many flowers who never find a good chance to open themselves to the same ways as those who are at the point to show their beauty to every eye who finds the good chance to contemplate them and not hesitate to express themselves about their mystery of beauty. Some others fade too soon and do not arrive at the term of glory to contribute to the garden's beauty. As the beauty of the flowers can contribute to the glory of the garden, each human can contribute to the beauty of a community, to the glory of a city, to the beauty of a nation, to the glory of the world. But that is not the case for everyone, as the flowers that don't have the chance to open; unfortunately, some people never have the chance to open their hearts, to express themselves inside for the benefits of others, even though some of them hide enough good things in their hearts that can please the whole world. For some reason, they don't find a good chance to offer anything at all to the world. *

*Some others who contribute to a community, to a city, to a nation, and glorify the world are like the flowers who were open and contributed their mysterious beauty for the glory of the world. Whether many other eyes see them going too soon and leave a scar in the heart of everyone in the world who knew them and those who are going to love them in the future by adoring the trace of their feet in the world.

As a flower that never gets a chance to prove its beauty in a garden, a human might never explain his heart to the life condition of a community, to an individual, to a nation, and to the world. When raising eyes to the sky, some heavy clouds always hide the blue. That way, their eyes might never see the blue color of the heavens. For them not to see the color of the sun in the morning, the heavy cloud is posted at the east where the sun rises and follows the sun until the west direction where a portion of the earth is hiding the sun, so they must not see the sun at all. The travel occasion always catches them by surprise, so they must walk barefoot overnight on the mud, thorns, and thistles. The apparent large road never takes them to a source of potable waters but only to the dry land where the wilderness is ready to say welcome to them.

After many years of labor to build a house for them to rest, at least then, a day they find themselves homeless. After a ton of hard work to make a farm for them to have food to eat, when it is the time to harvest, they must stand far away and look at those who did never know how to plant a tree eating their good fruits while their stomach becomes storage for hunger to be stored at all times. Their mind rules over peace and beauty while they are in the middle of chaos, and their eyes cannot see more than the darkness in the ugly wilderness.

A young man was learning to keep himself from becoming a criminal against those who were consistently doing wrong to him. He was the one training himself because, when he was young, he found himself in a family where love did not reside. He was sometimes mistreated by his mother, father, brothers, and sisters, even strangers who, seeing that, took advantage to do wrong to him.

Not only him, but also some other kids in that family. Some tried to live together, but not because they benefited from family love.

Upon leaving the family, the young man recalls a period when he worked very hard for months or even a year to buy a piece of clothing. On the next day, that clothing was found bleached and destroyed, a new piece of clothing that was hung in his closet. This was like a dewdrop for him because his training meant a lot to him, reaching a level he had never known. When it was time for him to make his way to another place where he would deal with other people, each time they did something bad to him, when he thought about vengeance, he returned to his mind and analyzed his past. He said to himself that kind of life was born with him, and he must avoid those situations as much as he can, but not try to do anything bad in revenge for himself.

When something wrong happens to someone, the wise take the lesson, and the fool criticizes. But most of the time, before their critics are over, they carry themselves to a dangerous area where it can never be easy for them to look back to where they were before. So, the wise, who see the rain and take themselves to the shelters, protect themselves against that rain. If you know how to put yourselves in a shelter against the rain, you will also know how to put yourselves in a shelter against a hurricane, that is for sure. But those who did not prepare for the rain will not be protected against the hurricane and will know adversity.

Never at any time minimize that; those who are well-prepared might never grant the chance to even wear a single piece of clothing that can sometimes compare to the kind of effort you made to go behind the darkness where the good spots are, and what you currently find is darkness. When you are the one who is working hard night and day to make a difference in your life and suddenly find yourselves among those who were refused to do anything for themselves that can make them happy, and believe you were a fool, but that is not the truth. It is what you can call an event because that does not happen to everybody who is working hard, but sometimes the bad leads to the wrong direction which is what people call human error or bad action against the others.

Sometimes humans can do something good, and next to it are many bad. Most of the time you are prepared for a dry season, and a flood happens. Next time you are prepared for the flood at that same season, then instead of the flood, a dryness happens. One thing you should never forget is there is nothing lost under the blue sky, there is nothing less nor greatest; there is what you can call power, whether it can be a power of humans, who are collective power that can disappear. If it is a natural power, you can change places at all times as a routine not to be there at the wrong time, but remember that a single human cannot do much; it has to be many humans to form collective power. Natural power has nothing to do with a category of life, but human power can be created especially to destroy lives and the witness of life, slaughtering as much life as they can with their powers. In reverse, their powers destroy themselves, and everything returns to normal.

You just don't want to be caught on the street by the heavy wind. If so, you can destroy, and a minute later there will be no more wind to be afraid of. Yet it can be sad to see what humans with short lives can cause to resemble them, but sometimes it is good to know when you ignite a fire what that can cost to you also. Because the power a single human uses to destroy millions of lives has been granted to him by most of his victims, one way or the other way. But in conclusion, all humans are the same as a harvest of oranges; one or more might be rotten in advance, but each one of them will go through the same process to make space for the new harvest. That is why humans always regret their bad actions not far away in their life.

A young man was visiting a very high mountain where there was a forest with some very high trees around bushes, thorns, and thistles. Not far is a lot of big rocks and gravel that can sweep away any object. It is like the current of a river that can sweep you until the ocean. At the top of the highest palm tree, that is the place a bird chooses to build her nest, lay her eggs, hatch them, and have her chicks. The sun was so hot during the daytime that the bird must stay there at the nest and open her wings as shadows to protect her chicks from dying as a result of the sun's heat.

This is good protection because the chicks survive without any scorching of the sun's heat. The mother is suffering and waiting for the chicks to fly fast so she can take a break from the sun's heat. A day arrives, and every chick is growing big enough to fly and leave the nest. But a trial should be done for the chicks to fly as a jump from that height to get to a lower altitude until the ground. Before the nest was built, the parents saw it as good protection to prevent predators from destroying their harvest. But now it appears to be a significant danger for the kids who do not yet know how to fly. So, the mother and the kids must accept that situation they cannot change, for instance, the kids must put faith in their mothers and do what the mothers currently ask them to do. The mother is flying away and gives them a signal to follow one after the other. The chicks must believe and trust their mother. Indeed, the mother is going and gives the first signal. One chick jumps to prevent it from being injured by thorns, thistles, or hitting a rock or the ground too hard. The mother keeps flying below the chick, and each time the chick touches her back, the strength to hurt diminishes until the chick finally gets to the ground. She continues the same process for every other one until all the chicks get to safety. Accidents do happen sometimes, but risk is risk. You know when you take a risk, what result that can give you if you do not win that risk.

When people put another on top as a leader for them and give him power, if that is really serious, you can be a billion or more, but all of you are like a single chick who puts faith in a mother to give a good and serious signal that can lead to a safe place. If that signal is confused or misled, there will be chaos. The higher you are, the harder it can be for you if you are falling to the ground. The reason humans must run is never to give them a chance to examine where to end up the run and examine a chance to turn back.

Since you were born, you can see that most people prepare to receive a newborn baby, but they do not know when a life will be ended. That is one of the reasons why people cannot control other people's actions, especially when they get the power to do so much. You can tell about a season, and with so much knowledge, you can have the chance to notice and receive notices from certain people about natural disasters, like hurricanes, tornadoes, and more. As for human power, even they are not sure about what is in their hearts to do and regret afterward. If it is possible to know how much greatness or danger there is when your life is in somebody else's hands, just think about the baby birds who were born at the top of a palm tree where the sun's heat was extremely hot, and that palm was the tallest palm tree in that mountain forest. Thorns and thistles were around every big rock at the ground, and any little mistake can be fatal. For that reason, it is not plentiful to hope everything that carries your name is yours. At a time, you might run and leave behind you a plume feather, an organ like an eye, foot, hand, or any other part as things or objects you might always memorize.

Visit to the Town

One day, a mother was taking her son for a walk in town by a river, with his beautiful clothes on him. But while approaching the river, the boy falls into the mud. By chance, the river is close, and his mother takes him to the river and washes him together with his clothes. As they are about to leave the river, there are some children playing by the river sand. One of them loses her shoes; the river's current sweeps that shoe away. Fearing punishment at home by her mom, she is crying a lot.

Another girl, who sees her friend crying, asks her mom to give her shoes to the girl who lost hers. Her mom agrees, and the girl is so happy and thanks them for preventing her from punishment. Upon entering the city, where many people must walk from store to store to buy what they need, the mother and son see another little girl crying bitterly. Her mother bought her a beautiful dress that she likes, but while walking among many other people, someone grabs the bag with the dress in it and runs away. The mother has no more money to purchase another dress, and that is not sweet for the girl.

During that time, people who fell in the mud got washed by their moms and started getting dry. Nobody can steal the clothes worn by their owner; if you cannot steal the owner with his clothes, all together. So, that is not everything. Not too far away, they see a couple crying in the dust because their house is catching fire, and they have lost the house with everything in it. When a person asks them what they have left, they answer and say only the clothes they are wearing.

Now the boy believes that if his clothes were not on him, something worse could have happened to him too. But he learns that everybody is not crying for the same problem, but every problem hurts. After all, the clothes you are wearing are only what you own and only for the time you wear them. Yet, even a mosquito is smart enough to attack you behind your neck so it can escape without being struck by you.

Most of the time, you must have that in your mind. If trouble does not reach out to you, then you yourself will reach out to the trouble. It is clear: if you are not the one who is looking for the problems, then someone else will bring the problems to you wherever you are. If you think about the people who are on the street, of course, they are facing some different problems than those who are at home. While the mom and son are on the road back home, they see a person who is walking slowly trying to cross a busy traffic road and gets hurt by a vehicle and dies right away.

At that time, the boy hears other people talking about getting a bag to put that person who has died by accident, and the boy hears another person say everyone who has problems should be put in the same bag. When the boy hears that person say everyone who has problems should be put in the same bag, the boy immediately remembers he had problems when he fell in the sliding mud. He says to his mother that he doesn't want them to put him in the same bag with the dead person; then they must leave before they put him in that bag.

When he says that, his mom tells him that they are seeing people who have problems, but that person who has died has no more problems. The people who must take him away from the street are the ones who eventually have problems. When someone dies, that person is immediately forgotten about any problem because problems can kill people, but problems don't live with dead people. Problems always want a living person to resolve them, but a dead person cannot resolve anything. That dead body is the loss of his life.

So, among everyone who had problems and resolved them or are on the way to resolving the problems, that one who has died, the problem has resolved instead of him resolving the problem. When many are running, some can be fatal, some can lose objects, some might lose organs. In the manner of the bird, humans were born in the middle of serious dangers that are surely serious for those born too close to the view of predators and born closer to certain forms of dangers.

That can be anyone who does not care about their daughter's actions, who can create a problem and put others in a vulnerable position in life. Tears in the eyes of a little girl can be for clothes, a beautiful dress that she lost. But tears in the eyes of big people can be for many years of hard work that disappears in one day or less than a day. If your clothes get dirty, that can be cleaned with water or with another object. If your clothes are lost, you can buy new ones soon, even a more beautiful one. But when that happens to be the loss of everything that you possess, eventually, you can feel different. But remember, you are the one who can resolve the problems because you are still alive. The life you have is the only one you can run with, and if you have clothes on you, that is when you have the chance to wear clothes. The most important thing is your life. Then, with more experiences, you can live easier and peacefully in life.

Whether you can move or not, if you are breathing, your soul is alive. Then you exist. If you are not dying, you are currently living and existing among every other life. The main cause of human problems is power. Everyone might need some source of power to live, but somehow, associating with too many ambitions can make it fatal. Indeed, you need some sort of power to survive, to learn, and to live, but the ambition to be the highest and the only one, or the ability to rule over every other, that can be the key to problems. And that kind of ambition is a fast-growing seed. If you sow it, your harvest will be great for a big name that will soon turn to bad reputations. That reputation can unfortunately sit on many souls that are slaughtered on it and under its covers of malice and betrayals of all kinds of associates with deceptive and shameless actions. Those who care for others sometimes live for others.

Children care the most about food and beautiful clothes, but children always depend on parents to provide care for them, like preparing food, buying clothes, and doing every other thing for them. Then the children learn how to love their parents from their parents. Now the parents who love their children become the ones to worry about their children's future. Most parents don't feel like they are living for themselves but for their children. Because everybody as human was a child of some parents, every human feels the need for someone to follow as the lead person.

Unfortunately, for most of the time, that can start well and finally turn as a baby shark who confuses a boat in the ocean with his mother and follows that boat until the baby shark completely loses the mother. And the baby shark, who cannot live without his mother, finds himself at the end of every future his mother visualizes for him. A boat does not go where the captain is not directing it; therefore, you can be in a boat, but it is not good to follow a boat. By doing so, you might find yourselves at a port where you never dreamed of being all the time. Never let yourselves be led by a leader who is led by other leaders. If you are sure you have a specific plan for a destination, always remember that even a law established is not for a powerful entity when that is not on the side of his way.

Everyone must respect the law; that is what everybody said. But as for you, indeed you must respect the law. If you don't, you will be punished, so don't hesitate to see those who are the most powerful going against the law. The most powerful family goes against the family laws by believing that only the children must respect these laws or principles. A child learns by his mom not to eat with his mouth at a high volume of speed, so his dad knows that too. But one day, that child sees his dad eating with a high volume. The child immediately does the same thing as his father. At that same time, his father tells him he cannot eat with a high volume like that.

Now the child understands that the laws are only for those who can get punished but not often for those who have the power to punish the one who goes against the laws. Of course, if a child is not respecting the law or principles of the family, that child can get punished. But never mind about any others who don't want to do so because a fence is not put to tell a human what to do; a sample sign is enough to direct the human path. Unfortunately, there are some people who violate that law. In antiquity, fences and walls were used only to prevent certain animals from penetrating where they didn't want them to be. Some animals, thanks to good owners and training, respect some limits and principles, especially about their behavior.

Good parents never skip the law of the family or any other law while their children are following their path. That is not only a local or family matter, but the world situation; the lesser nations are the only nations to obey the laws. When it happens to be the serious matters, those who have powers do not be among those who are not supposed to cross the laws. Now it has reached the point where it said the laws are for the children, so it is a serious matter, for those who are not children must do what they think is good. Whenever they get to that area, chaos is for those who are so vulnerable, those who cannot do anything to protect themselves, those who cannot and who should not cross the wrong path. Then, as an animal who is tired and tied, they see the fire but they cannot run away from it nor stop it in any way.

They not only respect the laws, but they also respect the greatest severity of laws for the lesser, and the law itself is born by the greatest. The same mind you can find in the heart and brain of the fire is the same mind you can find inside the human powers because humans always regret their wrong actions. If you are the victim of them, do expect one day before you die to meet face to face with one of them who were part of your calamity. At this point, you will be the one to help them out with their problems; always be sure of that, whatever your situation, you still have someone you can help. You are still important for someone who is in need of your help to survive.

There is an existing law that is worthy; that is the law of pineapple. At a garden where a child tries to make his own small farm in the middle of his parents' farm, he plants many different plants altogether. On a good day before his farm is good enough to harvest, the goats of his parents dashed to that section of the farm and unfortunately ate all his plants except for one plant, that was a pineapple plant. So the child cries and says the goats are out of the law then they enter the farm and eat his plants. Now he only has one plant left over, and the child says he will make sure he takes care of that plant in a way that can give him a lot of fruits to compensate for all the others he lost because of the goats who are eating them.

But his father tells him the plant he has is a pineapple plant, and the pineapple plant has a strict law and is worthy. Whether you take care of that plant less, that plant will keep its law as a worthy promise. Whether you take care of that plant a lot more, that plant will keep the same law; nothing will be less nor more. The child wants his dad to tell him what that law is; then his dad tells him that the pineapple plant will not give you any fruit before a year, and the pineapple plant will never give you more than one fruit per year. Wow! All this work, take care of a plant for a whole year and have only one fruit per year; that's not right.

Now the child is a little bit discouraged, but the father says to his son he will compensate him with some more plants and make his farm grow faster that way. While he is taking care of those plants, a year will be here faster, and the pineapple fruit might be the one to ripen when every other fruit of the harvest is over because there will be not too many fruits left from the others; the pineapple can be the one to welcome. There is a way to have many fruits, that is when you plant plenty of pineapple trees because one of them can give many baby plants. That can help you to plant many of them, and then the next year, you can have a lot of pineapple fruits in your garden. So, the pineapple can give you one fruit per year, but a lot of plants to compensate; that way, when you have a lot of plants, you can also harvest a lot of pineapple fruits at your farm.

Now the child not only knows how to make and take care of his garden, he then knows the pineapple law that will never change. Then he learns from that plant who has kept his worthy law and promises to give one fruit to the one who is taking care of it each year. And the child says if a plant can keep his promise, he also will never go under the reproach for not keeping any promise, and he will make sure for him to always keep his promises.

The little girl who had her dress stolen by a thief after leaving the store where her mom was purchasing the dress must go home without that dress because the dress was stolen by a thief.

In the next month, her mom has the chance to take her back to a boutique to purchase a different dress. After the agreement on the price, they have that dress in a bag and leave the boutique. While they forgot to pay for the dress, on their way home, they remember that they forgot to pay for the dress and hurry back to the store to pay for the dress. You can imagine if, by the door while they were leaving, a guard caught them, indeed, everyone will say they were stealing that dress. That is why it is important to establish some good judges to make some good judgments before definitively condemning somebody.

At this point, a person should never aggravate anything without listening with good judgment to make sure they can prove if that person was here with his money to purchase that item or not. On the other hand, when you make a mistake, you will be the one to pay for that if it happens to be a serious mistake than you are the one to prevent yourselves from making the mistake because there are not too many ways to know when a mistake happens what it appears to be is what they will consider it is.

That is for sure many people pass for what they will never want to be but the point of understanding is that nobody is able to detect anybody's minds just to make a good judgment for themselves. Everything can currently be done by the clear evidence of what they can see, and everybody else can absolutely view. Despite that, after the clear concrete and solid evidence, if a serious judgment proves that without a doubt a person is a big thief or big criminal, that person should not be allowed to have access to the security of others and should not be everywhere among good people.

The thieves and big criminals will never teach their children what is good, and if their children become friends with the good children, that is a ninety-nine percent chance for the good children to become the same as the bad children, that is for sure. It has never happened for one rotten orange to be at the same spot with some good oranges and for the rotten orange to turn out to be a good orange. But for sure, all the good oranges will be rotten soon.

If the big thieves and big criminals tell their child that they were bad and try not to be the same as the person they were, maybe it is because they are changed for sure. So if every big thief and big criminals have more than one kid, if the kids also turn out to be the same as his or her parents, then the numbers of thieves and criminals will double each time they have one child. It might not happen for the child of a big thief and criminal to turn the same as his parents but, who knows?

If you must choose between preventing or accepting, for sure you will choose to prevent. So if you have knowledge that a person is from the thieves or the criminal's family, there are too many ways to go than for you to prefer a road of thorns and thistles. Even though there are so many who are not worried about that because they suppose thieves and criminals are never going to prison and have never been punished nor accused for certain. So when your children produce with that kind who were highlighting, your grandbaby might be the one who inherited his father's or mother who were highlighting as the bad persons.

There are no good reasons to look at a child badly because of his parent's bad actions. Most of the time what people say and write as the laws have never been respected. As many people know, a mistreated dog can be the worst dog who can attack and even kill whoever is found on his path. That is why it is better to prevent a disease rather than cure it, which is better to not walk in the darkness, to not step over any thorns and thistles.

A drink can be considered bitter but excellent for your health; a word can be funny and sometimes even hurt for many people. After all, time can be proved that the word does not deserve the bad considerations; it is a prelude for the better tract for a train to make its way to the good areas.

People Travel to the Planet Nowhere

Long ago, people did not build bathrooms inside their homes. Every bathroom was located some yards away from the original home. Of course, everybody can see that it makes sense because that is the only good way to protect the atmosphere of the home with the residents.

Many years later, somebody came up with the idea that people could have bathrooms inside their homes. For many people, it did not make sense to build bathrooms or restrooms inside the homes. For sure, they had never heard that idea before, but that is never a reason for that idea to not become a reality after some generations.

Nowadays, most people have never known what a house without a bathroom inside looks like. This proves that everything is not limited just by what you know today or what you can see, but later it can be much greater and more marvelous, like a mystery. Many things that cannot happen today will happen tomorrow, even though for sure that time will be a far distance from today, perhaps a century or even less.

In the future, anybody who wants or can buy it may have their own airplane like a helicopter that can land at their own house and travel around the world. Then, wherever you want to go is just like using your car today. If you decide to go to a different country, then you will take your airplane and go. Today, if you are living in a world where a mirror has not yet been created, you may never believe that it is possible to happen, that somebody can produce a mirror that you can use every day to look at things your eyes cannot see.

If, by a strange dream in your sleep, you see yourself living in a world without telephones, then you will never believe that it is possible for someone to invent the telephone. So, right now, if you open your eyes and see you are living in a world where the name "computer" is not here and someone is trying to tell you about a computer, of course, you might not believe it one hundred percent. Not only those things, there are many other things, even the airplane itself. Like for the first time, when people talked about building bathrooms inside their houses, because at the time they were saying there were no bathrooms inside the houses, everyone saw that as a wrong dream. But today, no one wants to live in a house without a bathroom inside that house.

A time will come when people will no longer bury in cemeteries anymore. Many people who are on Earth today will never believe it because that seems to be just a word. People of this century might never see that, but it will happen at a time where nobody will take a deceased person to a cemetery to bury them. Sometimes, words are revealed as true after many generations, except for those that are just not true from one percent to one hundred percent. This is like a group of people who entered a city and told the inhabitants about a planet that is much better than Earth, and the name of that planet is "nowhere."

They told the people that the planet "nowhere" is only one step beyond the planet Earth. They said that if you want to go to the planet "nowhere," you must organize your trip and head to the planet "nowhere" without any problems. All you need to do is choose your direction. You can go north if you prefer, south if you want to travel from the south, or the same for east and west. Regardless of the direction you choose, you must go straight. If you encounter a river, you must cross it. If you encounter an ocean, you must cross it. The reason for going straight is that the planet "nowhere" is at the edge of the planet Earth. This means that if you start from the middle of the Earth and travel in any direction towards the planet "nowhere," your trip will cover half the circumference of the planet Earth.

Because at that time, people did not know how to determine their exact location on Earth, it was important to go straight. This way, they might not miss a minute of that long trip they were undertaking in the direction of the planet "nowhere." The people of that city believed it was a good idea to make the trip and find the planet "nowhere," something better than the planet Earth. They were willing to spend a lot of time, aiming to be the first to reach the planet named "nowhere."

So, the people of that city listened to that group of people and organized trips together to find that planet according to the information provided by the group. They were going to find it at the edge of the Earth and just skip one step beyond the planet Earth to enter planet "nowhere." The preparations were organized, and many people took the direction they had chosen to follow to reach the edge of the planet Earth and finally enter the planet "nowhere."

The trip has begun; night and day, people are walking straight ahead. If these people's point of departure is at the middle of the Earth, it's going to take them half of the planet Earth to reach the planet "nowhere," if the information is accurate. If you are still living, you will know whether the planet "nowhere" can be found or not. Remember, if you encounter a river, you must cross it. You cannot change direction just to avoid the river and continue in a different direction until you can bypass it. That's not in the plan. The deal is that you must go straight ahead, regardless of obstacles in your path.

After following one direction from their own city, they are now passing that city and heading to the next city. After many days on that trip, the people are very far away from their own city. From road to road, city to city, they are crossing rivers, one after another. Now, they are facing the sea, the ocean. They are going to need a boat. Now, it will take a significant amount of time to build a boat large enough for all of them to cross the ocean. Imagine the people of a city who have never traveled before finding themselves at the shores of the sea. They don't know if they are far or close to their destination or their own city. In case they change their minds and decide to turn back home, they need to know which way to go. However, at the present moment, everyone still wants to go to the planet "nowhere."

They enter many forests to cut trees and gather materials to buy from stores to build the ship they need to cross the ocean. It's a serious issue for them right now. It's not a matter of days or weeks, but months and years on the road. During this time, children grow bigger, old people become older, and sick people become worse. Water and food are not easy to come by. But the hope for a planet "nowhere," better than the planet Earth, keeps them working hard to build a boat that will take them on a journey to the edge of the Earth, with the intention to step onto the planet "nowhere."

After years, the people believe they have completed the ship they need to cross the ocean. They work out the logistics and get the ship onto the sea as they wanted. Now, they bid farewell to the land where they spent a lot of time building the ship. The ocean is their new reality. Day after day, heavy rain, wind, scorching sun, hunger, and all the challenges of a journey keep them company.

After some days, and weeks, there are no more ways for weeks, but months over the ocean. Now that trip starts looking like some too comfortable people in a city on earth who

are creating their own troubles. The group of people who led them to that trip disappears just after everybody gets on the boat.

The group of people who did not join the trip is making their way back to where they came from.

Now, the city people at sea have been on a trip for years with the belief they are going to reach the edge of the Earth and step onto a planet better than Earth. Now, it happens to be years into that trip, there are people who have died during the trip to "nowhere", but the loss of an eye doesn't stop the war. However, after years of the trip, there are no indications that the city people are going to make it to their intended destination. Currently, they are landing on an island where people speak a different language, and no one can understand the others. The islanders believe that these people are immigrants feeding some nations currently at war.

After some days, they finally have someone to translate for them. After the translation, no one agrees with the declaration they made, saying they are on the way to a planet called Nowhere. In a time when people have no airplanes, only the very smart can understand where a country other than their own is located on the map. And no one else, other than the authorities, has the right to send anybody to a different nation because there was no plan for a situation that had never happened before.

A trip to nowhere can take you anywhere in the world if you don't pass away during an event in that trip. So, the people from different countries were different than today, and the authorities gave them a temporary place to stay until they could be accepted to live and work like everyone else. Indeed, they were obligated to put a lot of effort into understanding the other people, their language, and the laws of the new land.

The people who dreamt of going to a planet better than Earth now find themselves in a country where they don't understand the language when someone speaks to them. One of the great mistakes they made was to ask the group of people what language they would speak on the new planet called Nowhere. A rich person who never expected to face any economic problems in life doesn't worry much about language as a difficulty. After all, the city people become part of a different nation, immigrants who need opportunities to work and live like everybody else.

As for the dream of the heavenly planet called Nowhere, it is nowhere to be found so far. Those who died during that trip are no longer there, but the living ones don't know anything about returning to their city of origin. At this point, it is time for them to understand that they belong to the planet Earth, and there is no way for them to skip that planet like they believed and switch to a different planet with just one step. The truth is evident in their current experience.

You can be born in one corner of the world and, for some reason, move to the next corner. Whether you regret it or not, it can happen because of a significant event you cannot prevent or due to a false belief or mislead. Either way, the conclusion is that you were born on Earth, and wherever Earth covers as a planet, if humans live here, your place is here too. When errors happen, people always accept that they made a mistake that caused them troubles. To regain control of themselves, they need to accept the example of three of the most dedicated workers on Earth: ants, honey bees, and chickens. These creatures do not often rest from their work, engage in labor all the time, rest while working, and eat the fruits of their labor. They do not lose a second of their time when at work.

The city people, instead of sitting down on a planet better than Earth, eating good food, wearing beautiful clothes, and being entertained without thinking about difficulties, were misled by a group of people who were telling them about that planet. Some of them died on the road to the planet "nowhere." The survivors had to start a new life, engaging in hard work day and night, with hopes for a better tomorrow. Not a better planet, but a better tomorrow where they could guarantee their food for the day. If they didn't work for a few days, even due to health reasons, they would not be able to find bread to put on their tables.

Before taking any significant action, always remember that a water source may be small, but it does not often dry up. A water source does not leave its spot to shift to a river and draw more water. Rather, a source of water is the one who nourishes the rivers. That means, a water source can be considered as a source further along on his way who turns itself into a river; that source of water may be the head of a river.

So, the reason for a source to be a great source of water is because that source continually diverts its waters in abundance for the great benefits of everyone dependent on that water. This is not really different from people. The more a person shares what they possess with others, the more others want from that person, and that person also becomes great in their eyes. They respect and honor him as a great person, and, for sure, that person becomes great by exercising the actions of great persons.

Actions like these are not limited to a single person; they can go step by step until nations. Those who want to receive all the time will continue to be the poorest so they can keep receiving. But for those who give all the time, they continue to be great, and they can still find enough to give away.

So, the city people must be vigilant enough to live like everybody else who are the original of that nation because they cannot go back to the country where they are coming from; it is far away, and as for themselves, they don't know if their country is to the north or the south. Besides all that, their energies are diminished, they have no more hopes for a planet whose life is better than planet Earth. So, no matter the degree of your happiness, you cannot laugh every second, night and day, and no matter how hard your pain is, you cannot cry every second, night and day. Therefore, the city people must forget about their city and work hard where they are granted favors to be together with those who don't even know them before and make a good life for themselves. They should never complain about anything because better is the enemy of good.

They were taught about a planet called Nowhere, which is better than planet Earth. They are trying to leave planet Earth for something better, which is the enemy of the good Earth, which is misery. In that time, everyone must understand that there is no planet by the name Nowhere that exists in the universe where humans can live better than planet Earth. Yet, that planet is not known in accordance with any human knowledge. If it is supposed to be, it is not known yet among any human knowledge on Earth.

One thing is for sure: some people are ready to obey any kind of mislead, even when it is the craziest action one could imagine. Indeed, humans can obey the worst, craziest leaders in the world. Some people might not openly agree; they will obey any bad leaders on Earth. But when you put your leaders in occupations, you must obey your leaders. Besides that, some of them become mentally sick just after being chosen as leaders, and leaders often will not tell anybody about their incapacity or their mental disorders. The world might not deny that some leaders were only mistakes for the entire world. And suppose a bad leader is ahead and orders his power control agents to go ahead and destroy a very important place in the world. Do you think anyone is going to declare the knowledge of his mental disorder before they obey his bad order? Yes, many people are going to say that it does not make sense, but before these people's voices can be heard, the bad actions will already be accomplished by the one who is supposed to obey the orders of their superiors. Even though, when everything really turns bad, they will be the ones to pay the price. But as for their superiors who ordered the bad actions, these leaders will walk away with their mental disorders and be put in secure places, satisfied with every comfort of the world until death.

A baby whale who mistook a boat for his mother is following the boat and loses his mother. Finally, the baby whale unfortunately moves to shallow waters where many people know nothing about whales. Some say it's a shark that can kill people, while others claim it's a crocodile that can eat them. Despite their conflicting beliefs, they all gather behind the baby whale to push it ashore so they can use it as normal fish.

Imagine that they are all behind that baby whale. If, by accident, it was a crocodile or a shark, as they suspected, you might imagine how many of them could get injured by that fish. Most of the time, people hear about danger but at the same time minimize what that means to them. Standing behind a leader appears to be the same as that baby whale that lost its mother in the ocean, following a boat weak and unable to breathe as it should. The baby whale was defenseless without his mother to feed him milk to make him strong. Of course, there will be no more life for that baby whale. Those who were there can always believe it was a big animal. If they knew at the moment it was a baby whale, maybe some of them could have tried to help it get back to the deep ocean, with the hope that its mother might find it again.

The baby whale was missing his mother and following a boat that could not help him but lead him to chaos. It is the same for those who sometimes follow leaders and don't understand for sure when they are behind the wrong one. It is not easy to control everything, and suddenly things can turn around in catastrophic situations that may not be easy to repair at all. So, when that happens, whether anybody says it or not, you need to agree that they were obeying the crazy leader. Sometimes they don't want to say the leader is crazy; instead, they say the leader is doing some crazy actions or making crazy decisions. After all, decisions and actions can be good or bad. When decisions and actions are good, they are made by good people. When they are bad, they are made by crazy people. Decisions and actions of humans often don't happen by accident but always happen by somebody's power. Whoever causes the bad actions is the one who is crazy, but not the actions or decisions.

Where you are living your life is the place you will die. But it is not the same as when people say the way you live is the way you are dying, so pay attention. When they are saying the way you live is the way you will die, sometimes what it looks like is not what it is.

Cat Chooses to Be the Leader of Democracy

A cat was chosen to be the leader of democracy to rescue rats and mice from a long-time atrocity by the snakes, who are continually eating rats and mice and preventing them from going where they want to go. At the same time, the cat dedicates himself to teach rats and mice democracy so they can live together as brothers and sisters without fear of one another. The cat is also the one who presents himself as the power lawyer and speaker for rats and mice. So, every night, the cat wears his gray costume with a silver tie around his neck and goes to the field where rats and mice live. This way, the cat can teach them how to live with democracy. Each time you see the cat, the first thing the cat must say is democracy. After all, the cat is a professor of democracy. The cat puts plenty of limits and checkpoints for the snakes so that rats and mice can be protected and live freely at all times, night and day, with no fear of any snakes attacking them.

Cats have so many big lawyers and judges assigned to hear rats and mice with the snakes in case a tragedy happens to a rat or mouse. Cat even says dogs are also allied with his firm of the law against snakes, not to mention honey badgers, mongooses, and eagles. So, snakes must behave and seriously heed that measure against them. Time after time, the cat proves he is a good teacher, lawyer, and everything for the benefit of the rights of rats and mice. Now, mice and rats can go at any time to every territory where the cat puts his checkpoints and prevents snakes from crossing into these territories by means of looking for any rats and mice to put under arrest as meals for the snakes. Because rats and mice are the most victimized, everyone not against mice and rats agrees that cats are doing a good job by stopping the snakes' penetrations into the territory of mice and rats.

At the same time, the cat is promoting democracy from mice and rats to lizards and snakes, even though snakes refuse to accept that democracy from the cat on a long scale. The cat's current dream is to include doves and chickens in his democracy so they can live together in peace as birds in one democracy. Therefore, the cat is calling the doves on the trees and letting them know the cat is now a teacher of democracy, and they must not be afraid of him. At any perfect moment for them, they can accept to join the cat in a meeting of democracy so the cat can help them understand how to live with no fears of any other animals like snakes and even falcons or hawks. So, the cat makes himself the head of a democracy to unite every fearful animal of these categories. Then the cat community is the most helpful for those helpless, making it very easy for a cat to travel to any territory without any problem at all. Snakes get killed every day, but snakes are enemies, so everyone knows that a mouse cannot kill a snake, a rat cannot kill a snake, a dove cannot kill a snake; therefore, there will be no investigation, as an investigation is not often conducted among those big authorities who are there to conduct investigations.

As for rats, doves, and mice, cats are the ones conducting those investigations. Sometimes the suspects are dogs, but cats are never yet ready to get dogs under arrest. But a complaint has been filed, just a complaint as a signal to prove that dogs are suspects. Every day, rats and mice disappear; eventually, cats take that as a serious matter, as the cats say, and the cats will catch every snake involved and bring them to justice. Every so often, cats put under arrest some of the snakes believed to be the ones eating the rats and mice, even the doves who disappear by leaving their feathers on the ground. Cats have the authority to go everywhere they want without any fear. Cats are the most prestigious democratic figures, so nobody has control over cats about whether cats have done good investigations or not. Cats can travel wherever they want and whenever they want, but cats are always in the field after sundown when darkness arrives so they can control everything about snakes, and in the morning before the sun arrives.

One morning, this time, the sun had already arrived, and a big snake who thought cats were no longer in the field was living inside a big tree trunk but sometimes traveled overnight and came back late in the morning. That snake laid himself on a big rock to catch some sun before getting back in the tree trunk where he lives. So, that day was not a good day, unlike every other day, for him. The snake is going to face a cat, yet when the snake sees the cat, he tries to hide himself, but that does not work well for him. He tries to run, but the cat has already told him not to go anywhere; he is under arrest by the cat for trespassing. Snakes are not supposed to be in that area at all times So, while the cat is questioning the snake and slapping the snake at the same time, the snake is playing rebellious by trying to fight back with the cat. At that point, the cat gets so angry and grabs the snake directly under his neck, continuing to slap the snake more rapidly. The snake, who was so big, ties himself around the cat so tightly that the cat, unable to carry that much weight over himself, is laid on the ground. This goes on for too long until the snake finally passes away because the cat has already cut his jaw and throat. As for the cat, it appears to be a no-win game because the cat can no longer handle the dead weight, cannot breathe anymore, and drowsiness has overcome the cat. So, the cat community decides to have the cat see a doctor who can find out what they can do to save the cat's life.

The cat is a big teacher of democracy who has a lot of respect, a lawyer for the rats and mice, and a peacekeeper for them as well. The cat doctors can be doctor vulture, falcon, and doctor Andean condor, one of them or both of them can be doctors for the cat because that is the cat, and he must have some good and excellent doctors. When the doctors examine the cat, they find out the cat must undergo immediate surgery to remove some things that are blocking his intestine during that long fight with the serpent. If the surgery goes well, the cat will have a good chance to live, but the doctors must remove those things stuck inside the cat's stomach before they can guarantee anything like life for the cat. The doctors know exactly what might be done.

Indeed, the surgery is done on the cat. What the doctors find inside the cat, who was teaching democracy to rats and mice for them to live together in peace, are ten mice and seven heads of rats. The doctors declare the cat did not survive the operation, and they take him to several mugs that refuse to accept the cat because of the nature of his death, which was illegal. The doctors are swallowing the cat by pieces and finishing with the cat, they are also swallowing ten mouse carcasses and they are swallowing seven carcasses of rat's head, so that makes those swallow thrice.

Now, to what conclusion will the cat's community come about those investigations cats are conducting on snakes and others for the disappearances of rats and mice? What kind of leaders are cats? How did those rat heads and mice enter inside the stomach of the cat? Everything is clear. Cats are the most deceptive teachers of democracy who exist at all times. From the beginning, cats were the entity destroying the most rats, doves, and mice. Sometimes cats even try to teach their democracy to dogs.

So, the accidental fight between the cat and the snake sheds light on the hypocrisies and deceptiveness of cats who mislead rats and mice, betray them, and eat them. Cats continue to deceive the rest of them by saying investigations are on the way to catch and punish the guilty. So, cats are guilty for neither rats nor mice. Now it is known that cats are the real entity causing the disappearance of rats and mice, but what can anyone do to help themselves? So far, they can only retreat deeper into their hiding places where a cat might not grab them easily because it's always good to know your enemies. If you ignore your enemies, you will continue to die easily, and no one will ever know the real entity of your killer.

Cats are everything for mice and rats, protecting them from snakes, limiting the snakes' territories so that rats and mice can be free to go wherever they want. At the same time, rats and mice are the best and favorite meals for cats. Sometimes people say a secret stays a secret, but for me, a secret is what never happens. Until a cat eventually dies, it never talks about what happened between him and the other cats, and what they are doing with those who trusted them. So, after a cat has passed away, that dead body reveals a high degree of cat deception. Cats enjoy themselves every day with some meals who have trusted them for their protection and good leadership, so they were completely deceiving and betraying them to death.

After the operation, cat doctors Andean condor, vulture, and falcon flew away. Right now, dogs have a job to inspect the place where the operation was done by these doctors. After that inspection, dogs found nothing left over for themselves. Yet, dogs accuse the doctors because they did not leave anything for dogs to take as evidence to conduct the investigation against cats.

Now, it is no longer a quiet place for cats. Dogs are all over the place looking for cats. If a leaf falls down, dogs say, "You!!! Hoop! Hoop! If you are a cat, let us know now!" The only thing is that neither rats or mice have any trust in dogs as well. But dogs promise to eliminate every bad cat in that area so that no more rats and mice may die because of cats.

The only big handicap of dogs that limits them from putting all the cats under arrest is that dogs did not complete the grade to be investigators. To be such investigators, dogs must not limit themselves to the places where cats can go most of the time. So, dogs did not reach the level where they can climb trees. When their teachers taught them how to climb trees, dogs failed to that degree.

Eventually, each time dogs must face cats, cats use that weapon against dogs and climb trees where dogs must stay on the ground and call for backup, which does not always come. After watching a cat sleeping on that tree for so long, dogs must quit and fail at that attempt to put a cat under arrest. Imagine that if only dog had completed his grade and knew how to climb on the trees, dog might have been a good leader. However, dogs, in general, are not happy when they must face situations where their enemies must go over the trees.

Dogs went to the highest entity of the world and applied for the permit to go back to school just to learn how to climb trees. However, there is a denial record that indicates dogs were prevented from climbing trees because they quit school too early when they were supposed to learn how to climb trees. Other than that, ants submitted an application with a contract in which they agreed with the authorities. They declared that the day the authorities accept dogs' application and grant them a permit to learn how to climb any trees, on that same day, ants would be authorized to be a species of animal bigger than a lion.

Yet, the authorities stated that if dogs learn how to climb trees, they would become a dominant animal without the human control, which could be too miserable for other animals. As for ants, if the ants become a species as big as the lion, ants will be the only one to stay on Earth. Then ants will kill and eat every other creature, including humans. For that reason, ants must remain as ants, and dogs, for the sake of other animals' lives, will never be permitted to learn how to climb trees. So, dogs, the most high-entrepreneur, the highest defender, the handiest, the highest in faithfulness and fidelity, loyal to the rich and poor, and the worthiest who never deceive or betray, refuse the permit to climb trees.

That is one of the ways to understand that knowledge has limits according to what each category is supposed to do depending on the brain or an organ inside. Dogs want to climb trees; they say no! Dogs want to fly away; they said no! So, dogs don't get mad with any commandant. Dogs say they don't want them to go on the trees or any way like climb; dogs will jump. They don't want dogs to fly away; dogs will run, yet dogs are happy.

Indeed, when dogs are ahead, nobody can take over easily. But when dogs know they are the ones to obey, dogs obey with no difficulty. By the way, dogs cannot resolve this responsibility to get all cats under arrest for the crimes cats committed against rats and mice. But dogs do their best by putting some checkpoints where cats can be afraid to step, and dogs use their voices to panic cats so that cats stay away from the territories of the rats and mice.

If you want to approach an analysis of the minds and actions of the so-called leaders who say they stand for you, through that analysis, do not hesitate to find nothing different compared to what was inside the cat. At all times, they can say they are your guardian protectors, but how many times do they block your way to a good life? How many times do they make efforts to keep you in poverty so they can continue to build their wealth and their fortress on you? At the same time, they keep their eyes on others who may be thought to help you out of poverty, so they can find a way to stop them from helping you.

Most of the time, they present themselves as your owner, the only entity who owns you. Therefore, you have an owner, and your owner is the only one to take care of you. Your owner always watches over you and doesn't want anybody else to come and give you too much food, so you might not overeat. Your owner doesn't want anybody else to feed you with fast food, so you must not be overweight. Your owner wants your belly to be halfway full all the time so you can always remember his food. If someone else gives you more food, you might turn your back away from him. If that happens, he is going to lose interest in you. Your owners will make sure all your needs are met by half or at least less than half. That is the only way they can make you turn back your eyes and look at your owner and ask, "What to do, my owner?" When you turn back your eyes, your owner will know it is time to let you have a half-loaf for you and the family. Then the owners know you will not sleep because your belly doesn't have enough food, and the family is there under your eyes. Then you have a feeling they don't have enough to be pleasant. So, if you can at a simple time verify those actions, there will be nothing better than the actions of the cats on behalf of the mice and the rats.

A serious plan is always at hand, a program is always in place; big promises that are not for sale, everything is free like a democracy taught by the cats. So, what makes you an uncomfortable person? Listen to your owner; you can sleep with your belly empty tonight. Do not accept any bread from anyone else; tomorrow your owner will feed you and your family. By the way, they are smart enough to see you and your family will not be able to make it until tomorrow. In that situation, they just want you and your family to die. They are encouraging you not to accept anything from nobody else, then wait for tomorrow so you can die with your family. If you are able to see, as an operation can prove what's inside the cat's stomach, you will be able to view and understand what's in their heart.

The only snare that always catches his owner is that they must watch you at all times so you must not take the good step for yourselves. Eventually, they forget that by watching you all the time, they will not find any time for them to sleep. When they are not sleeping enough, they will lose their strength to perform for as long as they want. Their health will reduce to the minimum unacceptable. Yet, that is a snare that catches his owner overnight while none of them paid attention to it. By means of that, there are no winners when it comes to malice or wrongdoing.

The snake was squeezing the cat until death while the cat had already cut the snake's throat to his death. As a result, the wrongdoing of the cats is all revealed to everybody. But as for a winner, neither cat nor snake knows the pit or the graveyard where the rats and mice were killed and eaten are snake and cat themselves. So, at this point, cats, snakes, rats, and mice are the losers; none among them is a winner.

If a person doesn't want you to sleep, of course, that person will continually watch you so you might not sleep. Never mind, at that same time, that same person will not sleep as well. You can choose to live like the cat who is at all times teaching democracy, what is good but, to be at the same time an enemy and killer, that is not good at all.

After all, those who belong to the forest are living in the forest, those who are domestic are living as domestic animals. When it comes to animals' life, that is continuous in the forests, at homes, and elsewhere. Cats and dogs, who are the highest compared to mice and rats, then where dogs and cats are living, often they have names. But rats and mice, their names are not repeated so often; they are lesser to mention if not needed for a duty the others cannot accomplish.

A powerful worker can retire at a certain point in his life and continue to live well. As for a beggar, there will be no retirement until the breath of life is given up. So, if you are chosen to be a good worker, if you are granted a chance to do that peacefully at the right time, you will be a retired person. But, if you have a feeling that you are the beggar, do not hope to be a retired person but, the one who will give up. Give up your strength, unfortunately, when the breath of life is given up on you. You may be a great fighter, but you might never win anything. So, at this point, your honor is to keep up the good fight. In the end, all you will gain is your life as your gift until your old body must rest in peace. That is your victory, stay alive until you pass away without the cause of your enemies.

In a forest where many kinds of animals are living, all the big animals depend on the small animals for their food. Every day, the big animals have to eat some small animals. A small animal lives in the middle of many big animals, and that small one must come outside every day to look for his food, just as the big animals do. Yet, each time the big animals see that small animal, they run to catch him in vain. That small animal always finds his chance to run fastest and hide himself in his spots where he lives. After this happens many times, finally, all big animals in the area know that small one, and they are not worried about him anymore. Whether he runs or not, there are no big animals who try to catch him anymore until he gets old. When he is ready to pass away, he steps outside and renders his last breath. No other animals attack him, and after he dies, his dead body stays at the place where he passed away until it dries and turns to dust. No other animals disturb his body.

The strength to resist also means many things in life. That capacity to run until the predators completely see their chance on that small animal as too weak was a key for that small animal to win his life. As much as you can resist your enemies, so much are your chances to achieve victory. That victory cannot only be a victory of glory but also a victory of strength, security, and respect. Like that small animal, many small groups of people suffer under those who consider themselves the greatest. Some small nations are on the path of other nations who always use them as tools to protect themselves against their enemies. For that reason, they want to keep them from doing anything to redraw themselves from their misery. Instead of helping them, they continue to plunge them deeper into the pit where their expertise cannot allow them to help themselves. Stepping on so many does not mean one of them might never find a way to protect himself from these kinds of atrocities.

The small animal did not move from his habitat, as a country cannot change its spot. But, as a life like every other, he continues to resist and never acts as a fool who doesn't know what an enemy can cause to him. So, he remains alive. A simple life cannot just come over and put an end to it. A big life is not more than one existing life, and a small life is not less than a big life; both have one existence. May you continue to be solid as a rock, so that even when you are weak or as you die, your enemies will no longer be worried about you as an easy prey for themselves.

There are no trees without branches, and branches cannot exist without the existence of the trees, whether it's a group, a small nation, or a big nation. The many powers you can have all depend on the others who are in front of you, at the side of you, and behind you. As trees can lose their branches and turn into poles, if those who are around you turn their minds away from you, that is enough to turn you into a simple pole. Even a strong wind will not make any ears hear your voice. Many roots can help a tree stand strong, but without the many branches that produce some multiple leaves, there will be no guarantee of solidity at all.

Even though in some cases you might have to trim some branches from a tree, that can be just to protect that tree. Because bad branches can cause severe damage to a tree, if they are too heavy and finally tear asunder from the existing tree. At that time, unfortunately, a tree can be split in half, and half is gone down with the branch that quits. The other half stands there, waiting for any event like rain, wind, or any vibration to finally get to the ground as well as the first branch. If some branches can cause the life of a tree, of course, power without balance can destroy groups of peoples and nations. For sure, that can be the grade no one ahead of a power will not pass because when humans have power, they want to be greater at every time. Any others who don't submit to them make it hard to tell when the boat is overloaded with unnecessary things.

Yes, human power can be too unbalanced when it is abused to satisfy strong desires, hypocrisy, betrayal of one's roots, or the destruction of major parts or branches of itself. In the end, a good conclusion will prove that power destroys itself by loading too much of its own powers and abusing them for self-destruction.

If a power can destroy itself when its conductors abuse it, what can you say about those conductors who choose to abuse their powers against it? Most of the time, it's good to hear, but witnessing the reality is not sweet. The main reason it's not good to witness anything like this is that for many people, just seeing something like an atrocity can leave a scar in their minds, haunting them day and night. It's not good for their hearts. If you've never seen where a serious natural catastrophe happened, there's no reason for you to even think about anything like this if you're not in an area where such events occur often.

So, if a natural catastrophe is about to happen, sometimes people are alerted by others who are qualified to do so. But sometimes, people have no alert about anything until they are caught by surprise. How about human catastrophe? That is much more dangerous because humans try to hurt and destroy specific targets without any specific time to stop, unlike a natural catastrophe that always has a short period to stop. As for human power when it happens out of control, you will never want to witness that. Unfortunately, sometimes you can be very close to it, or you must escape it, or even be a serious victim of it. After a person who witnesses a war must run away from what he was calling his wealth and, for the most part, see the destruction of everything, then that person knows the difference between a natural catastrophe and the madness of humans against others because there will be no winners. When you witness these, you will not be happy at all, except for those who are doing the bad actions at that point.

It is good to imagine that those who make those actions may never want to do that in the first place but have no choice. That is why, after those people accomplish such actions, they are surely not the same person anymore. If that person was a superb husband and a good father, after going through these, now you need to beware. It may be sad to say, but that person will not be the same. That is why no country ever wins the war. If a country enters a war and never loses a soldier, it is too early to cry victory. Only one of those who were at that war as a soldier to defeat the others, called enemies after the war is over, can post himself at a place. Then, for no reason, he can defeat a considerable number of his own friends, and he will not worry if they are kids who belong to himself. Be sure of that, most humans cannot see a severe atrocity and remain the same person. If, for any reason, that person comes from that dangerous sport of atrocity, that person, after a short period of time, will no longer be a real peaceable person. But, at any moment, that person can highly act as one with a serious mental disorder.

Happiness Should Not Face Any Deception

If you consider what it takes for a parent to raise a child and make them somebody, if you consider what it takes to build a nation, if you consider how long a person can work hard to build a fortress, if you consider the time and energy of your strength you put out just to build a house for you and your family to live, if you consider the misery you face to put some food in the corner for yourselves and your family, food that you wish to be left behind for the one who might live after you, and at a simple order of another human, everything can be swept away like water currents washing the shores. In a single second, you and a person who never did anything good are in the same bag. Your wealth is disappearing under your eyes with great thanks if you are alive. For many others, there is no sunshine at all. Maybe life is not the way everybody thought it was supposed to be. It is not the same for everybody, but in the end if someone doesn't hurt, you are not sick at all. So, age will come over and put you under some restrictions and finally take you away peacefully. That is the truth. So, if you choose to enjoy yourself, you can do that. But as for what many people call happiness, that does not last long and is not easy to catch back. Because even when you enjoy yourself, later you will face situations that are going to completely erase your joy. After all, whoever believes happiness exists, they are not living forever.

If you cannot live forever, then you are a person who only can enjoy life and die. Happiness should never face any deception; happiness should never face any defeat by any means. Happiness should be forever without interruptions at all times. How will you feel when after you spend all your young age on a none appreciated opportunity, one day before you die, you hear someone else say you have become rich, you are a person who can do whatever you want? Then, if someone calls themselves rich, you are also a rich person. So, what are you going to do with that wealth while you are making your way out of life? Your time is over before you can even see your name among those they call happy ones. That means happiness did not exist for you. If you are a person who always has a chance to assist yourself when you need anything, that is good. Then you can also enjoy yourself. But as for happiness, forget it. You can go on vacation with your family. Unfortunately, some of you can die in any kind of accident just before you are back home. If that can happen where every joy of the heart can be off faster than a second, happiness is not at the table. Nothing with life has happiness because happiness should never be associated with any pain or suffering.

A young couple was freshly married, started a family and started building a wonderful house for their family to live in. The construction of the house started after some months, and it's almost complete. They are preparing themselves to move into the new house, which is located not far from the intersection of two major highways.

One evening, they went to pick up their child from school, and upon their return, they wanted to stop by and pay attention to their nearly completed new home. Unfortunately, a big truck struck their vehicle, ending everything for them, but the child was safely withdrawn. There is no happiness at all. At that point, they were only enjoying themselves with the good moments they had and when the event happened, everything was over. All they have to do is rest forever.

However, accidents happen at any level, but humans are the most accountable for their troubles and chaos. For example, war is not an accident; it's a great concern for humanity today. Whatever problems come into existence today, it's not wrong to say that these problems are like simple leaves on the big tree of human trouble.

Many people understand that all forms of war are seeds sown by humans, whether it's anti-wealth, anti-health, or against life in general. Wars are anti-enjoyment, creators of every wrong, and agents of death at all levels. Sometimes, when major nations are at war, some smaller nations are at peace. Therefore, in these smaller nations, people can experience peace for some time, where problems are less at every level. People didn't get sick easily; they produced their own food. Everyone learned how to live with the products of their own country, and nobody worried about thieves coming to steal what they had. There were no major problems at all.

At a time when nations that are always at war turn their attention to those small nations, they say, "We are the big nations; we must conduct some study to find out what we must do to help the small nations." Just after they send what they are designed to send to those nations, they come up with some ideas. They claim that these nations are small, but the people are suffering from many diseases that cause them too many troubles. The people are sleeping in houses and outside wherever they are. Now, as the big nations, they are the only entities that can resolve this problem. But to do so, they must create many units to deal with the situation. So, they create many units and send them to the small nations just to keep them from sleeping too much.

This becomes the "gnats' organization" for many. Yet, they decide to use five kinds or more to help the people stay awake all the time, day and night. In each community, they place five bases of these agents to keep the people from sleeping too much. These bases include mosquitoes, ticks, fleas, bed bugs, and lice. The big nations claim that these agents are there to help keep the people awake and teach them how to exercise. Every second, the people must put a hand over their head to scratch a bit, and the process continues for every part of their bodies, night and day. Those who believe they have trouble with mosquitoes quit and go inside. Then, the bed bugs are there waiting for them inside. Some believe they can hide inside a new box to protect themselves for a little bit, but what happens with the lice? Even if people can stay underwater for a few seconds, the lice continue to bite them under their hairs. These are the prices to pay when you put too much faith in the help of others.

They are at war, then you proclaim yourselves the peaceable nations. Now, everyone is at war. The peace that allowed them to sleep whenever they wanted, day or night, now poisons their beds with bed bugs, their clothes with lice, and their bodies with ticks, fleas, and mosquitoes, which become their bodyguards behind their ears all the time. The peace they had is draining overnight, thanks to the help of the big nations.

If you always slept well and woke up when your sleep was over, now even when your sleep is in your eyes, you will not sleep. Your sleep will become a disease for you. Who were never sick before don't forget, there were promises to help you make exercises, so these exercises are now permanent. At each time, you must scratch your body when the bed bugs continue to bite your skin. Whenever you are scratching the flea bites you are exercising. When you bend over to move a tick on your back, you are doing exercises. When the mosquitoes bite you and you try to repel them, you are exercising. When the lice bite your scalp, and you scratch, you are doing exercises.

Somehow, people who learn how to own themselves, before saying yes to accepting any help from somebody else, analyze that help to see if they really need it. After that analysis, if they realize that help can create some chaos, they refuse that snare just to prevent so many nightmares.

After that, an organization sprays its five kinds of help over people who have never been sick. Now they are dying every day. People who never knew the road to hospitals are now going to hospitals every day. Now, people even need to take medicine if they want to sleep. If that was some help, now they are in need of no help so they can own the rest of their skins. If they were suffering from too much sleep disease, they are now in need of medications to sleep. If they were at peace, they are now at war with the help that brings tears, pains, and finally death to them.

It's easy to have what is not desirable, but it's not easy to absolutely get rid of it anymore. It is possible for those who never want such help from others, but it is not possible for those who always need help from others. A wild animal falls into a pit, fights for its life until it gets itself out, and continues to live a normal life. But a domestic animal, caught in a snare, waits for rescue when it thinks an accident is about to happen. Instead of a rescue, that was his predator, a hunter of animals. The animal will never see its owner again, even though the owner lost it. The animal loses its own life because of its dependence on human help.

Now, its mind doesn't have a chance to do the same as the other animal that used its own strengths to get out of danger. If you are in need, of course, you may need somebody's help at times. But you should be the first one to help yourselves before someone else even thinks about helping you. Sometimes, help from others can be worse than the problems you are trying to escape. This is good not only for one individual but even for a nation.

Some nations never had a real criminal until others entered with a mission to help them. Later, everyone realizes their mission was not to help but to train the young men and women to become criminals. For most, it is too late to stop anything. Moreover, if you are not good enough to identify the bad plants, how would you find out the bad seeds? The seeds are sown, grow, and bear fruit. Then you have no recourse but to harvest what was sown in your farm, whether good or bad.

Each time doctor mosquitoes visit you, believe it that you are losing some blood. It's not only the mosquitoes but every other bloodsucker. If any of those creatures invade your territory, they will not leave without something you can compare to your blood. They are there at all times to help you, but you are the only one who can put some sense in your brain, analyze their activities, and find out if you are dealing with bloodsuckers or real helpers.

From your own analysis, you should see if you are continuing to step back or if you are moving forward to the better steep from the way you were before. Check for anything amiss or out of control because sometimes you might not be intelligent enough to identify a seed or a tree, but you should be able to identify a tree by its fruits.

You cannot continue to call yourselves farmers and never be able to prove yourselves as farmers who can protect the good plants against the bad plants. If you cannot identify anything between the bad plants and the good plants, you will continue to harvest the wrong seeds and store them as good seeds, resulting from the same chaotic errors that cannot be repaired anytime soon. You need to know what you are supposed to know. The opposite of that is just building some luxury bases for those organizations which harbor lice, fleas, mosquitoes, bed bugs, and much more to defeat. They will take all your efforts into captivity, including you and everything surrounding you. This way, you might continue to be a parasite over what is good only for fire.

A couple was at a furniture store to purchase a sofa bed when a so-called friend arrived and told them not to buy it. He claimed he would give them a good one, so the couple agreed and obtained that sofa bed from him. Initially, the bed looked good, and the couple perceived it as a good gift and a helpful gesture.

However, inside that bed lodged more than twenty cobra snakes in their nest. The couple, unaware of the presence of these snakes, temporarily placed the bed in a corner of their house before installing it in the intended spot. When the couple woke up the next morning, they were terrified to find a couple of cobras in each corner of the house. In panic, they sought help from a neighbor and called for assistance.

The first thing they were told was to ensure they left the house to protect themselves because nobody could guarantee the capture of all the snakes. Fearing for their safety, the couple had no other option but to dash out and abandon the house, whether their friend knew about the snakes or not remains uncertain. The only truth is that the couple now had to find a different place to live.

In the future, when someone wants to give them something, they may have to verify whether there is anything that could cause them a nightmare, as the serious nightmare they experienced could no longer be prevented.

After the animal control went over and captured those cobras inside the house, the local authorities declared that it is not wise for anybody to live in that house anymore because of the many venomous animals who were inside, and nobody is able to declare that the house is free from snakes. So, that house can be demolished or sold only to the agents of animal control. This way, they can control the animals. After the final inspection has been done, the agent who buys the house can do whatever he wants with it. In that country, it is legal when animals take over a house, and the authorities order you to leave that house. An animal control agent can buy that house for a very small price and make sure he removes every single animal before he can sell that house or live in it himself. At this point, the couple has no other way to go except to sell that house for a tiny price and find a different place to live.

Yet, that is what's on the table for the couple who very much loved their beautiful house. At the time they put that house for sale with that record, an agent of animal control comes over and buys it for a tiny amount. The couple is no longer owners of a beautiful house; it goes to an agent of animal control. So, what is interesting is that after the couple accomplished the sale of that house for a very small amount, they are very surprised to learn that the person who gave them the sofa bed is the person who actually owns the agency company who purchased their home. This person sends the agent to buy their house for a tiny amount and resells it for a big amount. Now they fully understand they got into a snare of a bad person who meant to make a serious bad action to steal their beautiful home from them very easily. As for that person who knows how many snakes were inside the bed, and he knows how much they have grabbed, yet if one or more of the animals are hiding somewhere, that person knows how many snakes to look for, and looking for them is easy for them. The couple who received the gift are the ones who lost a house for just accepting a gift.

Everyone can be happy sometimes to accept a gift, but remember most of the time people don't give a gift to you if they never know you and do not expect anything back from you. Sometimes other people can use you as a bridge to cross to what is your feature, your wealth, your family, even your country for their purposes. If someone can put snakes in your house to make you leave that house so that they can take it, then believe that if your house had ears to listen and hears what a voice can say, those people could talk to your house and ask your house to do something wrong to you and put an end to your life so they can get that house for themselves.

So, if at any moment you can just prevent any unimportant relationships with the ones you don't have enough trust in your heart, do so to prevent yourselves from too many things you might never want to know because most of the events that are prevented are the events nobody will ever know how much bad they can cause if they were not prevented somehow. So, anything that can happen to an individual can also happen to more than one individual, and even an entire nation can be a victim. No one can tell how many times people of some nations enter other nations with promises to help the people, and finally, those help turn out to be some personal interests which, for the most part, turn into some serious chaos, which can be compared to some cobras inside their countries that they cannot control at any time, especially when you are not at a point to understand the deepest roots and pivots of the problems.

Among the people who can hate you to your death is the person you are giving your own food, and you are giving your food to his enemy. That person can hate you just because you are giving food to his enemy, and he never renders himself accountable that you own your food. If you can give your food to him, then you can also give your food to anybody else.

The second group of people who can create serious problems for you is the one you are receiving anything from. Also, receiving something from his enemy. These two entities can be the worst parties to pay great attention to because at any moment, they can try to put you under their control so that you could do what they prefer you to do. If they actually want you to be like the couple who abandoned their house, you will abandon your house and later sell that house to them for a tiny amount. Who knows how to remove what they have put into your house, your nation? By the time you open your eyes, the title of sale will already be signed by you and given to them as the owner of your house. At this point, you will look at yourselves who worked hard to build your house sleeping at a different spot for a temporary time. As for them, they will contemplate themselves and laugh at you as the fool who did not know how to prevent the kind of people they are and keep yourselves away from them.

The hunters are in the field every day, hunting the birds and all other kinds of animals as their prey. If you think you can be a victim of them, you are the only one to exercise yourselves as the one who knows any kind of bluff, any kind of snare, and any colors of the hunter's costumes. That is the only way you can live your life among them and never get caught by them at any time as prey. When someone wants to catch a chicken, the first thing he thinks about is corn because chickens love corn. So, when the wrongdoers want to harm you for whatever reason, they will present to your face something that can take your soul out of your own control. But often, those who cannot identify these tricks, of course, will go to the wrong side of that and pay the wrong price.

Never believe that what happens to one person cannot happen to a full nation because there are many different roads going to just one place, many roads but one direction. In every developing country, a road doesn't only mean one subject. On one road, you can find a part for vehicles, a part for bicycles, and a part for humans who are pedestrians. So, if you are not a person who wants to drive a bicycle, a motorcycle, or a vehicle like a car or another kind, you are not left behind; you can find a place for you to walk. But the predators are at each one of these roads. That means the road of life is the road you must be cautious of how you walk, whether it's a road to go somewhere or a road of dealing with other people every day of life. More precautions are always needed because some of the people who are victims from the others later become part of those who harmed them. Therefore, even when you know you are a victim, you might be at the side of a wrongdoing by any mistake of yourselves.

A multiple-times victim by the wrongdoing's bad actions even deserves a diploma for not becoming a criminal as well because often when someone continues to be the victim, that can push him to run for any kind of vengeance as justice for himself. When his actions are against the law, everyone will call that person a criminal. That mostly happens when justice is never accomplished in favor of any victims. For a person who is continuing to be a multiple time victim and trying not to be out of control, that means a lot of good qualities and endurance to cross that as a serious trial that can leave many scars in a life.

Good Actions without Measures Could be Regrets

A family of five people were pretending that they were stuck on a road in a situation where they needed someone who could help them. A young man encounters them and believes they are at a point where he can help them step out of that situation. That young man takes that family to a place where they can stay for some time and helps them find food and everything they need. However, the young man's good actions turn into many regrets for him just after that family finds access to his important spot where he stores many things, including a bag he had prepared for a trip containing a lot of important things, including money.

In a short period of time, everything disappears with the family. At this instant, the young man understands that the family was not a good one, as they pretended, but they were all thieves looking for easy prey to rob. The family grabs everything and goes away. Now the young man learns a lesson on how to help someone he doesn't know. If you don't know the person and you really want to help, just give something and turn away, leaving the rest for someone who knows them better than you. It is for sure that many people pretend they are in need when it's not really true; they are just looking for an easy way to steal from others. When you give them something and turn away, that is the best way to protect yourself against them. If you are not an organization, don't be the continual help for some individuals. Don't even be a friendly helper; you can help a person today, and tomorrow just help a different one. That way, wrongdoers may never have a chance to follow your path until they can get to your nest, carry it with your eggs, and leave you like a poor dog waiting for its deceased owner at the gate of the house.

Bad people close many gates where good people cannot get in; that is for sure. But rather than fall into a pit by helping someone who doesn't deserve your help, it is wise to just give something and walk away before you even hear the word "thanks." If you give to someone with good caution for yourself, you are doing your best and saving the life of the hungry in need. Never forget that in your life, the people who eat your bread are the same people who want your soul. While eating your bread, they are craving everything you own, including your life; they are digging your pit and numbering your days before you while they are drinking your pure wine.

This is the action of a man who always goes to the sea on his fishing boat to fish. One day, he catches a creature he doesn't have clear knowledge of. However, he chooses to bring that animal home and put it in a pool of water he has at his home back porch, thinking he is doing nothing bad. At that time, the man had a beautiful daughter who was just about five years old. One day, unfortunately, that beautiful girl, who has a beautiful gold ring on one of her fingers, is nowhere to be found. The beautiful girl disappears and cannot be found after many serious searches. There is no trace of that girl, and it's sad for the family and their good friends. After some days, they look at the bottom of the pool where the man put the animal and see only the beautiful gold ring she had on her finger. What a hopeless situation! So, eventually, that animal swallowed that little girl, and at that animal's feces, they could only see the ring, which did not turn to nothing. It is clear that the animal was the one who swallowed that girl.

So, the man who did not know anything about that animal and took that animal to the companions of his family is the one who made that mistake—a mistake that can never be repaired. A most unnecessary mistake that cost them an enormous loss of a beautiful daughter who cannot see anymore. Do not believe that a person you invite to your house may not be the same as that animal. You can invite a person into your house and later find out that person causes you something worse than that situation. So, it is not a good idea to have a dangerous animal around your children, as that may not be necessary at all. If you don't know someone, you should never trust that person with your child. It should be the same for an animal—if you don't know anything about that beast, never trust that animal around your children.

A family stole what a young man had at his house because their titles were grand thieves, and they were wicked. But a wild beast eats a child of a family because of someone's negligence or error. The wild beast was hungry and believed he just found the food to eat. If humans find in the animal menu, then humans who have the reason must be responsible for their own protection against wild animals. Whether some people might not want to call them wild animals, any animal can be wild and, for some reason, cause injury at any time; therefore, humans are responsible for both animals' injury and humans' injury. Animals have nothing to worry about except for their food, safety, and territory. After all, you must keep in mind that humans are the most dangerous animals who ever exist.

Animals of the sea will never attack if they are not looking for food, but if someone touches a poison beast at the sea, of course, they can get poisoned. Animals on land will not attack if they are not trying to defend, looking for food, or by mistake when the animal thinks they are trying to harm him, then he charges them as defense to protect himself. But humans sometimes just look for any other life, whether a beast or their resembling humans, and kill them to satisfy their wrong desire. Since no good reason can justify, humans are the most dangerous life on earth.

If you can imagine how many humans and animals who were believed to be at peace and suddenly destroyed by humans' unjustified actions, that is an absurd and horrible thing to imagine as a human. Most of the time, actions like these are considered as missions accomplished. If someone destroys a part of the world and nobody at any level condemns them for what they are doing, they have accomplished a mission apparently good to be executed where a judgment is not anything to be afraid of them at all. When a serious action happens, there are two options to be considered—whether they can judge someone or they can honor the one who accomplished that action. Eventually, if they cannot judge him, then they are agreeing with his action.

Among the worst, some may believe destroying the whole world can be easy and accepted by most of the wrongdoers who believe they are right to do whatever their anger incites them to do against the entire world. A longhorn is enough to make humans and other animals afraid, that is true. But a longhorn can break its horns even easier than the short horns, so a good demonstration is always better than a war. Whatever comes into existence can disappear at any time when you are not expected.

A powerful king was preparing his army for a great war against his neighboring nations, but this king had a cane. Each time he wanted to go to war, the king would stand at the front of his palace with the cane. One of his strong generals would then strike one of his iron statues about seven times with the cane. After this ritual, the king would appoint that general to lead the war against the neighboring nations, to destroy whatever pleased them and finally bring what they chose as spoils before the king.

When the king met his generals at the front gate of his palace and chose the one to strike the iron statue seven times before going to war, the chosen general, unfortunately, broke the cane into more than three pieces. Imagine, a cane the king thought would never be destroyed, saying goodbye to the king at the second strike. Now, the king faced a dilemma with most of his soldiers ready for war. His only concern was to send them quickly for a swift victory and return home satisfied.

What about the cane, shattered into more than three pieces? The king always had a general test the cane on the statue, indicating that the king knew the significance of its destruction. When it comes to humans making judgments about power, they would never agree to a defeat until they turned to real dust. Despite the feeling that he might not win the war and that his power could be at great risk, the king didn't want to be like a ripe fruit falling from the tree by itself; it had to be by somebody else. So, the king decided to send all of his army to what he claimed would be the shortest war ever.

Even though the war might be short, it wouldn't be a short victory for the king as he predicted. There would be a lot of losses for the king. Indeed, you must not ignore a principle for your own interests. For the king not to respect the test he set before the war, he should not have executed the test in the first place. If the king agreed to perform the test, it meant he was also prepared for any result. For a long time, the king always used that cane, and it always stayed strong, ensuring the king's victory. However, this time, the cane shattered into more than three pieces, and the king decided to go to war. Did the king hope to win the war for real, or did he make a mistake? Not too many people can answer that question except the king himself as he headed to his last war because his kingdom would be shared.

After a significant defeat, many soldiers who survived avoided going to another war where they might lose their lives. Some soldiers schemed against the king, forming their own parties to rule over their cities. The kingdom became a tiny power, unable to find the right way to control the entire nation. Instead of continuing to dominate other nations with its great power, things changed. There are some opportunities for the kingdom to build its power as strong safety for themselves that way they may never get back to the ground as the caterpillars for any ants to come over and put their lives in misery without control.

Meanwhile, the big king, who has seen his kingdom and his powers slipping away, has finally given up, much like his cane that shattered into pieces. These pieces have divided the country into more than three powers. They continue to rule the country in this manner for many years until a different nation comes over and fights them one after the other. Finally, this different nation takes control of the entire nation.

After that loss, it takes them many years to understand what can cause a different nation to enter a nation, fight, and ultimately win that war. Whether a big nation or a small nation might never lose a war conducted by a different nation at home. So, the real reason to win or lose all depends on your surroundings and the people of that nation. If no one from that nation betrays it by allying with the one considered an enemy, a nation can never lose a war at its own home. That should not and will not happen at all if not even one person from that nation betrays and deceives the nation by allying with the enemies. No enemy can win any war in your own country.

A fight happened between a crab and a rat who wanted to eat the crab. It wasn't so easy; a big crab could just grab the rat with his double claws and keep the rat under serious pain until it died. However, this wasn't the case for the rat and crab. The rat kept running behind the crab until the crab got tired and laid on the ground. By that time, the rat ran behind the crab, grabbed a leg, and when the rat pulled that leg, the crab released it to the rat. Now the crab was considered to have lost one of its legs. In a war, if a soldier is lost, the war can also be lost because most of the time wars can be won by the wisdom of one soldier.

So, the rat continued the same strategy, fighting until it removed eight legs of the crab. Now, the crab only had its two claws attached to its body, but it was too disabled to turn around or to the side. Now, what the rat did was lay itself in the way behind the crab, and the crab, with its two eyes and two claws, looked at the rat eating itself until its life was over. The rat left crab bones on the ground as proof to others that the crab no longer existed but was defeated.

This strategy of the rat frightened the crabs enough, making them worry about who might turn over where the rat could find an easy way to eat them. But the way the crab chose to do it was wrong. The crab believed sacrificing its legs would help, but it didn't take the time to think that its legs were the only way it could be safe from rat attacks. The crab didn't even know that if it sacrificed its legs, it wouldn't be able to walk. Then, when it couldn't walk, the rat could easily kill and eat it as a meal. Whatever way an enemy finds to deceive you is a great chance for them to defeat you.

If you are a single fighter and your adversary removes one of your legs or hands, you should know you have lost a significant percentage of your ability to survive because you lost your strength. Then you cannot make any miracles to win without the possibility to fight until you win. Yet, if there is more than one person, you need not lose any of yourselves unnecessarily. If you are a nation, you need to beware of turning yourselves into a crab by excluding important members among yourselves to benefit the strategies of your enemies who want you to do so. That way, they can defeat you.

If that happens, just after that, you will become too weak because of your continual decrease in important members of support. This will prove to you that you were wrong to let them play you like a cat plays with a mouse when he is no longer worried about a disabled mouse being able to escape because it is already paralyzed, to the point where the mouse cannot make a fast move anymore. Each time a power loses an important member, that power is weakened to a great percentage. Whether through betrayal or any other reason, as with a crab with its weapons and looks as the rat eats him.

Any big nation with weapons and strategies can just watch as another nation comes as an enemy to destroy you if you currently don't have enough ways and wisdom to defend yourselves. Like the crab who sacrificed everything to survive and finally found out it did so in the interest of its enemy, in the wrong way, instead of helping itself, it made it easier for the enemy to defeat it. So, even though you can see the snare at a point, you can be at an angle where somebody else must rescue you. So, at all times, people who have two feet must not wear only one shoe; you must wear both shoes, right and left, to ensure you will not be lost like a person who doesn't know what to do to defend himself and takes an airplane to the sky without a pilot's knowledge or a destination to land down.

Supposedly, a long time ago, there was a world where only the science people knew how to make rope. The big authorities of the world were those who dealt with the scientific people, sometimes commissioning them to make ropes, especially to restrain inhabitants who were living in ways displeasing to the authorities. Science people depended on these leaders for their livelihoods, and science itself required a continuous flow of money. Sometimes, leaders who didn't even know how to count large amounts were the ones tasked with finding and providing the substantial funds required by the science people.

It is not allowed for anyone to use words like "kidnapping" and "hostage" especially in reference to important people. So, those leaders who are not able to find that much money all the time to give the science people for them to continue to watch over the world, preventing anything from happening before they can see it and stop it from happening. At this point, the science people are the only entity that can foresee and prevent events. To do all that, they are in need of significant funds. When the leaders cannot find that large sum quickly, they start to look to the rest of the inhabitants of the world to help them find that money for the science people, even though it takes a little time for the science people to secure it when they need it.

Now, the science people decide to make some very strong ropes. Each time they want a large sum of money, they can only tie those leaders with a strong rope. Once they are tied, they must give the money away so that the science people can release them. Now, the leaders order the same kind of ropes for themselves to tie the inhabitants of the world, making them stop living the way they prefer. To get under the ropes with them is the only way for the leaders to pay that large sum to the science people. Now, the science people put their ropes on the leaders and tie them up. The leaders themselves make sure they put those ropes over every inhabitant of the world, making them part of those who are supposed to share in giving the big money to the science people. Therefore, everyone must remember not to say at this time that the science people are the ones kidnapping these leaders. Also, everyone must remember not to say the government people are kidnapping the inhabitants of the world—don't you ever say that. The only thing happening is that science is tying the leaders with their strong ropes prepared specifically for that reason, and the leaders using the same ropes to tie the inhabitants of the world, making them part of those responsible for giving the money to the science people.

At that time, the science people were the only entity that could foresee what could happen even many years in advance. They were the only ones who could do anything to prevent serious dangers based on what they currently saw. Therefore, they were the only ones to determine the cost of getting out of the wrong ways. Sometimes, you must move quickly to do what you are supposed to do to protect the populations of the world. If they tell you that your world is going to disappear if they don't do something, the only question you can ask is, "What can you do to protect us?" Nobody wants to be destroyed, and whatever they can do is considered good as protection, especially when they are the only ones who can protect others from a bad situation. If that is true, they must receive what is necessary without interruption while everyone wants to follow the right direction. When you don't know where the airplane will divert, it might not be the one you want to travel with. However, if you currently know where to go, you must not worry, even if that takes a long time on your way.

Two persons who didn't know each other had been traveling for the first time and met at a station where both of them must take the same transportation because they are living in the same town. While they are waiting for their right transportation, which will travel to the town where they are going, another person, a third traveler driving a vehicle, stops by and offers them a ride. When they ask him about his real destination, they realize that they will not get to their town before that destination, which is about halfway to the town where they are going. One of them says if that is halfway, then he will be closer to his town, so he decides to take that trip to get closer to his town. Then the other person makes a different decision and does not take that ride; he prefers to sit and currently wait for his true transportation. So, the one who is taking the wrong ride leaves first and goes, knowing that the ride will leave him at a halfway point before his town. Right now, he is halfway to his destination. But how would he get to the other halfway until where he wants to be?

Eventually, by the time he must think about how he will get to his destination, the person who was waiting for the right transportation has already reached his destination. He, as the person who was taking the first trip just to get closer, is currently closer. But the only thing is he must wait here at a station until the next day to get transportation to the same place where he was a day before to take the same right transportation he was supposed to take to finally reach the town where his destination is.

No matter how worried you try to be, that will never make the presence of a day earlier than it's supposed to be. There are no miracles to repair any errors; the only way you can repair a minor mistake is by spending time, energy, and money. Then you can be sure the big mistake may never get repaired. The person who was at the level to understand that he must wait for his right transportation did not spend a night outside; he just waited for the right time and made his trip without any interruption. But the person who wishes to go quicker is the one who spent two days before he can finally go back and make a return trip to get to his destination.

Now, if he must travel to a different place in the world, would he follow his trip guide schedules? No one may know, but if you want to go somewhere, don't listen to anyone who may tell you about any other place that is closer. You need to worry only about the right way to get where you want to go. But as for that man, his error granted him a chance not to go to the war because one day before he gets into town, the king of the nation was sending authorities over each corner of the streets and house to house to grab anybody they find and take them to a camp where they are preparing them to go to war. So, his mistake adjusted him as the survivor by luck because most of those who were going to that war unfortunately did not return home; they have been captured by a different king and sent to a different nation. After everybody was captured and did not return, that king became like a tree without any roots or pivot. The rest of the people who are still living demanded that the king accept a law they are going to make for the world. Now the king has not too many choices; then, to accept the population's proposal to him because the great losses happen right now. It is not the time not to please the rest of the people who keep him in power. But the king accepts while he does not yet know what that law is going to put in force. But the moment the great king does accept that law, all the rest of the world will be going to join them in that law. So, what is that law?

The populations are asking that king to grant them permission to establish that law for the whole world. There is the law; they are asking the king that each time two countries or two kings want to make war, the first thing that must happen before the soldiers go to war is that a physical battle must be done between the two kings. Whoever wins that battle should be considered as the king who has won the war. By doing such a smart thing, both of the nations might never continually lose any others' lives most of the time unnecessarily. So, the king is already accepting and promises them the law will be granted. So, beginning from that day, there should be no more people going to war, only a battle between the two kings who really want to open the war. Then that law becomes a real law over the whole world. Each time a king wants a war to happen, he must sign for himself to engage in a physical fight with the next king. Then if he wins the other king in the physical fight, he is currently the king who wins the war. If he considers himself lost, then he is the king who currently lost the war. No more soldiers or populations need to be engaged in a war if that is not something as an unpreventable war. So, the king who lost too many people at the war and has in his mind to make everybody else go to war so he may win the war is now trapped with his ideas. While he cannot cross that red light, which is a law he must obey as a king because that is a part of his promises to the population who was not revolting against him when he was sending too many of them to the war and never returning home.

Yet, by the time a king analyzes the size of the other king to find out if that is a king he can physically win. Many of the people and soldiers who could be all dead will be here with their family and friends. Thanks to that law, the world knows what everyone can call peace because no kings want to engage themselves in face-to-face physical fights. The kings are afraid of dying and afraid of losing the kingdom to the other king. Every rooster stays in his cage, and each torus stays behind its checkpoint. When every country in the world knows what it means to have peace, from that time, they try to estimate the number of people who died in each country before that law existed. It is not possible for anybody to reveal the real numbers even if they start with one country at a time each year until now.

So, what is the merit of the people who activated that law? Maybe the existence of so many who did not wish to die in a war in their land or elsewhere in the world. While every road has an end and every lock has a way to get it open, there are solutions for every problem. Of course, a tiny part is apparently negative, but that might be too small to be compared to anything but nothing. Many years before that, some people always said they sat down with the intention to find the best way to stop that problem between the kings, but it always came with no outlet. It seems that the more you talk about it, the worse it can be. No one ever knew that someone without extreme force could come up with a law that currently hangs over two columns, and every other has to line up on them. It is for sure the right way to get good results from every war they were suffering from for many generations. Why destroy chicks and hens when only two roosters can resolve the problem? Find the right way to get it done; let them both go against each other, and whoever prevails is the one to rule, and the other must listen and obey the real and legal winner. Do not let anybody ignite a fire that can burn your home by believing he will destroy wasps. Instead of a fire, if you don't buy the spray that can get the job done, just use hot water with some caution and remove the nest. That is what the people do: they put a hot law that can only hurt the real cause of their real problems, and finally, their kings keep gnashing their teeth, but they cannot cross that law because they are kings who know what it means to respect or not respect the law. So, they prefer to always respect the law.

Now they must not worry about any war; they only can concentrate themselves on doing what is really necessary for the wealth of the world. So, instead of being jealous about other nations' wealth and trying to destroy everything they can view, then every king has more chances to verify everything that needs to be done so they can create better education systems, good communication systems, good hospitals, better roads, and better structures in general. All countries are at the right stand. Wishing that to be today at our time might look funny, but if that is supposed to be, who can tell what is impossible? It might look funny at night without the light shining, but when the earth turns away from the sunlight, at that point, everything will be clear. If you have never seen people making paper from wood or learned that from someone, you will never believe that paper can be made with wood. Not only that, today, many things look like miracles compared to a long time ago. So, what is the real future? Only the one who sees it will know. As for those who saw the beginning of the twenty-first century, your path will remain far behind yourselves. Whatever might the good light continue to shine for those who are there to see it.

Humanly talk, the whole world, without exception, sits on a pivot of lies from a very long time. Because of that, many lies turn out to look like the truth, resulting in a mix between bad and good. Near that scenario, you must be wise to win your path. If you minimize wisdom, the number of times you stumble up will be the number of times you will fall. It is important to know that the number of steps you climb well is the number of mistakes you avoid on your way. It is never too late to know how to identify the right and true way to make things better.

Like a hen who laid her eggs over a ditch, each time she laid one egg, that egg would roll over and break, destroying it. After many losses, she realized that was not the right way to lay her eggs. The hen then goes to a flat area, builds a nest herself, and lays her eggs there. After twenty-one days incubating her eggs, she hatches her chicks. If not laid in a flat place, the eggs can continue to roll over and break each other. Many people know that humans are not different. Most human problems are caused by humans, like the eggs that can roll over and destroy each other. Humans continue to destroy each other. Fortunately for the hen, she figured out a good result for her and her eggs, and she became successful. But as for humans, so far, nobody yet knows how to remove among them hypocrisy, jealousy, lawlessness, and selfishness, which are the bad sports where humans are causing them to destroy each other.

The castles of the kings are built by the prisoners who will never be set free. The fortresses of the wealthy are built by poor slaves who will never be granted the chance to be free. If any young one tries to escape, no matter how far he steps, he cannot be a winner. There are many fake golds ahead in your way, like some shortcuts reserved especially for you to become successful. They can turn you into a gang, an illegal drug dealer, and to consume them not far from your mind. All your good dreams to be a free person will disappear, and your life will be worse than destroyed. Only one thing is truth: if someone can scheme and fake to turn you into trash, and you are listening to them, you also can listen to those who want you to have a good life. It's up to you to know if you want to walk, or if you prefer the violent wind to take you where you want to go.

Not too many people will tell where the original sea begins and reinforces, but as for the rivers, everyone or most maybe knows a source of water is the beginning of a river. It joins some ravines and torrents, and then a big river can divert to the sea. Rich without wisdom is not a source of water but a source of enemy favors who will take it back from you and put you into inactivity because you are not wise. They are using you as the bridge to kill yourself, so you cannot escape from them as a slave. Most of the time, they know that you cultivate in your mind if you become rich; that can be the best way for you to get free. That is why they offer you some fake, fast way you can get rich. But some ways they know are illegal. That way, whenever you get there, they can find a good reason to destroy you for your rebellion against them by trying to free yourself from their burden on you.

When you are among enemies, your knowledge is the only territory you own for yourself. Whatever you plan to do as good for yourself, your enemies will be the first to come over and counsel you without order. As you should know it, your enemies will never give you a pass to paradise but rather hell for you. Put your enemies in a bag out of your plan so you can do that wisely without breaking them like a bottle so they may not have the chances to cut you out. If by any mistake you let yourselves be guided by the ideas of your enemies, you will sweep directly into your pit.

Besides selfishness and hypocrisy of humans, sometimes on earth, whoever starts as the best never has any chance to terminate as the best. Those who never begin well most of the time prove themselves as the best. That is truth, but where everything must come to an end, whether good or bad, it appears to be sad. The one who is watching you to stop you from sleeping will also lose his sleep just to stop you from sleeping. After all, it does not appear to be a winner; everyone is lost. Tears for the eyes of the slaves, tears also at the end for the eyes of those who cause the tears of the slaves. Whatsoever, the wicked will never have a good heart. You must not waste your time explaining nor try to negotiate anything; all the wicked want is your destruction.

The Musician Bird

A musician bird, who knows what an enemy is, learns how to train himself to play his music by himself only, at the same time controlling all his territory from the sky to the land. If any other bird comes into that territory, the musician bird runs him out immediately. If any other animals like snakes enter his territory, the musician bird runs that animal out, whether it's big or small. The musician bird is his own better security and never lets any predators come into his territory to disturb him and kill him.

The human community also has some great musicians, that is for sure, but for many of them, they don't learn how to avoid enemies. For that reason, most of those supposed great musicians never live long. A bird knows how to create a limit between him and his enemies or predators. Why a human intelligent cannot? That may be because humans who turn themselves wicked and want to destroy others always present themselves currently as the best friends. It's up to you, as the bird taught himself how to identify enemies, to do so for yourselves.

When they come over and offer you something wrong like illegal drugs and tell you to try anything just for one time just to know how it tastes, you are the one to know that they are your enemies who come by just to get some dimensions about your pit in the graveyard. They just don't want you to occupy too much space at the cemetery; they want to put you in a tiny pit so they can have enough space left over for their future slaughters.

Be like the musician bird. Each time they come over, run them away from you by not accepting their offers. Why drink and eat often with someone you don't even know well at a great percentage? Even some of your good knowledge can be the worst problems sometimes. You are the one to know a bad friend can even put drugs in your drink or food if you are refusing it from them. Wise ways are to refuse what they are giving you and refuse to be where they are. The musician bird is not eaten in the same spot with a snake or any other birds rather than a bird like him.

You can be a person but not the same as other people. If those people want you to smoke something and you don't want to do that, you are not the same as that one. If you want, you can distance yourself away just for your protection. You may not be one of the many musicians, great superstars, who died because of illegal drugs. Everywhere in the world, there are many kinds of illegal drugs that are destroying people every second. Most of the ones who die maybe have it at their first time by a so-called friend or even parent and did not know they are swept away by a current of fast water they will never get back out anymore. Then they will switch right to their pit, the so-called friend was preparing for them.

Everyone who lives today can name one great singer who is destroyed at a very young age because of bad illegal drugs. If a dealer knows you have money, and he cannot come to you to introduce that to you, he may send your friend to introduce that to you. If that happens to you, will you keep a friend who introduces you to the bad ways? You may be the one to know, but whoever sits in a pot of water over the fire will be the burning person. If you have the feeling you are not among the ones you can trust, you are the one to get out and protect your life, which is your territory. Your life is your territory; you need to protect your territory as the musician bird does for himself.

You can be a celebrity, a famous diva, or whatever you are in sports activities. Everyone can call you a great champion, but there are many people who are continuing to make their money on you so they also want you to do what is the way for them to make money. Only whenever you put your eyes on what is good for you and to have a free life, they will accuse you of something somehow. That way, you will never enjoy yourselves. They will put you in their mouths like a chocolate bar and suck you to your finish until you die.

You may be in jail, a prison, or back and forth until you are unable to do anything for yourselves. If you don't want to do what they want you to do for them to continue to make money on you, even if they want to turn you into trash, beware of that. Some false accusations might be reserved on your path. So be like the musician bird, defeat every bad idea, and be wise to yourselves. Then you may be at a point to protect yourselves. Sometimes people use what they call democracy and freedom to destroy fools or those who misunderstand. A person should never let your freedom be like a bucket of water overflowing and pouring on the ground. No one should let anybody tell you that because you are free and part of a democracy, you can put your arm to live power electric or jump into a pit of fire. You must know that the world we are living in has a limit; that is why we know the estimation of the earth. So, our path and whatever we must do also have a limit. If by any mistake you are crossing your limit, that is an error that maybe cannot be repaired anymore.

The wicked, who wants to introduce you to your grave, is no one else than the one you thought to be a super friend for yourselves. A shelter may not be good to eat as a meal, as you know everything has a way in life, but you can taste the shelter of your life, which is your wisdom. A physical shelter can protect and save your life at the time of a cyclone, but your knowledge is your shelter that can protect and save your life when your enemies present themselves to you as a best friend.

In a world where you live among greed, selfishness, jealousy, and wickedness, life is like a serious fight. For many people, it is the same as a person coming from too far away and losing too much energy during that trip. Then that person becomes too tired to eat a meal, too sleepy to take a shower, and then that person lays down on the ground and goes into a deep sleep and rests forever. Because all life is a fight for him, the day that is a rest for him is a lasting rest.

Wicked people can rise among all ranks of people, especially when a so-called democracy and so-called freedom are over the floor or over their limits. As an example, a good man was living close to a city where many young people did not have a job to make any money. So, that good man created a business where he hired many of the young people during that period. With his help, they can make some money and help themselves with many things in their lives. But after some years, everybody in the city started saying that the employer is keeping people of the city as slaves. Then they must stop him from doing that, so everyone turns crazy against that good man. Then he has no other choice than to close that business. So, the people of the city are destroying themselves by being jealous, selfish, and hypocritical.

Not too long after that event, they are paying the big price for their foolishness. They were forgetting if the breads they are currently eating are the fruits of that good man's business. They thought they were destroying him, but he is the one who already has food on his table. So, they are taking the wrong direction for themselves. Misunderstandings and disagreements should never build enemies between employees and employers. In one way or the other, they are helping each other. That happens because the real enemies are never identified at the early time.

Under many stresses, you can find all kinds of animals who are here at the refuge as animals who are in need of shelter. Unfortunately, some of them are not there to take true refuge but to hunt those who need refuge. Such attitudes cannot only be found among the beasts but also among humans. Despite that, humans cannot completely prevent that situation, just as the beasts can never be able to protect themselves against some serious attacks of those predators.

After all, the true enemies are against every life; they are not only hunting for a meal when hungry for food, but they are destroyers who destroy lives without exceptions, whether vegetable, beasts, or humans. In some cases, enemies can be diseases, and age itself, which is a general who is not worried about fences, walls, or stone refuges. No matter between rich and poor, the lesser to the greatest, every life must face the ages and obey death. Anything built can be destroyed; anything born can grow; anything that grows can die; anything dead and destroyed can turn to dust. Any destroyer will be destroyed without doubt.

Today, humans are victims of some kind of powers operated by their resemblance. Believe it; before they are satisfied with themselves, only their names will stay behind themselves. Today, when a wealthy person becomes wicked and destroys a thousand lives per day, that weighs no more than a thousand mullets destroyed by a hawk at the waters just to eat a small portion that he likes for his meal and dumps their remains to the ground. Believe it; if you are living among the wicked, your life is no greater than the life of a bee hummingbird who lives among predators.

Your protection can only be your wisdom, not the promises of security for all, which do not exist at some point for everyone. Punishments are for the backs of the poor, whether you are right or wrong. The only path the wealthy and strong one cannot deceive, despite selfishness and wickedness, is the grave. If they want, they can buy your rights and destroy your life with a word from their mouth. But when the general age arrives, whether they are wealthy and wicked, ages will not accept any bribe from them just to back away from them; they must obey the same way as everybody else. Wicked retreat toward the grave. A good adult was a good baby at a time, but as time goes by, a baby grows until an adult. A wicked person also was a baby, but as a baby, everyone saw a beautiful baby instead of a wicked one.

Two Men Sowing Seeds

Two people went to a supermarket where there was also a section selling seeds of all kinds—the good plants and the miserable ones. The two individuals were preparing a piece of land each for cultivating some fruit and cereal, and they were interested in buying some seeds. One of them looked and found some corn seeds, then he bought the quantity he wanted. The other one just grabbed a bag of seeds. When the men got back, they sowed their seeds with great hope of harvesting some good fruits.

This was true for the one who knew he had gotten corn seeds, as when he harvested, beautiful corn grew. However, the one who didn't know what kind of seeds he got unfortunately found that his seeds only produced thorns. All his work turned out to be in vain because he did not exercise caution. He didn't pay enough attention to his plants, from the time of purchasing the seeds to the time they were growing, and this negligence cost him everything. What you sow is what you reap. Fortunately, his friend helped him with some corn, enough for him and his family. Hopefully, he learned a valuable lesson.

The snare that catches a bird today will not be the same one tomorrow; the next traps are further ahead. The next season approaches, and the man who planted corn has enough seeds to plant in his farm; he doesn't have to buy seeds anymore. Moreover, the man who planted thorns will not buy thorn seeds this time because his friend, the corn man, gave him enough seeds to sow on his land. Things are going well, and both men have a lot of corn. At this time, each man has a boy with his wife to raise.

From the start, the corn man uses garden flowers, animal portraits, and school children portraits with his boy for fun. On the contrary, the thorns man uses images of wars, soldiers on horses riding over other people and shooting them to death. Those are the things the thorn man exposes his boy to. After a year and more, the corn man buys a small house as toy pieces for his son to put together; he buys him a bunny and a small car as toys. The thorns man, however, buys a small gun weapon toy for his son. As the boy grows up, he continues to buy him bigger toy gun weapons.

When both boys are growing and watching TV, the corn boy watches animal channels, geography, and engineering. At this time, he has a small guitar his dad bought for him. The thorns boy only watches war channels and war games where people shoot each other. After years, both boys become adolescents. The corn boy knows how to play music, especially the guitar; he is an engineer and more. As for the thorns boy, he becomes a different person, liking weapons a lot and always wanting to fight. One day, he buys his own weapon, goes to public places, and kills many people. After all, he goes back home and kills his own parents. Unfortunately, the thorns family gets to the worst point, and there is no pity for them.

What you practice every day is what you keep in your mind; as a seed sown can grow and be identified. What grows inside the heart can be brought to light as a harvest. If it is good fruits, that is good, but if they are thorns, it is bad. Strong families will not exist without the belt of discipline as corrections for the children. If a parent makes the mistake of not having a belt, one day they will find themselves being whipped with the children's belt. This doesn't just happen to parents; it's the same thing in the case of nations on earth who cannot have the necessary belts, today or later, whoever has the belt will use it to whip you and order your own people to do the same to you.

Before you even think about being a head, you must verify your weight to see if there is a belt. If you cannot have a belt, believe it; you do not deserve the name you carry, and time will prove it. This will happen when those who are wearing belts come over and tell you what you must do. If you refuse, they will pull up their belts and make you pay the consequence of your rebellion by not obeying them immediately. From that time, you will render an account to yourselves that you were nothing. There are no strong parents without the belt of discipline, and there are no strong nations without the necessary belts. Among many choices, only one is reasonable, logistic, and true. While the success one cannot be determined in advance and can only be as a chance to win.

Three men were shepherds, one of them built a park and put his sheep inside the park. The second one decided to tie his sheep in a large land and take care of them. The third man decided to free all of his sheep so they could feed themselves and then return together at one place before night. Every day, all the sheep came back to his place until the next day. If someone asks which is the good shepherd among the three shepherds, many people can say the one who uses the park. As for success, that can only be known by analyzing the information of all three shepherds.

For many people, freeing the sheep is not a good idea, but it can be the choice of some others. Choices can be made in many aspects of life. As an example, a man who lived a long time ago had three sons. He sent one of them to school; then he wanted the second one to be a shepherd without going to school. He had to stay home and be the shepherd. As for the third one, he wanted him to be a farmer without going to school. If anyone asks you which is the good choice, you will easily answer and say that the one going to school is the good choice. As for success, no one can tell, but it is always good to prepare yourselves for many tracks of professions. Believe that school is a door open for everyone to learn many things, but always remember the waters you may not want to touch. All the time, that water can be your drinking water later depending on the circumstances of your life.

After all, your knowledge is greater than any viewing materials as wealth. Because your knowledge is the only way you can protect and be safe from any snare against you, something wealth cannot do for you. Riches are not as close to knowledge as many people thought, even though all are important to live. A good profession can help a lot in life; that is for certain. It is just a good baton to fight the bad dogs of everyday harsh life. A fence at a land might not be as strong as a concrete wall, but it can protect and prevent many things you don't even know in your days. When you have a dog that sleeps outside your home, that dog may never be able to report to you how many snakes and other bad animals it prevents from entering your yard. But that dog only solidifies its loyalty to a good owner. Your knowledge is the good dog that can prevent a lot of bad events in your life.

A family suddenly found a box containing some venomous snakes in their house. The family decided to take the box away from the house as they thought it was the only way to guarantee the safety and security of the family. However, after the family removed the venomous snakes from the house and took the box to a forest, one of them decided to open the box just to contemplate the snakes. At this instant, a venomous snake spit over them and contaminated them. The family that owns the house can put the snake out of the house, but in the forest, any wild animal could attack, especially to protect itself. If the venomous snake was good to look at, anybody could keep them in a safe place to observe, but taking them to the wild and trying to contemplate them is a serious and irreparable mistake. What kind of friend do venomous snakes want to be with you after you take them out of the house and put them in the wild? This lesson stays for anyone who believes they are putting out strangers and trying to embrace them as best friends; it can be a deadly mistake for anyone who makes that error. Running after a dog today and trying to pet him tomorrow; at that time, he can make you scared of him for sure and continue to bite you on each occasion he can. This is just to remind you of what you thought you did to him. Everyone must remember what animals can do to humans, whether in the past dealings with them were good or bad, as it is not erased nor forgotten by them.*

A soul who is running a lot because of his predators, after getting to an area where he cannot win anymore, even if his predators become too tired to currently grab him to turn him to pieces, raises his head to the sky and finally says- the water he did never want to touch in his life, that water become his drinking water. The land he never wanted to step on in his life, that land turns out to be his land to lay and rest with his absolute peace.

Old Man on the Mountain Valley
for His Last Time

* A family was living in a small village for a very long time; all the children grew there and got married, forming their own families. The old couple was getting very old. The man had a routine where he always climbed a low part of a mountain near his house. As he got very old, one day, he said to himself that day would be his last day to climb that part of the mountain because he felt too weak to climb it anymore. While sitting at a section of the mountain for the last time, as he thought in his mind, he looked at the top of the mountain and saw two young sheep coming to drink water at the river valley below the mountains. As he continued to look, he saw one of the sheep walking to a space like a free road. The other sheep was trying to walk into a space where it must face many thorns, thistles, and stones. Each step he currently made, he was already hurt by many thorns, thistles, and big rocks. The old man continued to look and saw both animals, who were young, become like adults. The trip continued the same way—one of them on the free road, and the other facing many problems and difficulties. By the time they reached the river, both were no longer young but old and weak.

Now, the old man started to think about how those animals, who are getting old, would be able to return to the top of that big mountain. The old man also wondered greatly about why the two young animals became old. Currently, it was the time for the old man to see closer with his own eyes the two sheep who reached the river. While he continued to look, he saw the one who encountered many difficulties lying by the river and not able to stand up, even though his mouth was in the water he spent his life looking for. He had passed away with his face in the river. As for the sheep who walked on the free road, he was stronger because he made his trip without any problems. So, after mourning his partner's death for a little time, he entered the river to a point where he could drink some water. Eventually, an alligator unfortunately approached, and that alligator grabbed his neck. The old, tired, and weak sheep couldn't defend himself against the alligator, and he gave up to that predator.

The old man woke up in the place where he always sat down and looked to the other side. While he looked to the other side of the mountain, he saw two young men coming from the top of the mountain. This time, the old man did not see any animals like sheep but two very young men. As he stood in that place and looked, he eventually saw one of the men walking on a free road, and the other one was walking like he was trapped by many bushes—more like thorns, thistles, and many big rocks and stones.

While both men continue to walk, they both turn to look like adults and are no longer very young. One of them is very much hurt by some big rocks, thorns, and thistles in the forest where he is walking. The other man, walking on the free road, continues on a very good path so far. While the old man continues to look, he sees the men getting closer, and at that same time, they are seriously old. Because they are both no longer young, at this instant, the old man starts thinking about the similarity of what he has been seeing on the other side of the mountain where the two sheep were making a trip, which was no different.

Now the old man, who was standing up and ready to go back to his house, sits back and starts thinking while looking at them. The man walking on the free road is walking a little slowly. As for the one facing difficulties in areas with thorns, thistles, and rocks, he moves apparently fast but is not going anywhere quickly because each time he moves, he is hurt by an object, keeping both men at the same distance.

Now the old man poses a question he did not pose in the sheep situations. The question is if both men are coming from the same place at the top of the mountain, why are both of them not walking on the same free road? At that time, the old man cannot have an answer for that question; he just asks himself. But by the time the men approach the bottom of the mountain, they are extremely tired, getting old, and weak. The old man continues to look and sees the two men arrive by the river guest, and the one who was walking among the thorns, thistles, and rocks no longer stands up straight. While he tries to bend himself down, he lays himself down where the waters of the river continue to float to his face, and then he passes away by the river. His partner, who was there with him, looks at him, but he himself is too weak to do anything.

Now the old man asks himself how that weak, aged man will be able to get back to the top of that mountain? No one else is there to answer him. While he continues to look, the last man tries to sit on a rock while he slides to a deep portion of the river and is immediately swept away by a fast current.

At this point, the old man wakes up to the place where he was sitting and starts walking to his house, feeling very sad. His sadness discourages him a lot, and then the old man hears a strong voice in his mind telling him, "You must not lose your strength. Be courageous. You are so lucky to see the way of life. But you might not tell that to many before you get to the last place you will return to, to stay forever."

The old man, who is a little bit afraid, thinks maybe he is going to stay at his house and not return to the side of the mountain. That is what the voice means to tell him, but he is not sure. However, that also means courage for the old man. He currently walks to his home with good courage, as the voice orders him to do for himself.

The old man has a source of water by his house gate, which he has been using for all the time he has lived there. He always takes enough water inside his home for him to use for about a week, just to make sure that if heavy rain comes and changes the color of the waters, he will never have a problem with water. This time, while the old man is approaching his house, there is a big mango tree that has been there for a very long time. The mango tree has fallen down and covered the source of water the old man always uses. While the old man stands and looks at that mango tree that has fallen down and covered the source of water he has used for a very long time, for the second time, he becomes very sad because he is an old man. Now he cannot make many moves to go to any other places far to get water, and he does not have the strength to cut and remove that tree covering his source of water.

While he stands and looks with great sadness, he hears the same voice that addressed him before. The voice says to him, "You must not be afraid and sad anymore. You currently have enough water at your house for you to use. You will not need to get back to that source of water nor force yourself to get any water somewhere else. Just go into your house and rest for your good times."

The old man enters his house as normal and continues to live without any worry about anything. Then, on the day the old man is going to deplete his last reserve of water, his beloved wife and himself lie in their spots and rest forever. The old man passed away, and he did not have any answer to his question about why both men did not walk on the same free road. Later, when the voice tells him, he just sees the ways of life, he probably understands that it is also the answer to his question, but he was sad in his heart.

Sometimes, you can have a super friend, and between you and your friend, one of you is a curse of misery in life and one of you is very wealthy to the top grade. The things both of you can share forever as good friend memories are age and finally death. Life can always be easy for you as a free road you are walking, but for your friend, life is a hell. Believe it, that is not easy for you to understand, and you will never be able to resolve that for your friend. Even when you do whatever you can do for your friend, the missions that don't have exemptions are age and death. It can be sad when the wealthy people look and see the poor people get old and die, and the wealthy also get old and finally die. The water you are afraid to touch with your shoes, that will be your last drinking water. The land you are afraid to step on with your horse, that land will be the land you will lie on and rest forever.*

Sadness in Your Heart

Among the people who are living on earth, certain names will not be removed as long as the earth itself exists. When a woman runs and leaves a little girl behind her, the little girl talks to her baby doll and continually says to her baby doll, "Here is your mother. I'm your mother. I will not run and leave you behind. I'm your mother. I will never leave you with the other people. Wherever I go, I will go with you. I'm your mother, and I will never leave you forever.

It is clear that the little girl has the feeling of both ways — her mother, who is going to work and leaving her with a person who does not care for her. So, whatever road you are on, the river will not change its spot just for you. The head will face the feet if you want to have a circle. Many words and lies have been put into the world just to ensure the poor and the most vulnerable sleep well with the hope of a better tomorrow and not engage in some sorts of violence, revenge, and vengeance. To that point, everyone must say every day, "Hope makes a living." Nobody must think about defeat because of a current adverse situation. Good ambition is the hope to see the end of everything as your trial mission. The work of your hands, the power of your arms, and the sweat of your forehead. Summer is not always worrying about winter, but when winter arrives, a quick look at the summer behind you is the most moment of sadness in existence in life. Sadness can happen unexpectedly as bad events that can break your heart and abort your plans for eternity.

When you cannot open your eyes to look at the beauty of the moon, when your skin is not able to feel the taste of the sun, when a bend of your knees before enemies buries you in the mud, when your eyes and your heart must contemplate your beautiful flowers in the garden of others, when your mind prefers your grave to your entertainment, when what you hear takes you to the sky of your memories from your first step to a step you have not yet attended. That is the world for you and I and our friends. Where all flowers fade when they pretend to be stronger and most beautiful. Woe to anyone who, by any means, gives a bitter drink to his friend during a dark moment; if that happens when the light arrives and shines, you will be blind. Never stay at the lowland, and always let the trees grow high on the mountains; when the waters rise high, someone might try to climb a tree. When nature is crying, humans are thought to be happy, but if nature cries too much, humans will carry some tears.

*When you must eat your food, never try to eat for tomorrow. If you ever eat for tomorrow, when tomorrow arrives, tomorrow will eat you too. Eat only for today; then tomorrow you will eat again. That again will be against tomorrow; that way, tomorrow may never be able to eat you. When the old man decided not to go back to the low part of the mountain as his routine exercise, that was a time when his courage and strength currently left him. Then he was known and felt he would not see that valley and mountain anymore for him to contemplate every day. At that time, he is feeling weak just for his memory of the mountain, valley, and beautiful river being removed from his heart. That way, he must not worry himself too much. The old man was himself in a free way of life when his courage was with him, but when his courage was away, at that time, he was hurt by many bad objects like rocks, thorns, and thistles, just for a short period of sadness when even his source of water and his mango tree were not on his menu anymore.

So, when you go to a festival, you might want to stay there for a lot more time, but the festival was set to terminate at one specific time whether you want it or not. When that time is there, if you don't say goodbye, someone will tell you goodbye. The old man did not clearly understand that he was not going to use any more water in his life, but he was listening to the voice telling him he had enough water at his home for him to use, so don't be sad anymore; be courageous and enter his house. He was listening and did enter his house and used the water he had in his possession. Before the last reserve of water is over, the old man himself rests in eternal peace. Then his final goodbye; that is what he has received from his loving village who was missing him for his lovely kindness and respect for the value of his village's nature and arts of humans. Never mind about what is not on your path; don't wonder about what you cannot do in your life. However, somebody else must accomplish what is supposed to. Your friend goes left; you are going in the right direction. You both will enter the same gate. Do honor what is right with as much respect as you can. Then, at last, every existence will prove your name deserves respect and honor forever.

Today, you can be a happy person or maybe suffering because of the bad actions of wicked people, but every good human has a seat in his heart for peace. Therefore, whoever turns away from certain values that can help turns into a self-enemy. The eyes and faces you have, others can see them and tell you how they look, especially how you look. But you, yourself, in order to see your face, you need a mirror made by somebody else to help you see your face. If, by any means, you refuse to use that mirror, you must believe that you will never have any other chance yet to see how you look; you will not know how you look. The beautiful face you have can only be seen by you through a mirror. Believe that today you will not find a person who doesn't want to see how his face looks every day in his life.

If by choice anyone does something that can be compared to the refusal of value, you must eventually understand why a heart can be separate from the rest of the body and the knowledge of the reason. The best friend by heart died apart as a condemned enemy. If life on earth had a second term, that second term should only make sense if it starts with knowledge of at least forty years of age. Yet, people can look as twenty years old, then their knowledge capacity equals forty years old; their knowledge is older than their age. Unfortunately, on earth, life does not yet have a second term, so there is no current space to gain back anything regrettable in life.

When best friends live as enemies for special reasons, that is a mountain behind the third mountains until dust the news will remain unknown as a marrow disease. Every heart continues to suffer forever; no one knows who will rest first to their eternal peace. Sad it can be; it is a bitter drink for the heart. For some of you, of course, you may never feel you win anything in life on earth; that is true. One thing you can still win is your strength with a mind that can engage yourselves as the most hopeful people who have ever been known before. Hopeful only for the retired in peace, a lasting rest in peace. Even those who are subjects of yours and most of the others' calamities and unhappiness will not skip. Joy and peace are for the world you were born in, not for those who contemplate your calamities. There will be no winner among anything who will be destroyed after destroying most of what was under his power on his path; everything will go like the cloud to the sky, which is wise for the wicked. There will be no power if the power doesn't have anything under itself. So, whoever rules should understand they are responsible to protect but not to destroy. Often, destruction happens by jealousy, selfishness, and bad ambitions to gain more power at all times. That can stop, and everyone can have a better condition of life. Yet, that can be different from bad to better, at least if the kings who rule can think about life.

A king has only one life. A soldier has only one life. So, a good king or a good ruler should never underestimate the life of the other humans, the value and importance of one life to many others. Humans can do much better than what is happening at this time in our day, especially those who rule over so many others. That can be changed only when the king of fire agrees to stop using his power in the wrong ways, and stops abusing his power against the dry forests. When a king can take enough courage to say to his soldiers that each one of them has a life that is the same as his life. Then the king will never send his soldiers to nonsensical wars to destroy their lives because the king and his friends want them to be here with them at all times, and their families and friends also want them to be there for them at all times. There is no reason to continue to lose life unnecessarily. When everybody will be able to stand before a judge by themselves to resolve a problem where no one will be forced to hire a lawyer who does not often plead in their favor. When everyone can understand it is not a crime for a rich or a poor person to stand before a judge without the prejudgment done by somebody else. When everything you say, everything you do, everything you agree to, are you and coming from your heart, then you forgive whoever causes you heartbreak, and you are ready to live better. *

When Your Eyes Can Not Be Open

A heart slides away from everything cherished and never surrenders like the roses of the summer adopted by the winter where sadness, bitterness, stress, and nightmares reside. However, for many, life never has the chance to explain itself. Sadly, shaking hands and saying goodbye with the hope to see each other in the near future, and that never happens. No realistic expectation is enough to promote pain and suffering, sadness and stress like the heart and soul abandoned in a deep dark pit without any hope. Where the regret of every moment enjoyed prevails over the bright future. Where all roses close themselves in the early morning before the dewdrop says goodbye to the sunrise. Where every best friend is living as an enemy. Where a heart loses its only wish to explain, Where the mystery is never revealed. That is the way the unhappy soul is as a nonexistent soul. Where the most important turns to ashes. When the beautiful city becomes nonhabitat, there are some gnashing of teeth. Where the bed is sweet and sleep is happy for the eyes, here are ways your sun will set, while you are laid in the middle of your roses, no one must see a space of the missing roses but a beautiful garden of the arts that was your preoccupation between the spring through winter. Now, minds and hearts are to the invisible as mysteries. Wish love and peace, yours and mine forever.

**Variety and Mystery Forever in Mind. GDtML.*

Dr. Thinker D. Gardiner is the author and writer of "Variety and Mystery". Author and writer of seventy-five titles of variety and mystery including sixteen star paragraphs.